MARKED BY OBSESSION

A PSY-IV Team Novel

JAMI GRAY

Cover Art: Robin Ludwig Design, Inc.

Publisher: Celtic Moon Press Revised edition, 2018
ISBN: 978-1-948884-09-9 (ebook) ISBN: 978-1-948884-08-2 (print)

First edition, January 2017, MuseItUp Publishing ISBN: 978-1-77127-890-4 (ebook) ISBN:
9978-1-77127-889-8 (paperback)

Sign up for free reads from Jami!

Join Jami's newsletter to be the first to hear about new releases, free books, special prices and other nifty events.

Sign up at: https://www.subscribepage.com/jami-gray-books

What Readers Say...

About Arcane Transporter:
"Taking a refreshing approach to fantasy magic, this fast-paced, economical thriller is told from a highly likable perspective." —Red Adept Editing

About PSY-IV Teams:
"This story is an emotional roller coaster, from betrayal, anger, fear, love..." —InD'tale Magazine

About the Kyn Kronicles:
"...a fantastic paranormal action novel is quite possibly the best book I've read this year. I could not put it down, and had to exercise serious self-control to keep from staying up all night to finish it." —The Romance Reviews

About Fate's Vultures:
"...if you like your characters with a bit more bite, with secrets, with hidden agendas, and all those sorts of things, and your worlds are a far more deadlier place, then this is for you." —Archaeolibrarian

Also by Jami Gray

ARCANE WONDERLAND

Last Call

Bitter Spirits

Rune & Tonic

ARCANE TRANSPORTER

Ignition Point (*Prequel Novella*)

Grave Cargo

Risky Goods

Lethal Contents

Collision Course

Blind Spot

Terminal Drift

THE KYN KRONICLES

Shadow's Edge

Shadow's Soul

Shadow's Moon

Shadow's Curse

Shadow's Dream

Shadow's Fall

Tangled in Shadows (*Short Story Collection*)

FATE'S VULTURES

Lying in Ruins

Beg for Mercy

Caught in the Aftermath

Fear the Reaper

PSY-IV TEAMS

Hunted by the Past

Touched by Fate

Marked by Obsession

Fractured by Deceit

Linked by Deception

BOX SETS

PSY-IV Teams Box Set I (Books 1-3)

The Collapse: Fate's Vultures (Books 1-4)

The Kyn Kronicles Box Set (Books 1-6)

Arcane Transporter Box Set I (Books 1-3)

Arcane Transporter Box Set II (Books 4-6)

For my real life Knight,
Who knows when to hand me back my sword and when to walk me
off the battlefield.
Thanks for keeping my heart in one piece.

Acknowledgments

Thank you to my fellow Four Horsemen for your endless support and encouragement. Even when you pull me by the ear and drag me back in line. Love you guys!

Muwha!

Contents

Chapter 1	1
Chapter 2	7
Chapter 3	18
Chapter 4	29
Chapter 5	39
Chapter 6	47
Chapter 7	59
Chapter 8	71
Chapter 9	83
Chapter 10	92
Chapter 11	103
Chapter 12	113
Chapter 13	126
Chapter 14	137
Chapter 15	156
Chapter 16	169
Chapter 17	175
Chapter 18	185
Chapter 19	202
Chapter 20	212
Chapter 21	222
Chapter 22	232
Chapter 23	243
Chapter 24	254
Chapter 25	261
Chapter 26	271
Chapter 27	279
Chapter 28	285
Chapter 29	293
Chapter 30	304
Chapter 31	310
PSY - IV Teams Books	313
About the Author	315

Chapter One

O*h, for Pete's sake, Meli, just hit send.*

It didn't matter how much I yelled at myself, I couldn't get my finger to hit the stupid button. The violent slam of a door made me jump and drop my phone, which then disappeared in the dark recesses of shag carpeting oozing out from under the questionable queen-size bed.

Outside the thin walls a shrill screech turned a string of Spanish obscenities into an abusive litany. A basso rumble answered and suddenly an argumentative duet erupted outside the door of my no-tell motel room.

Hot frustration pressed against my eyes, and I rubbed the heel of my hand hard to keep the lurking tears in check.

The angry concert outside picked up pace and volume, and my stomach clenched. My fingers curled into useless fists as I glared at the limp, sun-faded curtains.

The crescendo hit with the sickening sound of flesh impacting flesh, which was accented by a feminine scream of fury. It was a song I understood all too well, but tonight I had enough.

No more stupid excuses, I needed help.

Dropping to my knees, I tried to ignore the biohazards cultivating in the worn carpet, as I felt around for my phone. When my fingers hit familiar aluminum, the breath I held escaped on something sounding suspiciously close to a sob.

Phone in hand, I scooted back until my spine hit the wall. Huddled behind the bed as far from the door as possible, I touched the screen, scrolled through the abysmally small list, and despite my shaking fingers, hit send on the number I never expected to use.

Staring at the bedraggled bedspread, I listened to the line ring while the harsh rumble of a motorcycle roared to life drowning out the feminine curses gathering volume outside.

Once. Twice. Three times.

Panic dug desperate claws into my chest until little white starbursts decorated my vision. *Please.* The silent plea was all I could manage, my hold on calm and rational beginning to slip.

"Talk."

I opened my mouth to do just that, and all that emerged was a choked sob. I tried again. "Wolf?"

A momentary quiet filled the line while the muted sound-track of jumbled conversations and laughter played in the background, then, "Meli? What's wrong?"

As if the rough rasp of his voice shattered the lock on my throat, the words tumbled over one another, spilling in a frantic rush. "I'm sorry to bother you, but do you know where Risia is? I've been trying to reach her since this morning."

"She's out of town on assignment with Tag."

Of course she was, because that was how my luck was running lately. "Oh, okay. Sorry to bother y—"

"Vete a la verga culero!"

I winced as my temporary next-door neighbor found a new level of forte before slamming her door so hard the thin-paned window in my room rattled, even as her companion's motor-cycle left the parking lot in a squeal of rubber.

In my ear, Wolf growled, "Meli, where the hell are you?"

Obviously, he hadn't missed the telenovela drama on my end. Dropping my forehead to my knees, I pressed the phone closer to my ear, torn between the urge to laugh hysterically or sob. "In a motel."

"Why?"

Because someone shot up the vacation villas where I worked and lived but giving him that answer might not be in my best interest.

Time for a little down playing. "There was some ahh… trouble at Vientos Salvaje yesterday and the police asked me to stay at a hotel until tomorrow."

"Trouble?" he bit out as a door slammed shut somewhere on his end. "What kind of trouble requires police involvement?"

Right, as if he wouldn't want specifics after that rather lame answer. "It's nothing," I lied through my teeth.

"If it's nothing," he growled, "why are you looking for Risia?"

I thumped my head back against the wall, twice. This was why I hadn't wanted to call. "She's my best friend, I needed someone to talk to." More like someone to run to for help, but guess I was on my own. No surprise there. "Look, Wolf, I—"

"Meli, what the hell is going on?"

The edge of command in his question served as an obvious warning of his waning patience. Unfortunately, my patience had disappeared under the churning mass of frustration and fear dogging my heels for the last twenty-four hours. "Someone thought it would be amusing to shoot up the villas," I snapped.

"You were shot at?"

Oh boy.

Deafening silence rang through the line, then, "Where the hell are you?"

"Dead Miner's Motel off the 215."

"Are you safe?"

Part of me wanted to snipe, 'define safe', instead I managed to choke out, "For now."

The sudden explosion of canned laughter as the TV next door blared to life made me jump.

"Keep the damn door locked and don't fucking move, Meli. I'm on my way."

"Okay." Because it wasn't as if he left me any choice on my answer. Besides, I couldn't argue with the relief turning my legs watery. Right now, I'd take what help I could get because whatever was happening around me, I could deal with it, as soon as I got a chance to find my feet.

"I'll text you when I'm close."

Panic seeped in at the thought of losing this fragile connection and my fingers tightened on the phone.

I lifted my head, blind to the cheap motel room. "Wait, Wolf, don't hang up. I'm sor—"

"Don't you dare apologize."

I tangled my free hand in my hair and pulled at the strands. The minor bite of pain kept the choking cloud of terror at bay, loosening the tight bands on my chest. Dragging Wolf into my mess was never the plan, but then plans had a way of imploding lately.

"I told you to call me, woman. I didn't think you'd make me wait four fucking months." There was a burst of distinctive noise in my ear as the line was muffled. "Don't hang up."

Without waiting for my response, he said something to someone on his end, then the sound of a car door slamming was followed by his very irritated, "You are damn stubborn."

Despite the crummy situation, the frustration in his voice made my lips twitch. "You do know curse words aren't valid forms of communication, right?"

"They work just fine for me," he grumbled.

Privately, I agreed.

There was a shift on the line, then he was back, his voice sounding a bit hollower than before. "Want to start from the beginning?"

When my teeth found a particularly sensitive spot on my raw lower lip, I winced. "If I thought I had the time, I would, but my phone's battery is dying, and I don't have a charger."

I was lucky to remember my wallet and driver's license, much less my phone when the police herded me away. The charger would've been a massive bonus. Because when you're trying to figure out how your world could change on a dime, a phone charger is not what you're thinking of.

"How long do you have?"

Pulling my phone away from my ear, I checked the status bar and put it back. "I'm at twenty-six percent."

"Hang on."

Leaning my head back against the wall, I closed my eyes, grateful my frantic pulse was finally slowing. Not surprising, because just hearing Wolf's voice acted as a stabilizer.

Which was strange, since when he was actually in front of me, I couldn't decide if I wanted to run to or from him.

"The GPS has your location at roughly five hours. I want you to text me every quarter hour, and call me on the hour, understood?"

"Okay." It came out shaky, but clear.

"Meli," he paused, muttered something I couldn't make out, then the line filled with the steady thrum of an engine.

I waited, unable to read his mind, but cherishing the tentative connection we currently shared, no matter how flimsy it was.

When the silence began to stretch, I blinked my eyes open and stared into reality. "Yeah?"

"Are you really okay?" The softness in his voice was so at odds with the flesh and blood man.

His hidden questions—Are you physically hurt? Do you need a hospital? Who do I have to kill?—echoed underneath and his worry warmed long-frozen spots in my chest. "Yeah, just scared and probably paranoid."

"It's not paranoia if they're really out to get you."

His unexpected humor surprised a laugh and I covered my mouth, before it could change into something crazed.

Breathing through my nose, I slowly dropped my hand and whispered, "How very true."

"Text me."

Swallowing hard, I reached for my fading confidence, needing to fake it so the man rushing to my rescue didn't end up in a ditch. "Yes, sir."

When the line went dead, I dropped my head to my knees and clutched my phone to my chest. Staring into the gathering afternoon shadows, I took my first full breath in hours.

Wolf was coming.

Chapter Two

WOLF

Dead Miner's Motel was a fucking dump and the last place I'd ever consider finding Melisande Dwyer. Four hours and ten minutes since she called me, fear making her voice tight and leaving my stomach a mess. The squat building crouched in the heavy shadows of the desert night. Only half the outside lights worked, and they barely made a dent against the November evening.

Rolling over the cracked asphalt of the parking lot, I brought my truck to halt next to Meli's aging sedan. When the rumble of the engine faded, a heavy silence filled its wake. My spine itched as I scanned the shadows.

Most of the rooms appeared empty, but it was early yet. Give it a few hours and there was no doubt it would turn into a bustling hive of wretched villainy.

Next to me, teammate and friend, Bishop, leaned forward and studied the motel over the top of his shades. "You sure this is the right address?"

"Yeah. Shit." Rubbing a hand over my bare skull, I kneaded the tension gathered at the back of my neck.

What the hell was I getting into? Not that it mattered. Walking away wasn't a damn option. Meli was like a puzzle with the ultimate solution just out of reach. A fascinating, alluring, and frustrating puzzle who hit all my buttons without even trying.

Bishop jammed a ratty baseball cap over his mess of curls and reached for the door. "I'll go get us a room." The door popped open, he stepped out, laid an arm on the roof, and peered down at me, waggling his eyebrows. "Should I be asking for two queens or a king?"

"Don't be a dick," I growled. Leaning over, I pulled my USP 45 from the glove compartment, trying to ignore the vivid images my dirty mind decided to provide at Bishop's not too subtle hint. And he wasn't my co-star.

As I slipped the gun into my shoulder harness and readjusted the unbuttoned chambray work shirt I wore over my T-shirt, I scanned the U-shape motel. The curtains twitched on the room at the far end. Number twelve. "She's in room eleven, see if you can get ten."

Bishop snapped a half-assed salute, rust colored curls brushing his knuckles. "Yes, Chief."

Opening my door, I got out and glared at him over the roof of the cab. "Cut that shit out."

A white flash of teeth was my only answer as he turned and sauntered to the office. A few steps in he turned back and kept walking backward. "So, a king, right?"

I sent him a one-finger answer. "I'm going to find out what's happening. We'll go from there."

He dipped his chin, turned around, and kept going.

Stepping off the running board, I headed to Meli's door, noting the blaring Spanish dialog seeping through the thin walls from number twelve. Must be the screaming woman behind the asshole comment when Meli first called me.

I laid knuckles to door eleven.

Silence answered.

"Meli, it's me."

A lock clicked free and the door opened, spilling yellow light over a frazzled female. I didn't wait, but pushed my way in, closing the door behind me. Vivid green eyes outlined in purple shadows didn't match the dyed brown hair haphazardly pulled back into a ponytail. Freckles stood in stark relief against her pale face as she stood back from the door, arms wrapped around her waist, biting her bottom lip.

The lone bedside lamp didn't do much to alleviate the shadows in the room, but there was no missing the fact she was second-guessing my presence. Then there was her recent weight loss evidenced by her baggy, well-worn jeans.

Just how damn long had shit been hitting the fan before she called? "When did you eat last?"

Her arms went from her waist to her hips, and that temper she tried so hard to tamp down eked out. "Seriously? That's your first question?"

Nope, but my other questions could wait until she wasn't in danger of falling over. "What would you like me to ask you?"

"How about just a plain, 'Hello, Meli'?"

She existed to drive me nuts. Fighting back the urge to bang my head against the nearest wall, I blew out a breath of impatience. "Hello, Meli, when's the last fucking time you ate?"

The little minx's lips twitched. "Hello, Wolf. Sometime early yesterday."

"See how easy that was?" In an effort to ease her tension I forced a smile. "When Bishop gets here, we'll eat."

She inched back. "Bishop?"

"Yeah, he's with me."

She craned her head to look behind me, even though the door was closed, then turned away. "This isn't like last time. I appreciate you coming, but you shouldn't—"

"Don't go there." No way did I want to get into the particulars of my last visit to Vegas. "We're in between assignments.

Things are slow with the holidays coming up." Shoving my hands into my pockets, I hitched my shoulders. "It's not a thing. We grab Bishop and get some food in you before you fall over."

Her slender shoulders snapped straight before she edged around the bed and picked up her wallet from the nightstand. "I'm not hungry."

"Didn't ask if you were, sweets."

She huffed out an audible breath and spun around, temper adding much needed color to her cheeks. "Sweets?"

I raised an eyebrow. "You'd prefer honey bunny?"

She winced.

"Sweet cheeks."

She frowned. "I have a name."

"A beautiful one, but it won't get you out of coming out to eat." Fighting my smile at her pissed off pout, I held out my hand and waited.

Seconds ticked by and she finally reached out and put her hand in mine. It was ice cold.

I tightened my grip and tugged her closer until I could wrap an arm around her waist. She was stiff, whether from fear or reluctance I didn't honestly know. It was obvious whatever was happening stretched beyond her ability to cope. Good thing my skills were up to a challenge. "I think we passed a diner down the road. That work?"

She nodded.

"Meli." I waited until her gaze met mine. "You're okay now."

For a moment, her guard dropped, and heart-rending grief darkened her eyes, touching things in my chest better left alone. One long, slow blink later and it was gone. "Maybe. Maybe not."

There was nothing more I could say, not yet. Instead, I led her out of the dreary motel room and to my truck.

Unsurprisingly, the diner wasn't busy. Eight in the evening fell between the dinner and late-night drunk crowd. The three of us settled into a horseshoe-shaped booth, Bishop and I taking the ends. A scrawny teenager plopped three sweating glasses of ice water down and handed out menus before moving back behind the register near the door, his saggy-ass pants so low I wondered how they stayed on.

We studied our menus, discussed choices, and when we finalized, I motioned the No-Ass-Wonder over to take our order. Order placed, I turned my attention to Meli who was methodically shredding a napkin into confetti. "Where do you want to start?"

Her fingers stilled, then curled into a fist. She stared at me, a frown furrowing her forehead as she mentally picked her way through an explanation.

One, I'd bet, wouldn't come close to the actual truth. "Meli, stop."

She flinched at my harsh tone, but my patience was stretched to a breaking point.

I rubbed a hand over my face. "Start at the most logical place. We don't need all your secrets." Yet.

No-Ass-Wonder delivered our drinks, granting her a momentary reprieve, then wandered away. She flicked her gaze to Bishop who was sprawled on his side of the booth, his arms draped over the padded seat back.

Despite his intimidating appearance, he managed to offer her a gentle smile.

She cleared her throat and dropped her gaze to her fist. She uncurled her hand until it lay flat on the nicked Formica surface. "Early this morning someone shot up the main house at Vientos Salvaje."

The breath seized in my lungs, but I managed to force out a question. "Were you inside?"

She shook her head, her limp ponytail brushing her shoulders. "I was in one of the villas with Robert, fixing a leak in the bathroom sink."

"Robert?" Bishop asked, nabbing her attention.

She nodded. "He's our handyman. At first, I thought it was a car backfiring. We didn't have any guests scheduled, but we get occasional drop-ins."

The small group of buildings that made up the B&B known as Vientos Salvaje sat on the outskirts of west Las Vegas near a series of state parks. "Do you have guests staying there now?"

She rubbed her forehead and sat back in the booth. "Thankfully, no. Generally, this time of year, it's fairly quiet. We had a reservation set for Thanksgiving weekend, but they called and canceled."

"Means we can rule out the drive by being connected to a guest." Bishop picked up the white coffee mug and took a sip.

Drive by? Vientos Salvaje was not a place I'd connect to a drive by, but then my brain clicked into gear. Bishop had been stuck in Phoenix when Rabbit, Jinx, and I joined Tag, Risia, and Meli in Vegas back in July, which meant he didn't get it.

"Trust me, man, the villas are too out of the way for this to be a random drive by," I explained.

He took another sip, his dark eyes studying me over the rim of the mug. "If it's not random—"

"It's deliberate." There was the barest tremor to Meli's voice.

Trepidation curdled my blood. "Care to explain?"

Furrows formed her in forehead as she nibbled on her raw, bottom lip and she suddenly found the tabletop highly interesting. With that face she should never play poker.

Dammit, she was going to say something I wouldn't like.

Bishop set his coffee down and leaned forward, his arms on the table, watching Meli. "This isn't the first incident, is it?"

Her gaze flickered to him, then slid back to me.

I didn't need my specialized skill to know she was waging an internal war on what to say next. Time to take that option off the table. "You know who we are and what we do, Meli, so spill."

Her mouth opened, but before she could say anything a plate hit the table. "A number four, no onions, medium well; a number five, medium rare, and a salad and soup." No-Ass-Wonder dispersed our orders, all the while maintaining his supremely disinterested air. "Anything else for you?"

"We're good," Bishop answered, snagging the ketchup. Our intrepid waiter shuffled away.

Meli began picking at her salad as I salted fries and accepted the ketchup from Bishop.

"I know Risia, I don't know you." She took a bite.

In a way, she was right. Risia was her best friend and just happened to be involved with another member on our team, Tag. When he and Risia were in trouble, they landed on Meli's doorstep.

Setting the ketchup on the table, I did a quick scan of the diner. No one lingered within earshot. I waited until she finished her bite, before asking, "You know what Risia can do, right?"

She nodded.

Good, it was a workable starting point. At least I didn't have to shovel through a bucket load of disbelief. I snagged my burger. "We're different in the same way Risia's different." I took a bite, my stomach thanking me.

Meli forked another bite of lettuce and kept quiet.

Fine, then. Swallowing, I kept going. "Where Risia can see the future, Tag can tell if someone is lying, and Bishop, here," I waved a fry in my friend's direction, "can recognize patterns most people can't see. Each member of our team has a unique psychic ability, and we utilize our skills to accomplish mission objectives issued by Colonel Delacourt. Think of us as a psychic special ops team."

Meli's full fork rested against her plate forgotten. "Risia's never been military, and she told me Tag was out."

Bishop shrugged. "We're all out now, but we all served at one time. It's how Delacourt knew who to approach when she set up the PSY-IV Teams."

"Cipher?" she repeated.

"PSY-IV," I stressed. "Think psy, for psychic and the Roman numeral four."

She blinked. "Wow, so the urban myth about psychic soldiers is true?" She didn't wait for an answer, wary interest lurking in her green eyes as she studied me. "What kind of psychic are you, Wolf?"

Tension crept through my shoulders. Here came the stumbling block. "I'm a telepath."

She straightened so fast I thought she'd give herself whiplash. "You can read minds?"

Her instinctive flinch acted like a whip against my skin, but I hid my wince by taking another bite of my burger. Hers was an all too familiar reaction, one that would get worse if she knew what the full package contained.

Before I could respond, she went on, "Wait, can you read my mind?"

A sliver of relief crept in. What caused me undue frustration, would reassure her. I shook my head, mouth full, grateful when Bishop stepped in.

"Nope, you've managed to throw him for a loop." Despite his teasing tone, his gaze was serious as he watched Meli. "Congratulations, you're one of a very, very few with a solid, natural mental shield. Didn't think I'd ever see the day someone knocked him down a peg or two."

An intriguing smile began to form, wiping away the signs of her earlier stress. "Really?"

Really, but I wasn't about to encourage her.

Bishop's dig was an old one. He claimed because slipping in and out of the minds of those around me, I'd become too complacent with the ease of my telepathic ability. There may be some truth to that, but I spent years wading through the murky depths of mental minefields of others, and when I met Meli, it was a relief to get nothing.

In fact, because her mind was locked behind a natural shield that Fort Knox would envy, it meant I didn't have to work to keep my mind blocked from random, unwanted thoughts, like I had to with everyone else.

Well, unless the thoughts were mine.

With her, I would never have to wonder if her reactions were her own or merely a reflection of my own dark desires. Still, my attraction to her wasn't just the challenge of unlocking her shield, but something more, an innate sense that she was made to be mine. A total caveman thought, but I didn't argue with it. She was the closest I'd ever get to a "normal" relationship.

Whoa. Relationship? Where the hell did that come from?

My appetite disappeared leaving me glaring at my half-eaten burger. Wiping my face with a napkin, I shoved my plate aside. Time to get this conversation back on track. "What happened before the shooting?"

That fast, her smile dimmed. "It started with the phone calls."

"Phone calls?" Bishop pressed.

She nodded. "A couple weeks after Risia left, the phone at the main house would ring, and when I answered, no one was there." Her face scrunched, and she waved a hand, as if wiping a chalkboard. "Correction; someone was there, but they never said anything."

"No chance of a wrong number?"

She grimaced. "Nope, because later there were a few that came through my cell as private numbers. I called my carrier, but they couldn't get me the number."

Bishop drummed his fingers on the table. "Did you tell the police about those calls?"

Faint color stole over her cheeks. "Yes."

I didn't need my ability to grasp the reason behind her blush. "But not until the shooting, right?"

Her hand tightened on her fork until her fingers were bloodless. "Until bullets started flying, I thought I was paranoid. Or that maybe they had something to do with why your team was here before. I mentioned it to Risia, and she told me everyone who was involved was in custody."

Or dead, but that wasn't spread around. While we managed to stop a black-market sale of information regarding a flaw in the government's communication system, we uncovered the existence of a new threat—customizable nano-viruses. One of which almost cost Risia her life. Unfortunately, there were two individuals who attended that sale still unaccounted for and tracking them down was turning into a unicorn chase.

I met Bishop's gaze, and he gave a short shake of his head. Right, we'd check out that possibility on our own.

Meli missed our exchange and kept going. "There was nothing tying any of it together. I didn't want to come across as crazy."

I don't know what was on my face, but Bishop took over before I could respond. "What else happened?"

She blew out a breath. "Someone threw a rock through one of the villa windows." She paused and stared down at her food. "I thought it was kids screwing around." She lifted her head. "Last week I came out and all of my tires were flat."

An unsettling mix of anger and fear rose at the thought of

her being stranded at the villas while someone singled her out. "Were they slashed?"

"Strangely enough, no. They were just flat." Metal chimed softly against the edge of her plate, drawing my attention. Her hand was shaking.

Unable to stop the urge, I reached out and covered her hand. "What else?"

The tip of her tongue snuck out to wet her lips. "You'll think I'm nuts."

"You're not nuts." I sank every bit of my confidence into that statement. Someone was targeting her, and judging by the steel in Bishop's dark eyes, he had arrived at the same conclusion.

She braced. "In my house, some of my things were moved." Her voice was low, as if saying it aloud wasn't something she wanted to do.

"Like?" Bishop matched her softness.

She searched his face as seconds ticked by. "Books, music CDs, movies, pictures, and..." She turned back to me, worry and fear clouding her gaze. "Clothes."

That did not fit the actions of an international terrorist bent on revenge.

That sounded personal.

Chapter Three

The warm strength of Wolf's hand chased the chill from my fingers, even as my heart beat hard in my chest. Recounting the events of the last few months, even those I couldn't prove, was a relief. Of course, part of that relief could be attributed to the presence of the two very large and intimidating men at my side.

At six four and built like a linebacker, I thought Wolf was big, but his friend, Bishop, was right there with him. If Wolf hadn't vouched for him, I would have run in the other direction. Together the two would make anyone think twice about approaching.

The explosion of Bishop's long auburn curls combined with dark chocolate eyes, and a goatee with a five o'clock shadow, lent his strong face a strange, compelling intensity. He vibrated with a barely leashed sense of energy, while Wolf took after his namesake, quiet and watchful.

Like a perfect point and counter-point brought to vibrant life.

I gently tugged on my hand, until Wolf let me go. Clearing

my throat, I went back to our conversation. "I can't prove anything was moved, but I know it was."

There was no missing the exchange of glances between the men. I filed their reaction away to bring up to Wolf later, right next to processing the fact these two men were psychic like Risia, because that little fact was still sinking in.

Wolf rested his arm on the table as he leaned back in his seat. "If I remember right, the main house has an alarm system, right?"

"Monitored by Diamond Protection Services, but when I called, they said nothing registered on their end." Another one of those non-verbal exchanges occurred and frustration rose, driving me to speak. "Look, I'm not making this up."

I dropped my hands to my lap, trying to hide my fists. My emotional roller coaster ride took a sickening lurch as I considered how frantic I sounded. Fear, frustration, worry, it all gathered speed, tearing through my resolve. As hot pressure gathered behind my eyes, I wished we were sitting at a table instead of a stupid booth. I couldn't get up and take a moment for myself, because that required getting one of my bookends to move his butt. Unfortunately, if I moved now, I'd lose it.

"When did the police say you could go back to Vientos Salvaje?"

Wolf's question jerked me out of my impending pity party. I squeezed the one-word answer around the lump in my throat, "Tomorrow."

"Good." He waved our waiter over and waited until he approached before saying, "Check, please." The boy walked away, and Wolf shifted his weight to a hip and pulled out his wallet. "We'll head over first thing in the morning. Tonight, you need to sleep."

His autocratic tone rubbed me the wrong way and I stuck my tongue out before I could check the impulse.

He raised an eyebrow and leaned close. "Put that away unless you plan on using it, sugar lips."

I winced. "Definitely not sugar lips." Behind me, I caught Bishop's choked laugh. Grabbing my purse, I reached in for my wallet, only to have Wolf stop me.

"I've got this."

Of course he did. "You sure?"

He didn't bother responding, simply drew the receipt over and threw his card on top of it. "We have the room next to yours. What time do you want to head out? We can do a once over at the villas and see what we can find."

Cocking my head, I watched him. "You do know the police have already gone through everything, right?"

He didn't say anything, just arched an eyebrow.

Narrowing my eyes, I studied his face. "You think they missed something?"

While Wolf remained stubbornly mute, Bishop spoke up, "It doesn't hurt to get a second, or third, pair of eyes on scene."

Huffing out a breath, I turned to him. "I get you two are good at your jobs, but I'm pretty sure the police are as well. There's no reason for you both to get involved. I'm sure the police are doing everything they can."

Grim resolution stared back and I stifled the urge to roll my eyes. Granted I had called Wolf first, but it wasn't with an expectation of him riding to my rescue. "Look, my bosses already contacted their insurance company."

The owners, a lovely older couple, spent many, many months on the road visiting family and friends while exploring the country. When they decided to hire an on-site manager for the villas three years ago, they took a chance on a recently graduated business major, and I fell in love with the job and the location. "They're sending out an adjuster tomorrow so we can get the repairs started."

"Then we'll stay until they're complete," Wolf finally rejoined the conversation.

Feeling like a ping-pong ball as I swiveled my gaze, I frowned. "Why?"

"Why what?" he shot back.

"Why are you doing this?"

Holy Matilda, was that a blush rising on his face?

"Because it's obvious you're in someone's crosshairs, and I'm not comfortable leaving Risia's friend hanging in the wind. She'd shoot first, then ask questions."

Nope, not a blush, anger. "Neither Risia, nor I, expect anything from you." Oh wait, maybe that wasn't the best way to put that, but his cranky tone ruffled my feathers.

"That's just too damn bad," he snapped back before I could figure out how to rephrase my words. "Something's going on and until I figure out what, you're not heading back alone."

There was no way to win this illogical argument. Besides, if I was being honest, part of me was extremely grateful not to be going back to the villas alone.

The last couple of months—correction, the last year—had erased any sense of comfort I found at Vientos Salvaje. I managed to regain some of it, but then four months ago Risia brought Wolf to my doorstep. When he first stepped out of the rental car, I was torn between fear and fascination.

Where his big body and grim countenance should have been off-putting, the unshakeable man under the skin managed to slip past my guard and somehow become my talisman against my constant worries. Maybe it wasn't fair to use him as my imaginary shield. Heck, chances were most of what I believed of him was in my head, but I couldn't seem to let it go.

And maybe that was crazier than my paranoia.

Gathering the tattered remains of my composure, I wrapped my threadbare dignity close. "Fine. You and Bishop can stay in one of the villas." I shared my hardest stare between the two men. "Only until the repairs are done. If your boss calls you back before they're done, you go. I won't be the reason you jeopardize your jobs."

Our waiter came back and collected the card and check without a word. Bishop snagged his almost empty coffee cup and drained it, but his dark eyes laughed at me. When something brushed my cheek, I jumped and turned to Wolf.

He continued to tuck a loose strand of hair behind my ear, undeterred by my skittish reaction. "We're staying until we're sure you're safe."

His finger moved to my chin, the lightest pressure warning me not to speak. "We'll keep Delacourt apprised of the situation, but it's better we ensure there are no loose ends from our earlier visit. If it's not tied to our team, then it won't hurt to have some help figuring out what it's all about. Copy?"

His gaze searched my face, and realizing he wouldn't let go until I agreed, I gave a short nod.

Our waiter came back with Wolf's card, breaking the moment with his mumbled, "Have a great night."

I followed the men out of the diner and to Wolf's truck. The sound of releasing locks accompanied the flash of the truck's taillights. When someone's phone rang, we all came to a stop.

Bishop dug into his pocket. "I'll catch up." He thumbed his screen. "Yeah?"

Wolf's arm curled around my waist as he guided me to the passenger side. He opened the door, and I used his arm for balance as I stepped inside the cab. The old fashion move wiggled its way into my foolish heart.

Stupid Meli, a guy shows you a little kindness and you melt. Keep it together, girl, you know better than that. I bit my lip.

Wolf left the door open for Bishop and rounded the hood to the driver's side. As he settled behind the wheel, I kept space between us, staying on the far side of the middle console. Soon enough I'd be stuck between them.

He started the truck and then sat back, his attention focused on me.

His gaze held a heat I wanted to play with, but I knew better. Still, old habits die hard, and I couldn't resist. "What?" My voice came out soft.

He opened his mouth, but nothing emerged as the sound of gravel underfoot drew his attention behind me. He shook his head. "Later."

Bishop filled the open space of the passenger door. "Scoot, shrimp."

Folding my arms, I settled back instead. "Are you talking to me?"

His grin was bright. "See any other shrimps around."

"I hate to break it to you, but five seven isn't considered short." I shifted over, straddling the console hump and letting him in. "Besides, anyone's a shrimp compared to you two. Where do they grow giants like you?"

He chuckled as he settled into the seat. "Oregon."

"Seriously?" I bumped his shoulder. "Wow, guess all that tree-hugging pays off."

"Tree-hugging?"

Wolf backed out of the parking space and headed back to the motel.

Strange how easy it was to tease Bishop. "Everyone knows Oregonians revere trees. They even adjust their roads around their wooded lords. Makes driving there a GPS challenge."

"Sounds like you visited."

Memories crowded close, dimming my mood. "Yeah, a few times." Needing to change the topic, I gave it my best shot. "So, now you live in San Diego?"

Bishop shifted until his shoulders were braced against the window and the back of the seat. His position forced me closer to Wolf. "Yeah, I just moved from an apartment to Rabbit's condo. With Tag and Risia getting their own place, Rabbit was looking for a new roomie."

I knew Rabbit from when he came down with Wolf in July. "Risia mentioned they finally found something she and Tag could agree on." And that wasn't envy pinching me with little green fingers. Being on my own was a good thing. A very good thing. Not wanting to ignore Wolf, I pulled him into the conversation. "What about you, Wolf?"

"What about me?" He flicked on the turn signal and glided into a turn. We sat so close I could feel the muscles in his arms bunch with the movement.

"You living with a roommate?" It was a perfectly acceptable question, right? Just because I was holding my breath for his answer didn't mean a thing.

"Nope, have my own place."

"And it's a beaut," Bishop chimed in. "Older home, three bedrooms, and took him over three years to restore."

"Would've taken less if I hadn't kept getting deployed," Wolf muttered.

"I hear ya," Bishop said. "One of many benes of working for Delacourt is being able to unpack." He bumped my shoulder. "What's your story?"

Maybe I should've expected his question considering I started this, but it didn't stop my stomach from bottoming out. Striving for casual, I kept it general. "I got lucky and picked up my job straight out of college. Since I was looking for a change in scenery, managing the villas was a perfect opportunity."

"Where was college?" Bishop adjusted one of the vents in the dash.

"Seattle University."

He flashed a sly grin. "Ahh, explains the tree-hugging comment."

"Why Vegas?" The question came from Wolf.

I shrugged, unwilling to share and then desperately scrambled for a valid reason that wouldn't lead to more questions. "It's a good first job which will do wonders for my resume. Besides, the Nelsons offered a great benefit package."

That got me a sidelong glance, but thankfully he turned into the motel's parking lot.

Silently, I blew out a sigh of relief. Just a few more minutes of being polite, then I could hide in my room. The headlights bounced over the line of doors and my parked car. As Wolf pulled up next to it, I began fumbling with my seatbelt. "Thanks for dinner, but I think I'm going to call it night. How early do you want to leave tomorrow?"

Next to me Bishop shifted in his seat.

His soft expletive brought my head up as rattled nerves sparked. "What?"

He ignored me and instead said, "Wolf?"

"Yeah, I see it." Wolf's hand covered mine, stopping my fumbling. "Stay here, Meli."

The way the two were acting left me shaky. I peered through the windshield trying to see what caused their reactions, but the outside lights were dark and the one on the far corner wasn't reaching far.

Squinting, I could make out a thick black line along my door. "Is my d—"

Bishop opened his door, cutting off my sentence. He set one foot out, while his hand pulled up his T-shirt and wrapped around the dark butt of a gun nestled against his back. Frozen in place, I stared. Not because of the gun, but because processing what was happening was beyond me.

"Meli?"

Slowly I turned my head until I faced Wolf. There was a sudden rush of empty air as Bishop left the car.

Wolf's gaze was steady and his jaw set. "Did you leave anything in your room?"

I swallowed, as my mind skipped over his question. Eventually it got on track. "No, I only had my purse and I brought that with me."

Wolf's gaze snapped above my shoulder and there was the barest sound behind me before the seat cushion dipped a bit causing me to jump and turn.

"Whoa, sorry Meli, relax, it's just me," Bishop soothed. The hand wrapped around the gun rested on the seat, the other along the top of the doorframe as he looked at Wolf. "The car's clear, but we'll want to double check with some light once we clear the room. Ready?"

"Yeah." Wolf got out, turned to me and in a stern voice said, "Stay put."

Since I wasn't sure my legs would hold if I tried to get out and my mouth was drier than the surrounding desert, I nodded.

He straightened, reached under his loose shirt and pulled out a gun. A distant part of me noted the familiar lines of a Heckler & Koch 45. Then he was gone, closing in on the open motel door with Bishop, while all I could do was watch from the cab. For such big guys, they moved with uncommon grace.

I watched them come up on the door from different sides, Bishop crouching until he was below the window frame, Wolf coming in wide from the other side. They exchanged nods, and then Wolf pressed his back to the wall before using his free arm to push the door open wide.

Bishop rushed inside. Interminable minutes ticked by, before Bishop's low "clear," drifted through the open driver's door.

Wolf lowered his gun, the edgy atmosphere slowly dissipating. I released a shaky breath.

A yellow light chased some of the shadows from the room and made the drawn curtains glow. Bishop's shadow appeared next to the bed, probably because he turned on a lamp inside.

Wolf looked to me and before he could issue another one of his "stay put" commands, I managed a weak "go ahead" motion, more than happy to sit right here for another minute or so.

It didn't take them long to search the room, and when they came back out, their faces were grim.

Bishop went to the door next to my room, while Wolf headed my way. He stopped and leaned in. "There's no real sign of anyone in your room, but that doesn't mean anything. We're going to double check your car. If it's clear, we're moving to a different hotel for the night." He didn't wait for my answer but straightened and left.

Twisting in my seat, I watched him open the truck box sitting in the bed and pull out a heavy-duty flashlight. He clicked it, and eye-searing brightness sprang to life.

Bishop rejoined him and threw two duffel bags into the bed of the truck. Then he followed Wolf to my car where they proceeded to prowl around it like mechanics. They even popped the hood.

It was all so surreal it left me numb. When had my life gotten so out of control?

They slammed my hood into place and came back. I scooted over and pushed the door open to get out. I made it as far as standing on the running board, before being blocked in by two male bodies.

"Where do you think you're going?" Wolf growled.

Wasn't it obvious? "To my car."

He leaned in and the doorframe kept me from crawling back in the cab. "Get your sweet butt back into the truck and hand your keys to Bishop." I opened my mouth to argue, but he shut me up. "You're not safe behind the wheel since you're about ready to keel over from exhaustion. Bishop will bring your car to the new hotel." His sea green gaze held mine, waiting.

Scowling, I ducked down and grabbed my purse, then sat on the edge of the bench seat. Digging in the bottomless pit of holding, I withdrew my key ring. "Here." I shoved them at Bishop, who held his hand out from behind Wolf. "It's the third silver one."

Bishop's grin was faint, but there. "I promise not to trash your car."

"You'll be buying me a new one if you do," I muttered. Then with one last fulminating glare at Wolf and his macho attitude, I settled into the passenger side and pulled the door closed.

It wasn't long before Wolf got back behind the wheel and cranked the engine. "Put your seatbelt on."

My lack of sleep was playing catch up. It took a couple of tries, but I got the belt in place and propped my head up on my hand as I rested it against the window and closed my eyes.

The truck was moving when I finally spoke. "If nothing was disturbed, maybe the lock didn't catch."

There was a pause, but it was too much work to open my eyes. "Do you really believe that?"

After all the strange little and not-so-little things that had been happening? Nope, not for a minute, but it would be nuts to consider the open motel door had anything to do with the shooting. Right?

My thoughts were muddled, and I couldn't make heads or tails out of them. But it wouldn't do any good for Wolf to know how long my ride on the crazy train had been. "I don't know."

"Regardless, I'd rather be safe than sorry."

Too tired to guard my mouth, the words spilled out. "Too late."

Chapter Four

I woke the next morning with only a vague recollection of our arrival at the new hotel. For the first time in what felt like forever, I didn't wake under a smothering cloud of fear and panic. It was a welcomed relief.

Even our breakfast, held downstairs in the hotel's restaurant with Wolf and Bishop, was thankfully uneventful. The only bump occurred when Bishop wouldn't return my car keys as we were checking out of our rooms.

"Don't be ridiculous." I lunged for the keys he held out of reach. "I'm perfectly capable of driving my own car." Giving up on reclaiming them, I put my hands on my hips and glared. "In fact, I prefer to drive."

"Wolf said no."

His reply made me want to stomp my foot. Instead I layered my words with as much sickening sweetness as possible without going into sugar shock. "That's nice, but that's not Wolf's decision."

"Actually, honey bear, it is," Wolf drawled from behind me.

Since I believed in equal opportunity, I turned and shared

my glare, refusing to comment on his ridiculous use of pet names.

He shifted his duffel to his shoulder, ignored me, and drew their door shut. "You're riding with me."

"Why?" I gritted out.

His smile broke free, generating a remarkable transformation from macho solider man to teasing teddy bear. "Because I said so. And Bishop is lousy company."

Behind me Bishop laughed.

I threw up my hands to hide the beginnings of my answering grin. "Fine. Whatever. Let's go." I stomped down the hall to the elevator.

"What's the rush?" Wolf didn't have to do much other than lengthen his stride to keep up.

I hit the down button and folded my arms across my chest. "Stupid phone is dead, and I don't want to miss the insurance adjuster's call."

"You can use mine," he offered.

I bit my lip and brushed my chin on my shoulder. "I don't remember their number." In this day and age of instant information, memorizing numbers went the way of the dodo bird.

The elevator chimed, and the door whooshed open. Stepping inside the empty compartment, I waited until both men were on before hitting the button for the hotel lobby.

The shiny reflective doors acted like a mirror. Behind me, Bishop leaned against the wall, and Wolf's gaze was focused on my butt. The intensity of his stare left me barely resisting the urge to tug my shirt lower.

As I watched him watch me, dreams that crept in at night decided to brave the bright light of day. Heat fired through my veins, lighting up spots that, until this point, remained dormant. What was he thinking?

His gaze finally lifted and met mine. The heat smoldering inside burst into burning life across my cheeks and I silently cursed my fair skin. Thankfully the elevator ride was short, and I stumbled out as soon as the doors parted.

A warm hand wrapped around my arm, checking my rush. Wolf dragged me close, slowing us both until Bishop passed and moved ahead. "Relax, Meli." Even though it was muttered under his breath, the puff of warm air drifted over my ear and left chills in its wake. "What are you running from?"

You. "Nothing, just eager to get home." I plucked at my T-shirt, forcing a lame wince. "Clean clothes are under-appreciated."

He pulled me to a stop and tugged until I faced him. He searched my face, his early humor gone, replaced by a something I couldn't quite place. "Nothing's going to happen between us, unless you want it to. You know that, right?"

All the air in my lungs stumbled to a halt. "What?"

"You're more nervous than a cat-nip-laced mouse in a spinster's house."

That image garnered a surprised giggle. It also managed to dislodge a bit of truth. "I'm not sure what to do with you."

Desire and interest flamed in his eyes, brightening the green and blue swirls. "I'm more than willing to let you do whatever you want with me."

And, wow, didn't my body and heart perk up with that comment even as I tried to reassemble my powers of speech. Instead, we were interrupted by Bishop's, "You two coming?"

Since words were beyond me, we went.

⸻ •••• ⸻

The drive to Vientos Salvaje didn't take long, and Wolf let me retreat into silence. As we bounced over the gravel drive to the main house, I leaned forward until the bullet ridden exterior came into view. Staring at the shattered terra cotta pots that once stood along the porch and the pitted surface of the pueblo style home, I was torn between fury and tears. Fury won. "Immature, cotton-headed, ninny-muggins."

A choked laugh sounded from beside me. "Swear words have an actual purpose Meli. What the hell is a 'ninny-muggins'?"

"Someone who lacks brain power," I muttered as he pulled to a stop, Bishop right behind us.

Reaching for the door, my hand was on the handle when Wolf pulled me up short with a tug on the back of my T-shirt. "Don't."

Shooting him a frown over my shoulder, I paused. "Don't what?"

"Let me come around and get your door."

"I can open it myself, Wolf."

He held my gaze. "I know that, but just let me come around. I want to make sure no one's lurking around who shouldn't be."

He didn't wait for my answer but got out and came around.

I was still struggling with my response when my door opened, and he offered me his hand. I took it. His fingers tightened on mine, and the callouses pressing against my skin bore silent testimony to the inherent strength of the man before me.

A new appreciation for that type of strength unfurled in my chest as I prepared to face my home's damage wrought in violence. For the first time in a long time, I didn't have to be the sole source of strength. It made walking into the mess ahead easier.

Bishop joined us, his sunglasses firmly in place, his attention on the house. "Looks like warning shots."

Studying the damage, I shifted the strap of my purse before it could slide down my arm. "There's a difference?"

"Impacts are above and below window height," Wolf answered. "If you're looking to incapacitate, you aim mid-level."

Sure enough, now that they pointed it out, I noticed two clear lines of holes, one above the window and one along the edge of the porch. "I don't care what height bullets are flying, they're all scary."

Neither man said anything, but Wolf tugged me up the short set of steps to the front door, while Bishop stayed at the bottom.

Twisting my hand free, I dug in my purse for the keys to unlock the door, not that it was holding on by much. When I put the key in, the entire lock shifted. Great, another item to add to the repair list. "I'll get you a key for Maravilla, it's the largest with two queens."

I got the door opened and stepped inside. It was surreal to see the undamaged interior.

Wolf stood in the doorframe, then leaned back to look outside and then back in. "You're damn lucky the walls are so thick." He stepped through, leaving Bishop on the porch.

"Adobe." I moved through the living room to the kitchen cabinet where I kept the villa keys. "The main house was originally built with five-inch adobe bricks, but when the owners updated the interior, they insulated." Nabbing the ones I wanted, I turned and held them out. "Here."

"You're not staying here."

I shook the keys until he started towards me. When he was close, he reached out and took them. "No, I'm not." I went back to the other keys and found Pequeña Estrella's, our smallest villa. "I'll be just on the other side of you, across the path."

His hand tightened around his keys and a frown etched lines in his forehead. "How close?"

Leaning against the counter, I curled the keys in my hand and folded my arms across my chest. "Close enough."

A low rumble was my only warning. Between one blink and the next, he crowded in until my entire field of vision was filled with his chest. His arms kept me trapped as he gripped the counter behind me. His T-shirt did nothing to hide the hard muscles underneath.

My thoughts went from nice and polite to hot and dirty pretty quick. It didn't help that my every inhale was filled with a woodsy spice that dared me to put my nose at the base of his throat and just breathe. Forcing my hormones back in their attic room, I tilted my head back enough to meet his eyes. Too busy trying to regain some semblance of control over my wayward body, it was all I could do.

Wolf lowered his head until our faces were so close if I dared wet my lips, I'd taste him.

Something curled low and hot in my belly, and a wicked voice whispered, *"Just do it."* I dug my nails into my arms.

The sea glass of his eyes darkened, and he whispered, "Tell me no."

Not a chance. Very few good things had been offered to me lately. No way would I pass this up.

Holding his gaze, I did something that was a long time coming. I leaned in and traced my tongue over his lips, needing just a taste. While the simple touch rocketed through me, he didn't move.

Mortified, I drew back, eyes wide.

Red rode high on his cheeks and the muscles in his arms flexed. "Again," he growled.

My nails dug deeper into my arms. If I let go, I'd be wrapped around him like ivy. Instead, I slowly leaned in, refusing to take my eyes from his, and once more licked along his lips. This time, taking my time and relishing his taste.

Another flex of muscle and he was leaning closer, until our lips met, and his tongue tangled with mine. A slow, heated glide, drawing me ever closer while the rest of my body hovered on the edge of bursting into flames.

His taste was dark and decadent, coffee-laced chocolate

with a bite. It left me craving more. A gentle press of teeth against my lower lip made my eyelids flutter, and I leaned in, hunger stretching awake.

Bishop's sharp rap on the doorframe out front broke the spell, snapping my head back as I fought for air.

Wolf shifted and brought his hand up to cup my face, his thumb brushing over my swollen lip, while other, more tempting parts of him, brushed my stomach. "Your taste is addictive."

In what I was beginning to recognize as a pattern, he turned away without giving me a chance to respond. He ran a hand over his head and raised his voice to Bishop, "Don't get your shorts in a wad, we're coming."

He was feet ahead of me and I heard Bishop's voice but couldn't make out the words. Wolf shot a quick look at me before turning forward. His large frame filled the doorway, blocking my view. Obviously, he heard Bishop just fine, considering his scowl and his, "Fuck off, Bishop."

Embarrassment crowded out my achy want, and I was glad not to catch whatever Bishop said. I stopped behind Wolf. "I'll show you your villa." My voice came out amazingly steady considering my insides were a massive wreck.

Wolf turned, and through the open front door I could see Bishop, duffle bags on his shoulders, at the bottom of the porch stairs, grinning like a lunatic.

Squeezing around Wolf, I ignored them both as I led the way to Maravilla. The sooner I got them settled, the sooner I could escape and…and what? Hide?

Self-disgust rose in a choking wave. I was so tired of hiding, of looking over my shoulder. Just because—I ruthlessly cut my thoughts off before they could form.

Now was not the time.

First, get Wolf and Bishop settled, then take a shower and

deal with the insurance company. Maybe later I could afford to indulge the ghosts that haunted me.

—————•◆◆••—————

After leaving Wolf and Bishop, I went to go to the small villa I'd chosen, only to remember I needed clean clothes. Which were back at the main house. Heaving a sigh, I trudged back.

Here near the foothills of Red Rock Canyon the desert temperatures were offset by breezes, laced with juniper, especially during the onset of winter. Nature was rarely silent, even when the sun beat relentlessly down. The insectoid choir provided a continual, natural white noise filter.

At the main house I climbed the stairs, unlocked the door, and slipped inside, closing the door behind me. I made short work of gathering clean clothes from my dresser and my essential bath accessories. Arms full, I stepped out of the bathroom, only to stop short at the sight of a shadow drifting past my door.

Fear sank vicious teeth deep. Never taking my eyes from the door, I managed to dump my things on the bed and edge to the nightstand where the Glock 30S I inherited was stashed.

Holding my breath, I slowly pulled out the drawer, wincing a bit with the soft scrape of wood over wood. Slipping my hand inside, I wrapped my fingers around the familiar texture of the Glock's grip and pulled it out. Keeping it pointed down and my finger along the slide, I inched to the door.

"Meli?" My name in Wolf's voice made me stumble as the adrenaline rush weakened my legs, just as he filled the frame. His gaze went from my face to the gun. He winced. "Shit, I'm sorry, I didn't mean to scare you."

Instead of answering, mainly because it would come out in a squeak, I turned and went back to the bed to gather my stuff, carefully setting the gun on top. After that induced cardio adventure, I wasn't putting it back. I cleared my throat. "No worries. I came back to get some clothes. Forgot to get them earlier."

Arms once again full, I turned around to see him leaning against the doorjamb, arms folded across his chest.

"Considering how you were holding that," he nodded to the gun on top, "I'm assuming you know how to use it."

I gave him a wan smile. "I can manage." I wasn't ready to dive into explanations. Right now, the only thing I wanted was a hot shower.

We stood there, holding each other's gaze, as the seconds ticked by. Whatever he was thinking, he reconsidered, because he shook his head and stepped back. "I'll follow you back."

My arms tightened around my bundle as I found my fading spine and straightened. "You can't shadow me twenty-four seven, Wolf. You and Bishop go do whatever it is you need to do and let me do my thing."

"You're all I have to do at the moment."

Something in his voice slipped under my skin and irritated. "I'm going to take a shower. Alone." His lips twitched, which pissed me off more, so I gritted out the rest. "Then I'm dealing with the insurance adjuster and touching base with the police."

"Bishop and I'll talk to the police."

I looked to the ceiling in hopes of finding some secret to dealing with over-protective males. Nope, nothing there. Darn it.

Stay and argue, or let him have this? Easy decision. I walked forward and squeezed past him. "Fine, just let me know what they say."

He followed me down the hall. It wasn't until we were at the front door and he reached by me to open it, that he responded, "How about I tell you what they say over dinner, when we get back?"

"Whatever."

Unruffled by my bad-tempered response, he simply followed me back to the villas. He was hard to ignore, but I tried. He was temptation of the worse sort, solid, strong, and willing to put himself between me and whatever danger lurked, but I didn't want a savior. I wanted to save myself.

Problem was, I didn't know who or what I was fighting. Except the overwhelming need to find out what it would be like to crawl into his arms, just for a little bit.

We reached my cabin and I went inside, determined to stay silent.

Wolf wasn't having any of it. "Meli?"

I turned, and he took advantage of my full arms. He leaned in and pressed a heated kiss to my mouth before I could retreat. Then I didn't want to. Instead, I followed his lead, and my body rioted with cheerleader intensity.

When he pulled back, he brushed a finger along my jaw. Without a word he stepped back and tugged the door closed, shutting me inside alone.

Chapter Five

Standing on the porch of the main house, one hand shielding my eyes from the early afternoon sun, I watched the insurance adjuster drive off. *Hallelujah, I was finally alone.*

Wolf and Bishop left shortly after the adjuster arrived to meet with the officer in charge of my case. Wolf hadn't wanted to go, but after some fierce arguing (on my part) and growls (on his) I convinced him I would be perfectly fine without him. After watching me drill a few dented cans with lead during an impromptu target practice, he did insist I keep my gun with me at the house. It was currently tucked in a kitchen drawer. No sense in freaking out the insurance agent by greeting him armed. However, the meeting with the adjuster didn't last as long as I initially predicted, which meant I was exactly where Wolf didn't want me.

All by myself.

Before I could wallow in my alone time, I made a call to the contractor the insurance agent recommended. Agreeing to an early morning time on the Monday after Thanksgiving, a week away, I hung up and rocked slowly in one of the porch chairs.

First things first, because if I didn't, I'd never hear the end of it, I shot a quick text to Wolf letting him know the adjuster was gone. In minutes, my phone rang, and since I figured it was Wolf, I answered without looking at the screen. "Hello?"

Instead of Wolf's rough voice, all that answered was silence. Dread spread under my flimsy sense of security. "Hello?"

Nothing but dead air. Pulling the phone away, I looked at the screen.

Unknown.

Stabbing the off button, I hung up. Too rattled to stay out on the porch, I got up and went inside. Part way to the kitchen, my phone rang again startling me. Hard.

"Hello?" There was no way to hide the shaky vibe in my voice.

"Meli, what's wrong?"

At the sound of Wolf's voice, I braced my empty hand against the nearest wall for support. "Did you just try to call me?"

"Yeah, my first one didn't go through."

My breath rushed out. *Sheesh, Meli, you're a freaking mess.* "It rang, but when I answered, no one was there." This time my voice was nice and normal.

No one could accuse him of being slow on the uptake. "I knew I shouldn't have left you."

Shaking my head, even though he couldn't see me, I sank onto the couch. "I'm fine, Wolf. I'm in the house, the adjuster just left."

"We're heading out in five. Keep the door locked and your gun near."

Either he was really paranoid or, "What did the police say?"

"They didn't say anything. There's nothing more than what they had yesterday, which wasn't a hell of a lot. I just don't like the thought of you being out there alone."

"You do realize I've managed to make it through twenty-six years all by my lonesome?" I reminded him gently. It wasn't a dig, more of a nudge for him to rein it in.

"You called me."

"I called you to find Risia."

"But you got me."

"So, what? Now I have to deal with you?"

"Yes, ma'am. That's how this works. Hang on." There were shuffling noises on his end and then he was back. "We're leaving now; we should be back in about twenty. Stay put."

Exasperated beyond belief, I muttered a "bye" and hung up.

Stupid, stubborn man.

Still, I got up and locked the front door, then went to the kitchen. Wolf's concern wasn't unwelcome, but it set off tiny emotional tremors, and I wasn't sure I was ready to deal with repercussions of their impact.

Taking the gun out of the drawer, I brushed a finger over the words taken from the Ranger creed etched along the barrel, feeling the rise and curves under my finger. I repeated them out loud, "Never shall I fail." The now familiar ache throbbed deep inside where it would never be seen, but always felt. "I miss you, Eric."

Needing an escape from memories I wasn't ready to deal with, I decided the best way to anchor myself in the present was to deal with the small stack of mail on the counter. The mindless task would keep me from thinking until Wolf and Bishop came back.

Perched on one of the counter barstools, I began to separate the trash from actual mail. At the bottom of the pile was a ragged looking letter, addressed to me in familiar handwriting. Shock ricocheted through me, but lasted only a moment before grief and anger swarmed in.

My hands shook as I picked it up, handling it like the bomb

it was. Except this would rend more than flesh, this would tear my heart into non-existent pieces.

Ripping it open, I withdrew the letter while a key slid out and bounced onto the counter. Picking it up, I turned it over and over. It wasn't familiar, but the shape made me think it belonged to a safe deposit box. Tucking it into my front pocket, I picked up the letter.

The lined paper was ragged on one end, as if it had been torn from a spiral notebook. Smoothing it out, I began to read.

Hey little sister,

If this made it home after me, I'm sorry. I know it won't take away your anger or grief, but I'll apologize anyway. I tried my best not to have you see this letter. Hell, I've rewritten this before every mission and each time doesn't get any easier.

Not sure what happened. Not sure it really matters. What matters is that you're going to be okay, Meli. You won't believe me, you never do, but you will be okay. You might be able to fool most people into thinking you're this quiet little thing, but I know you. That strength that got you through losing Mom and Dad, it's still there, despite you burying it because of what happened.

Oh yeah, little sis, I know what happened. I wanted to ask you why you didn't come to me about it, but I can just imagine your answer. Maybe it's my fault for leaving you on your own, but I'm your brother, and I can't ignore it. Nor can I forgive his part in whatever it is you're hiding, but I've done my damnedest to make it right and keep you safe.

I love you, Meli, and I'm proud of the woman you are. I wish I could be there but know that whatever took me from you I did it to keep you and others safe.

Love,

Eric

PS: I've left some things for you. Can you make sure they find their rightful place?

Even now, months and months later, there were no tears, just a pain-filled hollow in my chest. It hurt to breathe, and the anger I tried so hard to bury began to claw its way to the surface.

I didn't want a letter, I wanted my brother back. Alive and well, not buried under a white cross in a grass-covered plot far from here. But life never cared about what I wanted, it just kept rolling on.

Tucking the letter back into the envelope, I wondered why it took ten months to find its way home. Much like the hows and whys behind Eric's death, it was another question I'd never find an answer to.

Older by two years, he enlisted as soon as he hit eighteen, unwilling or unable to deal with the unexpected loss of our mother. When our dad followed her a year later, Eric was on-tour and unable to come home. So, at seventeen, I buried Dad by myself and finished high school.

While I ran away to college, he ran away to the Rangers. When he was home, I made time to be with him, never knowing when another chance would come again. Still, he was my brother and the last of my family.

Burying him wasn't an option, until it was the only thing left to do.

"I'm so mad at you Eric." Harsh, but true, the words squeezed out of my tight throat.

Pushing up from the table, I headed down the hall to my room. I stepped into the bedroom's walk-in closet and found the box of Eric's things up on the shelf. It was out of reach, but I didn't want to go and drag a chair all the way back to get it.

Instead, I set the letter down, then pushed and pulled a couple of boxes of books over and used them as a makeshift ladder. My footing wasn't exactly stable, but I was able to shift the box to the edge. As it toppled into my arms, the landline began to ring.

"Seriously?" The weight of the box in my arms shifted, and my precarious position wobbled. Flinging out a hand to one of the shelves, I managed not to fall.

I carefully made my way back to stable ground, and the phone stopped ringing. "Figures."

Backing up until I had enough room, I set the box on the floor, grabbed the letter that started this whole mess, and sank cross-legged next to the box. Staring at it, I wondered how such a big life could fit in such a small container.

My brother lived for the adrenaline rush, which is why him choosing the Rangers over me never came as a surprise. There was a time when I shared that lust for adventure, and a spontaneous trip wasn't out of the range of possibilities, even as I balanced it with a day curled up in cozy chair with a good book.

In the months before Eric's death, my life devolved under the constant barrage of stress, until there were no more spontaneous trips, no more trying things for the heck of it, instead I locked more than my emotions away. The final nail in this self-imposed jail was answering my door and having two uniformed officers solemnly offer their condolences as my world collapsed again.

Yet lately, even the most solitary endeavors no longer managed to fulfill me the way they had before. The most engaging books were set aside unfinished while worry became a persistent companion that demanded my constant attention. Yet under it, a craving to throw life the finger grew brighter by the day.

Funnily enough, I could pinpoint when that dissatisfaction began—four months ago when my best friend brought her troubles and Wolf to my door.

Despite the dangerous situation Risia uncovered, working with her and the others on Wolf's team was the first time in a long time I felt truly alive. It made me realize what it was that my brother chased with his commitment to the Rangers. A sense of purpose was an addictive drug.

Add in the lure Wolf presented, and the urge to travel that road was tempting. Too tempting, maybe.

"Be careful, Meli," I muttered to myself as I opened my brother's box.

Pulling back the cardboard flaps, I stroked a finger over the black box containing the folded flag. Instead of the answers I wanted, this was what I was given.

Even now, it re-ignited my frustration with the military powers that be. Experts at evasion and re-direction, you could never meet a more closed-mouth bunch. Hadn't stopped me from trying, though.

Setting the flag aside I found the bundle of letters Eric sent me through his deployments. Lifting it dislodged a handful of small action figures and the rabbit foot ring of keys and sent it all scattering across the floor. A few figures made a break for it under my bed.

"Dang it!"

Setting the letters aside, I twisted around until I could lie on the floor to retrieve the escapees. I managed to get the first two, but accidentally knocked the third further back. It took some maneuvering but after a dust induced sneeze session, I got the last one.

Scooting back out, I nailed my head on the edge of the bed frame. "Mother of pearl!" I hissed, rubbing the sore spot as I sat up.

Another sneeze hit as I sat the runaway figures next to the rest of Eric's collection. Right, I needed to get the dust off my face or it wouldn't be long before my eyes swelled.

Getting up, I went into the bathroom, each step punctuated by a sneeze. Twisting on the faucets, I finally dowsed my face with cold water and was drying it off when I thought I heard the front door. Wolf and Bishop must be back.

Throwing the towel on the counter, I wove my way through the scattered items and out the doorway. A few steps into the hall, I called out, "Hey guys, I'm ba—"

My voice snapped off when the figure coming down the hall wasn't the one I expected.

Barely getting a glimpse of jeans, dark T-shirt and the incongruous ski mask, I spun on my heel, my goal the bedroom where I left the gun.

Fear left a metallic taste in my mouth, but it wasn't going to stop me. Unfortunately, I forgot about the box and tripped. I tried to aim for the bed, hand outstretched, but my impact was cut short with a cruel grip on my ponytail.

The agonizing pull drew a short scream from my throat and instinct had me reaching back to get free, nails clawing at the grip. A distant part of my mind noted the plastic feel under my nails. *Gloves, he was wearing gloves.*

Unfortunately, between the vicious tug-o-war and my lack of balance, we bounced off the edge of the bed and tumbled to the floor. The box slid across the floor.

His heavy weight crushed me, drowning out the stinging bites of plastic caught beneath me. Instead of wasting breath screaming, I grunted, and scrambled to get my hands under me to push up. I couldn't afford to be pinned to the floor.

I got my head and shoulders up only to have my head shoved viciously forward.

The pain of the first hit stunned, the second turned everything black.

Chapter Six

WOLF

Shoving the accelerator to the floor, I couldn't shake the apprehension clutching my gut as I turned on to the graveled road leading to Vientos Salvaje.

Next to me, Bishop remained grimly silent, but since the team was well trained on mental blocks, whatever he was thinking wasn't leaking out. I didn't need my ability to understand the why behind his unhappiness. Neither one of was thrilled with our visit to the police. There was jack shit to go on, and it could take weeks for ballistics to be returned on the bullets dug out from the walls. Whether I liked it or not, I couldn't pull rank and take the case from them because Meli didn't fall under PSY-IV Team's jurisdiction.

But I was worried, something just didn't add up. That ugly terror sneaking around her polite mask didn't come from everyday shit. Nope, there was something darker at play, and it wasn't done with her.

As the truck fishtailed on a turn, Bishop grabbed the chicken handle above the door. "What's got your panties in a twist?"

"Gut's talking."

"Try and get us there in one piece, then."

Knowing it wouldn't do a damn bit of good to flip the truck, I eased off the gas.

"Delacourt's going to want us back by Monday."

It was easy to follow Bishop's non sequitur. "It gives me five days to figure out what the hell is going on." Or convince Meli to take some time off and visit Risia in San Diego. No way was I leaving without making sure Meli was safe.

The weight of his gaze settled on me. "What really happened between you two?"

"Nothing," I gritted out.

Sadly it was the truth, but there was something there I wanted to pursue. When we first met, I wanted her, but her haunting fear held me back, my instincts whispering for patience. Not my strongest trait. I waited for her to come to me, but not like this. I wanted her to feel the same pull I did, I just didn't think it would take her so damn long to come around.

Now, thanks to some twist of fate, the one damn time my ability could've paid off, and the son of a bitch was silent as a tomb where she was concerned. Not being able to hone in on what she was thinking may have played an initial factor in my attraction, but it left me relying on old-fashion lust and a normal male's inability to understand women. If this was how normal relationships worked, it was a miracle anyone ended up together.

Coming around the last bend, malevolence crawled over me, setting every hair on end.

I slowed the truck as training and instincts kicked in. Thinning the mental shield blocking the whispers of the outside world, I did a psychic scan as we came closer.

Furious anger lined with resentment swept through my mind, leaving a red stain over my vision.

It wasn't mine. The reminder helped me pull back from the

swamping, intrusive emotions as I jerked the truck to a stop. "Someone's here."

As Bishop and I stepped out, guns hot, the mental signature of whoever was inside began to recede. They were on the run. Dammit, we were going to lose them.

Utilizing hand signals, I sent Bishop around back as I made my way up the front steps, the overriding need to ensure Meli's safety larger than my need to give chase.

Even as I tracked Bishop and our target on a mental plane, I reached the half-opened door. Focusing, I tried to sense Meli. While I couldn't get a read on her thoughts, her presence hit my psychic senses as a quiet hush. It was there, but that was all I could get and it wasn't enough.

Gun at the ready, I used my free arm to push the door open.

The front room looked untouched. The drone of the air conditioner provided a constant low-level hum in the quiet. A quick check of the kitchen, then I inched down the hall. Passing a bathroom, a room doubling as an office, and then a bedroom acting as storage for sheets, toilet paper, and various other sundries, I hit the last room just as a soft, feminine groan sounded.

My stomach dropped. Reeling in my urge to rush, I kept my back to the hall and pushed the door wide.

Meli was sprawled on the floor face down amidst a mess of what looked like plastic toys, boxes, and papers. The bed was rumpled and the mattress was angled slightly.

Edgy rage gnawed my gut, but I couldn't afford to acknowledge the ugly stew of emotions. Keeping my gun up and my gaze moving, I knelt next to her and pressed two fingers to her carotid. Relieved at the strong, steady pulse, I cleared the rest of the room. Not that there was much to it. The bathroom was empty, but the closet looked as if a whirlwind had torn through it.

Another groan sounded and I knelt by Meli, setting the gun

on the floor next to me to do a quick check for injuries. My touch was enough to bring her to swinging life. Dodging a wild strike, I managed to grab her wrist, trapping one arm, as she tried to push to her knees and scramble away. Her inherent terror sent a sharp stab through me. "Meli, it's Wolf."

I kept repeating the reassurance even as I pulled her close, finally capturing her other arm so she couldn't hurt either of us. She managed to knock me a good one along my chin before I wrapped my arms around her, holding her close and tight in my lap. "You're okay, I've got you."

It must have finally made it through whatever was racing through her mind, because she stilled, and the thick lashes rose revealing dazed green eyes. Recognition seeped in, turning them a vivid emerald. "Wolf?"

Seeing the knot forming on her forehead, and the blood seeping from under her nose made me hope Bishop caught the fucker who was running. "Yeah, honey, I've got you."

She tugged an arm free and touched the rising bruise, only to wince. "Ow!"

I pulled her hand away. "Stop, and let me look at it."

Carefully, I ran my fingers over the surrounding area including her skull, checking for any other signs of impact. Thankfully, it was the only bump I found. "What happened?"

Her gaze drifted over my face, and the stiffness in her body melted until she was curled into me.

Now that she was awake and aware, my body had other ideas on how to offer comfort. Gritting my teeth, I forced my dick under control. The last thing I needed was her getting spooked. If she tried to stand on her own right now, she'd collapse.

"I heard the front door and thought it was you." Her voice was muffled against my T-shirt.

"Didn't you lock the door?"

That made her turn and glare at me, though the small lines

of pain took some of the heat from it. "Yes, but you had a key. Hence, why I thought it was you."

I refrained from riding her ass about checking her surroundings, since it wouldn't do a damn bit of good. Instead, I managed, "And?"

"And as soon as I realized it wasn't you, I went back to get my gun. It was on the bed." She turned to the bed in question, and pushed against my chest as she struggled to sit up. "Is it still there?"

"Settle down." I stretched my neck until I could see the top of the rumpled bedspread. "It's not there, but we'll check the room in a minute."

She bit her bottom lip eyeing the offset mattress, worry evident in the lines around her mouth. "Maybe it got knocked off when he grabbed me."

"So he grabbed you and…?" I prompted.

She turned her attention back to me, one hand resting on my chest. "He used my ponytail to jerk me back and we struggled. We hit the floor, and he was too heavy to get off. Then he shoved my face into the floor."

Her hand left my chest and she brushed her fingers under her nose. When she caught sight of the blood on her fingers, her face paled more than I thought possible, but there was no mistaking the indignant fury wiping out the panic and tightening her jaw.

That telling hint of hidden strength loosened the tension in my chest. She was going to need it to get through whatever the hell was happening.

First things first. "I'll get you a towel, hang tight."

It took some careful maneuvering, but I left her propped against the bed and grabbed a towel from the bathroom, taking a second to wet the end.

Making my way through the scattered objects on the floor, I crouched in front of her and gently cleaned her nose. Wiping away the last of the blood, I stroked a finger over her cheek, unable to resist the temptation of her soft skin.

Her breath hitched, and I met her gaze, taking in the mixture of caution and need.

That look left me fighting the overwhelming urge to gather her close and tuck her away somewhere safe. Something whispered she might kick me in the balls, if I tried. "Did you get a good look at him?"

She went to shake her head, winced, and stopped. "Couldn't, he was wearing a ski mask." The fist in her lap uncurled and rose as she flexed her fingers. "He was wearing gloves. I went to get his hand off my ponytail, and there was a thin, plasticky layer."

"Latex." Between the gloves and ski mask, it meant the break-in was a planned event. Did the son of a bitch know Meli was home? Not the right question to start with. "We need to see if anything's missing."

"Right, let's start with my gun."

She went to turn and stand, but I held her in place with a hand on her shoulder. "Sit. I don't want you moving yet. I'll search the room for it."

Pushing to my feet, I took a step and something crunched underfoot.

The sound brought a small, quickly smothered gasp from Meli.

I looked down with a soft curse. "What's with the toys?"

I picked my way through the plastic minefield, then shoved the mattress back in line with the bed frame so I could make my way around the foot of the bed and to the other side.

"Not toys, mini-figures."

With no sign of the gun on the floor, I laid on my stomach to peer under the bed. "They're toys, no matter what you call them."

Lifting the material draping the frame, it wasn't long before

I spotted the dull glint of the gun's matte grip lodged between the headboard and the wall. "Found it."

Stretching my arm, I nabbed it and pulled it free. There was something etched along the barrel.

"Thank goodness."

The bed bounced and I looked up from where my fingers rubbed along the etchings to see Meli on her hands and knees crawling across the bed. Lust hit with a hard sucker punch, seizing every muscle. Her oversized T-shirt gaped at the collar, offering teasing glimpses of lush curves, while the afternoon sunlight glinted off the subtle hints of red no longer hidden under the veil of the brown hair dye she used to try and douse those embers. It was an unintentionally sexy picture.

Clearing my throat, I held it out to her. "Gorgeous." And it wasn't just the gun.

Red slipped over her cheeks.

"What's on the barrel?"

Taking it from me, her voice was husky as she answered, "Never shall I fail."

There was a story here. "From the Ranger creed?"

"It belonged to Eric, he gave it to me before his last deployment." With slow movements and a few winces, she moved until she was sitting Indian style in the middle of the bed, the gun cradled in her lap. She traced a finger over the barrel, and even with her head lowered, I couldn't miss the tenderness softening her features.

"Hell of a gift." I shifted until my back rested against the wall, and I set my arms on my drawn up knees, fighting not to react to the green-eyed monster prowling under my skin.

Her head lifted and I refused to avoid her gaze. "Is that jealousy, Wolf?"

Unable to answer, I shrugged.

Her grin was full of mischief, giving me a glimpse of the hidden woman. "Afraid of a little competition?"

Catching the teasing note in her voice, some of my tension loosened and I drawled, "Competition implies I might lose, and I don't plan on losing."

Her unexpected giggle made me grin. "Good to know."

"Wolf?" Bishop's voice floated down the hall. "Meli?"

"Back bedroom on the right." Shoving to my feet, I walked around the bed, pointing a finger at Meli. "Stay put. I'll get some ice for your head."

Picking my way through the stuff on the floor, a familiar black box caught my eye. Crouching down, I picked it up, conscious of its importance.

I set it on the bed next to the no longer smiling Meli.

She reached out and dragged it close.

I tucked a finger under her chin and lifted her gaze to mine. "Then you can tell me about Eric while I pick up the toys."

The grief clouding her face hurt to see, but she nodded.

Hard as it was, I left her there and met Bishop at the door. "Let's go to the kitchen. Meli needs an ice pack for her forehead."

He stuck his head in the doorway. "You okay, Meli?"

"It's just a bump." Her fingers rose to rub next to the purpling bruise. "I'll be fine."

Giving her a stern look, I warned, "Don't lay down. I don't want you sleeping for a couple hours."

Those fingers waved me away. "Go, I'm not planning on moving anytime soon."

I led Bishop down the hall to the kitchen. As I rummaged in the freezer, he pulled out drawers. Finding the ice tray, I pulled it out and turned.

Bishop held up a plastic zip bag.

Taking it, I dumped some ice inside, and left the tray in the sink. "Anything?"

"He's damn fast, and had a car waiting." Bishop leaned

back against the counter, his arms folded over his chest. "Whoever he is, he's got evasion training."

That was damn worrisome.

Bishop frowned. "What the hell is going on around here, Wolf?"

I set the bag of ice on the counter and stared out the window over the sink. "Damned if I know, but whatever it is, Meli's the target."

"Did you email Rabbit?"

I turned to him. "I was going to wait until we were done with the police."

He rubbed the back of his neck and straightened. "All right, I'll reach out and have him start digging. I'll have him rule out retaliation for our last visit here."

"If anyone can unearth something, it'll be Rabbit." As the team's geek, Rabbit could perform magic with technology. I picked up the ice. "I need to get this to her."

Bishop followed me out. "You okay here?"

"Yeah, I'll bunk with her and sack out on her couch tonight. She's going to have to be woken up every couple of hours."

He stopped by the front door. "Do we need to call in the police?"

Since that would only result in a pissing match, I shook my head. "Until we have an idea of what we're facing, there's no point."

"Roger." Then he was out and gone.

I continued down the hall and went back into the bedroom. Meli was as good as her word and hadn't moved, but the gun rested on top of the black box at her side.

I handed her the ice. "Here."

"Thanks." She took it and held it against her forehead with a slight hiss. "Did Bishop find him?"

"No, but I'm staying with you tonight." Gratefully, she didn't argue. Spying the upended cardboard box, I set it upright and crouched down, collecting the bits and pieces spread across the floor. "Whoever he was, he went through your closet, so as soon as I clean this up, you need to let me know if anything's missing."

"There should be fifteen figures, his rabbit foot key ring, a box of medals, five books, three T-shirts, and his jacket." Her spine was slumped as she held the ice to her forehead, occasionally shifting it. "And a bundle of letters and photos."

She straightened and scrambled to the edge of the bed. "His last letter, is it there?"

"Meli, sit your ass down and put that ice back on your head," I snapped.

She jerked to a halt and glared.

Ignoring that fuming look I counted the figures. "Thirteen accounted for."

Scanning the rest of the stuff on the floor, I muttered, "Books check, T-shirts and jacket check. Letters..." I went to my stomach to search under the bed. "Letters, photo, two more figures, and..." My fingers tipped against another thin box. Pulling it out, I lifted the lid. "Box of medals."

Sitting back up, I offered the small box to her. "Should I ask how many?"

She took it from me, opened it, and checked. "Eight, all from high school."

Woman had a strange thing for exact numbers. Lifting the jacket, a sheet of notebook paper fluttered to the floor. Reaching down, I picked it up and handed it over. "This what you were asking about?"

Relief bloomed over her face as she traded me the small box of medals for the paper. "Yes, thank you." Her gaze caught on the field jacket. "I'll take that as well."

Handing over the jacket, I put everything else back in the storage box, then checked around the room once more. "No rabbit foot keys."

"Maybe they're in the closet?"

Running a critical eye over her, I asked, "You good at standing?"

She slid off the bed, keeping a hand on top of the mattress for balance, looking a little wobbly. "Yeah."

Using my foot, I moved the box out of the way, took the plastic bag from her, and gave her my arm. "Take it, I don't want you falling over."

With her hand on my arm, we moved to the closet.

She stared at the mess of her closet as she leaned against me. "Son of a biscuit."

I handed her back the bag of melting ice.

She pressed it against her forehead, still staring at the mess.

While most of her clothes hung in haphazard disarray, some spilled onto the floor. Empty suitcases were open and tossed aside; a couple of other boxes had obviously been ripped off the top shelves, their contents strewn across the floor, mainly books and photos, with a few random CDs.

My lips twitched. "I think the word you really want is 'bitch,' love bug." That one earned me a narrow-eyed glare and a pinch on my arm. "Okay, love bug is out."

She shuffled deeper inside. When she dropped the hand with the ice to her side and went to bend over, I stopped her with a hand on her back. "Don't. Just try to see if anything's missing."

Heaving a put upon sigh, she used her foot to move things aside.

Moving in front of her, I stacked the empty suitcases. "Sit."

I waited until she did so before righting the upturned boxes. Each one was clearly labeled, so it made replacing their contents easy. "Let me know if something's not here."

It wasn't the best solution, a deeper inspection would have to be done tomorrow. For now, if her attacker was after something obvious, we'd know.

It took a good thirty minutes to set most of the closet back to rights and by that time the ice had completely melted, and she shuffled to the bathroom to throw it away.

I shoved the last box onto the top shelf.

Behind me Meli said, "The rabbit foot isn't here."

"What keys were on it?" I turned to find her biting her bottom lip. If she didn't stop soon, I'd be tempted to take a nibble of my own.

"Key's to Eric's car, his old storage unit, and apartment."

Ah, yes, Eric. "And Eric…"

"Is…was my older brother." It came out soft, but there was no more teasing when she lifted her gaze to mine. "He was killed during his tour last year."

Chapter Seven

W olf blinked and stuck his hands in his pockets. "I'm so sorry."

Normally those stupid, useless words were empty of anything but pity, but strangely, his held weight. Studying the grim acceptance carving a ruthless edge to his face, it hit me that he was one of those who could understand the full impact of this loss.

And why his understanding caused my anger to crest didn't make sense.

Eric's death wasn't Wolf's fault.

Swallowing the choking bitterness back, I looked down at the letter I still held and tried to shrug, but didn't quite pull it off.

Needing off this topic before things spun out of control, I focused on something else. "Why would anyone take his keys? I sold his car and cleaned out his storage unit months ago, so they wouldn't work anymore."

All that remained of his stuff was in the box Wolf set back on the shelf. Then I remembered what was with Eric's letter and jerked to my feet, ignoring the spike the sudden movement drove through my temples.

Wolf took a step forward as I dug into my front pocket.

"Wait." I pulled out the long, flat key. "This came with his letter today."

Wolf's hands came out of his pockets and his brows lowered, his face dark. "A letter came today?"

My stomach pitched at his ominous tone and I realized where he was going. "Probably last week, but I went through the mail today and found it."

He straightened and closed the distance between us. "Your brother died a year ago—"

"Ten months," I corrected quietly, a small distinction, but important.

"Ten months ago," he amended. "And you're just getting a letter from him now?"

Okay, put like that, it was a little weird. I nodded slowly.

He cocked his head. "Can I see it?"

Part of me didn't want to share because there were things in it I didn't want to talk about. Not now and nowhere any time soon, but then logic interfered. I handed him the letter, watched as he scanned it, and braced.

When he looked up, I swallowed at the intensity burning in eyes and sent up a silent prayer he'd stick to easy questions.

"How did he die?"

Not easy, but answerable. "I don't know. I've sent numerous inquiries to the army, but the only response I get was he was killed during a classified op." Wrapping my arms around my waist, I hid my fists. "No one will tell me anything. They just expect me to accept it and stop bugging them."

He handed the letter back. "If it's classified, no matter how hard you push, you won't get anything."

I knew that, but it didn't mean I accepted it. "Doesn't make it right."

"No, it doesn't." His low agreement softened the brittle edges of my resentment. "You have any idea what it is he left you?"

I went to shake my head, but stopped when a wave of dizziness washed through me. When the edges of my vision wavered, I reached out and found the hard heat of Wolf's chest under my palms. Before I could process, he muttered a curse and swung me up in his arms with gentle care.

There was something breathless about being swept up in a man's arms. At five seven, playing the delicate female role was beyond me, not that I ever wanted to, but being held like this was…nice.

"We're going back to your villa, you need to be lying down."

Lying down sounded wonderful, but we weren't done. "We need to go to the bank and see if they have a safe deposit box for Eric."

"We can do it tomorrow." He headed out of the closet.

Right, the bank would be closed soon. The late afternoon sunlight painted my room in golds and reds. The smudge of black on my nightstand reminded me. "Wait, my gun."

He stepped up to the nightstand. "Can you reach it?"

Keeping one hand on his shoulder, I leaned over. "Don't drop me."

He snorted as I grabbed it. "Anything else you need before we lock up for the night?"

It was starting to hurt to think, but I went through a mental checklist. "Put me down, I need to pack a few things."

His arm tightened, then he set me down on the bed's edge. "Why don't you sit here and tell me what you need?"

I straightened and set the gun aside. Before he could turn away, I snagged his shirt, holding him in place. "I don't think so."

Puzzled, he asked, "Why not?"

I fought the threatening blush. "Because, I don't want you digging through my underwear drawer."

My inner hussy came to attention when his smile filled with wicked intentions. "You're delaying the inevitable."

Probably, but I wouldn't make it easy. "Rather confident aren't you?"

He stepped in until his legs framed mine, leaned over and placed his hands outside my hips, effectively trapping me in place. A whisper of touch brushed my temple, and drifted down until I could feel his breath trailing over my ear as he whispered, "Hopeful, actually."

I shivered and strangled my needy whimper, barely managing to reply, "You're not getting your hands on my underwear."

Oh so slowly he drew back until our faces were level and stared into my eyes, teasing seduction evident in the flush dusting his cheeks. "Want to bet on it?"

When his image wavered, I reached out.

He curled an arm around my spine, pulling me close as he broke our connection.

"You're trying to take advantage when I'm hurt."

His chest vibrated under my cheek as he chuckled. "Then we'll re-visit when your head's not about to explode."

Dang it that rough rasp should be outlawed. I pushed him away. "Whatever." That's me, the queen of the snappy comeback.

He stepped back with a grin. "You sure you up to getting stuff on your own?"

Sighing, I got to my feet with more care than before. Everything stayed level. "I'll be fine."

To prove it, I stepped around him and began picking my way to the dresser. Deciding if he was going to stay and watch, he could be useful; I said, "Could you get me the black backpack from the closet? It's just inside the door on a hook."

At the dresser, I sank into a crouch instead of risking bending over and face planting. Pulling out a drawer, I grabbed a T-shirt and old yoga pants, my standard nightwear, and set it on the floor beside me.

As I closed the drawer, Wolf set the backpack next to them. He tapped my shoulder with something. Bracing a hand on the dresser, I turned and looked up. He handed me my gun. "Thanks."

"Anything else?"

Stuffing the clothes and gun into the backpack, I answered, "Why don't you grab the left over enchiladas in the fridge? You and Bishop can re-heat them for dinner tonight." Each of the villas had a small kitchenette. No sense in the men running back and forth for food. "Take whatever else you think you'll need."

"You need to eat something."

My stomach didn't agree with him, but based on the order underlying his words, arguing was pointless. "Grab a can of chicken noodle soup from the pantry."

His only answer was a grunt, but he turned and left.

I blew out a sigh of relief as he disappeared. Not that I minded his presence, but he kept me on edge, and all I wanted to do was crawl into bed and sleep.

Taking advantage of his absence, I quickly packed my intimates and bathroom supplies. With one last look around the room, I nabbed Eric's jacket off the bed and walked out, pulling the door closed behind me.

Wolf met me in the living room, two full plastic grocery bags in one hand, a small foil-covered pan in the other. He eyed me critically. "Ready?"

"As I'll ever be."

Wolf made quick work of getting me settled at Pequeña Estrella. After washing my face, being careful of the darkening bruise on my forehead, and changing into the yoga pants and T-shirt, I stepped out of the en suite bathroom to find Wolf sitting on the edge of the bed, Eric's letter in hand. Stupid of me to leave it out, but too late to take it back now.

When he looked up, there was no missing the questions on his face. Questions I was in no shape to answer. Leaning against the doorframe, I folded my arms across my chest. "Don't ask."

He arched an eyebrow. "You channeling my ability to read minds now?"

Instead of answering, I took the escape route he offered. "Can you really?"

He patted the bed. "Sit, before you fall down, angel."

Normally I found his penchant for pet names annoying, but this one worked, wrapping around the lonely part of my soul like a hug.

I shuffled over, and when he lifted his arm, I didn't bother fighting the urge to curl into him.

He tucked me close, my head over his heart. At least this way I could avoid his too-knowing gaze. He folded the letter and set it aside, then used his free hand to comb gentle fingers through my hair.

My eyes drifted closed as the minutes passed in intimate silence. Bit by bit, the tension seeped away and in my hazy state, I didn't miss the press of his lips against the top of my head. Such a delicate touch, as if I would break. It made me smile, even as my heart melted a little more.

This man was so dangerous to me. Not willing to dwell on the whys behind his threat, I focused on something else. "What's it like?"

That mesmerizing stroke paused, then resumed. "What's what like?"

Opening my eyes, I tilted my head back until I could see his face.

His hand cradled the back of my skull. Fine lines etched along his eyes and mouth, his jaw tight.

Reaching up, I rubbed my knuckle along that hard line. "Being telepathic." I didn't shy away when under his dark brows, his eyes emptied. Some instinct whispered to keep going if I wanted to understand this man. And I did, badly. "It can't be easy."

His thick lashes drifted down as he turned and pressed a tiny kiss against my knuckles. When he turned back, his eyes were filled with uncomfortable things. "It's like being in a room full of people screaming at you to pay attention all the damn time, but I've learned to keep them out."

Bringing my hand down, I curled my fingers in his T-shirt. "Have you always been able to hear them?"

"No."

I waited for more, but he kept silent. "Really? You're such a tease, Wolf."

The darkness in his gaze lightened as he studied my face, searching for something. "Make you a deal, you get under the covers, and I'll answer your questions."

Pressing back until there was a bit of space between us, I twisted away to get under the covers. A couple of minutes later and we were settled in, Wolf on top of the covers on his side, with his head propped by his hand, me facing him on my side, hand tucked under the pillow. The quiet settled around us, the evening light casting a hazy glow around the edges of the blinds on the window.

I kept my question soft, "What happened?"

Those wide shoulders rose and fell as he took a deep breath. "When I was five, I was in a car accident with my parents. A driver missed a stop sign and T-boned our car. My parents suffered some broken bones, but I ended up in a coma for a couple of days."

My heart clenched. "Head trauma?"

"Yeah, the impact snapped the restraint holding the car seat in place, and I knocked my head against a window. My brain was rattled enough, it began to swell and doctors warned my parents if I woke up I might be brain damaged." He rubbed his free hand over his head.

I watched his movement, knowing just enough about brain injuries to conjure up scary images. "Did they have to drill holes in your skull?"

"Yeah, to relieve the pressure. It worked, but when I woke up, there were whispers in my head, and I couldn't get them to shut up." He winced and dropped his hand to the blanket.

When it curled into a fist, I reached out and covered it with mine.

He stared down at our joined hands and kept going, "It didn't take me long to realize I was the only one hearing them, and by then I stopped asking about it because I could see the worry on the doctors' faces and the fear in my parents'. Plus, I wanted out of the damn hospital and the only way to get out was to pretend everything was fine."

Such a young age to face such a frightening thing. "Couldn't have been easy, you were only five."

The muscles in his arm flexed and his throat worked. "Once I was home, it didn't take my mom long to figure out things were far from okay." He looked at me, his face carefully blank.

I couldn't read him.

"One day we were at the park, she was pushing my swing, and one of her friends came up and began to chat. There was nothing wrong with her, she was smiling and acting completely normal, while her daughter, Marybelle, and I ran around the playground. We were getting ready to leave, and I was standing next to my mom, when her friend hugged her, and I was hit by this avalanche of sorrow and anger. Unfortunately, I wasn't looking at them, but I heard mom's friend say how much she'd missed my mom when she moved after her divorce. So when I was walking home with my mom I asked her where would Marybelle move to if her parents got a divorce. My mom was stunned and asked where I heard such a thing."

Taking in his pained expression, I filled in the next part. "Let me guess, the friend never said a word out loud."

He nodded. "Three days later, my mom sat with me at the kitchen table as we colored, and told me Marybelle and her mom were moving out of state to live with Marybelle's grandparents." Gently untangling our hands, he rolled onto his back, folded his hands under his head and stared at the ceiling. "Mom's friend found out her husband was having an affair and filed for divorce. I never saw Marybelle again."

"What happened with your mom?"

"Mom was always sharp, and that day at the table, she played a guessing game."

"She figured it out."

"She did, and then she did her best to see what she could do to help me."

"What about your dad?"

"He was harder to convince, but he and my mom had one of those relationships, so although it took him longer, he followed her lead."

Thinking about my best friend Risia's experiences when her mother found out she could see the future, it was nice to hear that a unique gift didn't make a parent turn away. "You're lucky."

"I was, but it took years before we found someone who could help me learn how to block out most of the noise. It was like developing a muscle, so it took time, which meant I spent a lot of time alone. Eventually I was able to block out most of it."

"But not all?"

"No, not all. When it got too much, I kept to myself."

"To escape the noise."

"Yeah," he sighed. "You haven't done crazy until you're inundated with the thoughts of hormonal teenagers. Swear to god, they're scarier than anything I've ever run across."

Being alone as a teenager had to hurt, it was hard enough to make and keep friends at that age, but add in the fact you could hear every thought. I winced. Yep, that would suck. "But you survived high school?"

"Survived and graduated." Grim triumph lay under his words. "Then I joined the Marines."

That choice didn't surprise me, there was a core of innate strength to Wolf and add in his stubbornness to see things through, and warrior became a natural role. "For the discipline."

He turned his head, and his eyes, such a clear green, like the sea, watched me. "And to escape," he added. "The level of mental discipline needed to make it in the Marines was a godsend."

It took me a minute to follow. "Not just yours, but those around you."

"For the first time, even if my shields were shaky, I could work with others and not be bombarded about what shit was going down in their personal lives." He turned back to gazing at the ceiling, his lip curving up in a smile. "Even during the damn Crucible, we were so beyond exhausted, the only thought was the next step."

I reached out and traced his smile, before resting my hand on his chest. "You found your place."

"For a bit, then I was approached to join PSY-IV Team." He paused.

Ah yes, the infamous team Risia could barely talk about without having to threaten me with death.

Pulling my hand back, I tucked it under the covers as my fingers curled into a fist. "PSY-IV Team is a group of covert operatives with psychic abilities headed by Colonel Charlene Delacourt," I recited the facts Risia finally shared a few months back in a level tone.

He rolled to his side and pushed up on one arm, a frown replacing the fading grin. "Please tell me Risia didn't share more than that."

Seconds ticked by before I answered. "I may not be psychic, Wolf, but I'm far from stupid. Risia didn't have to share more than that. I've seen you in action, remember?"

He grimaced. "Yeah, and the colonel wasn't happy about that."

I'd never met the colonel, but what little Risia shared of her, made me wonder if it wouldn't be best to keep it that way. "Since you and your friends aren't supposed to exist, I'm not surprised."

His jaw tightened.

I sighed. "Look, whatever is happening now, I think it's safe to say, it has nothing to do with why your team ended up in my house four months ago. Even if it does have to with my brother, he wasn't psychic either, just an adrenaline junkie. Whatever this is, it's not your responsibility. I'm glad you're here, but I don't want you to stay and risk a job you love for a friend of a friend. Once we get whatever is in that safe deposit box, I'll turn it over to whoever I need to, and I'll be fine."

Between one blink and the next, he rolled on top of me until my entire world was him. My hands clutched his shoulders as he loomed above me.

"You are much more than a responsibility, Meli." That growl set off a series of quakes under my skin as the possessive tone of his voice tangled around my heart.

There was no way to stop my question, "What am I, then?"

"Mine."

Chapter Eight

I woke up for the second time to find moonlight sneaking its way through the bedroom blinds. This time, Wolf wasn't there asking me silly questions to see if I knew what day it was, or what my name was. While my headache had receded to an occasional throb, my body still felt battered. Of course, neither of those came close to the emotional whirlwind wreaking havoc in my heart.

Shifting to my side, I turned to the partially opened door. The soft gleam illuminating the space outside meant Wolf left a light on somewhere out front. Hopefully it wouldn't bother him while he crashed on the couch.

Strange that his presence didn't freak me out, instead it offered a comfort I hadn't felt in a long time.

Unfortunately, his 'mine' comment was hard to comprehend. He couldn't really mean it. He didn't know me, not really. How could he? Letting people in wasn't something I did anymore. It wasn't worth it.

So why was he sticking around? Was I a passing curiosity? Probably. He said it himself, I was one of those rare people he couldn't read. Translation: I was a challenge, and men like Wolf liked challenges, right?

But being seen as a challenge hurt, like a pinch to the heart. The last time someone marked me as a challenge, it hadn't ended well.

Tucking my face under the edge of the blanket until it rode just above my nose, I stared unseeingly at the dark doorway, too tired and confused to fight back the memories.

Eric was the epitome of the older brother, which meant dating became an endurance sport. Not that I dated much, but the few times I managed to wander into a situation, all it took was Eric home on leave and visiting before said date disappeared. It should've upset me, but instead the fact my brother cared enough to step in made me feel loved. Besides, if a guy couldn't stand up to my brother, I wasn't sure I wanted him to stick around.

But Eric's visits home became a rare occurrence, and then I grew up. Each time he dropped back in my life, he brought baggage. Baggage he tried to hide and refused to let me help with, even as it grew, shaping my once happy-go-lucky brother, into a grim, wary man.

During his last visit, after a particularly brutal night where all I could do was brew pot after pot of coffee, I watched my big brother's shoulders bow under that weight and decided then and there, I wouldn't add to it.

I thought I'd managed to keep my worries to myself, but from Eric's letter, I wasn't as successful as I'd hoped. Hurting him was the last thing I wanted to do, and what was happening at the time was mine to handle, not his. And for over a year, I dealt with it, maybe not successfully, but I managed.

Not until I lost him, did I understand I was still using him as a fallback option. Now, I was truly winging it. Unfortunately, I was woefully in over my head. A fact made starkly clear when it got downright scary.

Yet, I got through. Sort of. And that sliver of accomplishment is what I kept a death grip on while everything else crumbled around me.

The old me would've latched on to the safety and protection Wolf offered, but she was buried under the newer, wary me, the one who'd learned the hard way things were never what they seemed, and sometimes the price exceeded the services rendered.

"But not Wolf," whispered a voice that sounded a lot like my interfering brother.

Snorting softly, I chalked it up to wishful thinking, because other than being cast from the same mold as my brother, what did I really know about Wolf?

His career choice indicated he was a warrior and a protector. Since he was one of the good guys, honor and loyalty were an integral part of him. As demonstrated by how fast he came running when Tag called him in to help with Risia's situation. And again when I called.

But there was more to him than that. Sure as the sun would rise tomorrow, I knew there were depths, caverns of stygian darkness and veins of hidden treasures and dangers, lying underneath all that steely, calm control. Undertaking a journey to uncover those would be reckless.

Dangerous.

Exciting.

"Tempting."

Ignoring that whisper wasn't easy, but I whipped out the harsh spotlight and targeted my biggest fear—he would leave me.

Even though I tried to keep my heart out of it, he kept worming his way in and making a place for himself. Even though I'd spent the last four months trying to pry him out, he was still there, tucked in places that would leave me broken when he left.

And he would.

I wasn't an integral part of his exciting world, I was a friend of a friend, with secrets he wanted to unravel. That's it.

When duty called, I'd be alone. There was no missing the fact he thrived on his job and the dangerous work they did. There was no room for me in his life. And the sad truth was, I would give anything to be a part of it, but I knew better.

The first rule of physics, two objects can't occupy the same space. Wolf's heart didn't have room for his job and me.

Despite recent events, my life was quiet, routine, predictable, and where I found solace in such things, he'd go stir crazy and bail. What sucked even worse, I knew from the minute he stepped on my porch, he'd change everything and set my world on end. All my hard-earned caution faded like smoke when he was around. Instead, temptation beckoned, daring me to live a little, much the way Eric always teased me.

"I dare you, mouse. Take a chance and see what happens."

I wanted to, oh I so wanted to. I wanted to lock Wolf in a room and do every wild, wicked thing I'd ever read about and then some. Heck, part of me wanted to recapture that aching awareness I found in his arms as we danced in a ballroom while Risia and Tag set a trap for the international thieves and spies weaving through the crowd. For those few days, being part of Wolf's life was exhilarating and addicting.

"So, what's holding you back?"

Fear. Ugly, choking, demoralizing fear. What if I was fooling myself into believing I could be the kind of woman he needed? What if this sense of connection or whatever I thought I felt with Wolf was nothing but desperate wishing on my part?

"What if it wasn't?"

That question made me pause and consider.

Was I willing to risk missing out on a chance of something so life changing? Good or bad, the results would change me forever. There were no guarantees in this life, none at all. Losing my parents and Eric proved that. Did I want to spend the rest of my life bowing under the crap life threw at me? Or was I willing to suck it up and crawl above it? Maybe fly above it.

"How bad do you want it, little sister?"

What was it Mark Twain said? *"You will be more disappointed by the things that you didn't do than by the ones you did do...Sail away from the safe harbor"*? If I were brutally honest, I wanted to brave the waters, bad. Bad enough the ache brought tears to my eyes and the thought of watching Wolf walk out the door without ever really knowing what could've been left me hollow.

Whether he walked away now or later, the end result for me wouldn't change, so why not reach for what I wanted? Not only did I deserve someone strong and bright to walk beside me, but so did he.

I wasn't this half-broken thing other people's decisions had made of me. I was stronger than that, stronger than them. If I really wanted Wolf, it was time to suck it up and fight my way into the heart of the warrior.

Then I could go down in a blaze of glory.

The next time I woke, it was to the tantalizing smell of bacon and coffee. Taking a few precious minutes to do my morning routine, I walked out to the front room to be greeted with a plate of scrambled eggs, bacon and toast, and a bare chest.

Trying not to stare, I took the rather overfilled plate from Wolf and muttered, "Thanks."

"What makes you so sure that was for you, dumpling?"

I offered a coy smile and shoved a piece of bacon in my mouth.

His lips twitched as he turned and headed back to the small kitchenette on the right. "Coffee's on the counter."

Holding my plate, I shuffled after him, my gaze taking in the broad, tanned width of his shoulders. His naked, very defined shoulders. Now it wasn't just my stomach that was hungry. Sweet Mary, he was better than coffee.

Slipping onto one of the two chairs at the table, I set the plate down and nudged the slender flower vase to the side nearest the wall.

Just in time, because Wolf set his plate down, piled much higher than mine, and settled in across from me, coffee in hand. "How's the head?"

His question jerked my gaze up. "Fine," I mumbled even as heat rushed over my face.

He raised his coffee cup, but not before I caught his knowing grin.

Huffing out a breath, because you can't blame a woman for appreciating a fine chest, I pushed up and went to make my own cup of joe. Maybe the caffeine would clear out the lust-induced haze he seemed to bring on.

It didn't take me long to get my cup and settle back in to enjoy the morning breeze drifting through the front screen door. For a few minutes, the only sounds in the small villa were utensils against stoneware, broken by the occasional clink of coffee cup against the table. Strangely, it wasn't a tense silence, but a comfortable one.

I managed to make it a third of the way through the eggs and was nibbling on a ribbon of bacon, when Wolf pushed back his chair. Stretching out his legs, his big hands cradled the sturdy, white mug against his abs. "Bishop will be here soon, then we can talk."

Bringing one leg up until my foot rested on the chair, I

finished my bacon and reached for my cup. My hands needed a distraction, otherwise I might be tempted to do a little braille mapping. "Not sure what I can tell you."

One finger tapped an absent pattern on his cup's rim. "Won't know what we need, until we go over things. Besides, Bishop was planning on talking to Rabbit this morning."

Anxiety doused my hormones better than any cold shower. "About?"

A frown marred his forehead, and a muscle along his jaw flexed, but his gaze didn't waver. "Eric's death."

A fragile, desperate hope rose, even as logic tried to hold it back. "Will they really be able to find out what happened?"

Those intriguing shoulders rose and fell, but this time, they didn't distract me.

Wolf's answer was too important. "No promises, Meli."

"No promises," I repeated and quickly took a sip from my cup to hide my grin. If being hit over the head got me answers to what happened to my brother, I'd count the headache worth it.

A thought occurred, wiping away my delight. "Wait, Rabbit's not going to get into trouble for this, is he?"

Amusement quirked his lips. "Not if he does it right."

I frowned, not amused. "I'm serious, Wolf. I don't want you guys getting in trouble on account of me."

He set his cup on the table and ran a hand over his head. "Stop worrying, cupcake. Rabbit's a damn magician on a computer, no one will ever have a clue he was digging for information."

Dropping my leg, I leaned forward with a narrow-eyed glare. "Look, sugar plum, I don't want to bring trouble to you or your team. I didn't ask for that."

A flash of something came and went in those sea-glass eyes. "You don't like accepting help, do you?"

"What's that supposed to mean?"

"I'm not talking in tongues, here. It means exactly what I said." He cocked his head, his face unreadable. "Why are you picking a fight with me, Meli?"

His question made me pause, and I sat back.

Why was I picking a fight? Wolf and Bishop were only trying to help, and getting Rabbit to uncover the details behind Eric's death might give us a clue as to what waited in the safe deposit box.

Or maybe, it would just raise more questions.

And there it was, "I think I'm scared of what you'll find." Saying it out loud didn't do a darn thing to diminish the dread lodged like a weight in my gut.

Wolf leaned forward, one arm stretching across the table until he could cover my hand fisted next to my plate. "Why?"

Such a soft question to land so hard. The fears chasing themselves in my head were so disloyal, but there was no escaping the logic. Whatever Eric was involved in was at my front door, and there was no outrunning it now.

I raised my head and met him head on, even though the words choked me. "During the last year, Eric changed. He was darker, harder than before, and worried. If this is tied to him, or what was haunting him, and it killed him, how do I fight it?"

His grip tightened. "You're not doing it alone, angel. I won't let you."

The solemn depth to his words triggered another fear, even as shame scrambled underneath.

As much as I'd love to stand alone, keeping everyone else safe, I couldn't. I didn't have the necessary skills to navigate this dangerous new road. But I couldn't bear it if this man was hurt because of me, because of the trouble I brought. "Don't stand in front of me, Wolf."

His thumb brushed back and forth along my wrist, his gaze never wavering. "I can't walk away. I won't, so don't ask."

I shook my head vehemently because I knew beyond a shadow of a doubt I wouldn't survive whatever was coming without him. "Beside me, stand beside me." It came out rough and aching.

His smile was brilliant and fierce. "That I can do."

Uncurling my fingers, I turned my hand up until our palms met and our fingers laced. Staring at our hands, I blinked back the threatening tears as relief swept around my worries and fears.

Sucking in a deep breath, I reached and found an answering smile, before lifting my head. "Okay then. So, talk to Bishop, then bank?"

"Another cup of coffee, Bishop, then bank."

"Are you using my name in vain?"

The squeak of the screen door announced Bishop's arrival. He stepped inside, dressed in running shorts and a T-shirt, his attention zeroing in on the plate of bacon on the counter. "Sacrifice your pig meat to me, and I won't strike you down for such blasphemy."

He barely waited for Wolf's motion to help himself, before he grabbed the plate of bacon. Since there wasn't another chair, he leaned against the counter's edge, plate in one hand, bacon in the other. "No eggs?"

"You're late. Breakfast service is over." Wolf scratched his chest and lifted his cup. "Should be a cup or two in the pot behind you."

Bishop demolished the piece, and reached for another. "Because I am a gracious lord, I shall forgive you this time."

I nudged my plate toward the table's edge. "I can't finish, help yourself."

Bishop finished chewing and grinned. "Thanks, shrimp." He set aside the bacon, nabbed my plate, and shot Wolf a look. "See there, Wolf, that's how you're supposed to treat your friends."

Wolf's lips twitched. "Who said you were a friend?"

Bishop added a couple of pieces of bacon to the plate, then settled in on the floor under the counter, legs crossed, back against the wall. His unruly hair brushed the underside of the overhang. "Now you're just being downright mean." He turned to me, his dark eyes sharp. "How's the head?"

"It's good."

"Good."

Wolf stood up and stepped around Bishop.

Bishop paused with a forkful of eggs halfway to his mouth. "Grab me one?"

Wolf filled a second mug from the coffee pot. "Talked to Rabbit?" He turned and handed one cup to Bishop, then made his way back to the table.

"Yeah."

I waited while Bishop finished his bite and took a sip. It wasn't easy, but my best bet was to sit tight and listen.

He set his coffee on the floor next to him. "He wasn't able to get far, had a late start. Delacourt had him and Jinx tugging a few lines last night."

Wolf frowned. "Something new come up?"

Bishop shrugged. "Not sure yet, but if it does, we'll hear about it. So far, Rabbit's getting the same information Meli got."

He finished off another piece of bacon. "Sgt. Eric Dwyer was an 18B with Ranger 2nd Battalion out of Ft. Lewis, Washington. He was serving his fourth tour in Rocket City when a classified op went south. The team stumbled into a tribal dispute and in the ensuing exchange, lost four men. The details on what happened are skimpy at best, but until Rabbit digs a little deeper, that's all we got."

Needing some clarification, I interrupted, "18B?"

"A nickname from the 18Bravo Course," Wolf answered. "It's a training course, a Special Forces Weapons Sergeant course, to be exact. It means your brother liked to play with things that did serious damage and went bang."

"And considering the number of commendations in his file, he was damn good at it," Bishop added.

I wasn't quite sure what to do with that little peek into my brother's life. "Where's Rocket City?"

"It's a Forward Operating Base called Salerno in Khost. Think southeastern border of Afghanistan, right next to Pakistan. Not a fun place to be."

With a nickname of Rocket City, I could only imagine, but there had to be more. "Is this normal?"

Wolf cocked his head. "Is what normal?"

"Having a classified assignment—"

"Op," Bishop corrected.

I fought not to roll my eyes. "Classified op and stumbling into a 'tribal dispute'?" I used my fingers to quote the report.

Wolf grimaced. "Classified doesn't mean all knowing, angel. Half the damn time you're sent in on shitty information and just pray they got the majority of it right. Especially in areas like that, where hostilities are non-fucking-stop."

"Amen," Bishop muttered, his face grim.

Right, okay, so sore spot. Moving on. "How good are our chances at finding out more?"

Both men snorted, but it was Bishop who answered. "You do remember Rabbit, don't you, Meli? The boy's a technological bloodhound. He won't stop digging until he uncovers all the bones; we just need to give him a little bit of time. I'm touching base this afternoon, hopefully he'll have more."

He pushed to his feet and set the now empty plate on the counter. "In the meantime, you and Wolf go visit the bank. I'm going to do my run, then I'll see if I can't help Rabbit out a bit."

Wolf followed him to the door, but I didn't pay attention to their conversation, instead pulled up both legs until I could wrap my arms around them. With my chin on my knees, I stared unseeing at the floor, my mind spinning.

A weapons specialist? It wasn't such a stretch, Eric always had a love affair with firearms, but still, that sounded so... dangerous.

Not that I knew what a weapons specialist did, but since Eric never shared, it was guaranteed to worry me. Logically I understood his position as a Ranger put him front and center, but something about knowing this small piece of him, sank the grim reality of his job deep.

Living on an edge like that, where being sent off with sketchy information into hostile territory, something Wolf and Bishop made sound like the norm, would wear on any soldier. It wore Eric beyond bone, leaving him tormented by nightmares that left him screaming.

It was during one such visit, I tried to convince him to leave the military.

But I wasn't the only stubborn one in my family.

"That's not an option."

So many secrets and dark emotions locked in his eyes, it made me want to scream. Instead, I choked out, "Why not?"

"Not yet, mouse. When I'm done, then I'll think about leaving."

Then it was too late, the decision was made for him, leaving me to chase down the answers I needed to let my brother rest. Unfortunately, my instincts told me those answers were leading danger straight to my door.

Chapter Nine

To figure out which bank Eric's box of secrets was stashed, I began with the obvious—my bank. Unsurprisingly, Wolf drove. We left shortly after breakfast. With tomorrow being Thanksgiving and banks closing early, I didn't want to miss our chance.

Conversation on the way into town was sporadic. Wolf tried to distract me a couple of times, but finally gave up. My thoughts were ragged and disjointed as nerves and worry played a guessing game I had no chance of winning.

Once we hit town, I directed Wolf to the bank. It sat on the corner separated from the surrounding stores by a parking lot. It was part of one of those national chains, which meant anonymity was a given.

Wolf pulled into the parking space, a line of established trees providing a flimsy barrier between the busy street and the shopping center. He shut off the engine. I was undoing my seatbelt when he broke the quiet. "You sure about this?"

Lifting my head, I found myself staring at my reflection in his dark lenses, unable to read his expression. "Nope."

His jaw worked.

Letting the seatbelt retract, I leaned forward to get my purse. "But it's a starting point."

My purse tipped over, and two pens, a lipstick I didn't remember having, mints, and a wrapped piece of gum made an escape attempt. "Dang it."

I leaned down to gather the escapees from my bottomless bag of holding.

"Meli."

Intent on not leaving my stuff in Wolf's car, I didn't look up, busy dumping things back in my purse. "What?"

"If nothing's here, do you have a second choice?"

Mission completed, I sat up and reached for the door, ignoring the tight tug on my knot of worry his question brought. "Hopping a flight to Seattle and renting a car to Ft. Lewis, Washington?"

Because if Eric hadn't left stuff here, the only other place I could think of was his bank in Washington. I didn't really believe that would pan out, since I'd closed all his accounts months ago and nothing was said of any other accounts.

I shoved opened my door even as I caught his rumbled, "Right."

He met me at the sidewalk.

We walked up, his hand resting on the base of my spine as he held the door open for me. Having his solid presence at my back meant I made it to the counter and managed to give my name for the branch manager without revealing just how nervous I was. As we sat in the lobby, I dug out the key, then waited through ten of the longest minutes of my life.

"Ms. Dwyer?"

I rose to my feet as a man in his mid-thirties in dress pants, pressed shirt and tie, complete with professional flash of white teeth came forward with an extended hand.

"I'm Jonas Selliand, the manager, how can I help you today?" His gaze barely flickered over my appearance—taking in the poorly disguised bruise on my forehead—before switching to Wolf, his professionalism never wavering.

"Mr. Selliand." I shook his hand and felt Wolf reach around me to do the same. "I need to get into a safe deposit box."

Clear puzzlement on why I would request a bank manager for such a simple task echoed in his eyes, but he simply waved us forward. "Wonderful, why don't you follow me and we'll get you signed in."

"Thank you," I murmured, unwilling to get into the details in the middle of the lobby.

He led us toward a counter nestled next to a secured door. "Please, have a seat."

His fingers flew over the keypad, and he stepped through. When he reappeared on the other side of the counter, he had a small box with him. He sat in front of the computer terminal and flipped open the box. Index cards were located inside. Signature cards. He began flipping through the cards. "Do you have your box number?"

"I don't, and that's why I asked for you, Mr. Selliand."

He stopped flipping and looked up, a small frown marring his forehead. "Oh?"

"The safe deposit box would be under my brother's name, not mine."

His attention went to Wolf, who remained silent. "So long as you have ID, we can look it up for you."

"I'm afraid that will be difficult, seeing as my brother died ten months ago."

That put his attention back on me and I waited through another long blink as he processed my comment. "I'm sorry for your loss."

Inclining my head, I kept on, "I recently received a delayed letter from him with this key." I set the key on the counter. "I was hoping you could let us into the box."

He picked up the key, and studied it. "It looks like one of

ours." He glanced up, his expression cautious. "If you don't mind waiting while I do some research, I should be able to confirm if it belongs to one of our boxes."

I gave him a smile. "Not at all, we'd be happy to wait."

He rose from his chair, key in hand. "May I have your ID?"

"Of course." I handed over my driver's license.

Another quick smile and the manager disappeared.

Next to me Wolf shifted in his seat, drawing my attention, but he wasn't looking at me. Nope, true to form, his gaze was sweeping through the bank, taking in every detail. Despite his relaxed slouch in the chair, I couldn't fail to miss the subtle tension coming from him.

"You okay?" I kept my voice low.

His gaze came to me with a smile that didn't touch his face, but lit his eyes. "Yeah, angel, I'm good." He reached out and tugged on my hand until I released my purse and let him hold it. "You?"

I nodded, wondering how long the manager needed. We sat there quietly, holding hands until Mr. Selliand reappeared long minutes later. Catching his smile as he approached, tension seeped from my spine.

He retook his chair and slid my ID and the key back over the counter. "Ms. Dwyer, would you by chance have a copy of your brother's death certificate? Before we can let you in the box, we just need verification for our records."

"Actually I do." Another round of digging in my purse, and I pulled out the copy I used months before when dealing with Eric's accounts, and handed it over.

"Thank you." The manager did a quick visual scan. "Do you mind if we make a copy?"

"No, please go ahead."

He rose, went to the copier against the far wall, made a copy and came back, my copy extended. "Here you go."

Taking it from him, I dropped it in my bag while he pulled over his box of signature cards.

He flipped through it, and removed a card and pushed it to me. "If you could sign and date, I'll take you back." His attention went to Wolf. "Will you be joining Ms. Dwyer?"

Wolf kept his answer simple. "Yes."

"Then I'll need your ID and you may sign and date under Ms. Dwyer, please."

Wolf shifted his hips and pulled out his wallet, then handed over his ID.

While I signed the card, it didn't escape me that Eric's signature appeared only once, on the initial open date, fourteen months ago. Seeing his familiar handwriting tugged, but I finished signing the card and handed it and the pen to Wolf, who made quick work of it, then handed both back to the manager.

In minutes we were through the secured door and walking down a short hall to an open, heavy vault door. The ring of keys rattled in Mr. Selliand's hand as he led the way into a room filled with row upon row of safe deposit boxes. Larger boxes lined the back wall, while two solid blocks of boxes ran the length of the room, one made of mid-size boxes, and the last smaller boxes.

He walked to the end of the stack of smaller boxes, obviously checking numbers. Three quarters of the way down, he uttered, "Here it is."

Box number 843. It took me two tries to get my key in the lock, then I stepped back so the manager could do his thing with his keys. Finally, the little door was unlocked, and Mr. Selliand pulled out the long, wide box. He handed it to me.

I took it. It wasn't heavy, and something shifted inside, but I couldn't tell if it was an object or papers or both. Now that the box was in my hands, my heart took up a heavy tempo.

As my hands were full, Mr. Selliand handed my key to

Wolf. He led us out of the room and waved to the three privacy rooms lining the opposite side of the hall. "Take your time."

With that, he walked away, leaving us to find out what my brother had left.

•◉◆◉•

Wolf closed the door behind us and switched the lock. There were no cameras in the rooms, ensuring the customers' privacy. There was a narrow table and two chairs.

I set the box on the table and took a seat, Wolf standing behind me. I stared at the box, my breath coming in short pants. Whatever was in here couldn't be good. Not if Eric had kept it from me. It meant he was trying to protect me. The real question was, from what?

Staring at the box, dread and anxiety decided to make me their whipping girl.

"Meli?" Wolf's rough timber jerked my attention away from the metal container. "You want me to open it?"

I shook my head sharply and reached shaky hands out to flip the metal latch to release the lid. I lifted it, my gaze trained on the shadowed interior. As the contents came to light, I frowned in confusion.

Letting the lid fall back, I picked up the aged envelope and shook out a handful of timeworn photos, their edges curled and their color yellowed. Using my elbow, I nudged the box to the side and began laying out the pictures.

My anxiety drained away to be replaced by confusion. "I don't understand."

Wolf's arm came around me to shift a photo so he could see them. "Do you recognize these?"

Well, yeah, but why these photos? Realizing he was waiting for my answer, I nodded. "They're our camping pictures from the summer we spent visiting old ghost towns up and down the west coast."

I picked up one that showed Eric and me standing in a dilapidated doorframe leading nowhere, matching grins on our faces. "This one was taken at Rhyolite, an abandoned mining town outside of Vegas."

Shifting the photos around, I grabbed another one. Eric and I stood next to Mom outside a red, two-story southern style building with white wraparound porches. "This is the Oliver House in Bisbee out in Arizona. It's supposed to be the most haunted building in town, next to the Copper Queen Hotel."

Moving a couple more photos, I pulled out one, which could pass for a postcard. "This is the Jerome Grand Hotel. Arizona has tons of ghost towns, and Mom never missed a chance to take photos of the old buildings."

Lifting it, I handed it to Wolf and the one below it caught my eye. A strange shiver ran down my spine as I picked it up. It was a gag photo Dad took of Eric at one of Jerome's tourist photo stops. My brother was standing in an upright coffin with his arms crossed and his eyes closed while I leaned against the side, licking an ice cream cone. The photo shook in my hand.

Wolf crouched next to my chair and carefully took the photo from my numb fingers, then set it aside. "Meli, angel, look at me."

Swallowing hard, I lifted my gaze to his.

His hand rose and cradled my jaw, his thumb brushing over my lower lip. "You're okay. Just breathe."

Unable to look away, my breath came out in a shaky rush as my crumbling composure slowly reformed, gaining strength from his quiet encouragement. I clung to the assurance he offered for a few more moments before finally nodding. "I'm okay."

He studied me carefully. "You were hoping for something else to be here."

At that I did look away, because he was right. Needing to defuse the moment, I tried to tease, "Reading my mind, Wolf?"

His hand dropped away and immediately I missed the warmth of his touch. "Your face, cupcake."

He rose to his feet, his attention focused on the photos as he began moving them around on the table.

Taking his cue, I turned back to the photos. "Next you'll tell me never to play poker."

"Oh, I wouldn't say that."

I snorted. "Right, what would you say?"

I stood and reached over the table for another photo of my dad and Eric posing in an abandoned railcar hunkered in the desert.

Wolf's arm curled around my waist, dragging me close.

Off balance and startled, I turned to brace my hands on his chest and looked up at him. "What—"

"I'd challenge you to a game of strip poker."

"Strip poker?" It came out in an undignified squeak.

"Yep." The intensity in his gaze left a heated impression, and my body sank into his. He lowered his head, coming in close. "I like playing games I can win."

And while I wouldn't mind letting him win that particular game, an unexpected truth emerged. "I don't like games."

"Good," he whispered, then barely brushed his lips against mine before putting a few inches between us. His arm dropped away as he turned back to the photo-strewn table. "What did you think would be here?"

Taking a cue from his lead, I watched him separate the pictures until they were lined along the table. There were twenty-four in all, capturing our trip from southern California, through Arizona, and up into Nevada and Utah.

"I don't know, maybe a flash drive? Another letter? Heck, even a name?" Hopefully not the one I tried not to think about. "Just not pictures from a family vacation that took place thirteen years ago. Why put these in a safe deposit box and not tell me?"

Staring at the images, frustration rose, and I began re-arranging the photos. What was Eric trying to tell me? And did he have to be so darn cryptic? He loved brainteasers, but they tended to frustrate me, especially if logic couldn't dictate the outcome. "I don't get it."

Wolf's hand wrapped around my wrist, stilling my restless movements. "What are you doing?"

Realizing I was compulsively arranging the photos in chronological order, I tried to ignore the blush working its way over my face. Great, the stress was bringing out my weirdo tendencies. "Nothing," I muttered, and tugged my hand free. "I'll just put them back in the envelope and we can take them with us. Maybe if I stare at them long enough, something will come to me."

Wolf helped me collect the photos. I slipped the stuffed envelope back in my purse, as he collected the now empty box. We left the room, to find Mr. Selliand waiting for us.

Within minutes we were back outside heading for the car.

I was reaching for the door handle, when Wolf's low curse stopped me. "What's wrong?" I looked across the roof just in time to see him disappear on the other side of the car. "Wolf?"

His head popped up, his face thunderous. "We have a flat."

There was no mistaking his grim tone and my hand froze above the handle. My stomach tightened and a clammy sweat dripped down my spine. "A flat?" It came out in a breathless squeak. "They're brand new." Even as the words left my mouth, I wanted to slap myself for stating the obvious.

"It's slashed." His darn sunglasses hid his eyes, but his jaw was tense. "We're not sticking around. Come on."

He rounded the car, grabbed my hand, and began tugging me away.

Chapter Ten

WOLF

Disgusted at having to scare the shit out of her again, I gentled my grip on her hand as I beat feet away from the car. Based on the relatively smooth edges of the slice tearing through the rubber wall, it was an easy guess that the flat was far from natural. Scanning the parking lot, there wasn't much to see.

It was late morning, the bank's parking was half-filled, and most of the cars carried a heavy window tint in an effort to beat back the Vegas sun. Which made it a bitch IDing whoever the hell ripped Meli's tire open.

Going back to the bank wasn't an option. One, I didn't want my next steps caught on monitored security cameras. Two, I wanted to draw out whoever was stalking us.

The bank was stuck off to the side of a strip-mall-type shopping center. The main store specialized in whatever a consumer's heart desired, including replacement tires, so that was where we were going. Add in the ability to blend in with the milling shoppers if need be, and I was good to go.

Tucking Meli against my left side and draping an arm around her shoulders, I hauled her across the lot, staying along the main walkway tucked between the parked cars. Less chance of being run over that way.

Meli's ponytail kept brushing my arm as her head swiveled.

Lowering my head to hers and turning my face into her hair, I hissed, "Stop checking out the parking lot, angel."

Her muscles locked and her step faltered.

"Relax, we're just walking to the store."

Her arm crept around my waist and her fingers curled around my belt loop, as she pulled her purse around to her front.

Even though it would make getting my gun awkward, I didn't adjust her hold. Sorry SOB that I was, having her pressed up so tight felt damn good.

We were halfway down the long-ass sidewalk, when she finally spoke. "Why are we going to the store?"

"They sell tires." That got me a narrow-eyed glare bright with disbelief. "Fine, easier to identify any possible shadows." Because if someone was following us, they were damn good.

We could stay by the car, but my itchy spine indicated that might not be our best bet. Heading to the store served to throw off any unwanted observers while making them work around a crowd. Attacking in public was a big no-no, unless you were damn desperate.

This didn't carry an air of desperation, this was personal. Besides, if we were being tracked, they had to use our phones to get our location. And following that logic meant they could be tapped into our lines as well.

Since I wasn't into having uninvited guests with my upcoming conversation with Bishop, I needed a different, untraceable phone.

I waited as the rattle of wheels and metal over bumpy asphalt drew closer. On our left, just beyond the bumpers of the parked cars, a long line of shopping carts guided by a bored teenager snaked by.

I picked up the pace, timing it so when we hit the crossing in front of the entrance, we crossed with the carts. We stepped through the automatic doors and were blasted with frigid air and the low din of holiday shoppers.

Running through my options to reach Bishop, I spotted a trio of teenage boys gathered around one of those video rental kiosks to our left. *Ahh, a solution.* Nowhere near ideal, but definitely doable.

Ambling over to the bench sitting smack center of the entryway, I took a seat, pulling Meli down beside me as the boys discussed their cinematic preferences.

There was a sharp jab in my ribs and I looked down to find Meli glaring at me. "What are you doing?" she mouthed.

Since it was too hard to explain, and the possibility of her freaking out and running away was too high to ignore, I locked my hold on her hand and simply muttered, "Watch."

Between one breath and the next, I dropped my mental shield and focused on the kids.

Man, that movie was so fuckin' lame. Why did I agree to come again? That was the middle one currently arguing with the one on the left over which movie to get.

The one on the right pulled out a phone, ignoring his friends. *Why hasn't she called?* Normal teenage insecurity swirled around me and provided an unexpected opening.

With as much care as possible, I slid my suggestion into his thoughts. *"Call her. What can it hurt?"*

Since it was what he wanted to do, my suggestion anchored and took root frighteningly quick.

"Hey," the kid broke into his friends' argument. "I got make a call. Be back in a second." He turned and made his way to the automatic doors.

Keeping hold of Meli, I got to my feet, and we followed him out.

The kid went to stand off to the side of the doors, his focus on his phone as he leaned against the wall. As he went to press his screen, I ignored the pitch of my stomach as I took control of his mind. His face went slack and his hand dropped.

I caught the phone as it tumbled out of his hand. Then I stood in front of him, dragging Meli along to help block him from the view of those passing by.

"Wolf?" Meli's voice was shaky, but I gritted my teeth, refusing to meet her gaze, as I quickly punched in Bishop's number.

She pulled against my grip, and I shot her a quelling look as I listened to the phone ring. Her face was pale, but there was no missing the combination of fear and anger glittering in her eyes.

There was no time for apologies or explanations, not that I felt like offering any.

"Who is this?" Cold and cutting, Bishop's voice came over the line.

"We've picked up a shadow."

"Where the hell are you calling from?"

"I borrowed a phone. Meli's tire was slashed outside the bank."

"Location?"

I gave him the cross streets as I checked out our options. "We'll be at the coffee shop by the sports store."

"Roger." The line went dead.

It took a few seconds to go in and erase my outgoing call from the cell, and put the phone back in the kid's hand before gently releasing my hold on his brain. Undoing my mental hold was like relaxing a pressure point, and a dull throb started in my skull.

Thankfully it was easily ignored, because in a minute the

seething woman next to me was going to be an even bigger pain.

The kid blinked and shook his head as he jerked back against the wall, his face pale. "Whoa!"

"You okay, kid?"

"What happened?" Confusion just heightened his youth, and my gut soured.

I reminded myself my actions were a necessary evil. Wasn't fucking helping. "You got pale and unsteady. We were worried you'd pass out. You okay?"

"Um, yeah." He swallowed, his throat bobbing with the movement as he rubbed his forehead. "Yeah, I'm good. Thanks."

"No problem." I gave him an empty smile, turned and dragged Meli along as I headed to the coffee shop just down the way.

Meli didn't need to say anything. I could feel her shards of icy disapproval ripping along my spine.

I didn't bother to say anything, and knowing the argument brewing on the horizon was threatening to burst, I nixed the coffee shop idea. Instead, I turned into the narrow opening between the buildings, dragging Meli behind me.

The opening held a garbage dumpster near the entrance, and further down was a pile of discarded boxes and crates. Not exactly a private room, but there was no sense in making a public scene.

Half way down and partially hidden by the building's shadows and the dumpster, I let her go and turned to face her screaming silence, jaw set and arms crossed across my chest.

Undaunted, her glare was guaranteed to set my ass on fire. "What was that?" Her jaw was so tight I was surprised her words came out.

Holding her furious gaze with mine, I refused to acknowledge the guilt slamming up against my better judgement. We needed an untraceable phone, and our options were limited. In no mood to argue with her or my conscience about my decision, I snapped, "That was me doing what needed to be done."

The unmistakable sound of frustration escaped her. "What needed to be done?"

Any other situation her growl would've been cute. Instead it made me want to growl back. I refrained. Barely, but I sure as shit didn't drop my gaze. Sometimes hard decisions were all you had. "Slashed tires don't just happen, sugar pants. It's a fucking message."

She mirrored me, crossing her arms over her chest. "And your response to that message was to what? Mess with that poor boy's mind?" A sliver of fear wove under her outrage.

Hearing it, my stomach dropped even as my temper spiked. I didn't bother with a response. What was the point? She'd obviously made up her mind about what she'd witnessed.

At my silence, her eyes narrowed and she leaned forward. "Don't you dare pull the silent thing with me, buster."

Buster? Seriously? If that was the worst she could come up with, I had a lot to teach her. "What do you want me to say, Meli?" I kept my voice low.

"I want to know what just happened."

"What just happened, was that I needed an untraceable phone to contact Bishop. I made the best of a shitty situation."

"Has anyone ever told you that paranoia isn't a good look on you?"

She could not be that oblivious. Could she? The derisive note in her voice snapped the last restraint on my temper.

It was my turn to lean forward until mere inches separated us. "It isn't paranoia, it's being goddamn careful. If you haven't figured it out yet, Melisande, you're someone's target. Until we can figure out why, I will do whatever is necessary to keep you safe. Even if you end up hating me for it."

Color rode high in her cheeks, and it didn't do a damn thing except make me want to kiss the stubbornness right out of her. "I'm someone's target because of my brother and whatever ghosts were chasing him. It has nothing to do with me. I can hand these," she made an awkward motion to her purse, "over to you and be out of this."

"You really think it's that simple?"

She reared back, almost hitting her head against the wall behind her. "Isn't it?"

I couldn't decide if I wanted to shake her or laugh in disbelief. Instead, I rubbed a hand over the back of my neck as I stepped away from her.

"For fuck's sake, you can't hide from this. Whatever shit your brother stepped in is piling up on your doorstep and it stinks to high heaven. You are so over your head, you're drowning and don't even know it. Your house has been shot up, you've been attacked, and your tires slashed—repeatedly. The only way you're going to be safe, is to neutralize the threat. And I can't do that with please and thank you's."

She followed me until we faced off in the middle of the narrow alleyway. "But you're completely okay with messing with someone's mind? Because that's what you did, isn't it?"

Her gaze, dark with fear-tainted worry, stayed locked on mine. Her voice shook, but I had to give the woman credit, she kept pushing. "Your ability isn't just reading minds, it's manipulating them."

Locking my jaw was the only way to ensure damaging words didn't escape. The snarl of resentment and hurt gathered steam, looking for an easy escape valve. *What did she want from me?* It wasn't as if I went around willy-nilly and screwed with people's minds for the fun of it. If it wasn't for the fact she was in danger, I would've never touched the kid. Instead, here she was, all but sitting in judgement of something she had no hope of understanding.

Undaunted she waited for me to respond.

Finally, I managed, "Yeah, Meli, I can manipulate minds."

She paled, the dusting of freckles standing out in stark relief, her eyes widening, fear dilating her pupils before her sense of self-preservation finally kicked in, shuttering her expression. "You said you couldn't read my mind, that however your ability worked, it didn't with me. That means you can't mess with my mind, right?"

Her question was a fist to the gut, complete with razor sharp claws. Feeling mean at her unintentional betrayal, I snapped, "Maybe, maybe not."

Instead of slapping her back, my response seemed to piss her off, because red infused her face, her eyes narrowed, and she stepped forward, one hand curled into a fist, the other equipped with a stiff pointing finger, which she proceeded to jab into my chest. "Don't be a jerk, Wo—"

Her voice cut off as her eyes flicked beyond my shoulder and widened.

It was all the warning I needed.

I pulled her in close, keeping my body between her and whatever was coming, and dove to the side for the dubious protection of boxes piled along the wall just as the report of a bullet echoed.

Twisting so my shoulder and hip took the brunt of the fall, I rolled Meli under me and close to the wall, her squeak drowned out by the rush of adrenaline as I reached for my gun. Ignoring the sting of scraped flesh, I pushed up into a crouch, careful to stay low, and faced back toward the opening, gun up and pointed.

The shadows between the buildings kept things dim, but sighting on the figure at the end of the opening, I dropped my aim and pulled the trigger just as the shooter went to dive behind the dumpster. There was a grunt, which translated to a hit.

Faint screams erupted as the sound of gunfire began to register with those out in front of the store.

Great, 911 had to be lighting up like the Fourth of July about now. "Stay put!" I hissed at Meli. Staying close to the wall and keeping an eye on the dumpster, I advanced down the alleyway.

Since there were curious faces popping up along the edges of the alleyway and the flash of cellphones, I went by the book. "Come out, hands where I can see them!"

The scrape of metal over asphalt made me pause.

A gun slid out from behind the dumpster, followed by a pained, "I'm unarmed, don't shoot."

I held my position and waited.

Hands appeared first, and were eventually followed by a dark ball cap that shadowed the face and a bulky figure in jeans and a T-shirt. The growing stain on the left lower leg explained the shooter's cooperative demeanor. Hard to run when you couldn't put weight on a leg.

Still, with the light coming in from behind, I couldn't make out his face. Keeping the gun on him, I moved forward cautiously. "Down on your knees, fingers laced behind your head. Now!"

He dropped to one knee, then awkwardly bent the other with a resounding hiss of pain. He managed to maintain his balance as he laced his fingers behind his cap.

Keeping clear of his reach, I circled around to his back. Pressing the barrel in-between his shoulder blades, I did a one-handed pat down. Unsurprisingly, I didn't find a wallet, keys, or even a gum wrapper.

I was reaching for his right arm when the store's security ran into the alleyway. "Drop the gun!"

Oh for fuck's sake. I wrenched the shooter's arm up between his shoulders and shoved him face first into the pavement. I knelt next to him, shifted my grip on the gun in my other hand, and raised it where the store's security could see it. "I'm with Naval Criminal Investigative Services. Badge is in my back right pocket."

I shifted my hold on the shooter's wrist until he groaned. "Don't fucking move," I hissed.

Behind me I could hear the security officer coming up behind me, his tread heavy. I kept my gun up and my grip loose, allowing him to take it. I held my position as he reached into my back pocket and pulled out my wallet.

"The police are on their way." The last word cracked under the strain of obvious nerves as my wallet was offered back over my shoulder. "Here."

"Thanks." Never letting go of my hold, I tucked my wallet away. "You happen to have any restraints I can use?"

"Um, yeah." There was the sound of fumbling, then a pair of flex cuffs was passed over my shoulder.

"Thanks. I'm going to call out my companion, okay?" I warned the nervous guard at my back. Making quick work, I had the shooter's wrists secured before I called down the alleyway. "Come on out, Meli."

As she appeared from behind the boxes and headed toward me, the shooter lifted his head, his body tightening.

With a palm against the back of his head, I leaned forward to snarl in his ear, "Don't." He stilled.

As Meli came closer I directed her to stand back by the guard. She disappeared behind me and I heard the security guard ask, "What's going on here?"

"The guy on the ground shot at us." Her voice was strong, if a little shaky.

"You okay?"

"Yes."

Their conversation was interrupted by the growing wail of sirens. I held my position and silence as the sirens drowned out the murmurs of the growing crowd milling out in front.

Meli inched closer and I met her gaze. There was no missing the fear under her concern. Seeing it twisted the useless guilt in my gut, adding a resentful edge to my frustration.

I turned away and shook my head, trying to dislodge the ugly whispers urging me to rip through the mind of the man at my feet. The whispers were winning until a soft touch on my shoulder brought me up short.

Meli stared down at me, pale but resolute. "You okay?"

I dipped my chin in a nod. When the sirens cut off midscream, I shifted to see two police cars pull to a stop in front of the alleyway.

It was all I could do not to sigh.

Now the real fun would begin.

Chapter Eleven

The downtown Las Vegas Police Department wasn't quite what I expected. Granted, I didn't spend a lot of time in police stations, but thanks to crime TV, I expected tons of fluorescent lighting, battered metal desks, and a general sense of grim reality. Instead, I was led through a reception area that could be found in any corporate office, past a cluster of cubicles, and asked to wait in what looked like a conference room.

Unfortunately, there wasn't anything to do but wait and stare at the walls. The shock of the attack was wearing off because my hands shook as much as my stomach. The scene between Wolf and the boy kept replaying in my head until I wanted to scream. I pressed my palms flat against the table, hoping to stave off the adrenaline-induced palsy. Forcing the rising tide of disbelief and paranoia down, I focused on the current situation.

Wolf hadn't said a word to me as we rode over. If he hadn't been there, I would've been a babbling mess. Even though we did nothing wrong, our only way to the station was the backseat of a patrol car. Staring at the cage separating us from the driver made it all feel so very unreal. I wanted to clutch Wolf's hand, but he was coldly silent, and I didn't dare.

Instead, after the officers searched my purse and handed it back, I kept a strangle hold on it. They kept Wolf's gun, but they didn't put him in cuffs. Hopefully that meant he wasn't in trouble. He disappeared into another room with another officer twenty minutes ago.

Questions chased each other in my head. How long would they keep us? Was Bishop here yet? What was going on? Where was Wolf?

My mental merry-go-round was interrupted when the door opened and a familiar face appeared.

"Detective Marsten, what are you doing here?" I rose to my feet.

"Ms. Dwyer, please, sit. I brought you some water, figured you might be thirsty." He set a water bottle in front of me.

Slowly, I sank back into my seat as he took the chair to my left. It didn't escape me that he positioned himself directly between me and the door. What? Did they think I was going to make a run for it? Something told me I was safer inside this room than outside. Not that I was in a huge hurry to test that hunch.

"First, how are you doing?" He set a folder on the table, and added a blank notepad before topping off the pile with a pen. Then he sat back and got comfortable.

Guess we were going to be here awhile. "Shaky, but fine."

I slid the water closer, twisted off the top and took a drink. The cool water helped with the encroaching lightheadedness. Setting it back on the table, I fiddled with the label. "What's going on?"

"Why don't you tell me?"

Blowing out a breath, I sat back, dropping my hands to my lap. "Wolf and I were shot at."

"Why?"

I shrugged. "If I knew, I'd tell you."

"You've encountered quite a bit of trouble lately, Ms. Dwyer."

I shook my head. "When we met the other day, I told you to call me Meli, Detective."

That got a small smile. "My momma raised me with manners, Meli."

Oh so true. When Detective Marsten first arrived at my house after it was shot up, he'd been unfailingly polite.

Polite or not, it didn't mask the hard edge lurking in his gaze. He didn't look away as he started in. "Your house was shot, you were attacked in your own home, and now your tires were slashed just in time to get mugged." He paused, watching me. "I've asked before, but I'm going to ask again, who do you think's behind this?"

"Like I told you, I have no idea." Maybe by repeating the same information, he'd get tired of asking the same questions.

He raised an eyebrow. "Really?"

He nudged the notepad off the folder, and flipped it open. Rifling through it, he pulled out a piece of paper and slid it across the table.

Automatically I reached out and drew it closer, noting there was a photo on the top right corner.

"What about Nicholas Breck? You think maybe he's behind this?"

Like a punch to the gut, his questions brought my world to a screeching halt. I could hear the clock on the wall count the seconds as I fought for balance, sucking in much needed air. My mind whirled and I stared at the clock, counting the seconds in time with ticks until they slowed.

Nicholas Breck. How could one name create such damage?

My muscles unlocked and I slowly inched the paper closer, taking my time to position it carefully in front of me, keeping the bottom edge straight with the table's edge. Each tiny correction meticulous as if one wrong move would unleash a monster. Maybe it would.

The color photo in the corner captured my gaze, refusing to let it go.

A cold sweat broke over my spine; my mouth went dry even as my stomach heaved in protest. I stopped touching the paper. Dropping my hands into my lap, I interlaced my fingers together as tight as possible under the table.

The world around me shrunk until my vision was dominated by the ice in the blue-gray eyes set above an arrogant half-smile surrounded by what most females would consider a sexy scruff. The mussed strands of gold and brown were longer on top, with shorter sides, but the entire picture added up to a man confident in his appeal to women.

I could mentally add in the rest of the picture. At just under six foot, Nicholas took pride in his physical appearance, and the sculpted musculature wrapped around that frame was a testament to his dedication to fitness.

"Meli?"

Jerking my head up, I flinched so hard my chair vibrated. It took a moment to bring Detective Marsten into focus because the light was being eaten by memories. Memories I couldn't afford.

I blinked the shadows away. "Ye…yes?"

The detective leaned forward, his hand outstretched across the table, pity and concern etched in his face. "Do you think it was Nicholas Breck?"

It was the gentleness in his voice that cut through my fear. I wasn't fragile, couldn't afford to be. Not anymore. It took concentrated effort to keep my gaze from drifting back to the photo, but I managed.

I straightened my shoulders and spine, unwilling to cede any power to Nicholas, whether he was physically here or not. "I don't know."

The detective studied me, his hazel eyes serious and watchful, even as he pulled his hand back and resettled in his chair. "You filed a restraining order against him a year ago."

Since the proof was sitting in front of me, there was nothing else to say but, "I did."

"Why?"

Residual fear began to crumble under a rising irritation. Unlacing my fingers, I brought out one hand and used a single finger to shove the RO back to the detective. "As the paperwork states, he was harassing me with phone calls, acting irrational, and making threats. Then he violated my home and attacked me."

That wasn't shame crawling through my chest, that was anger.

Marsten pulled the report back and tucked it into the file. "So shooting up your place of work, slashing your tires, even attacking you in your home again, would not be beyond him?"

No, not by a long shot, but… "Ever since I filed the RO, he's left me alone. It makes no sense that he'd suddenly start back up again months later."

"It would if he was out of town and returned two months ago."

Two months? The detective's answer hit with devastating force. If I hadn't been sitting, I would have collapsed.

My mind tried to piece together when everything first started. It was difficult, since all I wanted to do was get as far away as possible, but the timing might work. "He's back in town?"

"You weren't aware he was back?" Under the dark, spiky hair, frown lines marred the detective's forehead.

I shook my head.

"He returned stateside late August according to his military records."

I swallowed, which wasn't easy considering how dry my mouth was. "You're sure he's living in Vegas?"

He shrugged. "As sure as we can be, short of picking him up and questioning him."

Hope perked up. "Can you do that?"

"We need probable cause first."

Which meant the police wouldn't be much help unless there was evidence pointing to Nicholas, and he wouldn't have left any.

Deflated, I sank back into my chair. "Right, because unless he physically beats the crap out of me or kills me, you can't do a darn thing." The muttered comment was out before I could call it back.

Frustration twisted Marsten's face into a grimace. "The reality is, unless you can identify Breck as the one behind your recent attack or any of the recent incidents, my hands are tied. Since he fell off the radar two months ago, the best we could do is pick him up for questioning, if he makes an appearance."

He wasn't telling me anything I didn't know, but I couldn't lie, not even to escape Nicholas.

I worried my lower lip as I looked at the door behind the detective. I wanted out so badly I could taste it. Sitting here, knowing Nicholas was out there, made me twitchy.

I wanted my gun, which was currently tucked away at the villas. I wanted Wolf, but he was somewhere on the other side of the door, probably furious with me, and I didn't think the detective would appreciate me barreling through him to find Wolf. I wanted my brother. This whole thing sucked.

Hot tears rose in tandem with my fear and panic and my chin trembled. I sank my teeth deeper into my lip until I tasted blood, and the bright stinging pain steadied my jaw.

Sympathy drifted over the detective's face as he blew out a breath and gathered the notepad and pen. "You've had a rough morning, so let's see if we can go through the events once more so I can let you go, okay?"

I dipped my chin in acknowledgment. Grabbing the water bottle, I uncapped it, and took a long drink. Setting it back on the table, I kept my hands wrapped around it and my mind as blank as possible.

"All right Meli, start with coming out of the bank."

Following his prompts, I detailed the morning. The only stumbling block came when we reached the point where Wolf used the boy's telephone.

Marsten's pen paused and stopped. "Mr. Kincaid asked the kid to use his phone?" I nodded. "Why? Why not use his phone? Or yours?"

I rubbed my forehead in a lame attempt to ease the emerging headache, wincing when I hit the sore spot I had forgotten in the rest of my hectic morning. Stress did it every darn time. "I don't know, and I didn't ask."

I made the mistake of meeting his gaze.

It was sharp with suspicion. "Didn't that strike you as strange?"

My brittle laugh surprised even me. "Compared to what? Walking out of the bank and finding my tires slashed? Or getting shot at in broad daylight? The whole morning is beyond strange as far as I'm concerned."

Either my attitude or tone, or both, worked, because he backed off and continued taking me through the rest of the morning.

We were just finishing up, when a knock sounded. The door opened and an older woman stuck her silver streaked brown head through the opening. "Marsten, Mr. Kincaid is wondering how much longer Ms. Dwyer will be?"

"We're about finished, thanks. She'll be out in a moment." The woman withdrew and Marsten finished up his notes. "Okay, Meli, I think we're good for now."

He rose to his feet, and I followed suit, feeling stiff and sore. "Thank you for going over things with me. If we have any further questions, we'll give you a call. I have your number here."

Beyond exhausted, all I could offer was a weak smile. I came around the table and waited as he held the door opened for me. Stepping outside, I found the woman who'd interrupted us watching from a few feet away and Wolf leaning up against the opposite wall.

He took one look at me, zeroed in on my face, frowned, and then straightened from his position. "You okay?"

Not even close, but if I admitted it now, I'd crumble. No way would I break here. I just needed to hold it together until I was back behind the safety of the villas' walls, where no one was watching me. "I'm fine."

My voice cracked at the end, marking the comment for the lie it was.

Instead of calling me on it, Wolf simply pulled me close until I could hide my face against his chest as I wrapped my arms around his waist. The feel of him, solid and sure, gave my balance a much-needed boost.

Behind me someone cleared their throat, and Detective Marsten said, "Here's my card."

One of Wolf's arms shifted, reached out, and came back.

I didn't bother raising my head or opening my eyes.

The detective continued, his voice low, "If anything more happens, let me know. Especially if Breck makes a reappearance."

Against me, Wolf's body went rock solid. "Breck?"

The detective had a big mouth. Since my reprieve was up, I thumped my forehead against Wolf's chest, twice, carefully because of the tender spot. I only stopped when he cupped the back of my head with his hand and held me still.

"Who's Breck?" His chest vibrated with his question.

The detective wasn't done being Mr. Unhelpful. "Nicholas Breck."

There was the sound of papers shuffling, and Wolf's hand disappeared from my hair. He shifted a bit, and I rolled my head and opened my eyes to see him holding a copy of the RO.

I heaved a sigh and tilted my head back to meet Wolf's thunderous face. "Can you wait until we get back home?"

His jaw flexed as he pinned me in place with a disconcerting gaze. Finally, he shifted his focus to the paper, and I watched him read it. By the time he handed it back to the detective, even his goatee couldn't hide the white lines bracketing his mouth or the muscle jumping along his jaw. The arm still curled around my waist was tight.

Yep, it was going to be a long ride back to the villas. Maybe I should call a taxi? I could pretend to go to the bathroom and make a run for it.

Since Wolf wasn't dropping his hold, guess my escape plan was out.

"Thank you, Detective. We'll be sure to let you know if this Breck or anyone else shows up."

"You'll be staying with her, I assume?"

"That's the plan."

I turned in Wolf's arms to catch Detective Marsten's nod. "Good. That makes me feel better."

Wolf turned to the still watching woman. "Detective Valley, you mentioned I could sit in on the interrogation of the suspect once he's treated."

Her slow nod was accompanied by, "Once I verify your status with your superior, and clear it with my captain, we'd be happy to call you back in."

"I'll be sure to make time to be here then, thank you." He held out his hand to Detective Marsten, and the two men shook. He turned back to the female detective, "If you have any further questions after talking with my colonel, please let me know."

The woman's gaze drifted to me and back to Wolf, a bit of warmth leaking under her professional mask. "Will do."

With that, Wolf curled his arm around my waist and nudged me down the hall.

I pulled open the door only to have him catch the edge of it above me and hold it open as I stepped through. Out in the reception area, I dragged in a deep breath.

At the receptionist's desk, Bishop straightened, his attention zeroing in on us, but not before he flashed the dazzled thirty something a smile that left her blushing.

With Wolf's hand a warm pressure at the base of my spine, we walked over.

"Nice to see bail isn't required," Bishop drawled.

"Yet," I muttered, rattled by the silent storm brewing next to me.

Bishop looked between the two of us and hummed without further comment.

Wolf, unsurprisingly, remained mute. Considering how fast the distance to the door was shrinking, I didn't think that would last much longer.

Sure enough, as soon as we hit the concrete outside, I managed a whopping three steps before Wolf captured my wrist and tugged me off to the side, under a straggly Palo Verde tree.

Squinting against the late afternoon sun, I folded my arms and tilted my head back to meet his furious gaze.

Bishop stopped and watched with an upraised eyebrow. "You sure you want to do this within earshot of the station?"

Wolf ignored him and instead leaned in and snarled, "Who the hell is Nicholas Breck?"

Chapter Twelve

WOLF

It was all I could not to shake Meli when she lifted her chin, her mouth tightening mutinously. "He's nobody important."

Rearing back, I wrapped a hand around the back of my neck and squeezed, fighting for a grip on my fast dwindling patience. "You filed a restraining order against this unimportant nobody, Meli."

She caught her raw lower lip with her teeth and unable to watch her shred it into bloody ribbons, I reached out and gently brushed her chin to free it.

Hectic flags of color drifted over her cheeks and she dropped her gaze, her shoulders hunching as she half-turned away. "I don't want to talk about it here, Wolf."

Seeing that self-protective move added another layer to my anger. Someone would pay for leaving such a mark on her. Needing to step back from the edge, I tackled her comment. "Then we'll talk about it back at the villas."

Because getting into an argument about her keeping important shit from me in front of a police station wasn't the wisest move.

Her spine lost a bit of its starch, but before she could consider herself in the clear, I continued, "But we will be talking about it."

Ignoring her ungracious, "Fine," I grabbed her hand, waved Bishop on, and started out after him. It wasn't far to where Bishop had parked my truck, but my spine itched the whole damn way. Yet no matter how much I checked, nothing was pinging on my radar.

Ahead of us, Bishop was scanning as well, which helped ease my nerves. At the truck, he turned and lobbed the keys.

Letting go of Meli, I caught them and hit the unlock button. The double beeps were fading away when Meli reached for the handle. I nabbed her hand before it made contact. "Hold up, Miss Contrary."

I didn't bother addressing the puzzled exasperation she threw over her shoulder, but waited as Bishop did an unobtrusive scan for unexpected surprises. With the way Lady Luck was dicking with us lately, I wasn't in a rush to play fifty-two pick up with body pieces.

Bishop's head disappeared as he went prone to check the undercarriage.

My personal troublemaker decided to share her impatience. "It's a police station parking lot, for pity's sake. Aren't you being just a wee bit overly paranoid?"

"Nope."

My short answer shoved her last broken remnants aside, and she glared at me.

I'd take fire over tears any damn day of the week, so I kept my smile to myself.

When Bishop popped back up with a short nod, I released my hold on Meli.

She was quick to yank the door open and hop in.

To ensure her safety, I gave her a helpful boost with a hand on her ass. Of course, I took full advantage, and left it a little longer than necessary, but you couldn't blame a man for that.

Within minutes, we were heading away from the police station and back to the villas.

It wasn't long before Bishop broke the silence. "Spoke to Rabbit."

I kept an eye on the mirrors to ensure no one was tailing us, as I maneuvered through traffic. "Anything new?"

Bishop's elbow rested on the window edge, and his fingers drummed along the top. "He's hit a couple of unexpected snags, which means he has to pick his path carefully."

Of course he had, because this whole situation stank to high heaven.

Next to me, Meli shifted to face Bishop. "Snags? On what?"

I didn't have to read Bishop's mind to catch his hesitancy. It was there in the weight of his gaze. Shaking my head, I said, "Let me guess, the report details aren't adding up."

"That's a big negative." He stopped the finger drumming. "I need to head out tomorrow and do some home visits with Dwyer's old unit."

"Anything I need to be concerned about?" I caught his head-shake.

"What details aren't adding up, Bishop?" Meli was bound and determined to get answers. Problem was, despite's Rabbit's digging, I bet there were more questions than answers available.

Something Bishop's response confirmed. "We don't have enough to put it out there yet."

Undeterred, she pushed. "You obviously have enough to worry, and I'd like to know what's causing it."

Was she really going to sit there and read Bishop the riot act while she kept information like a psychotic stalker from us?

Not bothering to temper my tone, I let some of the frigid fury at her lie of omission leak out and freeze into a cutting edge. "You know what would have been helpful, Melisande? Knowing about that pesky restraining order you put out."

It was enough to redirect her attention to me. "I thought he was gone, so there was no reason to bring it up."

Disbelief hit first, but was quickly nipped in the ass by righteous indignation. My fingers tightened on the wheel as I gritted my teeth. "Are you fucking kidding me? Yo—"

"Whoa! Time out, kids," Bishop cut in, making a T with his hands. "I don't want to be on tonight's news cast, so let's table this part of our discussion for when we're not in two tons of speeding metal, shall we?"

"Fine by me," Meli muttered.

I growled, but it was that or our "discussion" would quickly devolve into a lecture where I set a certain, pig-headed female straight on what constituted "need-to-know" information. Something with which she was obviously not familiar.

Bishop waded in and played referee, redirecting the conversation. "According to Rabbit, the unit sent out the day your brother was killed requested a last minute substitution, but there's no record to indicate if it ever happened. Rabbit's trying to piece together if that substitution was one of the men the team lost, but there are all sorts of possible flags he's trying not to send up. Navigating classified ops is like making your way through a minefield blindfolded. Still, it's enough to warrant me reaching out to a couple of the men from your brother's unit who live nearby and get their take on what happened."

"If they'll talk," I added, knowing how tight lipped teams could get.

"Would it help if I came along? Would they talk if they knew I was Eric's sister?" It almost hurt to hear the note of hope in her question, and part of me was glad I wouldn't be the one snuffing it out.

Bishop was already shaking his head before Meli even finished. "Nope, they'd be more likely to clam up tighter than a v—" He coughed, interrupting a rather colorful description, not exactly fit for polite company. "Tighter than a drum."

I rolled my eyes as his lame recovery, but didn't correct it, because he nailed it.

If Meli showed up with Bishop, guaren-fucking-tee there was no way he'd get more than the standard, whitewashed response on what the hell happened. Her disappointment came through loud and clear as her shoulders slumped and her head dropped.

Time to give her something else to focus on. "You wouldn't have time to go with Bishop anyway, doll face."

She turned to me, her nose wrinkling at my current pet name. "Why not?"

"Because you and I need to discuss a certain Nicholas Breck and then decide if we're going to be doing a road trip of our own."

"Road trip?"

Nodding, I tapped a finger on her purse. "We need to figure out what those pictures mean."

"If they mean anything at all." She didn't bother hiding her exasperation. "It makes no sense why Eric would leave me family vacation photos."

"Not yet," I offered, knowing the key to unraveling mysteries started with figuring out the pieces. "But if you put all your cards on the table, we might just figure it out."

She blew out a long breath. "I wasn't deliberately hiding things, Wolf."

If that was her version of an apology, it sucked. But whether she was keeping things quiet or not, stuck in the truck wasn't the time or place for this conversation. "We'll discuss it back at the villas."

Her noisy sigh was my only response.

Once at the villas, Bishop made himself scarce, leaving me to follow Meli into her temporary home where she tossed her purse on the counter. I closed the door behind me and the resounding thunk of the door echoed through the space. Even turning the lock sounded overly loud, and there was no way to miss her jerk as it clicked into place.

Guess someone wasn't looking forward to the impending conversation. Good, because that made two of us.

Instead of pinning her against the counter and making demands, I went and sat on the couch under the window. The blinds were partially open, enough we didn't need artificial light. Stretching out my legs, I held my tongue while the atmosphere vibrated with her tension.

She was slow to turn around, but when she did, she pressed against the counter, her arms folded tight against her chest, watching me with an intensity akin to the rabbit watching a hungry wolf.

I winced at the lame play on imagery and spread my arms along the back of the couch, my gaze on my boots. The minutes stretched taut, but I remained silent.

Finally she broke. "You're mad at me, aren't you?"

Sure as hell was, but I wasn't an idiot. If I started in on her, she'd shut down so hard, it would take more than dynamite to get her to open back up.

A flare of frustration erupted at my inability to touch her mind. It would make navigating what were sure to be dangerous topics, a little less explosive. But no, that would be too damn easy, and one thing was for sure, anything having to do with the complex woman standing in front of me was far from easy.

Since answering in the affirmative would just create more problems than needed, without lifting my gaze, I flexed my jaw and shook my head slowly.

"Yes you are." Her arms dropped and she took a couple of steps forward. "Why won't you look at me?"

Right, so avoiding her question wasn't going to work and no way in hell would I lie to her. Not bothering to hide the turmoil churning inside, I looked up and caught those vibrant green eyes with mine. "Because I'm trying to give you a chance to explain to me who in the hell Nicholas Breck is, and why you have a damn restraining order against him."

Even though my voice didn't rise, she paled, her eyes widening and her pupils dilating. With fear.

Of me? Seeing her reaction made bile rise and I choked it down.

Dropping my arms, I leaned forward, arms on my knees, mindful to keep my hands relaxed and not curled into useless fists. "That, right there, is why I should have known about him from you and not some detective. What did he do to you?"

Her throat worked as her gaze skittered around the room, her hands rubbing her arms even though it had to be near seventy-eight inside. Her gaze kept drifting to the door. She was going to bolt.

Watching her struggle, it wasn't hard to keep my voice soft, "Meli?"

Her gaze jumped to mine.

"Angel, sit before you fall down. It's been a rough day."

Like a marionette with tangled strings, she headed to the plush chair tucked on the far end of the couch, her movements jerky, before she sank on the edge of the cushion.

"I thought he was gone." Based on how soft the words were uttered she wasn't talking to me, but to herself. Not surprising considering how much crap had landed on her today.

Now wasn't the time for me to indulge in my emotions, because she was floundering in hers. To make sure her head stayed above water I had to be the one treading currents. "Why?"

She blinked, those thick lashes dropping and rising hypnotically. "Because it all stopped."

"What stopped?"

She shifted back further into the chair, drawing her legs underneath her, and hunkered down. "The phone calls, the late night visits, even the 'accidental' run-ins in town." Her hands shook as she made air quotes around accidental, when she caught the telling movement she tucked them between her legs, then stared unseeingly at her lap.

Mirroring her, I forced my stiff body back to its previous position, legs stretched out, arms along the couch cushions. "How long was he stalking you?"

"I didn't realize he was stalking me." Her gaze skittered away and she mumbled, "Not at first." When she met my eyes, it did my heart good to see an edge of anger lurking under the shame and fear.

"You don't file a restraining order for the hell of it, Meli." I tried to temper my reprimand but based on her wince, I was unsuccessful. *Back off, asshole, that's not what she needs from you.* The mental riot act reined in my mouth and instead of pushing the point, I rephrased my initial question. "When did it all start?"

"About a year before Eric died."

"Did he know about it?"

Her gaze slid away, and her shoulders lifted in a jerky shrug. "I didn't think so, but..."

When she trailed off and worried her bottom lip, I remember what I read in her brother's letter. "Yeah, he knew."

Taking a visibly deep breath, she lifted her head and met my gaze head on. She nodded. "After Eric's last leave, Nicholas backed off."

"But it didn't last?"

"No, after Eric died, Nicholas came back around." Her gaze dropped back to her lap. "That's when it got bad, and I filed the restraining order." She began to pick imaginary lint from her jeans. "Things went quiet, so I thought the RO worked, or if I was really lucky, he'd been shipped back out."

Warning bells began clamoring for attention at that little tidbit. "Nicholas is military?"

She nodded. "He was Eric's best friend."

And the plot thickened. "Wait, best friends?" And it took her brother how long to catch on his buddy was a psycho?

"They met in basic, and when their leaves lined up, they always hung out."

Which explained the why behind her not sharing Nicholas's behavior with Eric. "You didn't want to interfere with your brother's friendship."

"Eric had enough on his shoulders."

Yet reading his last letter, I had a feeling if I wasn't here to give her the riot act, Eric would've gladly taken on the responsibility. "Hate to break it to you, but I'm pretty sure your brother would've wanted to know."

"Maybe, maybe not." A haunted look darkened her eyes as she hitched a shoulder to rub against her chin.

Recognizing the signs of guilt, I dug deeper, "Why wouldn't he want to know if someone was bothering his little sister?"

She stopped her nervous movements.

I dropped my arms so I could fold my hands over my stomach. It was that or pull her out of that chair and tuck her in my lap.

When her words tumbled out, one on top of another, I held my position, giving her the space she needed. "At first, Nicholas was charming. Even though he kept asking me out on a date, and I refused, it never seemed to bother him. Instead, even Eric teased him about not getting the point. Nicholas just laughed and said the most worthwhile things never came easily."

Curled into the chair's dubious protection, she stared over my head and through the window, lost in her memories.

"Eventually he wore me down, until I felt guilty for not giving him a chance, even though I knew it wouldn't go anywhere. So I accepted. Somehow, one date turned into two, then three. He was in town on leave for about four weeks, and he made sure we did something almost every night. I tried to refuse, but he'd just bowl right over me. Then one night when he and Eric were hanging out with some of their buddies here, he introduced me as his girlfriend."

Finally, her attention dropped to me and there was no mistaking her sincerity. "I didn't want to hurt or embarrass him, so I didn't call him on it. Then. After, when we were out in the drive watching the guys leave and Eric had gone back in, I kept Nicholas outside and told him straight out I wasn't his girlfriend."

"How'd that go over?"

She shifted uneasily. "He didn't do anything."

Maybe not then, but later I was damn sure Nicholas did something.

"But there was something off about his reaction, and it made me nervous. It didn't help that I was feeling trapped." Her voice dropped, "By the time he was ready to ship back out, I was so relieved."

It didn't surprise me. Even in the short time I'd known her, it was obvious Meli wasn't one to make nice with conflict. Not such a bad thing. She was intelligent enough to know when a situation stank to high heaven, it was best to retreat and reconsider your options. Unlike me, who had no issue with going in fast and loud. "But distance didn't help?"

My question brought her head up and she watched me warily. Made me wonder if she expected me to criticize how she handled things. "Some. He'd call and write letters. I managed to avoid the calls at first, then he started calling from unidentifiable numbers. When he got me on the line, he interrogated me on who I was with and what I was doing. Even his letters changed, becoming weirdly obsessive."

The picture she painted wasn't pretty, and my stomach lurched. It was a prime example of escalating behavior. "What happened when he came home?"

She swallowed hard, color rising in her face, only to fade away, leaving stark fear behind. "He came home a couple months before Eric died. Eric was due home the following week."

Which meant she was left to face Breck alone.

Determined, she kept going, "He showed up on my doorstep, and when I stood in the doorway, refusing to let him in, he got mad. I didn't think…" She trailed off.

Watching her fingers go bloodless from the pressure of her hold, it was all I could do to stay in place as she went quiet.

She wrapped her arms around her middle and when her shoulders curled in protectively, my blood began to pound in my ears.

The urge to go out and beat the living shit out of one Nicholas Breck gave a brutal shove against my common sense. I pressed my hands hard against my stomach until my knuckles whitened.

She finally looked up, her skin drawn tight, her eyes bright. "It got bad."

"How bad?" What would I need to do when I finally found the son of a bitch?

She shook her head even as she held my gaze. "I don't—" She choked off.

Seeing the depth of her pain and fear in those endless pools was worse than being torn open with a dull blade. "It's just you and me here, you're safe, angel."

"Not if he's back."

"He's not getting near you again, I promise." And it was one promise I had no problems keeping.

"You can't—"

"I can, and I will."

She studied me, and if I knew what she was looking for, I'd gladly give it to her. Instead all I could offer was my determination to keep her safe. Finally, she found whatever she needed and she continued, "I didn't want to let him in, but I wanted to make it clear I wasn't interested in him. Not as a boyfriend, not even as a friend."

She paused and rubbed a finger against the underside of her jaw. "He doesn't do rejection well." She stopped.

"No surprise there since he's a dickless wonder."

That earned me a tiny, shaky grin. "You've never met him."

"Don't need to, know the type."

She was avoiding going into details. It struck me to wonder how long she'd kept this bottled up. Meli was a solitary thing and with her brother gone, so were her options. Maybe Risia, but I wouldn't bet on Meli telling her best friend more than she needed. Especially since Risia wouldn't hesitate to castrate anyone who hurt her friend.

Something told me Meli needed to share with someone, and I preferred that someone be me. "What did he do when you sent him packing?"

She began to rock slightly. "He was furious. He shoved me back into the house and came in, slamming the door closed behind him."

All emotion was wiped from her voice, and my gut clenched, preparing for the incoming blow.

"The current group of guests had just finished checking out. Martha and Jorge were out cleaning up the villas."

"Which left you alone at the main house."

She nodded. "He was so angry, and he said…" she choked, her chest rising and falling rapidly.

Recognizing the signs of an impending panic attack and unable to sit aside any longer, I launched from the couch and ended up kneeling next to her.

Her eyes were wild, her hands clawing at her throat, as she began fighting for air.

Catching her hands, I held them still. Pressing my other hand just under her breasts, I began to rub her chest with gentle pressure, trying to relax her diaphragm. "Shh, angel." I held her gaze. "Breathe with me. In. Out."

I kept up the encouragement, and as the minutes dragged by, stuffed my own volatile emotions down.

Finally, fucking finally, she began to match my breathing.

Chapter Thirteen

It was hard not to think. But caught by Wolf's gaze and lulled by his careful circles against my diaphragm, I managed to follow his cue on breathing. Little by little, the steel bands clamped around my chest began to loosen.

I was so grateful not to be suffocating, tears pressed against my eyes. As air began to flow, embarrassment rose up to take center stage. *Way to go, Meli girl.* Here I had prided myself on showing Wolf how strong and self-sufficient I was, and all it took to reduce me to that weak thing of before was some fricking memories.

Granted they were darn scary ones, but still…

"Take in another breath, Meli."

It was automatic to follow Wolf's rough command even as I searched his face for signs of disgust. Instead all I found was a fierce concentration, laced with worry. My muscles ratcheted down another notch, and my next inhale was deeper.

"That's it angel. Keep going." He watched, offering quiet encouragement until I was breathing normally. His hand stopped its gentle movements, but didn't move away. "Better?"

I nodded. "I'm sor—"

"Stop," he growled, literally growled, as a fierce light made his eyes bright. "There is nothing to apologize for."

Logically I knew that, but logic didn't stand a chance against old habits.

He released my wrists and turned his hand to tangle his fingers with mine, giving me an anchor. "You up for continuing?"

He asked the question like I had a choice.

Despite the evidence to the contrary, I wasn't blind to the fact that I needed to share what had happened. If I could do that with Wolf, maybe it would dull the jagged edges of the memories.

What worried me was sharing and then watching Wolf realize I wasn't the type of woman he needed or wanted. Broken and barely mended didn't hold a candle to strong and sure.

Unable to look away, I slowly nodded.

"Okay." The hand under my breasts disappeared and he rose to his feet, still holding my other hand. "You're going to come sit with me on the couch. That way, we'll both be more comfortable."

Meli the Milquetoast I may be, but there was no way I was turning down a chance to be close to him while I could. Part of me warned to hoard the experience while I could because he wouldn't be staying.

Too battered emotionally, I chose to ignore the pessimistic voice. For now.

He tugged on my hand, and I uncurled my legs and stood shakily, waiting for the pins and needles to fade. Wolf stood patient and quiet, waiting for me.

We moved to the couch. He sat down, reached up, and pulled me into his lap. His warmth was better than any blanket and being held in his arms against his solid chest gave me the illusion of protection. Nothing could touch me, so long as he held me.

I tucked my head in the hollow of his shoulder. When his chin brushed my temple, I closed my eyes, gripped his wrist at my waist, and sank into him.

Finally, he broke the quiet. "What happened after he pushed you inside?"

My fingers tightened on his wrist. "He informed me that it didn't matter what I said, I was his."

Remembering the mad light in Nicholas's eyes, I shivered. "And what was his, stayed his. The only way I wouldn't be his was if he threw me away. He said a bunch of other stuff." Things I didn't want to share, so I rushed on, "He kept poking his finger into my chest, backing me up across the room. I slapped his hand away and told him to get out, then made the mistake of turning to get the phone."

The metallic taste of remembered fear flooded my mouth and I could feel my chest tightening again.

Wolf lowered his head over mine, his voice soft, gentle, "Breathe, it's just you and me."

I matched the rise and fall of his chest. Taking the time to distance myself from the memories was a necessary survival tactic or I'd never make it through this.

When I could recite the facts without it touching me, I said, "He grabbed my ponytail and jerked me back. The coffee table was beside us, and I ended up falling over it. When he wouldn't let go of my hair, he ended up wrenching my neck. He kept jerking me off balance. I couldn't get my feet under me. He kept ranting on about his expectations and what would happen if I didn't meet them."

It was strange how rational Nicholas sounded, even as he promised to break me until I learned my place. He was easily a hundred pounds heavier, and muscled.

At first, shock kept me quiet, but it wore off quickly as fear took its place. I clawed at his hands, ignoring the pain searing my scalp from his angry yanks. The only reason I knew I had done that was because afterward, I washed blood out from under my nails.

Then he tossed me across the room, sending me crashing into the shelves. The bruises on my shoulder, cheek, and hip took weeks to fade.

It was pure luck that had me dodging out of the way of his fist. His wild punch would have done serious damage, and would have put a stop to what happened next. "I made it to the door, yanked it open, and ran out to the drive screaming for Martha and Jorge."

I didn't realize I was clutching Wolf's shirt until he rubbed my arm, stroking his palm from shoulder to elbow. Uncurling my fingers, I began to smooth out the material.

He covered my hand with his, holding it against his chest. His voice rumbled under my ear, "Martha and Jorge?"

"They work part-time helping me with cleaning and maintenance."

Even now, months later, I thanked whichever benevolent being watched over me that day, because if they hadn't been there... A shiver course through me, and I cut off that dark train of thought. "They heard you?"

I nodded. "Yeah. Nicholas caught me halfway down the steps and began dragging me back inside. I managed to hold onto the railing until Jorge made it to the porch. He charged Nicholas with a rake, swinging it wildly and forcing Nicholas away from me."

Jorge and Martha were in their sixties, but the minute they heard my panicked cries, they came running. Armed with a garden tool, Jorge had been undaunted, determined to make Nicholas leave.

Martha had rushed over to where I had collapsed against

the railing, and kept her arm around me even as she dialed the police.

"When Nicholas realized the police were being called, he took off."

Under me, his muscles bunched then relaxed. "Did you file charges then?"

I nodded. Only because the responding officer had recommended it.

Frightened by Nicholas's behavior, and with Martha and Jorge as witnesses, I gave a detailed explanation of what had happened. It wasn't until everyone left that the shame and shakes crept in, leaving me a paranoid mess. By the time I managed to claw my way out of my self-induced hole, days had passed.

"Why wasn't he taken in?"

Awkward as it was, I managed a shrug. "Honestly? I'm not sure."

He stilled. "You didn't follow up?"

Nope, because I'm a coward. Instead of making the admission out loud, I choked out, "The officer in charge of my case left a message that they were still in process of following up with him."

When things stayed quiet and Nicholas didn't return, I stopped pushing for the officer to pursue it and let the situation slide. When Nicholas continued to stay away, I assumed the order was enough to discourage him, or if I was really lucky, he'd been sent back out on tour.

A very dark and damaged part of me hoped he never made it home.

Yep, not admitting that to Wolf either. "Days passed, then weeks, and nothing happened, so I went back to my life."

Wolf shifted his hold until his hands cupped my shoulder, holding me away so he could see my face. His expression was hard to read, but his gaze was intent. "You didn't go back, you hid."

My breath hitched at the brutal honesty in his accusation. I yanked away, scrambling out of his lap. On my feet, I began to pace, arms wrapped around my aching stomach.

Finally, I faced him. "I was dealing with Eric's death. Work took up my time, and then the whole situation with Risia happened. I wouldn't call that hiding."

Wolf shifted to the edge of the couch, his feet planted on the floor, elbows braced on his knees as his face darkened. Those eerie eyes pinned me in place, and then he blew out a breath, ran a hand over his head and cupped the back of his neck, his gaze shifting away before coming back. "Fine, you weren't hiding, but you sure as hell were avoiding things."

Frustrated that my flaws were on eye-searing display and so easily seen by this man I wanted to scream denials. Instead, I clenched my jaw and tried not to reveal how deep his comments cut.

Confronting the situation with Nicholas scared the ever-living daylights out of me. It meant admitting how much of what had happened, what was happening, was my fault. Did Wolf not get how demoralizing it was to realize that all the pain and fear you lived with, day in and day out, could be traced back to your one decision not to be the bad person and do something stupid like go out on a pity date? Or how much it scarred your soul to come face to face with the reality that the strength you thought you had was nothing more than an illusion?

When Nicholas stood over me, red-faced and crazy, my world shattered into unrecognizable pieces. I couldn't escape. My intelligence couldn't dodge his fists. My physical abilities were reduced to basic survival—trying to keep my head and stomach protected. It didn't matter what I did, or what I said, the only way Nicholas was stopping was if he decided to stop.

Getting away from him had been pure luck, just like Martha and Jorge being there.

"I was surviving." The three words came out harsh, echoing with bitterness.

He winced and stood. "I'm fucking this up."

The regret in his voice leached the heat from my ugly emotions.

No, he wasn't messing up, that would be me. How could I expect someone as strong and capable as him to understand my position?

Truth was, I couldn't. Wolf was no one's victim, it was one of the reasons I was so drawn to him. It was also why he would never understand, or ultimately accept, my decisions.

Sometimes it was too dangerous to stand your ground, safer to escape.

Proving he really couldn't read my mind, Wolf said, "The important thing is to make sure he can't ever hurt you again."

I didn't bother stating the obvious. Short of Wolf being permanently stuck to my side, that wasn't going to happen.

"To do that, we need to figure out if the trouble currently messing with you is tied into Breck or your brother."

Since we were stepping back from the drama of my past, my muscles began to unlock. "Those are two separate situations."

"You sure about that?" He waved me over to the chair. "Sit before you fall down, baby cakes."

I frowned, at the name and his question, but moved to the chair and sat. "What are you seeing that I'm missing?"

He went to the corner of the couch closest to the chair, and sat. Then he leaned forward, bracing his arms on his knees. He was so close I could reach out and brush the shadow dusting his jaw.

I tucked my hands under my thighs to quell the urge. Thank goodness he couldn't follow my thoughts. Hard enough to deal with my sappy emotions, much less have him witness it. He was seeing too much of me as it was.

"You said Breck served. So did Eric."

I cleared my throat. "Right, but they weren't on the same teams."

"Yet they stayed close?"

"Yeah, they tended to cross paths often."

"Your brother's letter indicated that he tried to make things right. What if he confronted Breck about his behavior with you? Would Eric do that?"

In a heartbeat. Eric took being an older brother seriously. "Even if he did, and they argued and had a falling out, what could that possibly have to do with pictures of our family vacation?"

"I don't know." Wolf's face grew grim.

My mind circled, trying to put the pieces together, but failing miserably. "Nicholas's behavior got violent when Eric wasn't here."

Something too fast passed over his face, leaving no trace behind. "That's because Eric was the leash that kept Breck in line."

I shook my head. "No way would my brother be a friend to a man who was abusive. Eric would never condone that."

"It's highly probable Eric had no idea of Breck's behavior until it was too late." The lines in his face softened, and his voice gentled, "Men like Breck are very, very good at hiding behind a mask."

"So you think the only reason Nicholas didn't strike out at me earlier was because Eric was here?"

"If your brother hadn't been killed, would you have kept the attack from him?"

I shook my head. During Eric's last visit, I wanted to spill everything, but it was too close to the heels of the attack. Plus, something had been worrying Eric. Still rattled, I hadn't been thinking very straight. But I knew me, I would have eventually told my brother everything.

Wolf tapped my knee. "That's the leash that kept Breck from hurting you again. He probably disappeared because he was worried you'd tell Eric. As soon as you told your brother, he would go after Breck. It's a whole different game fighting a man equal to you in size and strength versus terrorizing someone who can't hurt you."

His explanation detonated with a reverberating impact, freezing me in place, echoing through all my hidden spots. This time it made an impression.

Frozen by terror, I had remained deaf to the logic of Nicholas's need for power. Over me. Over the situation. Over everything.

It didn't erase my guilt and shame, but it gave me a logical shield to hold against the worst of it. The relief of that was so big it left me trembling.

Wolf kept talking, but my headspace was a disaster area. Good thing he couldn't read my mind because if he ever got a peek, he'd high-tail it away so fast he'd leave nothing but dust in his wake. Not that I could blame him. I didn't even want to deal with the mess, and it belonged to me.

Snapping my attention back to Wolf, I tuned back in.

"Let's assume Eric figured out what was happening and confronted Breck," Wolf said. "That would spark a huge argument, because I can't see a personality like Breck's taking shit lying down. What if Eric threatened to report him to his commanding officer?"

I tilted my head to the side and frowned. "What good would that do?"

"It could result in a disciplinary hearing. If there was enough corroborating evidence, it would get his ass drummed out on a dishonorable discharge."

I thought over Eric's behavior in the months before he died. Was anything different?

It took a few minutes, but I managed to pick out a couple of small, inconsequential at the time, things. "After his last visit, Eric called home more often. I teased him about it. He told me he just wanted to make sure I was okay. That worrying about me was his job." A lump grew in my throat. "I could tell things were tense wherever he was because the conversations were really, really short. A couple of times he acted as if he wanted to say something, but then changed his mind."

"Anything unusual before his last mission?"

I nibbled on my lower lip as I played back the conversations with my brother.

There were signs of exhaustion—bags under his eyes, new lines around his mouth, and he seemed grimmer, as if whatever was happening was sucking any of the lighter emotions out of him. But his conversations were general in nature. How was I doing, how was the job, meet anyone new type of thing.

"No, not that I can remember." I blinked and studied Wolf. "You really think the two can be tied together?"

He rubbed his chin. "I don't know. I could be grasping at straws, but something is off, I just don't know what it is."

"Maybe Bishop will get something on his visits." It was a fragile straw I wasn't willing to give up on yet.

"Maybe."

Seeing the frustration on his face, guilt rose. Here I was dumping all my garbage on him, just like I used to do with Eric. It wasn't fair to Wolf.

Needing to lighten the mood, I nudged his foot with mine. "You always like this?"

He raised an eyebrow. "Like what?"

"Intense, focused?"

My distraction worked, he smiled. "Yeah."

The suggestive note in his voice made my foolish heart sit

up and take notice. My mind went along for the ride, providing a host of possibilities on how having that much intensity and focus centered on me would feel.

Oh boy. Heat rose under my cheeks like a tidal wave. "That could get you in trouble."

"How so?"

I stumbled over my answer. "It could, you know, blind you to possibilities, or maybe send you down the wrong path." *Was I really going there?*

He leaned forward. "It hasn't yet. In fact, it's helped me get what I want."

The ever-simmering attraction flared into brilliant life and, caught in his gaze, I found myself leaning in to meet him.

The warm wash of his breath brushed my lips, when the sharp summons of his cellphone cut in.

Chapter Fourteen

WOLF

Sick with fury, hands covered in gore, I glared at the piece of shit on the other end of the gun, my ribs still aching from the punishing kicks they'd taken. Since taking a deep breath hurt like a bitch, it was safe to say one, maybe two, might be broken.

"Do it!" The harsh command came from the one bleeding out in the corner.

No sense in acknowledging the asshole, he'd be dead soon. Right now, all that mattered was the threat in front of me.

With Ricochet down and out, worry gnashed vicious teeth, but the silent countdown echoing in my head made pushing it aside essential to our survival. No way was he dying on my watch.

The man in front me raised his gun, the dark barrel pointed directly at my center mass from three feet away. At that range, even a blind man wouldn't miss.

His flat gaze met mine and with no time for finesse, I barreled into his mind, smashing through the natural barriers most people carried.

Under his belief in pulling the trigger was a hunger for killing, twisted and voracious, waiting to be fed. The depth of it meant changing his mind was out. The intent to kill was too deeply seated.

Fine, we'd do it the hard way then.

I wrenched hold of his body's reactions, trying to ignore the whisper of Mom's voice warning me on the dangers of taking away a person's choice. "It's the only thing a person has left that's truly theirs, sunshine. You have to respect that."

Unfortunately, sometimes survival counted for more than respect.

Clenching my teeth, I tightened my hold.

The man drawing down on me frowned, his gaze dropping to his hand. First, disbelief bloomed, seeping through the emotionless ice, and then he began to fight the unknown. As his hand holding the gun began to shake and slowly, torturously slowly, turn, his disbelief faded under rising panic.

Next to me, the pool of blood under Ricochet's motionless body spread. Added incentive to keep the pressure on.

The barrel began to shake, then turn. Finally, it rose, and the pleas began to spill out. "Man, fuck, don't...I can't..."

"What the hell are you doing?" This came from the one in the corner. "Shoot the fucker!"

Then my wanna be killer's age showed, as the flash of regret at meeting death at the tender age of nineteen hit home, searing across my brain, and still I kept ruthlessly pushing.

"I can't...oh Christ—"

The gunshot's echo shattered the grisly montage of nightmarish memories and jerked me upright. Darkness lay thick and solid. My harsh breaths were the only sounds in the room. Wiping a hand over my sweat-slicked face, I checked the clock. Just past two in the morning. "Fuck me."

Swinging my legs over the edge of the bed, I got up and hit the head. Bent over the sink, I washed away the sticky sweat with cool water. Avoiding the mirror, I grabbed a towel, made a couple of quick swipes, tossed it back on the counter, and flicked the light off.

With Bishop out on the road tracking down Eric's old teammates, I had the villa to myself. Good damn thing, because if he found me like this, I'd never escape the third degree.

Would've been better to spend the night wrapped around Meli at her villa, but by the time evening rolled around, I needed quiet and space.

Not verbal quiet and space, but emotional.

While I may not be able to access her thoughts, reading her face provided a ringside seat to her mind. Poor baby couldn't hide a damn thing if she wanted to.

Unfortunately, it was frustrating and heart breaking to stand witness to the garbage threatening to drown her. What sucked even more, thanks to previous experience with similar situations, my imagination could fill in the picture of what she was telling herself, until it was high definition.

And none of it would be good. For either of us. But there wasn't much I could do about it, especially when my head was a seething mess.

Pacing through the dark villa, I tried to ignore the other ghosts clawing for attention. It was my fault they were here. I practically sent the SOBs an engraved invitation when I used that kid today. A minor violation in the scheme of things, but the ripples of my actions could grow into unintended tsunamis.

The last bastion of freedom for an individual was choice. Growing up, my mom did everything but tattoo the concept into my brain once we realized what I could do. Choosing to take that freedom away put me on the other side of the white line. It was an ethical choice I faced on a constant basis.

Part of my reasoning for joining PSY-IV Team was to soothe that ache. If, correction when, I was forced into that situation, it had to be for the greater good. For the most part I succeeded in that justification.

Except once.

Memories of being sent out by the colonel with Ricochet to

get eyes on a suspected homegrown cult tucked deep into the Stanislaus National Forest scrambled for a foothold.

Small, but lethal, the group consisted of para-military men, not one above the age of thirty-five, all tied together by an agenda bent on wiping out the modern world and government. We tracked them for days, then stumbled into a primitive, but well-hidden trap.

They had us for three days, and Ricochet, being not white and not blond, took the brunt of their demented form of interrogation. On day three, Ricochet had enough and shot one of our two interrogators. This resulted in the other one retaliating with a shot of his own. Then he turned his gun on me, moving the choice to us or them. With no time to tread lightly, I chose us with brutal efficiency. While we remained breathing, it didn't erase the fact I consciously stepped across that line with deadly intent.

Paying the karmic cost was a bitch.

The walls closed in, the air stifling.

Needing an escape, on too many levels to count, I jerked open the door and stepped out.

Cool night air hit my chest, a reminder I was only wearing sweats. The walls were still too close, so I walked away from the villa until I could lean my head back and see nothing but stars.

Focusing on those pinpoints of white light, I breathed through the memories, until they broke apart like wind torn mists. Unfortunately, their chill lingered.

Dropping my head, I waited for the head-rush to pass.

A soft creak of metal chain links caught my ear and turning toward the main house, I noticed the front porch swing was occupied.

With moonlight illuminating the way, I walked over knowing the shadow curled in the seat would be Meli. Sure enough, I went up the steps to the porch while she watched, silent.

A quilt done in a Native American pattern was wrapped around her shoulders, like a cape, leaving her pale face and hands exposed and her feet tucked under. The darkness made it hard to read her face.

I didn't stop until I was sitting next to her. She didn't resist when I pulled her into my lap, arranged her and the blanket, before gently setting the swing to rocking. The feel of her in my arms soothed my ragged edges and steadied me. The ghosts retreated a bit more.

It was long minutes before she spoke. "Couldn't sleep?"

"Bad dreams."

No sense in hiding it from her. Maybe if she knew her decisions weren't the only ones difficult to live with, she might step back from the ugly edge on which she teetered.

She shifted, lifted the quilt, and pressed her palm against my heart as she resettled with her head on my shoulder. "If you want to talk about it, I'm here."

With that sweet offer, she managed to burrow a little closer to my heart. Even when crap was raining down around her, she didn't hesitate to share the load.

I ran my hand through her hair. Strands curled softly around my fingers, until it was like being caught with silk ribbons. "You should let it go back to red."

Her head tilted back so she could see me. "Red?"

I tugged gently on a strand. "Your natural color."

She ducked her head. "Darn, my roots must be showing."

The unexpected chagrin in her comment made me chuckle. "Nah, but between the freckles, pale skin, and green eyes, red becomes rather obvious."

The swing drifted back, then forward, then back as the night settled around us. The gentle sway of the swing and the night-critter chorus singing their tuneless melody provided a layer of privacy to the night. For the first time, her defenses seem to be absent.

Curious, I smoothed out another strand, and decided to push my luck. "Why'd you dye it in the first place?"

Tension tightened her spine. "Because."

Her walls were reassembling.

Determined to keep my foot wedged in the metaphorical opening, I ran a comforting hand down her back even as I nudged my way in. "Because why?"

It took a bit for her to answer and when she did her voice was low, melding with the night. "He said that it was my fault he couldn't stop thinking about me. That I used my looks to get what I wanted from men, but he wasn't going to be like the rest."

The cost of her raw honesty caused her to tremble, so I tightened my hold.

After a pause, she continued gamely, "Contacts are a pain in the butt, so changing eye color was out."

A violent curse echoed in my head as I picked up what she wasn't sharing. No matter how hard she tried to downplay it, there was no missing the number he did on her. When I got my hands on him, I would happily take him apart, one slow piece at a time.

Needing to back away from the edge for both of us, I switched the topic. "Why are you here and not in your villa, petunia blossom?"

At the silly pet name, her tension melted away and she heaved a rather beleaguered sigh.

I hid my grin by burying my face in her hair. Teasing her was quickly becoming one of my favorite pastimes.

"Just couldn't sleep."

"If you want to talk, I'm here," I gave her offer back.

"You wouldn't understand," she muttered.

"Try me. You might be surprised."

Her head burrowed deeper against my chest, and her voice was soft, hesitant, "I wish you could read my mind. It'd be easier. Maybe less humiliating than saying it out loud."

"Why?"

"Saying it makes it real."

God, angel. The depth of ravaged emotion in those five words flayed me alive. Looked like we were going to dive right into the deep end of this conversation.

Good thing I could hold my breath longer than most. "What do you have to be humiliated about?"

Her bitter, broken laugh shouldn't have caught me by surprise, but it did. All I could do was hold her tighter. "Everything?"

Even though she posed it as a question, deciphering the sub-text was simple. "Meli, what he did to you, it wasn't your fault."

Her small fist emerged from the blanket and pounded against her temple. "I know that here, but," her fist went to her chest. "Here, it's not so clear."

She was killing me. There was so much self-directed anger in her voice I was surprised she wasn't screaming in rage.

Unlike other teammates, psychology wasn't my strongest suit, but considering where my ability lay, over the years I managed to hone my therapist skills. One thing I knew for sure, pity was a sure fire way to get her to lock me back out.

Hard as it was, I tucked my need to protect and comfort away and gave her what she needed—undeniable truth tempered by logic. "What, exactly, could you have done to change it?"

"How about not giving in and going out with him in the first place."

It was never that simple. "It wouldn't have mattered." She

stiffened against me, a silent rejection, but I kept going, needing her to hear me, needing what I offered to sink in so she could finish healing. "If he fixated on you, he'd figure out a way to get to you no matter what."

"Maybe." Her answer was reluctantly given, but I'd take it.

"No maybe about it. Obsessive natures focus on their victim, generally on some minor detail. The color of a shirt they're wearing, their name, or even something as simple as they crossed the street at the same time as them. Whatever it is that flips their trigger, it's not something you or any rational mind can identify. It's how that personality type works."

This time when she sat up and pulled away, I loosened my hold but didn't let her go. She stared out over the railing and into the night. "Again, I know that, Wolf, but it doesn't help."

There was an impatient undertone to her voice, and it was the only thing keeping my frustration at her pessimistic attitude in check.

Still, I wasn't about to let her off that easy, because she was so much stronger than she thought. "So you're going to let him win, even though you walked away?"

That got me a glare. Sitting straight in my lap, wrapped in a blanket, she managed to convey an irate dignity even as she tried to fold her arms over her chest without letting go of the blanket. "Why does it have to be a question of winning or losing?"

Pleased by her spark of defiance, I laid it out for her. "If you let him determine how you act, then you've given him control. In my book, that's letting him win."

Her eyes narrowed, and her hand shot out complete with a stiff pointer finger she decided to drill into my chest to get her point across. "Giving him control? I'm not giving him anything. I'm trying to survive."

Since sporting another bruise wasn't high on my to-do list, I caught her hand and held it. "Hiding is not surviving, it's a choice."

We were so close I could see the battle raging in her gaze. For a moment, I thought I'd finally made in-roads, but then her eyes darkened and shuttered, but not before I caught her mix of fear and panic.

Before she even opened her mouth, I knew, fucking knew, she was going to fight dirty.

"Right, a choice, Wolf. What goes into making those choices isn't the same for everyone. Besides it's not like everyone sees things like you."

Got to love what self-preservation can do to the best of people. Meli was scared and fighting, but she was fighting the wrong thing. Unfortunately, just because I understood, didn't make it hurt any less. "What do you mean?"

Her gaze dropped and skittered away. Her shoulders hunched as she twisted in my lap, but her mouth pressed into a mutinous line.

Oh, hell no, she didn't get make a statement like that, then bug out.

Grasping her chin, I forced her to meet my gaze. "No, you said it, now explain what you meant, because something is obviously bothering you."

A sick feeling began gathering in my gut, as instinct screamed that what she said next was going to sting like a bitch. It was there, waiting in the shadows next to us, rubbing its hands with glee.

She searched my face, nibbling her lower lip. Finally, she whispered, "Why?"

And damn if she wasn't going to invite the bastard into our conversation. I waited her out, wanting her say it out loud, unable to give her an out.

Her next pause lasted longer than before.

The sick certainty gained strength because what she said next could do serious damage to the spark struggling to ignite the fires between us.

"Why?" This time it came out in a soft voice. "You could've just asked the kid to borrow his phone, but you didn't even hesitate." She maintained eye contact, but that minor victory was smashed beneath my rising anger. "You violated his mind to borrow a phone. A phone."

Guess it was time to try to explain the unexplainable. "I could tell you we were short on time and options. Or that we needed an untraceable line to contact Bishop."

"Neither one is good enough, Wolf."

"Not for you maybe, but both answers are true." When she frowned, I cut her off, "In my line of work, split-second decisions are the difference between staying alive or being dead. They aren't always pretty or nice, but I'm still breathing. I don't have the luxury of second guessing myself."

In my grip, her fingers curled and tugged. "And the next time? When things are dire or desperate, what then?"

I let her go abruptly and a harsh laugh, bitter and dark, erupted through the night. It must be nice to be able to view the world through such pristine glasses.

"Next time? Honey, there is always a next time, and I'm always scrambling to stay on the side of angels. Why do you think I was out here tonight?" Instead of shaking her, I ran a hand over my head, squeezing the back of my neck before letting it go and curling it into a fist I hid by my hip and under her legs. "You're not the only one haunted by past decisions."

Oh for fuck's sake, did that just come out of my mouth? I winced. Shit.

She frowned and leaned in to me. "What's haunting you?"

I shook my head, not wanting to get into it. Not now. Maybe never at this rate. "No, we're not going there."

I picked her up, and ignoring her squeak at my sudden

movement, sat her on the bench and got up to pace to the railing. I stared out over the drive, keeping my back to her. "This ability isn't fun. Hell, it's the worst kind of temptation."

The swing creaked and I turned, leaning against the rail, arms folded across my chest and pinned her with a cold gaze.

Time to shine the light of reality on her rose-colored glasses. "Sometimes there is no time. No good decision, but you react in order to survive. Something you should understand." I ignored her wince and kept going, knowing it was the wrong way to proceed. "You think I enjoy having this ability? That reading minds is some kind of power trip?"

"Isn't it?"

Sucker punched by her question, I could feel myself freezing, from the inside out. Christ, to ask that meant she didn't know me.

Hiding my rioting emotions behind heavy sarcasm, I sneered, "Guess we're clear on what you think of me, sugar plum."

Straightening, I moved, determined to get away from her. If she really thought I was the type to get off on being in control, then there was nothing more to say. Whatever I thought was between us was just in my head.

"Wolf, stop." Her small hand latched on to my wrist, leaving me unable to pull away.

There wasn't enough strength in her hold to keep me in place, but I didn't move, just stood there, refusing to look at her.

"I didn't say that to hurt you."

Her half-assed apology left me clenching my jaw. A couple of deep breaths and I finally looked down into her face. "Then why?"

Without letting go, she got to her feet, leaving her blanket pooled on the swing. Shadows and moonlight played over the boxer style shorts and thin T-shirt.

Despite the situation I couldn't help but notice she was braless, thanks to the cool night air, and that part of me that didn't give a shit what she thought, reacted.

She moved in close until she was standing almost on top of me, her cold feet brushing mine. "Because I'm worried."

She raised her hand and cupped my face. "About you. About the cost you pay, how far you'll slip before you disappear. You're a natural born protector, it's why you're so good at what you do, but how much are you willing to sacrifice to win? How far can you go to win the battle before you lose you?"

How could she be so clueless? I shook my head and her hand fell away. "It wasn't about winning, it was about keeping you safe."

I turned, needing distance to reconsider this whole screwed up situation. I twisted my wrist against her hold, breaking her grip.

She stepped in front of me and pressed her hands against my chest. "Don't."

Nope, wasn't going to let those big green eyes suck me under. "Don't what?"

As I watched, tears pooled. Not a deliberate move because that wasn't her style. That wasn't what got through my ice, it was the shadow of guilt, dark and heavy layering the pain within that clued me in. I wasn't the only one struggling here.

"Don't sacrifice yourself for me. I'm not worth it." The last bit came out in choked whisper that about brought me to my knees. She stepped back, turned away and crawled into the swing, dragging her blanket around her.

Shoving aside my damaged pride and bruised heart, I went over and dropped to crouch in front of her.

She wouldn't look at me.

My thoughts spun as I watched her. This wasn't some act to gain sympathy. Meli truly thought she wasn't worthy of being loved. I wasn't sure how to convince her otherwise, but swiping at her in retaliation was definitely not going to work.

It hit me then, if I wanted her to take her place by my side, maybe I should take mine at hers.

Her fingers were twisted in the blanket as she held it closed. Her head was lowered, and I had no idea if I could find my way through this treacherous maze.

Reaching out, I gathered her hands, her fingers were ice cold, and waited until she lifted her eyes to mine. "You are worth it."

When she tugged at her hands, I refused to release her. The damage Nicholas wrought was massive, and she'd been trying to fix it on her own for too long. It was time to help, no matter how hard she tried to keep me out.

"For this alone, I would gladly take him out, Meli." I let her see the truth in my words, every deadly intent I would keep when I crossed paths with that bastard. "That he managed to brutalize your sense of self is unforgivable."

When she went to duck her head again, I captured her chin and forced her to meet my gaze. "It's not a sacrifice to keep you safe."

Her tears spilled over and dripped like hot rain on my hand. She swallowed a couple of times before she managed a rough, "I don't want to be the reason you leave."

I brushed the wetness from her cheeks, but the tears continued. It hurt to watch, and I lowered my forehead to our hands in her lap. If she could bare this much of herself to me, I could do no less.

Taking in a deep breath, I raised my head to meet her gaze. "Angel, why are you so sure I'd leave you?"

"Wasn't that what you were going to do a minute ago?"

Yeah, but…wait a goddamn minute. Narrowing my gaze, I studied her lowered head. "You're trying to push me away." Yep, came out like the accusation it was.

She gave a shaky shrug, her gaze sliding away before coming back. "You deserve someone stronger, tougher." She tugged on her hands. "A woman who can watch your back."

I blinked, trying to process her answer. This must be the murky maze of female logic, so I had to proceed with caution. "Why can't you watch my back?"

"How?" The flash of feminine frustration laced with disbelief confirmed we were indeed deep inside female logic territory. This time when she tugged, I let her hands go. "I'm more liable to scream and then run in the other direction if we're attacked, or duck for cover when the bullets start flying. There's no way I'm cut out for all this warrior stuff. Just this," she waved a hand around, almost smacking me upside the head, "what's been happening here, has me stretched to the breaking point."

Maybe, but she hadn't snapped. Not yet. Did she not see that strength wasn't always about muscle and attitude? Since smiling now wouldn't be good, I fiddled with her blanket until I was sure I knew where to step.

I captured her gaze and held it. "I don't need someone to protect me, Meli. I need someone to stand beside me, to accept me, all of me. What I need is a light to anchor me so I don't slip too far into the dark. You can be that anchor, hell you're already doing it."

She fidgeted with the blanket. When her nose wrinkled, she rubbed it away with a finger. "Easy to say now, but what about later?" She snuck a look at me from under her lashes. "When things go back to normal?"

Seeing a faint light at the end of the conversational tunnel, I gently teased, "What's normal?"

That got me a roll of her eyes. "You know what I mean. This can't go on forever. You and Bishop will figure out who's behind the recent attacks and why they're happening, then you'll fix it and go back to your lives in San Diego, doing whatever it is that you two do with your team. Meanwhile, I'll be here, running the villas. How does that work?"

Resting my arms on either side of her, I cocked my head to the side. "I'm sure we can figure it out."

Her jaw firmed, then jutted out. "You'll get bored with me."

Silly, stubborn woman. There was no stopping my bark of laughter. "Are you serious?"

Totally convinced of what she was saying, she leaned forward. "I don't lead an exciting life, I don't have any nifty super powers."

She was so close I wanted to kiss her until she wasn't thinking straight, but the timing wasn't right.

It was getting harder to hide my amusement at her persistence that she was boring. "I get more than enough excitement from the team, and I wouldn't wish a psychic ability on anyone."

Something I couldn't catch washed over her face.

Turning serious, I studied her, wishing futilely that just once, I could see what was spinning inside her head. I sent out a questioning mental touch. No such luck.

Guess I'd stick to old-fashioned direct questions. "What do you think this is, between us?"

Her blush was fast and furious. "Lust."

There was no missing the lack of belief in her answer. I arched an eyebrow and drawled, "Really? Just lust?"

Instead of answering, she shifted in her seat, her blush bleeding down her neck and onto the sliver of her throat revealed by the blanket.

Pushing a bit harder, I didn't bother hiding the heat in my voice. A heat that had nothing to do with anger, and everything to do with the wicked images in my mind. "Hate to break it to you, but I didn't drive hundreds of miles just because of a pretty face. From the first time we met, it was more than lust, you know that." Or she wouldn't have reached out in the first place. "I spent the last four months thinking about you, trying to decide how to make my approach so you wouldn't run. Even Risia's evil eye couldn't deter me."

That got me a choked giggle. "Risia can be mean."

Damn straight. Talk about being frightened by a woman, Risia would make most men either drool or run for cover. Depending on what she wanted from you. But she was devoted to Tag, and those she considered hers.

"Yeah, and she's very protective of her best friend." I considered how much more to share, and decided to hell with it, it was time to lay all the cards on the table. "When we first met, you were still jumpy. While I couldn't read your mind, I could interpret that signal loud and clear. Not knowing the reason behind it and not being able to fix it, drove me nuts. I didn't need Risia's warning to keep my distance. No way did I want you to be afraid of me, so I decided you'd have to come to me."

She gave a delicate snort. "And how was I supposed to know that? Was I supposed to read your mind?"

Her snippy comeback made my lips twitch. "Didn't matter if you could or not, because your time was about up. So, it's a good thing you called me."

Her gaze drifted over my face, weighing my sincerity.

Since I meant every damn word, I hid nothing.

Finally, she offered a hesitant, "Maybe."

There's only so much a male can resist, and I'd reached my limit. Grabbing the edge of the swing to halt its movement, I leaned in and caught her mouth in a sweet kiss, taking my time.

Her soft lips parted under mine as I nibbled along the tender edges.

Despite my best intentions to keep it gentle, her simple touch lit the fuse and what was supposed to be an offer of reassurance exploded into heated demand. My fingers tightened on the swing's wooden slats, even as her hands left the protection of her blanket and curled around my neck, pulling me closer.

Her soft groan echoed mine as my body clamored for hers.

By some minor miracle, I managed to pull back, chest heaving as I stared into her eyes.

They were dark with desire and focused on me. Her arms tightened, and her chest heaved as if she had run a race.

I dropped my head to hers until our foreheads touched, careful of her bruise, my voice emerging rougher than normal, "You still think you're not my type?"

This close together I didn't miss the curve of her kiss-swollen lips, and had to swallow a new groan as that small movement made my dick twitch in greedy demand. Her hold loosened, as she coughed, once, then twice, before answering, "Maybe you're just caught up in the adrenaline rush."

Got to love a challenge.

I uncurled one hand from the swing and tucked a strand of hair behind her ear. Then just because I could, I traced a slow, hot line from her jaw, down her neck and along the gaping edge of her T-shirt.

As my finger dipped under the T-shirt's edge, she held her breath.

I smiled as I drew it back out. "Guess I'll have to convince you otherwise."

"Guess so," she croaked, but captured my hand with hers.

We stayed that way, simply touching each other as the minutes passed. I didn't know about her, but if I tried to move from my current position I was liable to hurt something I was planning on using later.

When it was safe to stand, I rose to my feet, offering her my hand. She gathered her blanket and fumbled with something under it, before weaving her fingers through mine and rising from the swing. Which reminded me of the question that started this whole thing. "You never did answer me."

She stopped adjusting the blanket with awkward one-handed movements, and tilted her head to look at me. "About?"

"Why you're out here?"

"Oh, because." She moved, and the blanket's edge parted as she brought out her hand filled with photos. "I was hoping to figure out why Eric left these."

The blanket slipped, and she went to catch it but since both hands were full, she dropped the photos with a muttered, "Darn it."

Watching her bend down to pick them up, I considered how to work with her on increasing her colorful vocabulary skills.

I dropped into a crouch and began helping gather the splayed photos. "Any luck?"

When she shook her head, her hair brushed my shoulder. She leaned over to nab a photo that slid further than the others and began to teeter.

I grabbed her shoulder to help her balance.

She patted my hand and leaned way over, her shadow shifting until a shaft of moonlight drifted over the photo.

I tightened my hold, stopping her, my gaze never wavering from the photo. "Hold up, angel."

Reaching beyond her, I grabbed the stray photo thinking there was something on it. But when I brought it closer, there was nothing.

Maybe I needed better light.

Rising, I walked over to the railing, turning the picture until moonlight fell across it, and a strange glimmer appeared. Shifting the photo carefully, the glimmers formed into numbers. "Holy shit."

"What?" Meli came up to my side, trying to see.

Instead of answering, I tugged the other photos out of her hand. She watched silently as I laid out the pictures in a line on the flat side of the railing where the moonlight could reach. I pulled some out and left others.

Meli gasped. "What is that?"

There were four photos sporting numbers in a luminescent ink. "A message from your brother."

Chapter Fifteen

Crowding Wolf until I could tuck my toes against his feet, I wrapped a hand on his bicep to keep my balance, trying to ignore the expanse of naked male skin so temptingly close. Despite the fact he wasn't wearing a shirt he radiated enough heat to double as a space heater. How was he not cold?

Reeling my wandering, libido-directed mind back into focus, I watched him rearrange the four photos trying to see what he saw.

He handed me back all of the photos but the four on the railing.

I leaned in, studying the remaining pictures. There were numbers lining the edge, but no matter how he arranged them, they didn't make sense. "I don't get it. What are those?"

"A lead."

His answer sent my pulse into overdrive, and my fingers tightened on his arm before I could stop myself. Excitement made me grin.

He caught it and grinned back. Picking up the photos, he turned and curled an arm around my waist, pulling me in close. "Time to go inside. You're toes are turning into ice cubes." He looked around the porch. "Where are your shoes?"

"Over there." I nodded toward the post where I left my slip-ons.

He nudged me towards them. "Put them on and we'll go back to your villa."

As much as I wanted to go to my actual room and not my temporary space, I knew it wasn't worth mentioning. No way would he let us stay in the house while the bullet holes were still fresh. Not to mention the fact I still hadn't gotten a chance to clean up or replace the lock from the last break-in.

Sighing, I got my shoes on. When he held out his hand, I took it and let him lead the way to Pequeña Estrella.

Once inside, he flipped on the light in the living room, headed for the small coffee table, and sat on the floor.

Wanting to see, I went to the other side and sat, using the couch to brace my back.

He laid the four photos out in a straight line. "First, are all of these of the same place?"

Leaning over the table, I pulled them toward me, and turned them so I wasn't looking at them upside down. It took me a few minutes of wracking my brain for memories of our trip before I could put it together. "Yep. They're all from Rhyolite."

"How far away is that from here?"

I shrugged. "I think it's about two and half, maybe three hours up US 95."

"We'll need to get an early start on tomorrow's road trip then." He slid the pictures back to his side. "Do you have a piece of paper and pen?"

I got up, leaving the warmth of my blanket behind on the floor and hit the kitchen. Digging through the junk drawer, I found a pen and the back of a takeout menu when he added, "And a flashlight?"

That took a bit more hunting, but I found one in the cabinet with the coffee. Why it was there was beyond me. When I clicked to check if the batteries still worked, I got a bright beam in the affirmative.

I brought my stash back and handed it all over. "Here."

"Thanks." He set the paper and pen aside, and kept the flashlight. "Since you're up, want to hit the lights for me?"

A quick trip back near the door, a flick of a switch, echoed by him flipping on the flashlight, and we were good to go.

Wolf, being Wolf, kept the flashlight aimed at my feet so I could make my way back.

This time I sat next to him.

He pushed the menu and pen at me. "Since my hand-writing is crap, you get to write this down."

While he studied the photos, I was left undistracted to ponder the night's events. Right now, I felt battered and bruised from sharing my secrets with him. It left me raw and off-balance.

Wolf, on the other hand, didn't seem at all fazed by our conversation.

There was no doubt he intended us to move on to the next level, and despite my doubts on our longevity, I was happy to follow even as I sent up silent prayers I wouldn't screw this up.

Still, it was strange how quickly he slipped into business mode, when I was still reeling from his words and his earlier kiss. As much as I wanted answers, there were other things I wanted to explore as well.

Not the time, Meli. Focus. Blowing out a quiet breath, I pulled the paper and pen close and got ready to take notes.

"Honey bear?"

Grimacing at the cutesy name, I looked up, mouth open to respond, when he swooped in and stopped my words with a heated, devilish kiss. His tongue was quick and wicked, setting my nerves alight, and leaving me craving more. When he drew back, I couldn't mute my hiss of displeasure. His teeth flashed as he grinned, illuminated by the beam of the flashlight.

"This first, then we'll get back to our previous discussion." Low and rough, his promise made me shiver in anticipation.

Needing to recapture some semblance of control, I narrowed my eyes. "Are you sure you can't read my mind?"

He laughed, a genuine sound of happiness, and shook his head. "No gambling tables for you, angel."

He turned back to the coffee table, angling the flashlight until the beam's edge bled over the first photo. Green, blurry numbers appeared.

Leaning over his arm to see the photo, the green marking took on a glow under the light. "What did he do? Write with super-secret spy ink?"

Tilting my head, I squinted, trying to make the wiggles out. They looked like numbers, and scratches?

"Super-secret spy ink?"

Turning to look up at his face wreathed in shadows, I shrugged. "Is that what that is?"

He grinned and shook his head. "Remind me to tell Rabbit about your spy ink." He moved the photos slowly under the lights. "Based on the bleeding edges of whatever he used as ink, I'm betting it's some homemade concoction."

Funny, it still looked like a leaky pen to me.

"Okay, first set is thirty-six."

Turning my attention back to the picture, I pointed out a mark. "Is that a line before it?"

Wolf shifted the light's angle and then tilted the photo. "Actually I think there's a dot there too."

"Or whatever ink Eric used may have smudged or dripped." Not that playing Negative Nelly was my preference, but it was best to consider all our options so we didn't get ahead of ourselves.

"Maybe," he muttered, clearly considering something. "But let's go with a line, dot, 36."

I wrote — . thirty-six and waited while he moved to the second one.

"Okay, I think we have two nines, a three, maybe an I or a one, then five and three." He leaned back, so I could move in. "What do you think? You're more familiar with Eric's handwriting."

"Yeah, but that's not saying much, he wasn't all that great at penmanship." Still, I studied the green markings. "Okay, I think the first one is a four, then nine, then three, then one, since everything else seems to be numbers. The last two are five and three."

"Sounds good to me." He set the second photo aside.

I wrote the second sequence under the first.

Photo number three required a few minutes of debate before we agreed it was a dot, two lines, two ones, and a six. The last one was smudged, so we had two options: 36684 or 35687.

When we were sure there was no other markings, Wolf got up and flipped on the light.

I blinked under the harsh illumination until my eyes adjusted, rubbing the white dots and bleeding black edges away.

"Where's your phone, sleepyhead."

"Not sleepy," I mumbled, despite the burn of exhaustion.

"Uh huh." He crouched in front of me. "Phone, angel?"

"Nightstand in the bedroom, charging."

He disappeared into the bedroom.

I braced my elbow on the low-slung table and propped my chin in my hand as I stared at the photos and my notes. Leave it to my brother to make things difficult.

Why Rhyolite? We hadn't stayed long, maybe a few hours at most. The only reason it stuck out from the other stops was the nifty house made completely of glass bottles.

And the numbers in funky ink, where did they come in? Maybe it would make sense in the morning.

Wolf came back, straightened the photos and my notes, then took a picture with my phone, spent a minute typing out a text, then dropped it into the front pocket of his sweats. He held out his hand. "Come on, boofish, let's get you to bed."

Taking it, I let him pull me up. He was so close, I couldn't resist resting my head against his chest. "Where do you come up with these names?"

His soft laugh was accompanied by a hand brushing over my hair. "I make them up as I go."

"Figures."

Heaving a sigh, I straightened and turned. Not letting go of his hand, I made my way to the bedroom, my silent invitation loudly apparent. With each step, my earlier symptoms of exhaustion faded under an onslaught of nervous anticipation.

As I stepped through the door, he stopped, his hand tightening on mine. I stopped and looked over my shoulder.

He was watching me with a strange intensity. "You sure about this, Meli?"

My mouth was dry and the butterflies in my stomach were going crazy. "Yeah." When my answer emerged in a squeak, I winced.

He didn't say anything, just arched an eyebrow in question.

I tried again, this time swallowing past my nerves. "Yes, Wolf, I'm one hundred and fifty percent sure."

That got me a small grin. "Just a hundred and fifty?"

He stepped in until he could wrap an arm around my waist and pull me close. He let go of my hand and cupped my chin, dropping his head, his gaze never leaving mine, until our lips were just a breath apart. "Maybe I should wait until you hit two hundred."

"Don't you dar—" My husky complaint was cut off by his kiss. Held as I was, all I could do was follow his lead.

His tongue traced my lips, once, then twice.

On the second pass, I met him with mine. Like adding gasoline to a lit match, the heat flared, breaking my desire free of whatever silly constraints existed.

Our tongues teased and coaxed, until I was trying to pull free to turn to face him. What I wanted was to run my hands over those shoulders and down his chest, taking the time to trace the lines of muscle and explore the expanse of hot skin with my fingers and tongue. If I were really lucky, I might discover what caresses would break through his steely control.

When he finally broke our kiss, my chest was heaving as I gulped in air. Funny, I hadn't missed breathing until he pulled away.

He brushed his thumb along my damp lip, his gaze hooded and hot, while ruddy color swept along his cheeks. Altogether, he was the picture of predatory male, and I was too happy to be his prey.

Maybe later, we could switch places. Maybe.

Tempted by the thought, I licked my lips, tasting remnants of him, dark and decadent, and oh so addictive.

His sea-glass eyes were storm-tossed as he narrowed in on my small movement. A near-silent growl escaped as his arm loosened.

Taking advantage, I twisted in his arms until I could assuage my need to touch him from chest to hip.

Pressing close I cupped his stubble-roughened jaw, feeling the soft bristles against my palms. Shifting restlessly against his chest, his heat seeped through my T-shirt and my breasts grew heavy and achy.

Drawing in a slow, deep breath, dragged my breasts erotically over his chest, my T-shirt adding to the friction. My breathing deepened as I slowly drew my hands down his neck and over his shoulders. I watched my hands, fascinated by the feel of his hot, silken skin, of being able to indulge.

There were small interruptions in my path, physical reminders that the man in front of me lived in a dangerous world. Each scar nicked my heart, and I leaned forward to follow my touch with butterfly kisses, hoping to kiss away any memories of hurt.

His chest rose and fell against mine, the friction not doing a darn thing to ease the ache in my breasts. Instead, it increased the ache until the need to assuage it had me arching closer.

I continued my exploration, drawing my fingers down a slow, torturous path from shoulder to wrists.

He wasn't unaffected; I could feel him watching me as I explored, his gaze hot and growing hotter by the second.

Raising his hands, I brought them where I needed them most, my hands cupping his, encouraging them to cradle my breasts.

He didn't disappoint. His warm palms cupped me, his hands molding with a gentle, but sure touch, his thumbs brushing over my stiff nipples. It was my turn to lose focus at his simple, but devastating touch.

He tugged against my hold. "Let go, angel." The deep rumble cut through the haze of heat and want.

My lashes were heavy. I managed to get my eyes partially open, only then realizing I had closed them to better savor the tumbling kaleidoscope of desire invoked by his touch.

He stared down at me while his hands continued to tease and torment.

My hands left his wrists and went to the low edge of his sweats and found a hold on his bare waist. When he tugged my nipples, the sharp edge of pleasure and pain blurred, and I swayed forward with a soft moan. A dark flame flared bright, adding a heated glow to his eyes.

His head dipped down, and I rose on tiptoe to meet him

more than halfway, craving more of his taste. My fingers dug into his waist, and I pressed closer, trapping his hands between us.

When one of his hands left my breast, I nipped his lip in retaliation. He squeezed my butt and caught my lower lip with his teeth, tugged it, then whipped his tongue over the captured piece of flesh before releasing it.

Not giving me time to respond in kind, his other hand left my chest and buried in my hair, holding my head still as he plundered my mouth. It wasn't about give and take, it was all about establishing who was in charge.

Him.

I melted, giving him everything. Only then did he begin moving us into the bedroom. Pressed so close, walking backward was beyond me, so my hands went to his shoulders for balance as I stumbled backward, being shepherded by Wolf. Even that stumbling shuffle stayed distant as his mouth continued to take mine.

He lifted his head, leaving me fighting for air. He shifted his hold, one arm curling around my lower back, the other just under my butt, then growled, "Hold on."

Following his guttural warning, my eyes widened as he lifted me. Automatically I tightened my hold on his shoulders and wrapped my legs at his waist, holding on. Then the world tilted, as he leaned forward.

A quick glance behind confirmed the bed was right there.

"Eyes on me, Meli."

My gaze snapped back to his while I did my best clinging-ivy impression.

He braced an arm on the bed, then a knee, and then we were moving to the center. His head dipped next to mine, and then his lips brushed my ear. "You can let go now, baby."

Then it wasn't a matter of choice, because when his lips found the secret spot just behind my ear my legs loosened and dropped to the bed, desire leaving water in place of muscles.

The heated press of his lips whispered over that spot producing another moan, this one softer, needier than before as I arched my head away, giving him better access.

His chuckle sent heated breath over my neck, leaving chills in its wake. "Like that do you?"

"Oh yeah." It was all I could do to get the two words out. As it was, they came out on a breathy whisper.

His tongue joined in and painted a delicate trail from that spot, down my neck, and then he nuzzled against the base of my throat as he crouched above me. Gentle, mind-shattering kisses, full of unspoken emotion.

With my back now against the bed, I arched, head back, fingers locked on his arms. "More, please," I gasped.

"So polite," his rough voice was like velvet. But he took direction well because his hands were drawing my T-shirt up, exposing my skin to his mouth. His tongue painted a path behind the trail blazed by his talented fingers.

The ache between my legs deepened. Needing more, I lifted a leg and wrapped it around his waist, digging my heel into his butt covered by the rough material of his sweats, and bent my other leg, bracing my foot against the bed, so I could press up.

Unfortunately, I was no match, strength wise, to Wolf, who held his position even as he continued tormenting me in all the best ways. He ignored my attempts to get him to drop his weight on top of me. Instead, he pushed my T-shirt above my breasts, and I stilled, watching him watch me.

His face softened as his warm, calloused hands slid over my ribs until they rested just under my breasts. Mesmerized by the mix of heated desire and something I wasn't ready to name, I could only watch as he slowly cupped the aching mounds, bringing them together until my nipples were proudly pointed straight at him, while plump flesh overflowed his cupped hands.

Heat burst over my cheeks at his blatant approval. When his lips closed over one achy peak and drew it into a wet, hot cavern of his mouth, I shuddered. The decadent suction brought my lashes fluttering down.

He changed it up, adding his tongue, flicking it over the sensitive tip, driving my need higher. The feel of his mouth on me sent a direct line of fire settling in-between my legs, and my hips began to writhe. For long, delirious minutes he shared his devious attention between both breasts, until I was sobbing with frustration.

For the first time I mentally cursed his decision to shave his head. With no hair to grip, I was forced to tug on his ears until he lifted his head.

His hands released their hold and he rested his chin in-between my breasts. "Yes, dear?"

With an undiscovered athleticism, I curled the muscles in my stomach until my shoulders and head were off the bed and I could stare into Wolf's amused face. "Stop teasing me, Wolf."

"Why?" His grin promised all sort of naughty things. "It's so much fun."

With a snarled screech of impotent sexual frustration, I shifted my hold, dragging his head closer until I could kiss him. I used my tongue ruthlessly, teasing and taunting, then when his tongue was just as crazed as mine, I shifted my weight, trying to roll him over.

He chuckled and we rolled, his hands at my hips, mine on his shoulders, our mouths fused, until I was straddling him. The feel of him hard, long and hot against me, had me abandoning the kiss and sitting up.

The thin barrier of my boxer shorts didn't stop me from bracing my hands on his chest, and shifting my position until he was nestled where I wanted him.

Lord have mercy. The feel of him, hot and hard, nestled right there, was more than I could take.

I adjusted my hips, dragging my heat over his and making us both groan. His hands on my waist tightened as I began a slow rocking motion. The rise and fall stoked the fires, and they began to eat at my mind, leaving behind a primitive need to have him fill the aching emptiness spiraling closer.

"Wolf." Half groan, half plea, it was all I could manage as I leaned forward, unable to continue my teasing torment without sending myself over the edge. Something I didn't want. Not yet. There was so much more to discover.

"Enough playing, angel," he growled, the muscles of his abs tightened under my palms as he curled up, nipping my chin.

My head fell back, and his nips moved down my neck, followed by gentle licks that soothe the tiny stings. His hand splayed at the base of my spine, fingers sliding under the edge of my boxers. He tangled his other hand in my hair, holding me there, head back, neck arched, my body bowed for his enjoyment. A tug on my hair was accompanied by a nudge upward. "Lift, baby."

Bracing my knees on the bed by his hips, I flexed my thighs and rose, panting.

The hand in my hair gently disengaged and smoothed over my spine, then joined forces with his other hand and burrowed under the boxers to grip my hips.

When he moved, my hands went from his chest to his shoulders as the world spun and I squeaked in surprise.

When he was done, I was on my back, under him, and his hands were taking my boxers down my legs, leaving me naked.

Holding his shoulders, I lifted my head, craning my neck to watch him as he shifted backward until his head was just below my breasts.

"Not—" I broke off as he pressed a soft, open mouth kiss against my abdomen. The next was a little lower, then lower again. Scrambling for my train of thought, I sank back to the pillow, my fingers kneading his arms. "Not fair."

The two words came out in a barely understandable groan.

His tongue dipped into my belly button, traced a circle, then drifted over to the delicate skin where my leg met my torso. So close. One lick, then another, closer.

My hips rose in a silent plea.

Another kiss just above my pubic bone, then. "What do you want, angel."

Meeting his gaze down the line of my body, I licked my lips and whispered. "You, naked, in me."

Chapter Sixteen

WOLF

Delicate and tempting. That's what she tasted like. Her scent was even more alluring. Spice and heat. I watched her walls crumble under her need, her green eyes hazy with a mixture of want and an emotion she was trying so hard not to feel.

My body was ramped, but that raw intensity she couldn't hide wrapped around my heart and found its place deep within, making this so much more than feeding a hunger. The aching hollows were filling up with her light, leaving me wanting to ensure there was nothing but beauty and pleasure, such pleasure, she'd never be able to walk away. I didn't want to move, enjoying my position immensely, but if she wanted me naked, she'd get me naked.

Pushing up, I shoved my sweats down one-handed. When they snagged on my dick, I gave them a rough yank and they pulled free.

I went back to resume my position, but she stopped me. "My turn."

God love a woman who knew what the hell she wanted. Between the color dusting her cheeks and fevered gaze, there was no doubt in my mind she wanted me. Before she could sit up, I took advantage and dipped my head, my tongue swiping out to lick her, taking her taste deep.

She sucked in a sharp breath that ended on a moan.

Fuck me, but her taste was hot.

I went back for seconds, but her hands on my face stopped me.

"My turn." There was feminine demand this time.

Since it was all about pleasing her, I licked my lips, getting one last taste of her. There was always later. I let her push me onto my back.

She sat between my legs, at my knees, her stunning breasts rising and falling, just begging for my touch, but this was her turn.

I watched her study me, barely aware of her hands curling around my ankles, then slowly stroking up to my knees.

Her focus was centered on my dick, which was standing at attention. Her hands passed my knees and drifted over my inner thighs.

I shifted my legs further apart, and when she leaned forward, her hands coming higher, closer, I groaned.

Those eyes rose to mine, and a wicked, wicked smile appeared. "What do you want?" She gave my question back.

Clenching my fists so I wouldn't grab her and show her exactly what I wanted, I growled. "You, beautiful, wet, hot, and naked on me. Riding me."

Her response was a grin, then she dipped her head.

My head shoved back into the pillow, my eyes closing as my world centered on the sensation of her loving me. Hot, teasing, and destructively beautiful, I gave her what time I could, but it was a struggle.

Lifting my eyelids, I stared down, watching her enjoy herself, but knew I wouldn't last long. "Enough, angel." It came out on a low growl as I tangled my hands in her hair and gave a gentle tug, lifting her head, until those slumberous eyes rose to mine, her tongue peeking out to swipe over the tip of me in gentle chastisement. "I want inside you."

She crawled up me, dragging her breasts over me, leaving fire in her wake. She nipped my chin and whispered, "You were inside me."

Huffing out a breath at her teasing, I wrapped my arms around her and shifted, putting her under me, right where I wanted her. She was laughing, even as she arched closer, and my dick slid along her heated dampness. The sensation caused both of us to rock our hips, repeating the motion.

She managed to gasp, "Condom?"

Taking time to indulge, I dropped a line of open mouth kisses over the slope of her breast, stopping as I reached the tip, giving it a slow lick. It got me another gasp, and she arched in mute plea, her nails digging into my shoulders.

It was my turn to smile and tease, "Now who's the impatient one?"

"Dang it, Wolf," she groaned. "If you don't stop teasing, I'm going to explode without you."

"Can't have that happening." I ravaged her mouth and when I was done, she was blinking up at me dazedly. "Don't move."

As I quickly and carefully as I could, due to my aching dick, I got up from the bed and headed to the en suite bathroom where I'd stashed my shaving kit earlier.

Behind me, I heard her mutter, "As if it was even a possibility."

I shook my head, found my stash, and rejoined her.

Between the two of us, we made quick work of the condom, and then I was right there, her legs curled around my waist, poised to enter paradise. As I slowly sank deep inside her, I dipped my head and kissed her. Even as I rocked my hips to sink in, inch by inch, I kept our kiss gentle, slow, letting the heat between us rise. When I sank that last bit in, she moaned soft and low as she flexed. The feel of her, the heat, the beauty of her, became a supernova, searing everything but the sense of finally coming home, away.

Our gazes locked.

Hers stunned and exposed, sharing the sweetest glimpse into her delicate heart. Unwilling to damage her tenuous gift, I did the only thing I could, I showed her my battered heart, trusting her to hold it safe.

Her eyes went luminous. Her hands drifted my shoulders to my face, holding me even as our hips continued to rock.

"Wolf?" There was a world of unspoken questions in my name.

I heard every damn one of them, but I knew what I wanted, and what I wanted was currently giving me everything she had. "Yours, Meli, if you want it."

She searched my face and I watched as she, finally, fucking finally, reached for what she wanted. She was braver than she believed, because she answered, "I'll trade you."

The silly offer made me smile as my heart shattered and reformed, the seams holding it together filled with her. "Deal."

Her answering smile started soft and slowly grew as she watched me. She shifted her hold to my neck and pulled herself up, sending me deeper. We both groaned, then her breathless, "Deal," was the last word we spoke.

Slow and gentle shifted to hard and hungry. Moans and gasps, mine and hers, filled the room, as we chased each other to the peak, jumping off together. The sound of my name shattering from her lips was followed by my rough, "Meli!" as we fell into a miraculous oblivion I hoped never faded.

———————— •••◆◆••• ————————

It was early morning, and still dark out when I began urging Meli to wake up. Last night took the edge off my hunger, but hadn't dulled my need. Unfortunately, we had a long day on the road ahead of us and needed to get a move on. Even as I nuzzled the back of her neck, she mumbled a complaint and burrowed deeper into her pillow.

Curling around her, one hand on her stomach, the other brushing her hip, I set my chin on her shoulder. "Time to wake up, sleepyhead."

"No." The mulish denial was damn cute, but time didn't wait for any warm, sexy woman or her horny lover.

Another brush along her hip, but this time as I came back up, I gave her ass a small tap. "Up."

The move got me a reaction, not the one I wanted though. Without lifting her head from her pillow or opening her eyes, she pinched my arm.

"Ow."

"Serves you right." Half turning to me, she blinked a few times, then squinted. "It's dark out, Wolf, why are you trying to get me up?"

"We need to hit the road."

She turned the rest of the way over, until she was on her back as I lay on my side, my head propped by the hand not currently occupied tracing patterns over her soft skin.

"Where are we going?"

"We're going to visit a ghost town."

Covering my wandering hands with her hers, she frowned. "It's Thanksgiving."

"I know," and I felt bad about messing up her holiday, but this was more important. "But we don't have a lot of time to get this shit straightened out."

"Before you leave." Sleepy contentment faded and worry crept in.

I tightened my hold on her hand. "We'll figure out how to

make us work after we make sure you're not in any more danger."

When her lower lip disappeared under her teeth, I knew she was inviting in trouble. "You sound sure we will work."

Yep, still had some convincing to do. "You with me, Meli?"

She searched my face, and a band wrapped around my heart and squeezed. In the cold light of day, was she having second thoughts?

She slowly nodded.

The band disintegrated. "Then we'll make it work."

"Okay," she agreed softly.

"Okay," I repeated, then gave her a soft kiss. When I was done, I whipped the blankets back. "Time to get a move on."

"Wolf," she snapped, reaching for the blanket and sheet. "I'm naked and now I'm cold."

I moved until I covered her, enjoying the feel of her under me. One part of me more hopeful than he should be, but I couldn't resist. "I can warm you up."

She melted into me. "Thought we had to get going."

Dropping my head, I muttered, "We do." I brushed her mouth with mine, feeling her lips curve.

"So, can you do fast?"

I grinned and gathered her close. "Keep up, angel."

She kept up and then some.

Dawn was cresting on the horizon when we finally hit the road, travel mugs of coffee in hand, prepared to chase ghosts.

Chapter Seventeen

WOLF

We were in my truck since Meli's car was still in town being repaired and about an hour and a half into the three-hour road trip when the first of the texts came in.

The first was from Rabbit. He spent time with the photos and numbers I sent via Meli's phone. "Best guess, you're looking at GPS coordinates. Give it a shot."

A list of possible combinations followed. The text was short and to the point, confirming my suspicion of what the numbers meant, but it didn't hurt to have a second pair of eyes on it. If it had been some strange code, Rabbit would've broken the bitch in a matter of hours.

I put Meli on running the combinations through the map feature on her phone.

"GPS coordinates?" She began typing in the first set. "What about the squiggles?"

What the hell was she talking about? "Squiggles?"

She raised her head and watched me. "You know, the smudges that looked like pen drippings and scratches."

Ah, got it. "Lines and dots, babe. Morse code."

"Huh." She went back to her typing.

On combination number nine, we struck gold.

"This one puts the location arrow over Rhyolite." When she looked up, she was frowning. "But we're already going there. How does that help?"

Sometimes I forgot that civilians didn't have much to do with GPS coordinates. "If you zoom in, those coordinates will probably adjust to an actual structure or something."

"Oh, sorry."

Puzzled, I turned to look at her before putting my attention back on the road. "For what?"

I caught her shrug out of the corner of my eye. "That was probably a stupid question."

Okay, time to nip this shit in the bud. "It wasn't a stupid question, Meli. It's not like you work with mapping coordinates on a regular basis." I waited a beat, then continued, "Don't apologize for asking questions."

"Sor—" She winced and waved her hand brushing the rest of the unspoken word away. "You're right, it's habit."

One a lot of females seemed to have, because she wasn't alone in that. Hell, even Jinx, another teammate, slipped and apologized for crap she had no control over. "No worries, I'll help you break it."

"I bet." Her face relaxed as she grabbed her travel mug of coffee and took a sip. "Okay, so once we're there, we just have to figure out where this spot is?"

"Pretty much."

Around hour two, Bishop's text came in. "Waiting on one last connect. Might be what we're looking for. Will touch base later."

It was about damn time our luck began to turn.

Between whomever he was talking to and our little jaunt, we should be able to get somewhere. The certainty we were on the right path vibrated along my bones, nothing concrete just an instinct that had saved my ass more than once.

Which was a good thing, because roughly thirty minutes later our cell phone coverage went spotty.

"What if we can't pull up the map when we get there?" Meli worried.

"Next time a signal comes in, let me know. We'll pull over, and get a more detailed idea of what we're dealing with."

Fifteen minutes later, I pulled off the side of the road and dug out my phone. Yep, signal was there, but sketchy. Not wasting time, I input the coordinates and brought the map up overlaying a 3D image of the terrain.

A few tense minutes passed as I zoomed in, trying to keep easily identified landmarks near the locator pin while Meli leaned over to watch. It didn't look like there was a structure there, but who knew.

"There," I muttered, locking the image and saving it to my phone's camera log. "We should be good."

"Since you've got it covered, I'll turn off my phone. At least one of us should have some battery life when we're done." While she settled in her seat, she put her phone in the glove compartment and then refastened her seatbelt. "Just out of curiosity, where are we going? It didn't look like anything was there."

I set the phone between us, and put the truck back in gear. "GPS images, especially in more remote locations, tend to run at least a year behind."

I pulled out on the empty highway and made tracks to our ghost town. The road was empty, not a surprise since it was an actual holiday. Most people were tucked in gorging on turkey and pie.

"So why ghost towns?"

She turned to me, a puzzled frown marring her forehead. "What?"

"Why did your parents decide touring ghost towns would make for a fun family getaway?"

The frown disappeared and her face relaxed as she shifted to sit sideways and tuck a leg under her. "My dad loved the old west. We grew up reading Zane Gray novels and enduring Spaghetti Western nights, complete with spaghetti and meatballs. Even Mom indulged his fascination with all things cowboy.

That summer money was a little tight even though Dad's work at the garage was steady, Mom's hours at the office had been reduced, so family vacation had to be scaled back a bit. We talked about what we'd like to see. I wanted to see the Grand Canyon and the Pueblo dwellings in New Mexico. Eric was all about the California beaches, and Dad wanted to cycle through the ghost towns."

Under her casual tone lay a soft layer of grief indicating how much she missed her family. In a sudden flash of insight, it hit me what my girl needed—family. Meli wasn't meant to stand alone. Not that she couldn't, she'd been doing it for a while now, but it wasn't where she'd thrive.

If what I already offered wasn't enough to make her stay, maybe offering her a new family, one bound by love and loyalty versus blood, might help my cause. Something to keep in mind.

"Sounds like your mom became the deciding vote."

Her lips twisted up a tiny bit. "Yeah, Mom tended to end up in that role."

"So ghost town tour won?"

"Kind of. She agreed to the ghost towns if we made a couple extra stops."

"Let me guess, the Grand Canyon, the dwellings, a beach or two?"

The tiny curve grew into a smile. "And a few stops at some wineries in Napa Valley."

That made me chuckle. "Everyone wins."

"Yeah." Her voice faded as she turned to stare out the window. "Everyone won."

Needing to pull her back from the past, I sighed and said, "If Eric left a sign behind, it may not show up."

Her focus shifted and came back to me and the present. Not the best solution, but one I'd take for now. "Maybe, or maybe we should have brought a shovel."

"Got it covered."

She twisted around trying to look behind her seat. Finding nothing in the narrow opening behind us, she gave me a raised eyebrow.

I grinned. "In the box in the truck's bed."

As she went back to her previous position, she teased, "Ah yes, the male version of the bag of infinite holding."

"Male bag of what?" Keeping on hand on the wheel, I nabbed my coffee with the other.

"Infinite holding." Something playful peeked out as I took a huge gulp, just in time to almost lose it when she continued, "Think of it like a purse."

Successfully managing to not lose my mouthful of coffee, I swallowed, and shot her a look. "Men don't do purses, buttercup."

She giggled. An honest to God giggle, so filled with joy and light, I could only stare.

For the first time I caught a glimpse of a carefree Meli before Breck the Bastard, and she was stunning. Seeing that made me want to get that back for her. Hell, at this point I'd rather pack her up and haul her back to San Diego with me, giving Vegas nothing but my dust.

The only thing keeping me from doing that was her.

If I tried, she'd have my balls, she was so determined to solve the puzzle her brother left behind. Since I liked my boys right where they were, it was safer to be at her side, keeping her safe from whatever trouble was barreling our way.

If it turns out the secrets Eric left, should stay buried, then what? Turning back to the road, my fingers tightened on the wheel. Then…well, then I'd deal with it when it came up.

"Wolf?"

I stumbled out of my thoughts and cleared my throat. "Yeah?"

"You okay?"

I forced a smile. "Yeah, I'm good, just thinking."

It took her a few seconds to accept that, the weight of her gaze lingering before she finally said, "Okay."

An easy silence fell between us, one I spent considering every possible scenario that might come from this adventure. Unlike Meli, my opinion on Eric and his intentions weren't colored by family ties, but by a healthy dose of cynicism.

She mentioned he'd been withdrawn and moody on his last visit home. His letter indicated he decided to check into the situation with Breck on his own. The fact Eric sent her a letter so it would arrive months after this death, didn't reassure me. Nor did the fact he'd hidden coordinates in a group of old photos. There was too much cloak and dagger shit that screamed clusterfuck.

The more I considered Eric's behavioral changes and the closer we got to Rhyolite, the more the niggling unease in my stomach grew.

Before Bishop headed out to gather more intel, he, and I quote, "didn't want to jinx it," which meant he might have more of the puzzle pieces. Pieces that might be crucial to what we were walking into.

Tangled up in my anger with Meli at not sharing about that damn Breck, I hadn't pushed it before he left. Now, I was moving that up on my to-do list.

We were missing something, and either Bishop would find it or we would. Part of me hoped Bishop would be the lucky winner, because I wasn't sure what it would do to Meli if it came to light her brother wasn't who she thought he was. It wouldn't break her, but it would do some lasting damage.

"There's the turnoff." Her voice broke through my slowly darkening thoughts.

Following her directions, we bounced over the well-used dirt road.

A boarded up Rhyolite Mercantile greeted us first. Layers of plywood covered its aged façade, while rickety stairs led to a sagging porch. A rusted out 1939 Studebaker that used to sport a black paint job sat tucked away behind it. The two blue port-a-johns on the side added a jarring modern note.

I pulled my truck to a stop in front of a tidy little house. A wooden bench sat on the raised front porch, surrounded by a red post railing.

Meli undid her seatbelt, and flung open her door letting in the cool air. She hit the ground before I managed to grab a couple of water bottles and close mine. She wandered up to the front of the house, while I checked things out.

There were no other cars around, and since we weren't far from the highway, the flat landscape made it easy to spot the crumbling buildings further down the stretch of asphalt on the other side. What was left of Rhyolite was scattered along the side of the highway.

Yep, definitely a ghost town, because we were the only two within miles who were breathing.

Turning back to Meli, I went to join her. Coming up on her side, I couldn't figure out what captured her attention so completely, but the small wooden sign at her feet was my first clue. It held two words: BOTTLE HOUSE.

She moved closer, her frame swallowed by her brother's faded field jacket I insisted she wear due to the cooler weather, and I followed.

What I first thought were stones covering every inch of the

walls, turned out to be glass bottle bottoms. It was strangely mesmerizing.

Meli didn't stop, but wandered up to the porch, her hand brushing over the walls. "Before we did our trip, Dad researched each town we were visiting."

I settled in to listen, standing at the foot of the stairs holding the water bottles. I watched her recapture her memories, my heart aching a bit at the mix of love and sadness drifting over her features as she shared.

"It was founded in 1904 when someone thought they found a rich vein of ore in the hills back over there." She waved a hand indicating the rolling mounds behind the house. "I think at one time the population hit close to ten thousand, but by 1910 the population dropped to several hundred, and it never recovered."

She reached out and touched another smooth base of glass. "This was one of three bottle houses to be built in Rhyolite in 1905, and ended up being the largest. Most of the bottles used were from Adolphus Busch."

"Can't say it sounds familiar."

She looked over her shoulder and gave a small smile. "Today, it's called Budweiser."

Since I wasn't a big fan of the beer, there wasn't much to add to that.

She wandered around the small porch, then came and leaned against the post at the top, looking down at me. "It took Mr. Kelly, the house's owner, five and half months to build, and he wasn't some spring chicken. I think Dad said he was in his sixties or seventies at the time. He used almost thirty thousand bottles on his home."

Leaning back and taking in the construction with a bit more appreciation, I muttered, "Hope he washed them first."

She laughed. "Eric said the same thing."

Turning back to her, I offered her one of the waters. She

took it, and I left my hand up, offering to help her back down. "So, did your dad have an answer?"

Her smile went soft, as she grabbed my hand and came down the stairs. "Yeah, since they had to buy water at the time, Mr. Kelly didn't want to waste it, so he just plastered over them on the interior."

When she was next to me, I curled an arm around her waist, tucking her in close. While she may cherish her memories, they were still making her ache. It was there in the flashes of grief she tried to hide. It couldn't be easy being the last one left in your family. It was something even I didn't want to contemplate. "It's cool to have lasted this long."

We wandered around the far side of the house, and the only other structures were two fairly modern freestanding garages. Empty, of course.

"There were caretakers here then," she said. "Not sure what happened to them."

"Who knows, but it's a good thing for us. Means no interruptions while we check things out."

We headed back to the truck. Digging my phone out, I brought up the image with the coordinates. The pixelated outlines of the garages were there, and our pin was off to the east. Not far as the crow flies, maybe just over half a mile. "Ready for a walk?"

She shielded her eyes with her hand and tilted her head to look at me. "To where?"

Turning the phone so she could see the screen, I answered, "There."

"You think it will be okay to leave the truck here?"

I flipped the lid on the truck's bed box, nabbed an olive green backpack with a few essentials and slung it on. "We're the only two here, and considering there isn't a line for admission, I think we'll be good."

Digging a do-rag out of my pocket, I tied it on over my

head. "I doubt anyone is coming out on Thanksgiving to check on a bunch of abandoned buildings."

Besides, I wasn't keen on leaving a dusty arrow to our direct location. Bad enough leaving my truck behind; I'd minimize what I could.

I laced my fingers with hers and began tugging her in the direction we needed to be going.

She grimaced. "Fine, but if we get ticketed or towed, I get to tell you I told you so."

Chapter Eighteen

Wolf led the way, cutting across the desolate landscape, aiming for the ring of hills surrounding Rhyolite. Since we were on foot, we could create our own path, which made for a more direct route than using the dirt roads curling through the desert terrain.

At least it wasn't the middle of summer, or even this minor trek would be miserable. Since it was the end of November, we were accompanied by a cloud-dotted sky and a frisky breeze, which kept us cool. Studying the drifting, light gray clouds above I wondered if it would rain later.

Probably.

We passed abandoned equipment and then there was a low cement wall curling around a stone formation.

Wolf constantly checked his phone and our surroundings. He stopped next to the wall, turning slowly, his phone held out like a compass.

I took the opportunity to drink from the bottle he handed me earlier. Screwing the cap back on and tucking it in his backpack, I saw the blocky structure just beyond the wall. "Is that where we're going?" *Please say no.*

The narrow opening was dark, and my imagination had no problem imagining what multi-legged creatures lived inside, big and small.

"Nope." He shifted and pointed. "We need to go down this road a bit more. It should be up on our left."

"Does this mean the cell signal is working?" Which would be great, since I was a little worried about being in the middle of the desert with no phone service. Funny, it never struck me how dependent I was on technology until it wasn't around.

Sheesh, maybe I needed to cut back on my electronics use.

He adjusted his pack. "Signal's a wash, but you don't need it to make a GPS work."

The apparent contradiction in his answer allowed me to continue to ignore my rising concern about what and why Eric had something stashed in the middle of nowhere. "That doesn't make sense."

"Quick lesson on GPS and Smartphones." Wolf didn't stop as he moved off the dirt road and began heading towards the nearest mini-mountain. "GPS works by bouncing signals off a series of military satellites, so while having a mobile signal will increase the phone's ability to pinpoint your location, if no signal is available, it still works, giving you a grid shot of where you're located. You just have to know how to read a map."

"Something you know how to do."

He shot me a sexy grin over his shoulder.

Between his well-worn camouflage jacket, with the same beige pattern as mine, bandana, sunglasses, and scruff, he was looking dang good, in a Rambo sort of way.

"Stick with me, sugar plum, I won't steer you wrong."

Oh, he wouldn't steer me wrong, but he was more likely to lead me down the rabbit hole. And just like Alice, I happily tumbled along, entranced by that grin and my curiosity.

The terrain began to ascend, and I grabbed his backpack a

couple of times to keep from stumbling. The combination of dirt and loose rocks required concentration to navigate, which kept our conversation to a minimum.

It took about fifteen minutes before he finally stopped.

Since I was using his backpack as my personal walking stick, I stumbled up alongside of him, chest heaving, while a thin line of moisture trickled down my spine despite the cool weather.

He barely broke a sweat.

So much for channeling my inner fearless adventurer. When I was sure I wasn't going to keel over, I let go and put my hands on my hips, trying to figure out why we stopped.

Dirt, rock, more dirt, more rock.

"There." He pointed up the slope.

A breeze blew an escapee strand of hair over my face. Catching it back and squinting against the sun's glare, I followed his direction, studying the side of the hill. I wasn't sure, but it looked like a dilapidated wire fence was strung up over a rock face. "What is that?"

"You said this town popped up because someone hit a rich vein, right?"

"Yeah?"

He started up the hill. "I think we just found the entrance to one of the mines."

My muscles protested as I plodded along behind him.

Great, an abandoned mine. Just how I wanted to spend my Thanksgiving, crawling around in the dark, praying the walls would hold so I wouldn't end up buried alive. Not to mention what would happen if it decided to rain. Flash flood, anyone?

I shivered. "Please, do not tell me, that's where the coordinates lead to."

"Okay, I won't."

I didn't have enough breath to growl at him, so I focused on keeping up.

As we got closer, it was easy to tell this wasn't a frequently visited spot. The wire fence was no more than chicken wire, rusted in some places, broken and lying in the dirt in others. There were posts missing and a couple leaned precariously to the side. One stiff wind and they would be on the ground with the others.

Wolf stopped and pocketed his phone.

Standing next to him, I took in what lay beyond the fence.

Weather-beaten wood framed a rough-hewn doorway, and the sunlight barely made a dent inside the narrow opening, the darkness within patiently lying in wait for whoever was stupid enough to come inside.

Which would be us.

Next to me, Wolf asked, "Got any phobias I need to worry about, princess?"

Plenty, but none that currently applied. Well, besides the whole being buried thing. "Don't worry, stud muffin, I'll keep up."

My attempt to match his name game was met with a grin and an unexpected head dip as he brushed my mouth with a quick kiss that still managed to make my exhausted body perk up. Darn it.

His eyes were dancing when he finished. "Stud muffin, uh?"

A stupid, silly blush rose before I could figure out how to stop it. "Whatever."

I moved forward and managed to step over the fence in one of the disassembled spots. Wolf followed.

At the entrance, we both stopped. A draft kicked up dirt and sent air tainted with dust and a strange metallic odor drifting out.

Sucking in a deep, bracing breath, I inched a little closer to his reassuring frame. "Don't suppose you have a flashlight in that bag?"

"Yep, plus a first-aid kit, and a few other necessities."

I could only imagine what those "necessities" were, but it made me feel better.

I waited while he swung his pack around, dug out a flashlight. Its casing looked a bit battered, but solid. He flicked it on and directed the strong beam into the yawning hole before us. He flicked it off, then handed it to me. "Hold this a second, would you?"

I took it and watched as he pulled his phone back out, hit the screen, squinted down at it, slowly twisting his torso one way then the other, his gaze never leaving the electronic compass.

A minute ticked by, and he finally seemed satisfied with whatever he figured out. The phone went back in his pocket, and when he held out a hand for the flashlight, I handed it over.

He shoved up his sunglasses, and gave me a searching look. "Ready?"

Nodding, I followed him in as he ducked his head to avoid the low-hanging ledge of the door. Stepping just inside the opening, the temperature drop was noticeable.

The surrounding walls were lined with mismatched wood beams. A couple were toppled on the hard-packed ground. That didn't bode well in my quest for remaining unburied by collapsing walls.

With enough room to straighten, Wolf took his time, running the light over the walls. The walls went from wood covered to hewn stone, and the opening trailed deeper back.

Since there were rusted-out rail tracks lining the floor, I kept one hand on Wolf's pack and my gaze on the ground so I wouldn't trip. We shuffled in about fifty feet before the first branch-off opening appeared to our right.

He stopped, shining his light down that tunnel.

Peering around his back, I stared in the inky abyss. "Are we going down that way?"

He shifted the light to his other hand, his shoulders bunching as he pulled out the phone. When the screen lit, it illuminated the tunnel's ceiling with a harsh light.

At the far edge of shadow something skittered across the rock, causing me to swallow an awkward squeak.

Wolf aimed the light in the direction of still rattling pebbles and it bounced off the dark eyes of a rather large rat, before it scurried back down the long, dark tunnel.

I stepped right into Wolf, fingers digging under his jacket and tucking under the waistband of his pants, my knuckles brushing warm skin as I plastered my front to his back, face buried in the backpack, fighting back the creepy crawlies dancing over my skin. "That thing is huge."

"And unfortunately going in the same direction as us."

That made me lift my head. "Seriously?"

"If I promise to keep you safe from the rodents will you stop shaking?"

My answer was immediate. "Nope."

He handed me his phone. "You take this, and tell me if the arrow starts to move from the thirty-six mark."

This would require me letting go and stepping back. Okay, I could do this.

Forcing my fingers to relax, I reached out, took the phone, and took the tiniest of steps back. Looking down at the screen, I found the familiar face of a compass.

Wolf began moving forward, and I followed, keeping an eye on the compass. Sure enough, going down the main tunnel kept the indicator fairly steady. We were following the rat.

We kept moving and as we shifted to squeeze past a pile of wood and rock, I looked back the way we'd come. Darkness greeted me. There was no indication of the opening.

It would be so easy to get lost down here.

My gaze darted back to the compass, and I noted we were sitting at forty percent battery life. If the battery died, we were screwed.

My breathing sped up, and I tried to slow it down, but I couldn't catch a deep breath. In fact, each frantic inhale became more and more difficult. A roaring filled my ears, like water rushing against stone. It was all my mind needed to fire off a series of morbid images of suffocating under untold layers of dirt and rock or drowning as flood waters filled the mine. On top of that, there was no air anymore.

"Meli, baby, look at me."

Wolf's voice filtered through my panicked haze.

I latched on to his gaze. "Can't breathe," I gasped.

He crowded me against a rock wall, dominating my space, and then he caught my chin in his free hand. "You're breathing too fast. Slow it down." His voice pushed away the wall of white noise.

I tried to shake my head, but couldn't because of his hold. Then I tried to move, but with his weight against me, I couldn't, which wasn't such a bad thing since I was about to shatter into a million pieces. He was the only thing holding me in place.

"Breathe," he snapped.

I opened my mouth and tried, but there wasn't enough air.

"Come on, in." He noisily sucked in air. "Out." He sent it out.

If he could do it, there was air. Yet no matter how hard I tried, I couldn't follow along, even after I flattened my hand against his chest.

The walls started closing in.

"Melisande." The sharp cut of my name jerked my attention back to him. "Breathe in now."

His merciless command demanded immediate obedience, and somehow I managed to squeeze in a shallow breath.

"Blow it out, now."

I did, and it came out shaky and spotty.

"Again."

The ruthless edge in his voice ticked me off. If I could breathe, I would. This time I managed a deeper inhale, a steadier exhale.

He kept at me and rubbed circles on my chest in time with my breathing.

Finally, my achy chest relaxed and my nerves shakily settled. A cold sweat coated my face, but he still kept on me.

Time to call the drill sergeant to a halt. I moved my hand from his chest to his mouth. "I'm good."

He took my hand away, but didn't let it go. "Why didn't you tell me you were claustrophobic."

Still peeved but also fighting embarrassment, I muttered, "I didn't know I was."

"Hell of a time to figure it out, angel."

I wanted to roll my eyes, because yes it was, but it wasn't like I went spelunking on a regular basis. "Do you have any idea how much further we have to go?" Because I wasn't sure how long this fragile calm would last.

"You still have my phone?"

Looking down at the hand not occupied with his, I found that yes, indeed I did still have the phone. Lifting it, I handed it to him, surprised my bloodless fingers hadn't left dents in the casing.

He lifted it, twisted his upper body to adjust, then said, "I don't think it's much further. We'll give it another ten minutes, then turn back."

He kept the flashlight's beam aimed away, but when he turned back to me, the edge of light played over his face.

For the briefest second I caught an unfiltered glimpse of the battle-hardened warrior under the teasing pet names and colorful vocabulary. It didn't do much for my breathing, but it was stunning in a rather primitive way. It was also reassuring.

Unable to resist, I cupped his jaw, rose on my toes, and pressed the gentlest kiss against his lips.

When I dropped back down, he was staring at me with a puzzled frown. "What was that for?"

Shifting my gaze to his lips, I brushed a thumb over the lower one, then dropped my hand to pat his chest. "Just because."

Who knew how he'd take it if I told him my actions were driven by a combination to protect him, while stealing some of his strength for my own use. He'd probably laugh in my face or think I was crazy. He wasn't the one who needed protecting, especially not from someone who could barely keep it together in the dark. Still, the driving urge lingered, whispering even warriors needed help.

Shaking my head in an effort to clear out my strange thoughts, I gave his chest a light push. "Lead on, Macduff."

He stepped back, shaking his head. He waited until I grabbed his backpack before he set off once again. His head turned and he asked over his shoulder, "Isn't it supposed to be 'Lead on, Macbeth'?"

Grateful for the unexpected topic change, I latched on like drowning woman. "Actually, it's a misquote from Shakespeare. The actual line is said by Macbeth to Macduff when they were in the midst of battle. He said, 'Lay on, Macduff'—"

"'And damn'd be him that first cries, 'Hold, enough!'"

Startled by Wolf's unexpected recital, I stumbled. "Wow, you're a Shakespeare fan?"

"Senior year, I wanted to impress Amanda, so ended up in a theater production of 'The Scottish Play' in the role of—"

"Let me guess, Macbeth?" It was my turn to interrupt.

He nodded.

"So, did it impress Amanda?"

He gave a low chuckle. "It's not nice to kiss and tell."

The little spark of jealousy surprised me. "She was impressed," I muttered under my breath.

"Like you didn't do anything to impress some guy in high school."

Even though he couldn't see, I shrugged my shoulders. "Not really, with everything that happened with my family, high school was…school."

"Ah, dammit, Meli, I'm sorry. I should've thought before I spoke."

Okay, not the reaction I expected. "There's no reason for you to apologize, Wolf, it's a perfectly normal question. I'm not that fragile." Despite all the evidence to the contrary.

He came to an abrupt halt and I bumped into his back, smashing my nose against the backpack.

"Ow, a little warning next time?" I rubbed my abused nose, blinking past my watery eyes to find him leaning down and glaring at me. Now what?

"First off, I apologized because sometimes I tease without thinking about how it can be taken. Second, I never said you were fragile. Third, what do you consider evidence to the contrary?"

Stunned, because I knew darn good and well I hadn't said that last part out loud, all I could manage was, "You…you said you couldn't read my mind!" Doubts crowded close, their whispers crawling into the cracks and widening them.

His head jerked back, his frown less angry, more confused. "I can't."

Oh no, he was not going to stand there and deny he hadn't peeked into my head. "Yes, you can, since I didn't say anything about evidence to the contrary out loud."

His face shuttered. I'd heard the expression numerous times, but this was the first time I witnessed it, and it was shocking. Every emotion disappeared, leaving behind an intimidating male. "It was unintentional."

I knew that. Logically, but emotionally I was unexplainably hurt by his violation. It didn't matter that I knew, down to the marrow of my bones, Wolf wasn't the type to invade someone's thoughts.

Unless it was a matter of life or death, a snide little voice reminded me.

Whatever, he wouldn't peek into my head, not unless I invited him.

He wouldn't lie to me, right?

The doubts gained strength.

I turned and shuffled away from him, my hands curling into fists, half hidden by the overly long sleeves of my brother's jacket, fighting my insecurities.

Behind me, Wolf stayed silent, wary and tense. Didn't need psychic abilities to pick that up, I could feel it in the enclosed air.

Wolf was not Nicholas.

Staring into the shadows, I faced my mental damage head on.

Nicholas had left scars, and no matter how much I tried to pretend they didn't exist, they did. They would always be there, waiting for me to stumble. The trick was to recognize them for the traps they were.

Wolf wouldn't lie to me. He wouldn't betray me. He would always put me first, no matter what the cost. The fact he waited months for me to reach out proved that. And last night...last night he'd been unashamedly open on what he wanted for me...for us.

Wolf was nothing like Nicholas.

Wolf was—*my heart,* from the depths of my soul a quiet voice supplied the answer.

Turning back to face him, I said quietly, "I believe you. I'm sorry, it was the wrong way to react." At my words, his tense body relaxed and emotion began to seep back into his face. I moved in until I was in front of him. "It just caught me off guard."

Despite the phone in his hand, he still managed to tuck a stray strand of hair behind my ear. "Apology accepted." His moody gaze swept over my face. "You aren't fragile, Melisande, not even close. You couldn't be and still be standing."

The belief in his statement seeped into my bones, easing the unexpected sting of his accidental eavesdropping. "Sometimes it's hard to see when you're the one caught inside the mess."

That got me an answering grin, fleeting though it was. "Yeah, I get that."

Straightening my shoulders, I said, "Okay, let's get this done, so we can get out of here."

"Roger that."

It took us less than ten minutes to run across the abandoned mine cart, the rusted steel pitted and disintegrating. It lay overturned against what looked to be a cave in, since there was a wall of loose rock and wood stretching across the rails creating a dead end.

Standing next to Wolf as he ran his light over the end of the line, I grumbled, "Well, great. All of this for nothing."

With his head tilted back, he continued to inch the beam over the cave. "Don't be so impatient, cupcake."

Despite my jacket the chill of being underground left goosebumps on my arms. I rubbed my arms, not quite able to keep the whine out of my voice. "I want to get out of here soon, say maybe before dark or the walls collapse or it starts to rain."

"Ha ha." He continued his meticulous search.

"Not joking, soldier boy."

That got me a look. "If you want out, help me search. What-ever your brother left behind has to be here, because not only can we not move forward, but this spot matches the GPS coordinates."

His confirmation that Eric's coded message led here, to this abandoned hole in the earth did not make me feel better. In fact, the uneasy feeling I'd fought to ignore since first discovering Eric's secret message, decided to blossom into a freaking giant beanstalk.

Deciding it best to get this over with, I started helping Wolf search. As he ran his light slowly over the far wall, I got closer, being careful not to touch the slimy surface. "What are we looking for?"

"Anything, a crack in the wall big enough to hide something, a box, a damn glowing, red X would be fantastic."

Couldn't argue that one.

Wolf was relentless, inching his way over the wall, up the ceiling, even going so far as to climb on unstable large rocks to peer into the crumbling beams overhead. We found metal galore, remnants of tools and dishes the long ago miners left behind. It would've been cool—in a museum.

When we finished with that side, I turned to the back wall, which was blocked by the cave in.

"We'll save that for last," he advised. "Let's do the other side."

We moved to the rotting cart. I was picking my way over the loose pile of debris, when the unsteady stones shifted underfoot. There wasn't time to do anything but snap out my hand and grab the edge of the cart to stop my fall. I hissed as the ragged edge cut my palm. The sting was sharp, but I didn't let go until my feet were under me. "Darn it."

I yanked my hand away, turning it up, trying to see the damage in the spotty light.

Then Wolf was there, shining his light right on the ugly gash. His low curse followed him stuffing his phone in a pocket, before he grabbed my wrist, gently twisting my hand until it was revealed in all its wounded glory by his light.

Why was it wounds never hurt until you looked at them? The sting grew barbs that set their nasty teeth deep into my bones. Tears welled, but I kept them back by sheer force of will.

It helped when he handed me the flashlight. "Hold this for me."

Gripping the solid cylinder, I kept it aimed at my palm, even as I avoided looking at it.

His fingers were gentle, but it still hurt as he examined it. "It's just a scratch, sweetheart. A little numbing gel and a pad, you'll be fine. Come over here."

He led me to an oversized rock next to the blasted cart.

I leaned against it as he shrugged out of his backpack. Setting it at his feet, he crouched, dug inside and produced his first-aid kit. Laying it aside, he handed me a roll of tape, then grabbed a white tube and tucked it in a pocket. "Tell me you're up to date on your tetanus shot?"

"Yes, sir."

"Good."

Next up was a small can followed by him putting a couple of gauze packages in his mouth before he stood back up. He braced his leg next to my waist and laid my hand on his thigh.

"Don't move," he muttered around his mouth full of bandages.

Biting my lip, I watched him work.

The only warning I got was a gruff, "This might sting."

Then my skin was hit with a cold wetness as he sprayed the wound. The initial shock wore off quickly, only to be replaced by an army of fire ants scorching their way across my palm.

There was no stopping my hiss or my instinctive reaction to jerk my hand back. But he anticipated my move and locked my wrist against his thigh, even as he bent over it to blow gently.

Now the fire ants were joined by shivers. "Ow, ow, ow."

Wolf continued to blow and finally the stinging sensation faded. Now my hand just ached.

He lifted his head and studied my face. "You okay?"

"Yeah."

He pocketed the can, and pulled out the tube. In moments, a thick layer of cooling gel was smeared over the wound and, thankfully, the ache began to fade.

He worked fast, securing the gauze and repacking his supplies in less than five minutes. When he turned back to me, he held out two white tablets. "Just in case."

"Aspirin?"

He nodded.

I handed back the flashlight to trade it for the nearly empty water bottle. I downed the pills, then dropped to my heels to put the empty bottle in the pack. The light was aimed off to my left and glinted off something tucked behind one of the few remaining upright posts.

I squinted, as if that would help bring whatever it was into focus. "Wolf?"

"Yeah?"

"I think I found something."

Rocks rattled underfoot as he made his way over to me and crouched down, his shoulders brushing mine.

Bracing my uninjured hand against the slimy wall carefully, I leaned in to get a better angle behind the thick beam. The light bounced, then steadied and illuminated what looked like the corner of an oversized, padded wallet tucked into a crevasse in the stone. Something you'd never see unless you were pressed up against the stone wall.

"I'm pretty sure this doesn't belong here."

"Switch places with me, buttercup."

Giving in to the urge, I stuck my tongue out in response to his name choice, even as I moved to let him take my place.

The childish reaction earned me a swift tap on the butt. "Save that for later, sweet cakes."

"Seriously? You need better name options."

He grinned even as he settled in. "Can you hold this for me?"

He offered the flashlight.

I stood up so I wouldn't need the wall for balance, took it, and aimed it over his shoulder. From my position, I couldn't see much but the muscles bunched in Wolf's back as he leaned forward and carefully began working the wallet thingy out of the wall.

"Damn thing's stuck tight." He shifted until his face was practically kissing the wall, readjusted his hold, and pulled.

There was a soft clatter of loose stone raining down, sounding louder in the enclosed space, and then he was pulling his arm back. He quickly adjusted his grip, using both hands to hold it.

When his hand came into the light, I got my first look at what we found. My earlier guess was spot on. It was a padded, leather wallet about the size of a thick, oversized book. "That has to be it."

"Time to find out what's inside." Wolf stood and moved back over to the rock we'd used for our impromptu medical services. Probably because it was the flattest surface available. "Bring the light over."

I followed and stood next to him, the light aimed down as he found the zippered edge and pulled. I was holding my breath as he opened it, and all that air came out in a violent rush as the contents hit the light. "Holy smokes! Is that—"

"Yeah, dammit it is." A restrained fury vibrated in his voice as we stared at the small, thin, rectangular bars of gold lining page after page inside the wallet. He pulled one of the bars out, and held it in his palm.

The surface was shiny, but smooth, which struck me as odd. "Aren't these supposed to have some sort of markings?" Not that I was a gold connoisseur, but living in Vegas, you couldn't miss the gold bullion offered at some of the higher-end shops.

He tucked the piece back in, zipped it closed with a rough jerk. "Yeah, it is." He turned and stuffed the wallet into his backpack.

His grim answer left ice snaking its way through my veins. "So why are these blank?"

He stilled, and his shoulders rose and fell as he blew out a hard breath. He turned his head, and the surrounding shadows were echoed on his face. "Because these are stolen."

Chapter Nineteen

WOLF

"**N**o."

Watching Meli back away as she shook her head did nothing to ease my anger at her brother, which quickly gathered steam. Instead of arguing with her, I looked away, zipped the backpack and stood, swinging it over my shoulder.

Cupping the back of my neck, I stared at the ground wondering what the fuck Eric was thinking leaving shit like this for her?

No wonder someone was gunning for her. The damn portfolio had to hold at least half a million dollars' worth of unmarked gold bullion. Granted, in the scheme of things, half a million could be considered chump change, but my mind began running scenarios. None of them good, all of them leaving me silently cursing Eric Dwyer.

Regardless of how dark my musings got, I needed more information before taking my suppositions any further. To do that, I needed to talk to Bishop and find out what he learned from Eric's previous teammates.

"Wolf." Her demand was accompanied by a tug on my sleeve. "Eric wouldn't steal from anyone."

Gritting my teeth, because current evidence proved otherwise, I faced her. "Look, we need to make sure this is what it looks like, and then get this in to the authorities at Nellis Air Force Base."

Meli didn't budge as disbelief, horror, and anger fought over her expressive face. "I'm telling you, my brother did not steal this."

God, I didn't want to argue with her, but finding a hidden cache of unmarked gold in an abandoned mine, placed there by a dead man who died thousands of miles overseas with most of his team, did not bode well.

Holding my hands up, palms forward I tried to get her moving. "I didn't say he did."

"You're thinking it."

Damn straight I was, but that wouldn't get her moving. "It doesn't matter what I'm thinking. We need to touch base with Bishop and see what he was able to find out."

Stepping in close, I held her shoulders and forcibly turned her around. "Now, help me check the rest of this place so we can head out."

It took another thirty tense minutes to clear the remainder of the mine, while Meli's silence fairly screamed accusations. While I could admire her loyalty to her brother, right now she was being a pain in my ass. I didn't have answers for her, at least not ones she'd accept. "Let's head out."

I took point, leaving her to follow. When I felt her fingers at my back curling around my belt, I released the breath I was unconsciously holding.

We went about a hundred feet when she spoke, "You're wrong."

"Maybe," I conceded, giving what little comfort I could without lying.

"What makes you so certain he stole it?"

It was a good thing she was behind me, because rolling my

eyes was liable to piss her off. "Let's wait and talk to Bishop before we get into this."

She jerked my belt. "No. Tell me why you automatically jumped to the worse possible conclusion."

What did she think was worse than this? Unfortunately, lying to her wasn't an option. No matter how I phrased my answer, she would end up hurt. That realization made me wish her brother were still alive so I could pound some sense into him.

"Wolf?"

Sighing, I gave in. "Baby, what do you want me to say here?"

"Just tell me the truth." Her voice lost its angry edge, leaving it shaky and lost.

I stopped, reached back and grabbed her hand, then turned to hold her close, offering what comfort I could. As strands of her hair brushed against my chin, I gave her what she asked for. "I'm not sure what the truth is, angel. However, I can take what little we have and paint a pretty grim picture. You said the last time he was home, something was off. He was moody and uncommunicative, right?"

She nodded.

"There has to be a reason behind his attitude shift. If he and his team were involved in something shady overseas, it would explain how he came to be in possession of the gold. It could also explain how his team managed to get ambushed during a classified op." I stopped because I did not want to keep going, but she wasn't stupid.

"So you don't think he stole the gold, do you?" I refused to react, but she kept going, "You think it's payment for something." She pulled back to look up at me. "He would never betray his country, his men, he wouldn't, Wolf."

"He had to have stashed it during his last leave, then he set up a trail of clues for you to follow. That is not the action of someone who wants to keep you clear of this shit."

Her mouth firmed, her chin set as she held my gaze. "No, it's the action of someone who wants the truth to be exposed."

Arguing about this was going nowhere. I wasn't going to change her mind, and she couldn't erase my doubts.

Looking down into her face, the depth of her conviction in Eric's integrity shone an eye-wincing light on my own cynicism. It couldn't be helped.

During my time in the corps, I witnessed good men convince themselves they had all the right reasons for doing bad things. There was no way I wanted her to lose that faith if I didn't have the complete story.

Cupping her face, I kissed the tip of her nose. Lifting my head, I held her gaze and made a promise I hoped to God I could keep. "We'll touch base with Bishop, get the facts, and if that was Eric's intent, we'll make sure the truth comes out."

She searched my face, and bit-by-bit, the tension eased away. "Okay."

"Okay."

The rest of our trip out of the mine was quiet. Too damn bad my brain was spinning in overdrive.

Over and over, I tried to fit the pieces into an understandable picture. No matter how I tried, I couldn't come up with a good scenario, one that would save Meli's heart from breaking. Dammit, I needed Bishop and his intel. I picked up the pace.

When we hit the entrance, I turned off the flashlight only to realize the light had faded. As we stepped outside, I realized it wasn't because of the time, but because the clouds had settled in for the afternoon. Looked as if we'd be getting rain on our way back in.

Tucking the flashlight in a side pocket of the pack, I offered my hand to Meli. When she took it, the tightness in my chest I hadn't realized existed loosened. "Looks like we might be running through a storm."

"I'm sure we'll survive." Quiet confidence added an unexpected depth to her answer, and it hit me how my comment could be taken.

My fingers tightened on hers. "Yeah, angel, of that I have no doubt."

•‑•●●●‑•

We made it to my truck as the first drops hit. "Hop in."

I nudged Meli to the passenger side, unlocking her door, then rounded the hood to the driver's side. Opening my door, I flipped my seat forward, and moved aside the liner. Underneath was a built-in storage compartment. With quick movements, I transferred the gold from the backpack to the floor compartment. Straightening the liner, I flipped the seat back into place, and stashed the backpack in the bed box before getting behind the wheel.

As I strapped on my seatbelt, Meli said, "Hidden compartments? Is that part of the secret agent package?"

Grateful for the reappearance of her humor, I responded in kind, "Only if you know the secret handshake."

Starting the truck, I flicked on the wipers as the rain mixed with the dust creating a filmy grime. A couple of passes and the window was clear.

Backing out, I executed a three-point turn and headed back to the highway. "Actually, it's meant for tools, but I figured it was a good place to stash that for now."

For a few moments she didn't say anything, then, "So what now?"

Sparing a glance to find her frowning as she faced the windshield, I answered, "As soon as we get a signal, you call Bishop and find out when he expects to be back. We need to pool our information and see what kind of sense we can make out of everything."

She sighed, then leaned forward, pulling open the glove

compartment. She pulled out her phone, and it beeped as she turned it on and set it in her lap. "You really think he'll have something?"

"Based on his last message, yeah."

She played with the edges of the tape on her wounded hand. "What if..."

"What?"

I set the cruise control as the empty road stretched before us. Shifting a bit, I could keep an eye on the road and still see her. Whatever was on her mind worried her. If she kept biting her lip, it would end up a bloody mess.

Her shoulders straightened and she turned to face me. "What if whoever Bishop talked to lied?"

"Why would they?"

"Why wouldn't they?"

Someone had been watching way too much crime TV. "What? You think there was some conspiracy happening with your brother's team?"

She huffed out a breath. "It's just as conceivable as your suggestion that he stole the gold."

She had a point, but I knew she was reaching for any rational reason to keep the image of the brother she loved untarnished. "Until we talk to Bishop, it's pointless to play the what-if game."

She shook her head and leaned forward, putting her hand on my knee. "Just hear me out, okay? Then you can tell me I'm chasing unicorns."

Chasing unicorns? What the hell was that about? "Um, okay?"

It couldn't hurt to hear her out. Gave me an idea of what I'd be starting with when the truth came out. Because the more I considered it, the more convinced I was the truth would be ugly.

Satisfied she had my attention, she settled back, pulling her hand back to her lap, leaving a patch of warmth where she touched. "Okay, say one of the surviving team members is the one behind the gold? What if Eric found the gold while he was on tour, but didn't know which guy it was, so he brought it home, to hide it until he could confirm who had taken it?"

That was stretching it. "If Eric found the gold, he would have reported it up the chain of command."

Not only was it the smartest move to make considering he was part of specialized team, it was the safest choice because the reasons on how that gold came to be in an operator's possession could lead to dangerously unpleasant answers.

"Not if he didn't know who it belonged to. He wouldn't want his whole team to get in trouble because of one person."

"Honey, your brother was part of a highly skilled combat team. If he discovered one of his guys had over half a million dollars in stolen gold, he wouldn't dare risk any future ops. He'd be pounding on his CO's door with the information. And his team wouldn't blame him."

"Maybe his commanding officer is in on it." Frustration added color to her cheeks.

Okay, it was time to nip this in the bud. "Baby, you're reaching."

"Wolf—"

I shook my head and reached out to grab her uninjured hand, giving it a reassuring squeeze. "Stop. Let's just wait until we talk to Bishop. There's no point in driving yourself crazy when we don't have all the facts."

A soft beep from her lap nabbed her attention. She tugged her hand free, and reluctantly I gave it up. It sucked not being able to reassure her.

She picked up her phone. "Looks like we have a signal."

"Why don't you call Bishop? My battery's about dead, and I forgot my charger. You have his number?"

"I'll get it from your phone."

Shifting my weight to my left hip, I pulled my phone out of my back right pocket and handed it over. "Here."

She took it and laid it in her lap, using her bandaged hand to hold it still as she pulled up Bishop's number.

I checked the mirrors by habit, since the road remained fairly deserted. We passed a couple of cars going in the other direction, but otherwise it was quiet.

A big SUV was coming up fast, but since I was in the right lane, he had room to pass. Still, I kept an eye on him because he wasn't shifting lanes and he was picking up speed. The hairs on the back of my neck rose as an unfamiliar ugliness began to seep across my brain, triggering every psychic alarm I had.

Gut clenching, I hit the accelerator. "Meli, hang on."

Startled, her head came up. "What's going on?"

"We've got unexpected company." While we managed to pull ahead, the SUV was still gaining. "Did you get Bishop's number?"

"N...not yet." Her answer was breathy.

I couldn't have her break into a panic attack now, because I was about to have my hands full and the dark fury ripping along the psychic airwaves was creeping closer, narrowing my focus. "Get it. Text him: SOS IRP."

"Okay."

I did a quick eye check.

Her face was pale, her hands shaky, but she was hitting the screen.

Please God, get the damn text to Bishop. He'd recognize my request for immediate backup.

The SUV crept closer, the heavy window tint made it difficult to tell how many tangos we were dealing with.

Gritting my teeth, I flexed my mental muscle, shifting my personal mental defenses enough to open a crack and see what I could pick up.

Thankfully we were on a straightaway so keeping the truck on the road wasn't difficult. At least not until you added the steady rain mixing with the oil and dust on the asphalt. The road was becoming slick, making hydroplaning a definite possibility, especially as our speeds increased.

On the downside, there were no turnoffs, which meant we were stuck.

Bitch is not getting away this time.

The ruthless fury in that thought had my grip tightening on the wheel as the SUV cut the distance between us.

Dammit, they were after Meli.

Worry for the woman beside me sent ripples over my concentration. When another thought hit me, I managed to swerve to the left, just missing getting my bumper kissed as the SUV gunned it.

Jamming a foot on the gas, I could feel the loss of traction and wished to hell I had better tires for this shit. That was cutting it too damn close.

Tightening my focus, I locked down my mental blocks so the actual thoughts didn't distract me, but the roiling emotion still lapped at the edges. Good enough. "Did you send it?"

"Yeah." Her voice was tight, but steady.

"Good." Watching the charging SUV, I knew it was just a matter of time before impact. "Brace, he's going to hit."

While both vehicles were heavy, the SUV had the added advantage of equally distributed weight, while my truck was front heavy.

The SUV surged forward and managed to slam against the tail end of the bed. Metal screamed and the truck bucked.

Using both hands, I fought the wheel, desperate to keep my truck on the road. "Mother fucker!"

Not wanting to keep the threat on Meli's side, I took the truck down the sloped edge of the highway, picking up speed to get ahead. The vibration rattled teeth and bone as we bounced over rock and asphalt while essentially straddling a delicate angle between the road and the embankment.

The gamble paid off because the SUV fell back and I yanked the wheel, forcing it to swerve so I wouldn't crush its front end.

Next to me, a feminine squeak was quickly choked off.

Weaving along the middle of the two-lane highway, I used the truck's mass to keep them back.

Then my luck ran out.

The SUV went to cut around, and as I forced the truck to block it, the tires hit pooling water and lost the battle for traction. The back end began to fishtail.

"Shit!"

A burst of black excitement was my only warning as the SUV took advantage and rammed into the side panel.

The impact reverberated bone-deep. Meli's scream echoed my litany of curses as I tried to stay on the road. The truck began to spiral, my hood coming in line with the SUV's bumper. Tires, mine and the SUV's, squealed.

The SUV went in for the kill, slamming along our side and rocking the truck.

"Hang on, Meli." I tried to work the steering and pedals to compensate, but it was a losing battle.

The truck began to rock. Another nudge from the fucker was joined by a vicious thrill, and my heart sank.

"Wolf!" Meli's frightened cry blended in with the shotgun blasts of rocks peppering the exterior as tires fought and lost to keep the truck upright.

The world outside my windshield tilted in slow motion. The screech of tortured metal meeting rock and sand grew deafening. Then the side airbag exploded and everything went black.

Chapter Twenty

I came to with the stench of burnt oil and gasoline searing my nose. Blinking my eyes open, I was met with a cloudy white, and it took a moment to realize it was some sort of ragged, white material.

Batting it away, images of a black SUV barreling towards us, the scream of metal, and jarring impact followed by a sense of sickening weightlessness, flooded my mind. An accident, we'd been in an accident.

"Wolf?" His name emerged as from a long, hollow tunnel, but there was no answer.

I coughed to clear the tightness in my chest, batting against what I realized was a deployed airbag. Once I managed to shove it aside, I froze, stunned by the chaos around me.

The windshield swarmed with cracks, adding a warped house of mirrors vibe to the outside world. Beyond it, the hood was up, but bent. Couldn't tell how badly through the webbed glass, but it was in rough shape. There was steam or smoke seeping around the edges.

I wasn't sure if the dashboard was buckled or if it was an illusion helped by the fact the cab's roof seemed much too close for comfort. The glove compartment gaped open, its contents scattered around me, the door barely hanging on by a lone hinge.

Looking down I could see my seatbelt still strapped across my chest and hips, but my lap was covered in pieces of hard glitter. Tempered glass.

Before daring to move I tried to figure out if everything still worked. Not easy since my mind kept fuzzing out.

First up were my legs. I was able to move them, not far, because there wasn't much room. Something heavy shifted and settled near my ankle. When I went to lean forward, I found the seatbelt had taken its job to heart, holding me tight against the seat.

So tight, the ache in my chest was increasing. Being trapped wasn't high on my list of fun things to do, so trying to relax instead of clawing my way free was enormously difficult. My involuntary jerks caused glass pieces to fall in a tinkling rain.

Breathe, Meli. The voice in my head sounded suspiciously like Wolf's, but it helped me find my focus.

When I was sure I wasn't going to turn into a screaming madwoman, I continued to take stock. My door panel was bowed as if a giant fist had plowed into it from the outside.

Raising a shaky hand, I pushed aside the airbag and got a face full of rain. So there was nothing left of my window.

Letting the material fall back, I brushed the wetness from my face, and when I held my trembling hand up, it was coated in rain and blood.

As if the crimson stain was what my body had been waiting for, various aches and pains came roaring to life. Dull fire ran from my shoulder to my hip, and there would be some serious bruises from the seatbelt, but nothing seemed broken.

"Wolf?" This time his name sounded a little clearer as sound began to filter back in.

There was a distant hiss of some kind of leak and sporadic

groans from the protesting truck. But what I wanted to hear most didn't come.

Panic began to set in. "Wolf?"

Twisting slowly, I sucked in a sharp breath, difficult to do with the overly tight seatbelt.

Wolf was unmoving in his seat, his face covered in blood.

My pulse picked up speed, which didn't help my pounding head, and I fumbled for the seatbelt. My fingers were thick and awkward, and my breathing shifted from choked to panicked as desperation set in. A sob escaped when I realized I wasn't getting loose.

My gaze locked on Wolf's terrifyingly pale face. *Where was the blood coming from? Was he breathing?*

Reaching out, I forced my trembling hand to steady so I could find his pulse. It took long, frightening seconds, but the reassuring beat steadied me. Unconscious beat dead any day of the week.

Ignoring the protest of my battered body, I stretched as far as I could, my foot hitting something as it sought and found something to brace against. Sparing a quick look down, a familiar black grip peeked out from under the clutter of plastic, paper, glass, and metal. Wolf's gun.

Right then, a problem for later.

Refocusing on Wolf, I managed to grab his T-shirt and shift him toward me the necessary few inches, so I could run my fingers over his face, trying to locate whatever wound he had by touch alone since all I could see was his profile.

My slow, clumsy exam wasn't much, but it was all I could manage.

When I reached his far temple, the blood was thicker. Then I found the torn edges of skin. I mimicked his involuntary wince at my touch. "Sorry, baby," I breathed as more pieces of glass fell around us.

Okay, so we had a head wound, which explained the blood.

Unfortunately, stuck in my seat, there wasn't much I could do to help.

Over my harsh breathing the dull thump of a car door closing sounded. It was followed by a second one.

Straining to hear, I wondered if maybe someone witnessed the accident and stopped to help. Opening my mouth to call out, the fragile bubble of optimism burst when it hit me that the only people around would be the ones who caused this mess in the first place.

Gritting my teeth, I forced my body to freeze. Holding my breath, I waited, my heart in my throat.

The crunch of gravel underfoot confirmed someone was coming closer.

This wasn't good.

Between the upright hood and the deployed airbags, I was blind, unable to see who was approaching. On a shaky exhale, my gaze fell to the half-hidden gun.

Right, now to get it, because I needed something to keep us safe until I could get Wolf to wake up. With that goal in mind, I decided to risk a whisper, "Oh God, Wolf, can you hear me?"

A voice called out.

I refused to answer, carefully twisting and shifting. Using my foot, I managed to nudge the gun along the floor. My ankle ached by the time I managed to wedge it between my calf and the side of the twisted wreck of the console.

Now came the difficult part. Gritting my teeth, I shifted against the seatbelt, ignoring the nylon edging cutting into my chest and wished my arm were longer. Straining against the seatbelt, I choked back my sobs of frustration as my fingers brushed against it, nudging it a bit further out of reach. *Dammit, Meli, reach!*

The low voices outside got closer and ugly tension seeped up my spine, leaving my skin crawling. Fear is a great motivator, and I jerked against the seatbelt, my fingertips catching on the grip and dragging it closer. Tingles ran down my arm, my circulation hampered by the belt, but I finally managed to wrap my hand around the gun.

"You did a fucking number on this, man."

The unfamiliar male voice left me frozen in place, and the only thing I felt safe moving was my eyes. From my new angle, there was a sliver of space between the damaged hood and the cracked windshield. Just enough to see the two men standing a bit away from the truck.

My hold on the gun tightened despite the pins and needles sensation slowly increasing in my fingers.

A soft groan, Wolf's, drifted through the cab.

Even as relief turned my muscles to water, I barely moved my lips to whisper, "Shhhhh, baby, please."

Something warned me I couldn't let the two outside know Wolf was still alive.

The two figures separated, one disappearing behind the airbag curtain. His footsteps deliberate and loud as he approached my side of the tuck.

Next to me, Wolf shifted and I hissed sharply. Then with every ounce of concentration I possessed I focused on getting a message to him mentally, whispering the words in sync, just in case. "Wolf, don't move, please. They're coming."

My mind raced with options, none of them good.

The numbness was spreading, so yanking the gun up for a shot was an iffy proposition. I'd probably end up shooting myself by accident. Not helpful. Not to mention if I did manage to shoot one of the men, that still left the other. Since they had no problems running us off the road, I wouldn't put it pass them to have weapons of their own.

So, shot by my gun or theirs? Neither one appealed to me.

Out of time and options, I made a decision, one I hoped wouldn't come back to haunt me. I tucked the gun into Wolf's lap, moving his hand to cover it, and then let my lashes drift down until they were barely open, watching the figure approach, feigning unconsciousness. Then time was up.

The truck rocked violently as with a loud, metallic protest, my damaged door was jerked open and the last voice I expected to hear seared through my brain, melting away rational thought. "Meli-girl, did you miss me?"

My eyes snapped open, my whole body jerked, and the primal need to escape took control. Slowly, as if in a nightmare, I turned and came face to face with Nicholas Breck.

The world stepped back and the only thing I could see was his boy-next-door grin that didn't do a thing to hide the cruel, sadistic light in his eyes.

He reached through gap of the damaged door.

I shrank back, but held hostage by the seatbelt, didn't get far.

At my obvious retreat, his smile faded and the anger I learned to fear seeped in. "Don't look at me like that, Meli."

Trussed up and barely able to breath, I tried to think past my panic. If I could keep him focused on me, I could keep Wolf safe. And right now, that was all that mattered. Why Nicholas was here or how he got here, were questions for later.

This time when he reached for me, with nowhere to go, I braced. It didn't help. The feel of his touch made my skin crawl and my stomach heave.

He cupped my chin and turned my head to face him, his fingers digging into my jaw, bringing unwanted tears into my eyes. "We have some unfinished business to discuss, darling."

Unable to look away, unable to fight, I could only stare as dread crawled through me leaving behind a soul-chilling fear.

When he flipped open a vicious looking knife, I couldn't tear my gaze away. He watched me, a disturbing smile on his face. "You look like you could use some help, there."

Before I could react, he leaned in, the blade flashed out and the restrictive bands across my chest and hips disappeared.

Now trapped between him and the seat, I didn't dare look away. It was like watching a snake. One blink and he'd bite. Except a snakebite would be infinitely more preferable, since it wouldn't be anywhere as slow and destructive as Nicholas's poison.

Without warning he covered my mouth with his in a cruel, punishing kiss.

I managed to keep my mouth closed as I tried to disappear into the seat, but it didn't stop him from mashing my lips against my teeth so hard the delicate skin inside split, spilling the coppery tang of blood over my tongue.

A whimper escaped, and only then did he lift his head. His gaze brightening as he took in my fear.

Buried under my soul rattling terror a kernel of anger flickered to life. He was getting off scaring me.

His gaze shifted to the side, his pleasure disappearing under a mask of calculation.

My small flare of anger surged and gained depth. No, it was one thing to terrorize me, but he did not get to threaten Wolf.

My hand shook, but I forced it up to touch Nicholas's face, regaining his attention. Better it be on me than Wolf. "Nic." It was all I could manage, but it was enough.

His gaze came back to me. "Let's get you out of here."

He ignored Wolf and locked his hand around my wrist, pulling me with him as he backed out of the cab's wreckage.

I couldn't stifle my gasps and whimpers as I finally managed to turn on the seat until my back was to Wolf. Nicholas shifted his hold to my waist and pulled me to my feet. Once upright, I was left to hold on to him as I fought for balance. The world dipped and swayed, making my stomach pitch and roll in tandem. A cold sweat broke out over my forehead, mixing with the soft rain.

"I don't feel so good," I mumbled, hunched over his arm.

"Considering the truck rolled twice, I'm not surprised." He began to lead me away. Part of me dared to hope he'd leave Wolf alone. He led me around the crumpled hood and toward the second man, who stood there watching, the brim of his baseball cap peeking out from under the hoodie, casting his face in shadow.

When we were a few feet away Nicholas stopped. "Let me have your keys. I want to get her out of the rain."

Hoodie Man's head swiveled between us and the truck. "What about the dude?"

"That's your job." Nicholas held out a hand. "Keys?"

"Shit, man, that's not what I signed up for." His shoulders hunched, and he turned and sent a wad of spit off to his right. "Cost you extra."

The arm around my waist went rock hard and I braced. Disagreeing with Nicholas never ended well. The complete lack of emotion in his voice set off a series of tremors, which left my teeth chattering.

"You want your paycheck, you clean up. Keys." The last word was bit out.

Hoodie Man pulled the keys from his front pocket and sent them flying through the air.

Nicholas caught them. "You have three minutes."

He spun on his heel, forcing me to move with him as he set off.

Panic crawled through me. I couldn't let him kill Wolf, but I had no idea how to stop them. "Nic, wait!" My voice was rough, and there was no hiding the frantic edge.

I pulled against his hold, stumbling.

He jerked my arm, pain radiating up my shoulder and through my neck at the brutal move. "Don't start, Meli."

Twisting, I tried to see where Hoodie Man was, as I fought to get away from Nicholas. "You can't kill him!"

He stopped, turned, grabbed my upper arms, and shook

me. My head whipped back and forth so hard black dots erupted along the edge of my vision, and my legs threatened to collapse.

Then he leaned in until his face was all I could see. "I'm not the one who brought him into this. You are."

Off balance and desperate, I pushed, "Brought him into what?"

He jerked back, letting go of my arms, and before I could brace, he backhanded me.

The impact sent me sprawling on the muddy ground, my hip and shoulder taking the brunt of the fall even as I tried to break it with my hands. Gravel tore into my palms, even as my face burned and my ears rang. I barely got a breath before he crouched next to me, wrapped his hand in my hair and yanked up, pulling me upright.

Torn between anger and fear, I scratched at his hands, desperate to get loose. "Let go!"

A vicious tug yanked my head back, forcing me to stare into his face. "Who is he to you?"

"A friend," I choked out. I knew this game. My answer didn't matter, but I wasn't sure I could play along.

He shoved my head forward and I barely managed to stop myself from slamming forehead first into the ground. He straightened, hands on his hips and turned back to Hoodie Man. "Hurry the hell up."

Taking advantage of his inattention, I scrambled on all fours, getting to my feet to run. "WOLF!" I screamed his name, praying he would wake up.

I managed to get to my feet even as the world stretched, time slowing.

Hoodie Man continued to walk toward the truck, a gun now visible in his hand. As he rounded the passenger side door, his arm rose, gun in hand.

My heart stopped and I screamed again, "WOL—"

Nicholas's arm hand wrapped around my mouth, cutting my warning off.

Beyond fear and fighting the sickening dread clawing its way through me, leaving massive wounds in its wake, I clawed and bit at his hand. *Not Wolf, please not Wolf. Don't let me lose him too.*

Behind me, Nicholas's violent curse meant nothing.

The rough shove that sent me stumbling forward was unexpected, but I didn't waste it. Chest heaving, I managed to get my feet under me and was picking up speed, mouth open to warn Wolf again, when a gunshot cracked through the air, quickly followed by two more.

My world shattered on a ragged scream.

Chapter Twenty-One

WOLF

My name screamed in Meli's voice penetrated the heavy blackness. I struggled to swim to the surface accompanied by a series of thoughts not belonging to me but connected only by their implied threat.

Situational awareness could be a fickle bitch, but mine kicked in with savage brutality.

The acrid mix of oil and engine fluid filled my nose. A twitch of muscle confirmed my hands worked, feet too. Under my right hand was the familiar hardness of my USP's grip.

The crunch of gravel underfoot meant incoming. The focused intent gaining strength confirmed the tango's priority wasn't to keep me breathing.

Habit kicked in and despite the pulsing ache in my temples, I tightened my mental barriers against the intrusive thoughts as I curled my fingers around my gun.

My eyes flew open as Meli's second scream was abruptly cut off, my arm lifting, gun aimed out the passenger door. A burst of rain and wind whipped the torn strips of the airbag like fringe, giving me a snapshot of the approaching target.

What happened next was almost too fast to process.

The figure appeared in the partially open passenger door.

I lurched back from the steering wheel, pressing back into the seat even as my finger squeezed the trigger. Gunfire tore through the enclosed space. I got two shots off to the hooded figure's one.

Through the ringing of my ears Meli's cry, full of pain and horror, ripped across my mind and heart, leaving behind invisible wounds that matched the line of fire searing across my chest.

Without lowering my gun, I used my other hand to figure out how badly I'd been hit. I sucked in a sharp breath when my fingers found a long, shallow furrow indicating a graze.

That had been too damn close. Thankfully, my aim was a hell of a lot better than his.

He stumbled back a couple of steps, hand to his chest, his other arm dropping, the gun falling from his loose grip as he turned. He managed another step or two before dropping to his knees. He knelt there in profile, staring at God only knows what, before toppling forward.

My arm started to shake, so I lowered the gun on the twisted remains of the center console. The ringing in my ears faded, but sounds remained muffled, as if coming from underwater. I couldn't hear Meli and didn't know who or what waited outside. As much as I wanted to call out to reassure her, I didn't dare. Instead I scanned my surroundings taking stock of the situation.

My truck was a fucking mess. Pieces of glass and white residue from the deployed airbags were everywhere. Streaks of blood decorated the white curtain on Meli's side. Her seatbelt lay limp, the straps cleanly cut amidst the tattered upholstery.

The sight of both made my gut knot.

Sound began to filter back in. Desperate for information, I thinned my mental barrier.

Fucking incompetent. Choices, choices, finish the job myself or leave his ass to rot?

The thoughts disappeared only to be replaced by a sucking morass of anger and jealousy. Someone yelled something, but I didn't catch the response. The thoughts tangled, warping into something not quite right, only to settle into cold practicality.

I'll teach her.

The deadly intent behind the thought froze my blood. The chill of dread sharpened my focus and I shook free of the twisted emotions of the sick fucker, slamming my barriers back in place. It was damn difficult to shove away the fear and worry gnawing their way through skin and bone, and work on getting out.

I fumbled for the seatbelt, but the release was jammed too far down to reach. Ripping away the last bit of the airbag, I uncovered the bent steering wheel. My left leg ached, but since I could move my toes without pain, I ruled out it being broken.

Good enough.

Twisting against the restraint, I gritted my teeth against the burn as the seatbelt rubbed against the graze and reached down to get the knife stashed in the lower pocket of my cargos.

The skin on the back of my hand tore as I forced it between the door panel and my leg. Seconds crawled by and I managed to snag the knife.

Bringing it up, I went to work sawing through the shoulder restraint.

When the faint sound of a car door slamming closed reached me, I began to curse steadily, yanking viciously against the fraying belt. It snapped as an engine turned over and then shifted into gear.

Frantic now, I tried to kick free of the disaster under the dash. Unfortunately my actions seemed to make things worse, not better.

Tires spun against gravel, gained traction, and then sped away, the heavy engine leaving a fading echo in its wake.

"Goddammit!"

Frustrated, scared, and sick, I slammed my fists against the steering wheel, failure choking me. All of my emotions escaped in a vicious bellow that left my throat raw as my mind kept stumbling over the fact that Meli was gone.

Taken while I was trapped in the fucking truck.

Furious at fate or whatever you wanted to call it, I kicked out, slamming my right foot against the canted center console. The impact sent it to its side, and my gun careened into the passenger floorboard. The truck rocked under the violent impact, and a burst of rain swept in and snapping me out of my haze.

Action, not reaction was needed now.

Falling back on years of discipline honed by the military, I centered my efforts on getting free. Ten minutes later I stood outside the wreckage, pants ripped, skin torn, and a mixture of blood and rain dripping down my face, gun in hand, gaze trained on the body sprawled in the mud.

Using the toe of my boot, I kicked it over.

Under the olive green hood, sightless eyes stared into the rain, and two dark spots, one chest height, the second just below, stained the front of the heavy material.

I dropped into a crouch, slowly because my thigh hurt like a bitch.

A wimpy ass goatee covered the rounded chin, the crooked nose looked as if it was intimately acquainted with fists, and the dark hair was worn long.

A quick search confirmed no wallet or anything else to help with ID. John Doe was average height, average weight. Tugging down the hoodie's zipper revealed some serious black ink curling above the collar of the gray T-shirt.

Using a finger to pull the shirt down to get a better picture, the artwork struck me as the do-it-yourself kind. *Prison art, maybe?* Question for later.

Reaching across his body, I grabbed the gun, careful to touch the barrel in hopes of preserving prints on the grip. Not sure if they'd be recoverable after the rain, but at this point, I needed every advantage I could get.

Forcing my protesting muscles to work, I stood up and went back to the truck. Ripping a piece of the airbag material off the liner, I wrapped the gun, and tucked it into one of my pockets.

Time to call in reinforcements, which required a phone. I began to dig through the debris in the truck.

It was slow going as ragged edges threaten to do more damage to my already battered hands. After a few minutes, during which I managed to fill the quiet by painting the air blue, I finally found my phone. It was under my seat, wedged between the broken seat bottom and the floor.

Getting it loose required more patience than I had, and sweat stung the cuts on my face by the time I pulled it free. The screen was shattered, but when I thumbed the power, I got a brief flash before it blacked back out. The damn battery was done.

Instead of throwing it away, I slipped it into my back pocket, and kept searching. This time looking for Meli's phone.

Part of me prayed I wouldn't find it, because that meant she had it. And if she had it, I had a way to trace her. It was stupid and delusional, but I held it tight because I could feel my emotions beginning to unravel as the minutes ticked by, stretching into an hour.

Forcing patience, I continued my search working my way back toward the passenger door. I dropped to a crouch to get an angle on the space between the door and the passenger seat so I could see under it.

I rested my forehead against the edge of the seat back,

closed my eyes for a moment. "Aw, fuck me," I whispered, the knot in my stomach rising to my throat.

Slowly, I reached out and pulled Meli's phone from the cracked liner of the door. It was dented on one corner, and a chip was missing in the surface glass.

I tried not to think as I hit the power button. The screen lit, the battery showed twenty-three percent, but hope rose despite my fears when I saw the texts from Bishop.

"We're en route, ETA 1:40."

Even better was the following text time-stamped twenty minutes ago. *"Sit-rep?"*

I typed, *"Not good,"* which was putting it mildly.

In minutes the phone rang, the bright tune jarring.

Knowing who was on the other line, I didn't bother with a greeting as I straightened and walked clear of the wreckage. "How far out are you?"

"We're hauling ass, thirty minutes based upon where we're pinging your location," Bishop's voice was tight.

"Who's we?"

"Ricochet's joined the party, the rest of the team's been tapped on another assignment."

Relief trumped curiosity, since the assignment couldn't be too critical if the colonel hadn't sent out a call. Besides, having Ricochet on board meant our chances of tracking Meli were slightly better than shit. "Good, we're going to need him."

Bishop read between the lines. "How bad?"

I looked over my shoulder at the cluster behind me, before turning away. "Fucker took Meli. I got a body with two holes in it, a surprise package, and my truck's totaled."

"What about you?"

"Upright and breathing."

There was a pause, but he didn't push. "Ideas on the who behind the fucker?"

Considering the cloying tendrils of possession, lust, and anger accompanying the mind, yeah. "Nicholas Breck."

"Shit."

His grim response left tension zipping through every muscle. "What?"

"Spoke to that teammate of Dwyer's, the situation is murky as fuck, but Breck is in it neck deep."

Staring at the deserted highway, as if that would bring them closer any faster, I gripped the back of my neck and squeezed, a futile attempt to ease the ache. "Of fucking course he is."

A quiet beep in my ear reminded me I was talking on borrowed time. "Fill me in when you get here, the battery's dying."

"Roger that." There was a muffled response from Ricochet, and Bishop added, "Any lookie-loos we need to worry about?"

"It's Thanksgiving, it's raining, and I'm in the middle of BFE."

Bishop's answering bark of laughter held no humor. "Copy that. Hang tight, Wolf. We're coming."

Call ended, I dropped the phone into a pocket and continued to stare unseeingly over the landscape.

The soft fall of rain couldn't stop the silence from crowding in despite the occasional pings as drops hit the metal carnage behind me. It was hard to shift my focus from the gnawing worry about Meli, and my futile wish fest of second chances to untangling what the hell was going on.

Turning on my heel, I studied the remains of my truck and forced my brain into gear.

First things first, retrieve the gold from the floor compartment.

I rounded the truck's bed. Strange that Breck hadn't come over after his partner in crime failed so spectacularly. Instead, he hauled ass, taking Meli with him. Based on Bishop's brief comment, chances were good he was involved with the stolen gold. Either he knew Eric took it, or they were working together.

Yet, that didn't fit with tone of the letter Eric left for Meli. My impression was her brother would rather visit some serious payback on Breck, but I'd witnessed stranger partnerships. Meli was convinced her brother wouldn't steal it, but I wasn't so sure.

Gripping the edge of the truck's bed, I used the tilted rear wheel as a step and climbed into the back of the truck. The bed-box was pockmarked with dents and scratches, but it was intact. Good.

The lid was jammed tight, and took a couple of well-placed kicks to pop it free. Inside, I found the crowbar and my backpack. Grabbing both, I hopped down, ignoring the flare of protest along my leg, wiped the rain from my face, and dropped the pack next to truck.

Then I shoved the end of the bar in-between the bent frame and smashed door and pulled. Metal creaked and glass cracked, but the door barely budged. I kept at, half my mind on getting the damn door open, half on the puzzle of what went down.

If Breck knew about the gold, whether he was part of it or blackmailing Eric, why did he leave without searching for it?

Easiest answer, he didn't know we found it.

Yet he managed to find us in the middle of nowhere. How? A question I filed away for later.

The metal gave. I stopped my mental gymnastics in order to concentrate on getting the door open. By the time there was enough room to maneuver I was sweating. Go figure.

It took a few more minutes with my knife to cut away the ragged remains of the airbag so I could get a clear picture of what I was working with. It wasn't pretty. Between the SUV's impact and the roll, the space behind the front seats no longer existed which made getting the driver's seat up and forward a bitch.

Applying muscle and a few choice curses, I managed to reclaim some space. Not much, but enough, hopefully.

Working in the confined area took concentration. Minutes ticked by, and I fought frustration and the urge to hurry. Eventually I got the liner shoved aside, and lifted the lid of the compartment. Then it became a tug of war, until I finally got the leather folder out. The backs of my hands were torn to shit from the jagged pieces of the seat, but the leather was battered and intact.

After stashing the gold and the tango's wrapped gun in the backpack, I tossed the crowbar back in the box. Keeping the backpack close, I went through the paperwork scattered across the interior until I found my registration. That went into my pocket. It wouldn't slow down any cop that came to investigate, but it didn't make sense to leave it behind. Knowing Bishop and Ricochet, they already called the accident in to the colonel, who'd take care of my truck and the body.

Trying to get an idea of what happened while I was stuck in the truck, I worked my way out, starting at the passenger's door. Thanks to the soft rain, it wasn't easy, but I found two sets of footprints.

One belonged to the dead man, and based on the heavier, larger tread, the other had to be Breck. There were a few scuffs from a smaller boot, which would be Meli. That she was mobile after the accident eased a bit of my worry.

About a hundred yards out, I found churned earth.

My stomach clenched, and I crouched to get a closer look.

Ricochet was a hell of a lot better at this crap than me, but it was obvious Meli tried to escape and didn't get far. There was a deep heel impression from Breck's boot, the toe print wasn't as clear, more scuffed.

If I was reading this right, it meant his weight increased,

probably because he picked up Meli, and he was turning away from the truck.

Looking out, I spotted the tire tracks.

Rising, I made my way over to the tracks, currently filling with rainwater. The weather was wiping out our only lead.

I grabbed Meli's phone, and managed a couple of photos of the tire tracks, then sent them along to Bishop. No need for an attached message, he knew what to do with these. In the meantime, I followed the dissolving tracks to the highway. On the asphalt the trail of muddy tracks headed back in the direction of Vegas.

A slim hope rose.

I sent a quick text to the guys to keep an eye peeled for a black SUV with front-end damage heading their way. If the highway remained as quiet as this patch, they might get lucky. Of course that was betting on the fact, Breck was a dense fuckwit which didn't jibe with his personality, but one could always hope.

In the meantime, all that was left was to start humping it and meet my ride. Walking would keep my muscles loose, but it wouldn't stop the memories of Breck's mental state or what that meant for Meli.

Even knowing she couldn't hear me, didn't stop me from trying to reach her, to let her know she wasn't alone.

Hold on, angel. I'm coming for you.

Chapter Twenty-Two

The world came back to me in pieces. First it was the sound of tires over asphalt, then the squeak of a windshield wiper scraping over glass. Then the tires bumped over a pothole, jarring awake a chorus of aches and pains, but it wasn't enough to drown out the sound of steady breathing close by.

"I know you're awake, Meli."

At the sound of Nicholas's voice, everything came rushing back. The accident. His sudden reappearance. The gunshots. Wolf.

The last cracked my heart wide, leaving it bleeding out in my chest, while my screams echoed only in my skull. The image of Nicholas's partner raising his arm, the gun bucking in his hand as he fired into the cab, it was etched in brutal detail.

I failed to keep Wolf safe, and because of me, he was gone. So much for watching his back.

"Come on, Meli-girl, stop your silly games."

Strangely it wasn't the expected fear that rose at his taunt, it was an animalistic fury. Unmindful that we were in a moving vehicle, I erupted from my seat, lips peeled back in a silent snarl, fingers curled into claws, my intent to inflict as much pain as possible. Even hampered by the seatbelt, I still managed to make contact, scoring deep scratches down the side of his face.

Caught by surprise, he yelled and jerked the wheel sharply to the side, his hand slamming out in an awkward punch.

Undaunted and lost in my grief-driven anger and pain, I didn't stop, clawing and striking out with a silent ferocity. Even when he slammed on the brakes, I kept going, my body jerking against the seatbelt.

Unfortunately, Nicholas was better at attacking than me.

With the SUV stopped, he twisted in his seat, one hand trapping my flailing arms, the other whipping out and slamming my head back against the window.

Stunned, I could only blink away the white stars peppering my vision as he wrapped something sharp and cutting around my wrists. Feebly, I tried to pull away, only to have him jerk my arms sharply, the stinging pain in my shoulders tearing a whimper free.

"Stop it, Melisande. You'll only hurt yourself."

Using the restraint on my wrists, he pulled me closer, capturing my chin in his hand, and forcing me to meet his gaze. He studied my face, his fingers tightening as I tried to pull free.

Whatever he saw, he didn't understand, because he frowned. "Why are you so upset?"

Hysterical laughter threatened to erupt. *Was he for real?*

Staring back, it struck me he was perfectly serious.

My stomach clenched as realization hit I was dealing with a man completely lost in his own delusions. It did not bode well for me. Maybe it should worry me more than it did, but haunted by the fact the man I loved was either dead or dying somewhere in the middle of nowhere, I really had nothing left to lose. "You killed Wolf!"

Nicholas shook his head slowly. "No, you did."

The absolute conviction in his voice froze my soul, robbing my ability to form any kind of response.

He didn't wait for one, but kept driving the knife in, twisting it deeper. "I told you, you're mine. I don't share. Not with another man, not even your brother."

My thoughts skipped and slipped because there was nothing to hold onto, the edge of sanity crumbling under my desperate grasp. What was it about me that kept bringing Nicholas back? If I could figure it out, maybe I could make this madness stop. And Eric? What did he have to do with any of this?

Ugly, traitorous whispers crept in, undermining a previously unshakable faith in my brother.

Completely unaware of the chaos erupting behind my silence, Nicholas dug his fingers into my chin.

The sharp, biting pain left tears welling, but I refused to blink and set them free. No way in hell would I give him the satisfaction of seeing me cry. It was just pain, and it was temporary.

He leaned in until his hot breath fell over my face and the cold, steel blue-gray flint of his eyes filled my entire field of vision. "We will be discussing your behavior when we get home, but for now, you either behave for the rest of the ride, or I'll make sure you have no choice but to behave. Which will it be?"

He paused, waiting. When I refused to answer, a muscle jumped in his jaw and the ice factor in his gaze dropped below freezing. "Answer me, Melisande."

There was no missing the spark of anticipation, as if he wanted me to fight, maybe even hoped for it. Too damn bad. I swallowed against the sting of answering, "I'll behave."

Sure enough, disappointment sparked, then was washed

away as triumph took its place. "Knew you could be smart, babe."

He squeezed once, keeping the pressure on as he watched. Only when a tear escaped and crept down my skin, did he let go of both my chin and my sore wrists. "Sit tight, we're almost home."

Then, as if nothing out of the ordinary had occurred, he put the SUV back into gear, and got back on the road.

I stared out the passenger window, trying to ignore my reflection in the heavily tinted glass, not wanting to face the obvious. I was so screwed. Fighting Nicholas was futile. I wasn't sure I could take another blow to my head without some serious consequences.

My cut hand throbbed. A high-pitched ring echoed faintly in my ears, and the ache had spread from my temples to encompass the entire inside of my skull.

Even my vision was off.

Of course, it could be because of the damn tears I couldn't seem to stop.

The evolving cityscape passed by in a blur. We were cruising along the streets, cars beside us, filled with people caught up in their conversations and laughter, completely unaware of the horror playing out in the vehicle next to them.

How could you be in the middle of things and still be so invisible?

I needed someone to see me. I needed someone to save me.

I stumbled to a stop at the edge of the yawning abyss. There was no one left to save me. Eric was gone. Wolf was gone. Neither one would be able to come back and help me. There was only one person left. Me.

It took effort to step back from the debilitating despair, but if Nicholas got me back to wherever he was holing up, my chances would go from slim to none.

Trying not to be obvious, I dropped my gaze down to the door. The power locks were engaged.

He began to slow, and a quick check confirmed we were coming to a red light.

Who knows what gave me away, but he didn't look away from the road. "Don't think about it. I've disabled the locks."

The SUV rolled to a stop.

In the glass, I watched as he slowly turned to me, his smile disturbing despite its apparent normalcy. "Go ahead and try, if you don't believe me."

The seconds crept by and his gaze didn't waver, and neither did mine. I didn't realize I was holding my breath until an impatient beep of a car horn behind us broke through our weird staring game.

He shook his head and proceeded through the light.

The rest of our drive was silent. I tried to figure out where we were, but the streets didn't look familiar. Not that I spent much time driving around the outskirts of Vegas, but based on the cookie cutter homes lining the streets, the neighborhood he navigated through was at least fifteen years old.

Most of the homes were one story, with a two-story here and there. The streets were quiet, a few lined with cars. Just before the road ended in desert, he made a right turn, turning into another cluster of homes. A left took us down a street that ended in a cul-de-sac where a house sat a bit apart from the rest due to the oversized lot.

He pulled into the drive even as he reached up to the visor. Since the garage door at the end began to rise, safe to say the opener was clipped above his head. He drove in, shut the engine off, hit the button again and waited until the door closed, leaving us in the dim garage while my chances bypassed none with a dull thunk.

Guess he didn't want his neighbors witnessing him in the midst of a kidnapping.

"Sit tight, I'll come around and get you." He hopped out of the car.

As if I had a choice.

I watched him round the hood and come to the door.

He reached behind his back, and when he brought his arm back around, he had a gun.

A distant part of me wondered how much it was going to hurt to get shot, because that would be a better than what I refused to consider might be waiting for me.

He opened my door and stood there, waving the gun casually. "Come on, hop down."

The gun was like a snake, mesmerizing, and I couldn't tear my gaze away. This would be an ideal time to channel my inner ninja warrior, but since she only existed in my dreams, I was left with nothing but a chilling numbness creeping through every muscle.

"Out, Meli, I don't have all day."

Funny, I did.

He sighed, grabbed the plastic tie on my wrists, and yanked, hard.

Hissing against the bite of plastic cutting into my skin, I managed to get out. It wasn't easy, my balance was off kilter thanks to his hold and my bound hands. Plus, the world swayed a bit with my uncoordinated movements.

He pulled me along, using the restraints like a leash. There wasn't much in the garage. The walls were empty, no tools, no equipment or cabinets.

He opened the lone door, and held it open. "Go on in, I'll lock up behind you."

I stumbled inside. It was dark, and only when he flicked on a light did I realize I was standing in a laundry room. The washer and dryer stood side by side, a broom and dustpan tucked in the corner.

His hand pressed between my shoulder blades, and I stumbled through the laundry room to emerge in a kitchen.

I stopped, leaning against the edge of a counter that divided the kitchen from a dining room. From there I could see into the sparsely furnished living room.

A couple of easy chairs, a TV table in-between, and a TV. Not new, but not too old. The shutters on the windows were closed against the afternoon sun. There was a chill in the air. Either the AC was on or he didn't believe in using the heater.

Right now, it worked in my favor, because the cold air kept me focused. Still, there wasn't much here to use.

"Why don't you sit, and I'll see what I can scrounge up for lunch." He waved me to the other side of the counter, where a pair of high-back barstools stood.

When I didn't move, he set the gun out of reach on the far counter by the fridge, grabbed my arm in a bruising grip and did a push-pull move to get me in place. Ever the demented gentleman, he then pulled one of the stools out. "I need to grocery shop soon, but I think we have enough for sandwiches."

He waited while I awkwardly got onto the stool. Once he was sure I was settled, he walked back to the fridge and opened the door. "Looks like your options are fried egg or peanut butter and jelly." He turned to look at me over his shoulder. "Which will it be?"

Keeping my expression empty, I raised my hands, my fingers long past numb. Even the cut had stopped aching. "Can you take these off? I can't feel my hands."

He shook his head. "When you're ready to eat, I'll take them off. For now, they stay on."

I wasn't going to beg, but I wasn't going to play along either. "I'm not hungry."

"Fine, then you can sit there while I make my lunch."

He pulled out a carton of eggs, half a loaf of bread, butter, and mayo.

I sat there, watching him make a fried egg sandwich.

There was a deliberateness to his actions. Every move precise. When he was finished, he washed the pan he used, and left it to dry on the drain board. He grabbed a soda can from the fridge, then brought his sandwich-filled plate over and took the barstool next to me, sitting so close his shoulders brushed mine.

It hit me that if I actually made it out of here, never again would I be able to have eggs without wanting to barf. My stomach pitched and rolled as he ate next to me.

By the time he was done, my nerves were stretched to the breaking point. When he finally spoke, I jumped.

"Want to tell me why you decided to hook up with that bald-headed bastard?" He shoved in the last bite of egg and bread and chewed. He watched me, his face calm. Too calm.

There was no way to answer him without tripping a trigger. I knew it, but it didn't stop me from saying, "Why are you doing this?"

He wagged a finger in my face. "No dodging the question, Meli-girl." He set his hand down on the counter, his fingers curling into a fist. "Were you fucking him while I was on tour? Was that why you tried to dump me?"

Tried? Hysterical laughter threatened to escape. "We weren't dating, Nic."

His face darkened, his eyes took on a strange glitter. "You were mine from the minute I saw you." He leaned in and hissed, "Were you fucking him?"

I jerked back, but there was nowhere to go. "I'm not answering that."

I didn't want to share something beautiful with the ugly creature in front of me. It was mine to hold close. He didn't get to take it from me.

His hand whipped out, snagging the plastic tie and twisted, sending the sharp edges deep.

Blood beaded along the edges and I choked back my pained cry.

"Were you fucking him?"

My wrists were on fire, and answering him wouldn't end well, but there was no escaping his demand. No way would I let him destroy what I shared with Wolf, warping it with his twisted version of reality. Instead I'd use it as a weapon, a way to tear through his arrogant belief he had me cowed.

Taking aim with vicious pleasure and uncaring of the consequences, I spat, "Yes, and I loved every minute of it."

He struck so fast I couldn't avoid it if I tried. His fist slammed into my stomach in a brutal jab.

The impact rocked the chair and nearly toppled me out of it. Bile burned up my throat, pain riding behind it, resulting in a gagging moan.

"Bitch." Low and mean, it was my only warning before he tangled his hand in my hair and yanked my head back.

I couldn't control my flinch, and he caught it. As sudden as his temper flared, it cooled. Calculation replaced the fury in his eyes. "You're lying." It came out as if he was trying to convince himself. He cocked his head. "Why?"

Since I could barely breathe, providing a verbal response was beyond me.

He ripped his hand free, taking strands of my hair with him.

Dropping my head, I curled in as best I could in the chair, hunching my shoulders and bringing my now numb hands to my chest. Right now, my only worry was keeping his fists away from my stomach and ribs, because I wasn't sure how much more I could take. As it was, I was shaking, torn between fear and my need to strike back.

Next to me, lost in his own demented world, Nicholas kept talking as if we were having a normal conversation. "It's because of Eric, isn't it? He turned you against me with his shit."

He picked up his soda and took a drink.

Hearing him swallow, my stomach churned. I coughed, trying not to throw up. Not that there was anything to bring up.

He set the can down in front of him, both hands wrapped around it. "He was just jealous, you know." His hands tightened on the can, and the aluminum began to give with soft cracks and pops. "He didn't want me to be with you, said I wasn't good enough." He shook his head slowly. "Never understood how he could say that to me."

The tender scars of grief tore open because with every word, Nicholas confirmed that Eric had figured out what I tried to hide. Treading the fine line of sanity in this conversation left my balance shaky. It was a tossup on which would set off Nicholas's triggers first, silence or answers.

My voice was rough with pain and unshed tears, "He was my brother, his job was to keep me safe."

Nicholas sighed and sat back. He switched his hold on the can to one hand, and began dragging it in circles against the countertop. The abrasive scratch of metal against Formica began to fray my tentative hold on my nerves. "You were always safe with me."

Squeezing my eyes close, I bit my lip to keep my bitter laugh silent. Screaming at him wouldn't make a dent in the delusional world he called home.

The can's movement stopped. "What did I do that was so bad you had to go crying to him?"

My breath hitched and I forced my eyes open, but refused to look at him. "I never told him anything. He had enough to worry about."

His unexpected bark of laughter made me jump. "You got that right, babe."

He shoved away from the counter and grabbed his empty plate.

From under my lashes, I watched him get up and walk into the kitchen, tension vibrating through every nerve ending, unable not to be on guard for an unexpected move on his part.

"Whatever you didn't say," he added a nasty twist to the last two words, "I didn't appreciate."

He stopped at the sink, turned on the faucet and rinsed his plate. "Being a pain in the ass has to be a family trait with you two. He wasn't happy with just warning me to back off. Oh no, he had to go and stick his damn nose where it didn't belong, trying to make me look bad. That boy didn't have clue when to back the fuck off, but he learned."

He opened the dishwasher, leaned over and put in his plate. As he straightened, he caught me staring. His smile slowly curled his lips, and a voice in the back of my mind began to lose it.

Something bad, really bad was coming.

"Just like you'll learn."

I swallowed against my dry throat and croaked, "Learn what?"

He rested his hands on the sink's edge and leaned in. "Betrayal carries a hell of a price tag." He reached out, and I flinched back, but he simply tapped my nose with a finger, my heart seizing at the dark menace lacing his words. "Hope you can afford it, Meli-girl."

Chapter Twenty-Three

WOLF

Fifteen minutes later, a sedan cruised to a stop on the shoulder of the road in front of me. The passenger door flew open, and Bishop stuck his head out, taking in my battered appearance with a wince. "Get in, before you keel over."

I hopped in the back of the rental sedan, tossed my backpack across the seat, and caught the dry bandana Bishop threw my way as he resettled in the front. Wiping the rain from my face, I braced my legs against the floorboards as Ricochet pulled a U-ey. "He's heading back into town."

"We didn't see anything on the way in." Ricochet met my gaze in the rearview mirror, before going back to the road. "According to the maps, that doesn't mean dick since there's a couple of ways back to the city that go around the highway."

My hands tightened on the now wet bandana as I turned to stare out the side window. "It was a long shot."

"But one worth taking," Bishop added, bringing my attention back around.

He shifted in his seat, setting his back to the door so he could see me and Ricochet. He rested one arm along the back of his seat, the edges of his tattoo peeking out from under his T-shirt, his face grim. "Managed to track down the last of Dwyer's team and cornered him this morning feeding a slot machine the last of his disability check. A couple cups of coffee to help ease the haze of lady luck and he shared an interesting story."

"Must have been a doozy, if you called Ricochet in."

That got a lip twitch from Ricochet, but it was Bishop who spoke. "Actually called him last night."

I frowned. "What happened last night?"

Bishop shrugged, an uncomfortable expression I recognized from past missions crossed his face. "Nothing, but I knew I'd need backup."

Because Bishop's ability to recognize patterns in events or behaviors gave him a leg up to predicting possible outcomes. Handy as fuck, especially now. "What does that make me?"

"Busy." There was a knowing light in his eyes. "You had your hands full, and the backup wasn't for last night, it's for today."

Yeah, my hands had been full. For a few blessed hours I held the world in my hands. I blew out a breath. Had it only been last night when I held Meli, and promised to keep her safe?

Failure churned in my gut, and I dropped my head, wrapped a hand around my neck, and squeezed against the rising tension. *Where the fuck had he taken her? Was she hurt? Would I make it in time?*

Breck was an unbalanced bastard, which didn't bode well for Meli's safety. Sick with worry, I sent up a silent prayer, *God, please let me make it in time.*

"Wolf."

I raised my head, blinking back to the present and focusing on Ricochet. "Yeah?"

"Worrying like that will make you fuck up." His eyes went

to the rearview mirror and locked with mine. Comprehension and steel stared back. "Stop."

Easier said than done, but I got it. Dipping my chin in acknowledgement, I turned to Bishop. "What'd you find out?"

"That tribal dispute the team stumbled into wasn't a tribal dispute. Dwyer's six-man team was supposed to be providing backup to an off the books meet between a local tribe leader with U.S. leanings and a suspected arms dealer out of Russia. When they got there, they walked into an ambush."

"From which side?"

Bishop frowned. "That's the weirdest part, the tribal leader led the charge. According to Corporal Thayer, the leader claimed the U.S. betrayed him to the dealer. Dwyer tried to talk to him, but he wasn't listening, and decided to voice his displeasure with bullets. The tribe managed to take out Dwyer and two others, leaving the remaining three wounded and pinned down. The team caused some serious population reduction of their own, but Thayer lost his left leg after being hit with a stray round that required a field tourniquet."

"How long?" Because to lose a leg, meant the tourniquet had been left on longer than a couple of hours.

"Five hours, before the other half of the team could get in and bring them home."

A somber quiet followed Bishop's answer, each of us knowing just how long five hours could feel in the middle of hell.

Bishop cleared his throat and continued, "According to what Thayer remembers, there was no talking to the leader. In fact, he's pretty certain there was someone spouting shit non-stop in the leader's ear because he kept screaming how Dwyer's team was protecting thieves and murderers. His words, not mine."

"Murderers and thieves?"

Bishop nodded.

Something wasn't adding up here, and the lack of information was going to bite us in the ass. "Who was killed and what was taken?"

"Not sure on who got killed, but as for what was stolen, I'm thinking it was the weapons promised to the dealer. They were never recovered."

I hated not having the rest of the story, but as soon as we hit town, that was going to change. Not sure how, but I'd figure it out. "And Eric? Did Thayer have any insight on what was going on with him?"

"Yeah, Dwyer definitely had something going on." Bishop scratched his chin. "It took some prodding, but I finally got Thayer to share. Dwyer's team tended to work in tandem with a couple of other special teams, one of which was Nicholas Breck's group. In fact, a few days before everything went tits up, Dwyer's team was tapped to work with Breck's team on an op, except Dwyer went to his CO, had a private conversation, and suddenly Dwyer's team was off the hook, which is why they were tapped for the tribal backup.

But here's where it gets interesting. A few days before, Thayer was coming back from mess, when he heard two men arguing. Since it was getting fairly heated, and he recognized Dwyer's voice, he went to check on what was up. He said Breck took a swing at Dwyer, who managed to deflect, and took Breck's ass to the ground with a wrist lock. Dwyer saw Thayer, but Dwyer waved him off. The corporal saw Dwyer lean down and say something to Breck, who, and I'm quoting our corporal here, 'got this scary-ass look on his face.'"

If Eric confronted Breck about his behavior toward Meli, that would make sense, but it didn't explain the gold. Which served to remind me. "Got another mystery for you."

I dragged the backpack over and unzipped it. Pulling out the leather folder, I handed it to Bishop.

He took it and set it in his lap. The sound of the zipper

filled the car and was quickly followed by his low, "What the fuck?"

Ricochet's attention dropped from the road, to what was in Bishop's lap. His eyes widened before he let out a low whistle.

"My question exactly."

Bishop raised his head and looked at me. "Where did this come from?"

"The coordinates Eric left for Meli," saying her name made my heart clench, but I kept going. "They led to an abandoned mine where that was stashed."

"Shit, Wolf, there has to be close to half a million dollars' worth here. Where did he get it? Better yet, how?"

I rubbed a hand over my face, the weight of frustration and worry eating at my patience. "It's unmarked, which means untraceable."

"You think he stole it?"

"Maybe, or it's a payment. But why and from who? Meli swears her brother wouldn't pull shit like this, even when the evidence is staring her in her face." And I couldn't quell my fury for a dead man who dropped his sister into the center of a shitstorm. "I'm thinking she didn't know dick about him, especially since she mentioned his behavior had changed during his last couple of visits."

"She could just as easily be right." This came from Ricochet.

"And if she is, then where the hell did this come from?"

"Breck?" Bishop offered.

I turned to him. "How do you figure?"

His face was locked down tight, not giving away shit, but his gaze was rock solid. "Let's come at this from a different angle. What if Breck wasn't stalking Meli because he was obsessed? What if he was stalking her to see if her brother left something for her?"

I shook my head. "Time line doesn't add up. Meli said Eric and Breck were friends, and her brother introduced Breck to her a little over a year ago. Breck kept pushing her to go out, she eventually gave in, and when he got shipped out, she told him she wasn't interested. Then, to be sure he got her message, she ignored his letters and calls."

Bishop held up his hand. "Right, but the violence didn't start until just before Dwyer's death, right? Before his last visit home?"

"Yeah, but I'm thinking Breck dared to lay hands on her because Eric wasn't there to keep him in check."

The pounding in my head was getting worse, and my muscles were stiffening up. Shifting in my seat, I adjusted my position so I could stretch out my leg to ease the ache. The move pulled along my wound, and I couldn't quite stifle my hiss. "Besides, I felt the fucker as he ran us off the road. He wants Meli, believes she's his."

And the memory of that sent a black rage seeping under my fragile control. When I finally caught up with Breck, I wasn't sure I'd be able to let him crawl away breathing.

Bishop watched me, his jaw flexing. "The question is, which does he want more, Meli or the gold?"

Considering the depth of possession Breck was sporting, the answer was easy, "Both. He doesn't like losing."

"We're still missing where the gold came from." Ricochet guided the sedan around a semi.

"Honestly? Not sure that's really a concern right now. We get Meli back, take the asshole down, then we can worry about where the gold came from." Because I couldn't care less if Eric was a thief or not, if he was working with or against Breck, I just wanted Meli back, safe.

Unfortunately, life was a damn good teacher and while I knew I could get Meli back, it was the safe part worrying the hell out of me.

"He'll keep her alive." Bishop's comment was quiet, but it still made me wince.

"Yeah, but for how long?" I growled.

"She's stronger than you give her credit for," Bishop said.

Echoes of her soul-shattering scream haunted me, more than I wanted to admit, because everyone had a breaking point. "She may think I'm dead. I'm not sure if, on top of everything else, she'll be thinking all that rationally."

"You're in love with her."

"You're slipping, Bishop. I have been for a while."

"She feel the same?"

The memory of her under me, sharing her bruised heart, that delicate link that snapped into place while I held her, I hugged it tight. "I think so, just not sure she trusts it. Not after what Breck's put her through."

He nodded. "Then she'll hang tough, long enough to make Breck sorry."

"How do you figure?"

His dark gaze softened. "Because your little spitfire has a hell of a temper. It's buried, but it's there. If she thinks Breck hurt you, she'll be focused on payback."

He was right, but what form that payback would take scared the shit out of me. What would it cost her?

I swallowed against the lump threatening to choke me. "We need to find her."

Bishop's gaze didn't waver. "We will, brother, we will."

I nodded, then turned away, closing my eyes, holding tight to the conviction in his answer, because the odds were against us.

Meli was running out of time.

• • ● ◆ ● • •

When we hit the city limits, I jerked out of my semi-conscious state, a nebulous idea gaining form. "Bishop, I need your phone."

He handed it over, and I did a quick phone number search, found it, and hit send. It was picked up on the second ring. "Marsten."

"Detective, it's Randall Kincaid, sorry to bother you on the holiday." From the front passenger seat, Bishop raised an eyebrow. I gave him a short head-shake.

"Don't worry about it, I pulled the short end of the stick. I'm just finishing up my shift." There was the sound of a chair squeaking under a settling weight. "What can I do for you Mr. Kincaid?"

"Meli's been a little on edge since the last incident, and I'd like to take her out of town for a few days."

"I don't see why that would be a problem. We have her contact information if we have any questions."

"I'd like her to relax while we're gone, and Detective Valley mentioned she would call me in when you were set to interview the guy."

"Actually, we managed an initial interview early this morning."

I frowned. "I was under the impression Valley would call me before that happened."

"I believe she tried, but couldn't reach you."

Probably because I was traipsing around a damn ghost town. "My cell's reception has been a bit shoddy lately; I must have missed her call. With everything that's happened, I'd like to reassure Meli there's nothing to worry about while we're gone. Were you able to find out what his deal was?"

There was a pause and I wondered if I had overplayed my hand, but there was a point to my questions.

Finally, he sighed. "I can request you get a copy of the report, but I'm not at liberty to share over the phone."

Translation, they had something.

Anticipation had me leaning forward as I clutched the

phone tighter. It took effort to keep my voice casual. "So you found something?"

"Yeah."

I met Bishop's gaze with a fierce grin. "Anything I should be worried about?"

Another pause followed by the sound of a chair scraping back. "Hang on a sec." I counted to ten before Marsten spoke again. "Off the record, and only because I know you're a tough SOB and your colonel vouched for you, I would suggest you keep an eye on Meli. Even better, maybe extend her out-of-town visit a few more days."

That snuffed out my spark of excitement. "Who am I looking for?"

"Nicholas Breck."

"The report going to contain the entire interview or pieces?"

Because he and I both knew, if there were possible leads under investigation, they wouldn't be in the report. Territorial pissing matches were a pain in the ass, but I got it. The detectives wouldn't want the military crashing their party. Didn't matter that PSY-IV Team wasn't on any verifiable books, our covers were linked to NCIS offices.

"I can request a copy of the interview be attached to the report, but it'll be a few days before the request is processed."

Meli didn't have a few days. But there was a way to speed up getting the recording of the interview, a way Marsten didn't need to know about. "I'd appreciate it. Could you please send it on to my colonel? She'll make sure I get a copy."

"Yeah, I can do that."

"Thanks."

"Kincaid, I wish I could do more." True regret echoed in his voice.

"I appreciate it, Marsten."

"Watch your back, because Breck's slick."

"Roger that." With that, we disconnected.

"Where are we headed?" That was Ricochet.

"Meli's place." I got a brief nod in reply.

As Bishop began giving Ricochet directions, I scrolled through Bishop's address book and hit the next number.

"What's doin', Bishop?" Tainted by the molasses of the south, Rabbit's greeting came through loud and clear.

"It's Wolf."

"Wolf, my scary ass mofo, what can I do you for?"

"I need you to hack the LVPD's system and get me a copy of Detective Valley's suspect interview this morning."

Bishop shot me a look, then shook his head.

Without a pause, Rabbit asked, "Got a case number?"

"No, but it'll be linked to Melisande Dwyer."

"Ain't that Risia's lil' friend, the mouse?"

"She's not a mouse, Rabbit," I snapped.

"Whoa there, didn't mean to be steppin' on your toes," Rabbit backpedaled, but continued in complete seriousness, "She in trouble?"

I blew out a hard breath, trying to reign in my impatience. "Yeah, big trouble."

"You need me out there?"

And that right there was why being part of the team was more than a job. You had a problem they were there, no questions asked. "No, man, I got Bishop and Ricochet. We should be good."

There was a snort of disbelief. "Yeah, you're so good Bishop's calling in for a cleanup crew in the middle of fuckin' nowhere." He didn't pause. "LVPD's security walls are for shit, I should be able to pull it in about fifteen. I'll send it over."

One of the multitude of knots in my stomach loosened. Time to see how much more Rabbit's genius with electronics could untie. "I know you're treading lightly on Breck, but I need you to dig deep and fast."

"How fast?"

"Like yesterday."

"Start talkin'." Grim and hard, Rabbit lost all sense of humor.

I laid it all out for him, knowing he needed every detail to figure what the hell was going on. And he would. It was just a matter of time. Time that was running out for Meli.

When I was done, I couldn't help adding, "And Rabbit, don't tell Risia."

Because the minute Meli's friend found out, she'd be here, and so would Tag, which would leave the team short and tight. Bad enough three of us were involved, but I didn't think the colonel would take kindly to our numbers of involved increasing. Especially since I wasn't sure how messy we were going to get before it was all said and done.

"Wolf," there was a warning note in Rabbit's voice. "You best tread lightly or Tag's woman will be all over your ass, not to mention the colonel."

"I know, Rabbit. As soon as we have something solid, I'll bring the colonel up to speed."

"Copy that. I'll get to work. Good luck."

"Thanks, man."

I handed the phone back to Bishop. I might be stuck spinning my wheels until Rabbit came through, but at least I could start digging through the muck to unearth Breck's hole. It didn't ease the fear burrowing into my bones, but it was something. And right now, focusing on that impeded the sickening sense of Meli slipping through my desperate hands.

Chapter Twenty-Four

Watching the arrogant satisfaction reflected in Nicholas's smile, a horrible, twisted suspicion began to form. One I wasn't sure I could handle.

"What did you do, Nic?"

"Me?" He adopted an innocent expression so patently false my pulse took on a heavy beat. "I didn't do a thing. Not really."

He shrugged as he leaned back, resting his hip against the counter's edge as he folded his thick arms across his chest. "Eric was bound and determined to keep you safe from me. He failed to watch his six. Since he routinely walked into sketchy situations with his team, that's not a healthy habit to acquire."

It was like watching a coiled snake preparing to strike. He was getting ready to sink his poisonous fangs into my heart, but I couldn't figure out how. "I don't understand."

"You never did, did you?"

His constant baiting made me want to scream, instead I scrambled for a handhold, something to hang on to as my already rocky world began to shake underfoot. "Nic." His name came out on a plea, but in the scheme of things, like figuring out what was happening, I couldn't afford to care. Even when his face softened with a weird happiness.

"You were always bothered by Eric's interference. Didn't matter if you tried to excuse it as being little Miss Independent, with your 'I can handle it on my own' crap. You couldn't hide the real reasons from me. You knew he wouldn't approve of our relationship, so you hid it."

How? How did he manage to twist everything into such a warped tangle?

He pushed off the counter, twisted, and opened a drawer. When he turned, he held a knife in his hand.

I froze.

He came around, hand lifted.

I steeled my spine in an effort not to cower, but couldn't stop my shudder.

He stopped, the knife raised, eyebrow quirked. "I thought you wanted the ties off."

I worried my bottom lip, studying his face.

He waited with a small, taunting half-smile.

Slowly, I held my bound wrists out.

He slipped the knife between my hands and sliced. The plastic loosened, but stuck in the bloody furrows cut around my wrists. He set the knife on the counter obviously not worried I'd try and go for it.

Going for the knife was pointless, since I was busy trying to breathe through the agony of the returning circulation coursing through my numb hands. I could barely curl the hand with the cut.

He ripped the cut plastic away from my wrists with a sharp pull.

I swallowed a pained cry, as blood welled and trickled over my wrists.

Uncaring of the bandaged cut on my palm he caught my

hands, holding them tight as he turned my wrists examining the cuts. "You really did a number on yourself."

He put my hands on the counter, including the injured one, forcing my fingers to uncurl and lie flat, as he slapped the back of them in a sham version of a pat. "We'll have to clean that up later."

I dropped my chin to my chest, trying to hide my face as much as possible because silent, angry, pain-induced tears coursed down my cheeks.

Released from the strangling hold of plastic, my hands burned with the return of blood flow. Even the cool interior air hurt. One hand felt thick and swollen, and moving my fingers made it worse.

When he brushed a loose strand behind my ear with a disquieting gentleness, I startled hard. I lifted my head to find him there, staring.

"It didn't bother me."

Following his train of thought was like diving down a rabbit hole, and I was completely lost. "What didn't bother you?"

"You hiding us. I was okay with that, because I didn't want Eric butting in anyway. He was always looking for a reason to bitch to my CO. God, him and his team of boy scouts were a clusterfuck waiting to happen."

A faraway look entered his eyes as he got lost in his memories, his finger absently tracing a chilling line behind my ear and down my neck. "Most of the time, I could deal with it. It's expected, that kind of shit attitude, when you move up fast and strong, leaving others choking on your dust."

Somehow, I didn't think it was wise to point out that Eric had outpaced Nicholas years ago. Especially when Nicholas was clearly a few crackers shy of a full box.

He blinked, his focus zeroing in on me. "But then you

changed the rules." His hand wrapped around the back of my neck, forcing me to straighten despite the protest of bruised ribs and stomach muscles. "Which makes it your fault, not mine."

Held fast by his grip and gaze, nerves and dread slithered through me. I brought my arms in, protecting my vulnerable parts. "My fault?"

He searched my face. "You really don't get it."

I managed to shake my head slowly, every muscle tensing as some sixth sense kicked in, a belated warning things were about to go from worse straight to hell.

A combination of predatory triumph and a creepy gentleness washed over his face. "When Eric introduced us, I knew you were mine, but you needed time. Or so I thought. And I gave that to you. Letting you play your games. But I watched, and I waited, knowing in the end, I'd win. But then you decided to sic your big brother on me. Telling him a shit ton of lies, until he turned on me. Baby, that places his blood on your hands. You sent him after me. Leaving me no choice but to clean up your mess."

The meaning behind his words detonated, washing my world away in a silent, nuclear blast of denial. "What did you do?" My question was nearly silent.

He turned the stool and trapped me in place by locking his arms on either side of me. His voice was cold, cutting, with not one speck of remorse or guilt visible in his arrogant response. "If you hadn't bitched to him, he never would've made it his mission to fuck with me. He got in my way and you put him there."

"What did you do?" Anger, so huge it was impossible to contain, swept through me. "WHAT DID YOU DO!" I screamed in his face, uncaring what it would mean.

His smile, that damn boy-next-door smile, was mocking. "I killed him."

Those three words shredded the last thread holding me together.

This…this demented fuck had taken away the two men who meant everything to me, my beloved brother and the man who'd become my world. The agony of his arrogance encompassed me in a level of hurt I couldn't comprehend. It tore through my soul, leaving it hollow and empty.

I had failed the two people I loved most on a catastrophic level.

One thought rose from the horror, consuming me. *Hurt Nicholas.* The need for his suffering became a kaleidoscope of emotions that morphed into a mindless storm. No plan, no tactics, no self-preservation survived. Only the impulse to inflict misery on the wretched thing standing in front of me.

Nicholas, the kitchen, the counter, the entire room pulled back, like a surreal camera zooming out at sickening speed. His mouth continued to move, but I couldn't hear over the deafening noise of my shattered universe.

As if from a distance I watched the woman in the chair explode. Fists, nails, teeth, feet, head, any, and everything, she could use she did without hesitation. Lost in her fury, she became a weapon.

I was lost. So lost I barely felt his return blows. In fact, it wasn't until he yanked me out of the chair, his arm a suffocating vise around my neck, pulling me up and back until my toes barely brushed the floor, and the lack of oxygen robbed my moves of their intended violence, that reality began to seep back in.

I stopped fighting Nicholas and fought to breathe. His arm was so tight, I felt my face turn red and my eyes bulge.

"Fucking chill out, Meli." The growl was accompanied by a violent jerk before he slammed me face first into the wall, his body pressing hard behind me.

I couldn't move, couldn't fight back, reduced to clawing feebly at his arm as my vision began to go.

Finally, his arm loosened, and I sucked in air. It hurt, God it hurt, but not as much as the overwhelming wave of guilt and loss sweeping in. Nicholas was right about one thing, Eric and Wolf were dead because of me.

It was the last straw. Something buried deep fragmented with an audible crash.

From far away someone choked on harsh sobs.

"Are you done throwing your little fit?" The hiss was right by my ear.

I jerked away. A stupid move since I had nowhere to go.

"I hate you." Flat, hard, and so cold it took a moment to realize I said it out loud. Then to be sure he heard, I forced every ounce of loathing into my voice and turned my head, ignoring the sharp pains of hair tearing free in his unforgiving grip or the rough scrape of the wall over my abused face. "I fucking hate you."

He whipped me around so fast, my head bounced against the wall. Fury, dark and deep, swept over his face, wiping away the false mask he wore, revealing the bastard beneath.

I refused to cower. I was done. He'd taken everything from me, there was nothing left he could do to truly hurt me. If it took until my last breath, I'd make sure to return the favor.

With his hands on my upper arms, he slammed me against the wall in time with his words. "Don't push me."

The bitter laugh that escaped surprised me, because I wanted to howl. It carried an edge so sharp, he winced. "Or what, Nicholas?" Despite his hold, I leaned forward and sneered, "You going to kill me too?"

I finally managed to tip him over.

His shoulders straightened with a jerk, and he inhaled sharply through his nose, his face set. He yanked me away from the wall and hit me with an unchecked backhand that sent me stumbling back.

What followed became a blur. Hit after hit sent me to the floor. Once down, he added in a couple of vicious kicks, then knelt next to me to keep hitting me.

There was nothing to do but endure. Endure the endless pain quickly becoming my entire world.

I kept my arms over my head, trying to ward off the worst of it, but my reaction time began to lag, while he warmed to the task of inflicting his punishment.

His voice became a droning backdrop that barely penetrated.

Deep, where he couldn't reach, what was broken began to reform, twisted by a craving for vengeance so strong it should have scared me. That it didn't, proved there was nothing left of Meli.

Rough hands tore my arms from my bruised and battered face. Nicholas crouched over my aching body, his face in mine, his breathing harsh and labored. There were small crimson specks dotting his face.

Distantly it registered that it was blood, my blood.

"You're not getting off that easy, Meli. We still need to talk about what your asshole brother did with my gold."

My tongue felt thick, and every time I swallowed, I tasted blood. It took a great deal of concentration to get my mouth to move. "What gold?"

He reared back and slammed his fist into the floor next to my head. If he expected a reaction, he was doomed for disappointment. "Don't fucking lie to me."

I forced my damaged lips to curl up. "Fuck you."

Whatever sanity remained disappeared, leaving the monster unleashed.

I began discovering a new level of pain.

Chapter Twenty-Five

WOLF

By the time we got to Meli's, the afternoon had settled in to stay. The rain was gone, leaving behind a cool breeze. It would take Rabbit some time to get back to us, and I couldn't stand around, I needed to keep busy, both physically and mentally.

After a quick shower, and letting Bishop practice his patchwork medical skills, I headed to the main house. First up, repair the lock on the main door.

I was tightening the last of the screws, when Bishop appeared at the bottom of the steps. "Video's in. Ready to watch?"

"Yeah." Straightening, I gathered the scattered tools and replaced them where I found them, in a drawer in the kitchen.

After flipping the new lock into place, I followed Bishop over to Pequeña Estrella, where he and Ricochet set up their laptops.

The door to the room Meli and I spent the night in was closed, but it didn't stop my gaze from going there first. A futile wish it would open to reveal her standing there with that shy smile in her overly large shirt hit me, landing harder than a sucker punch.

Deliberately I turned away, focusing on the two men crowded at the small table. "What do we have?"

Ricochet's long hair was pulled back, hands that could handle a rifle and nail the wings on a fly at inconceivable distances, flew over the laptop's keyboard. "I'm cuing the interview to the important parts. Your wanna-be assassin's name is Fredrick Canva, also known as Freddie." He turned the laptop around.

"Assassin?"

"Watch."

On screen, Detective Valley sat at a plain, battered table across from Freddie, a notepad in front of her. "Let me get this straight, you answered a want ad on the Dark Web for a hit on Melisande Dwyer?"

"It wasn't a hit, it was just to rough her up a little." Dressed in a T-shirt and scrubs, he stretched his left leg out in front of him. The bulge at his thigh indicated a bandage. He rested one thick arm on the table. "But nothin' was said about the big ass boyfriend she had tagging along."

"Who put out the ad?"

"Look, Detective, it's the Dark Web for a reason. Names aren't important, payment is. I don't have a fucking clue who hired me."

Valley's pen moved across the notepad, and she didn't look up. "So you do this a lot? Accept jobs to 'rough up' people?"

"This is Vegas, and lots of people need reminding to pay their bills."

"Ms. Dwyer doesn't have any outstanding debts, Freddie."

"Well, she sure as shit pissed someone off, because you don't get requests for collecting library fines."

Valley sat back, pen tapping absently against the edge of the table, while she studied him. "You realize we've seized all your electronics, and once we've swept through them we'll have you on various charges."

Her threat didn't seem to faze Freddie, who remained slouched in his chair. His reaction didn't surprise me, because it would take LVPD's techs weeks to unravel whatever maze he created to work behind. Weeks we didn't have.

When he remained silent, she continued, "How much were you paid?"

The cocky ass grin Freddie sported pissed me off, because he had no intention of answering any other questions.

Sure enough, Valley kept coming at him from different directions and got nothing.

Finally, even Freddie got tired of playing. "I want to call my lawyer."

Though she tried to hide it, frustration was evident in Valley's sharp movements as she ceded the round to him.

Unable to watch anymore, I hit pause, stilling the frame with Valley stalking to the door and Freddie wearing a shit-eating grin. Like a fly hitting a tripwire, that expression set a speeding wave of rage coursing through me, leaving the edges of my vision red.

A vise clamped over my wrist, clamping down on sensitive pressure points. The spikes of pain reeled me back.

I blinked and Ricochet's face came into focus. Harsh lines carved sharp edges through his normally expressionless face. It was his grip tightening on my wrist, increasing the pressure, stopping me from shoving the laptop off the table. "You back with me?"

My chest heaved, as if I ran through a minefield blind-folded, but I managed a jerky nod.

His dark eyes scanned my face, seeing far beyond what was comfortable. Even better, his mental shields were shut down tight, allowing nothing to leak out. Which helped since there was enough crap in my head spewing over. Yet, I didn't turn away, because I was too close to the edge. Far closer than I initially thought.

I slowed my breathing, pushing the rage and helplessness back into their box while he watched. Only after they were locked away, did I give him a verbal answer. "Yeah, I'm good."

A minute ticked by while he considered me, then slowly, as if worried I'd snap, he loosened his grip and let me go.

I shook my hand out, and turned away to begin pacing the living room.

Behind me, Bishop cleared his throat. "You ready for what else Rabbit found?"

Stopping by the chair Meli curled up in last night, I spotted a hairband lying on the arm. Picking it up, I wrapped it around my wrist. The fit was tight, but the pinch of it grounded me. "Yeah."

"Freddie wasn't lying about not knowing who hired him."

I turned around, folding my arms across my chest, and waited for the rest. "Not a big surprise. Most of those working in the Dark Web know how to cover their tracks."

Bishop was half-turned in his chair, one arm resting on the back, the other near his laptop. "True, but Rabbit thinks if it was Breck, he had help from someone."

"Who?"

He shook his head. "Don't know, and our tech guru indicated it would take a hell of a lot of time we don't have to find out."

"Yeah, I'm not good with that." Later, when Meli was safe, then yeah, I had no problems doing a little hunting.

"Didn't think you would be. So Rabbit dug around through some of LVPD's files and found the number Freddie used to connect with his boss. Turns out it's a burner cell."

Great, another possible dead end, since burner cells were easy to come by and just as easy to ditch. "Breck's?"

Bishop shrugged. "If he's the one behind the ad, then

maybe, but Rabbit can't tell for sure. It's still showing active though."

If it was active, we could use it to reach out. See who picked up on the other end. It was a long shot, a very long shot, but it was all we had right now. "Let's call it."

Ricochet was shaking his head before I finished. "Not you and not yet."

The faint sense of alarm coming from Bishop, jerked my attention to him. "What?"

As if a switch was thrown, he went as blank as Ricochet.

Goddammit. I stalked across the room. "What aren't you telling me?"

Ricochet stepped in front of Bishop, blocking my view. "You need to pull your head out of your ass, Wolf. Start thinking with your big head and not your little one. What the hell is wrong with you? Meli doesn't need you losing your shit."

Logically I knew he was right, but trying to separate the lover and the soldier was proving far more difficult than I would have guessed. The drive to move out, to rush in and save her, shoved strategy and skill aside.

Forcing my mind to ignore what was at risk, I caught sight of what the two men in front of me already knew. "He has to think I'm dead."

And, by extension, so did Meli.

My heart seized, imagining what that would do to her. The resulting denial almost dropped me to my knees.

"It's the only way we get close." Ricochet didn't move, but his tension level dropped now that I was thinking. "We can call the number, and tell whoever's on the other end, we have something they want."

"This isn't just about Meli." Bishop rose behind Ricochet and stepped to the side. There was worry in his gaze, but it was tempered by a steely determination. "It's about the gold.

Rabbit confirmed there are no reports of any stolen caches, but we all know that means dick. Especially since the arms trade went south. That gold could have come from the tribe or the Russian dealer."

Which would be why it never pinged on the U.S. military's radar.

Bishop kept going, "Breck's contract ended just under nine months ago, but he has a handful of minor disciplinary actions on record. His address belongs to a P.O. box, and his number is disconnected. There's been no movement on his accounts in the last four months, not that there was much to begin with. He's overdrawn and at his limit across the board. Whether he was trying to avoid bill collectors or the police, he basically ghosted after he timed out."

Meli filed the RO a year ago, Eric was killed two months later, and then not a month later, Breck disappeared? Yeah, the timing on all of this sucked. "Any indication he and Eric were working the same angle?"

Bishop shook his head. "Not a one. In fact, Rabbit's convinced it was more than being a protective older brother that had Dwyer turning on Breck."

"Why?"

"Remember how Thayer mentioned Dwyer's team got pulled from working with Breck's team? Rabbit was able to find a report from Dwyer's CO detailing some concerns with Breck's team and how they ran their ops. He didn't mention Dwyer by name, but the timing is spot on. The report mentioned complaints filed by the locals regarding the team's behavior. Words like 'threats' and 'unjustifiable detainment' were used. In fact, the CO suggested an inquiry be initiated."

My stomach churned.

The story wasn't a new one, but it wasn't as common as most thought. In fact, most of those in the hot zones understood the value of good relationships with the locals. It could be the difference between coming home upright or in a flag-draped box. "Was it?"

He shook his head. "No, because Dwyer's team was blown to hell and they ended up with bigger questions to answer."

Which reminded me. "Thayer stated he thought someone was filling the leader's ear with crap. Rabbit find anything to that?"

This time it Ricochet answered, "Nothing solid, but he's got enough crumbs to wonder."

"And I have enough crumbs to bake a pie," Bishop chimed in, snagging my full attention. "Follow along and tell me what you think."

Ricochet and I shared a look, the excitement starting to bubble in my veins reflected in his dark gaze.

Bishop's ability might not earn him tights and a cape, but it guaranteed a leg up on any operation we planned.

Right now, we needed every inch we could gain.

Turning back to him, I said, "We're listening."

Now it was Bishop's turn to pace as he talked. "We've got two friends, Dwyer and Breck. Dwyer zips his way up into a Spec Ops team, and his highly competitive friend is left behind to fend for himself. Breck manages to get on a team of his own, but they're not in the same league. It may burn his ass, but he gets off on hanging with his friend, because the attention spills over to him. We know Breck's a loner, and he's possessive as hell. He latches his star to Dwyer's, but it's just not turning out the way he imagined. Then, one day on leave, he traipses behind Dwyer and meets the little sister. From all indications, Meli and Dwyer were tight."

I nodded.

"Now Breck sees someone else he wants as his and begins to go about getting that. Not only will it permanently tie him to Dwyer, but because he gets Meli, he can chalk it up as a win in his column. Of course, her opinion means jack shit, because it's all about what he wants."

"And he's determined to win."

Bishop nodded. "At any cost."

"You're starting to sound like Cyn."

"She's not the only team member with psych classes under her belt." Bishop moved to the fridge, opened it, grabbed a bottle of water, unscrewed the cap and took a drink.

Setting it on the counter, he picked up his retelling of Breck's descent. "Dwyer's not stupid, and picks up on Meli's behavioral changes. I'm sure it didn't take much for him to put two and two together and get four. He was probably already harboring a few concerns about Breck's behavior on tour before their trip home, so he's watching closer than ever. Doesn't matter if Meli never said word, he knew something was up. Then they head back out, and because he's watching so closely, he finds more things to worry about. Maybe he starts to dig a little deeper, maybe he talks to the wrong people, maybe he sees something, but whatever it was he doesn't stop digging or watching or whatever it was he was doing."

As Bishop continued, the pieces began to come together in a very ugly, twisted picture. "You think he dug deep enough to find the gold?"

Which means Breck got hold of it before the arms-deal meet. Payment for other dirty jobs or simple thievery? The only one left who could answer that would be Breck.

Bishop leaned back against the counter. "Yeah, and I think on Dwyer's last trip home, he brought it with him, set up an alternate plan, just in case."

Which would make sense. "Meli said Eric was on edge and jumpy during his last visit."

"Makes sense," Ricochet added. "If he had stumbled onto something bigger than Breck being an ass, it'd make any man check his six."

Bishop's expression was grim. "Dwyer goes back over, and ends up arguing with Breck. He's had enough and goes to his CO, asks to be pulled off because things aren't adding up."

Time to play devil's advocate, even though my gut was running along the same lines as Bishop's. "Why wouldn't he tell his CO about the gold?"

Ricochet leaned his elbows on the counter. "Just having the gold wouldn't be enough to get his superiors to look in the right direction, because it would come down to his story against Breck's."

"Or," Bishop cut in, "he was using it to force Breck away from his sister."

Or the rot Eric stumbled onto may have spread further than he thought. Again, something else to sniff along, once I had Meli safe. "Either way would set Breck off."

I eased down onto one of the barstools, rubbing along the edge of the bandage on my thigh to ease the dull ache. Studying the shadows gathering in Bishop's face, I didn't need the flashes of worry, anger, and disgust to follow his next mental step. "And the gold?"

He shrugged. "Could have come from anywhere. Breck could have picked it up while clearing a building, he could have been paid it to do a job."

There was a lack of conviction in his voice, which made me think those options weren't what worried him. Which left the rumors of thievery Thayer mentioned. "You think Breck stole the gold from the tribal leader."

Bishop's nod was small. "I think the leader didn't know it was missing until right before the trade. I'm not sure why the tribe was unaware it was missing, but however it happened, Breck used it to set up Dwyer and his team. Once Dwyer was out of the picture, all Breck had to do was get to Meli."

Because without her brother, Meli was unprotected and unaware. "Why the hell didn't Eric warn her?"

"I can't answer that, but if there was one person Dwyer trusted, it was her. Maybe he hadn't finished finalizing his plan; maybe he intended to get the information to someone else. We'll never know. What this means now is that Breck will keep her alive until he gets his gold."

Alive and unharmed were two very different things, and from the grim faces around me, I wasn't the only one thinking that. "Which means we call, hope it's Breck who picks up, and offer a trade."

Ricochet arched a brow at my grimace. "The gold for Meli?" He shook his head. "He won't go for it. Not if he thinks Wolf's dead. He's not stupid. He knows we'll be gunning for him."

"You're forgetting Breck's an arrogant bastard," Bishop reminded them. "He'll play along with the trade because it gives him a chance to take us out, get his gold, and keep Meli."

"Maybe," Ricochet grudgingly admitted. "But turning tables on him only works if he falls for the bait." He looked down at the laptop, a frown creasing his brow. "If we're lucky, we might be able to pinpoint the cell's signal."

"It's a hell of a long shot." Just like grasping at ice-slicked straws, because it all depended on Breck being on the other end of the line.

"Right now, it's the best we've got," Bishop said.

It sure as hell beat pacing the floors. "Call the bastard and let's get her back."

Chapter Twenty-Six

WOLF

Ricochet was at his laptop setting up the triangulation program Rabbit sent along with the burner number. Not only would it narrow down the cell towers the signal pinged off, but it would also cover our location, burying it deep in case Breck tried tracking us back.

Bishop watched me wear a hole in the floor. "You going to be able to hold your shit together?"

Was I? Probably not, but we didn't have the luxury for me to lose it, so I'd suck it the hell up and hold on. "Yeah."

He watched me a second, then shook his head as he ran a hand through his already unruly mop. "Dammit," he muttered, then lifted his head. "Wish there was another way."

Yeah, so did I. But if it worked, maybe I'd get a chance to work out my frustrations on Breck. That was a plan I could get behind.

"Ready."

At Ricochet's call, I went to the table to stand behind him, my attention on the screen and my hands curled over the top of the chair's back.

Tension filled the room as Bishop dialed. Only the repeated

ringing of the line broke the quiet. With each successive ring, my grip tightened.

The ringing stopped. On the laptop's screen information began flowing, following whatever cryptic route Rabbit set in motion.

When nothing but the faint sound of breathing came over the line, I turned to Bishop.

He frowned, his gaze on the screen. A handful of seconds ticked by, before he finally broke it. "You there?"

"Who the fuck is this?" The words were a growl.

Bishop's voice took on a hard, lethal edge. "I'm the one who cleaned up the mess you left this morning, asshole. And guess what I found?"

Silence came back over the line.

The smile creeping over Bishop's face wasn't the least bit friendly. "What? No guesses?"

"What do you want?"

"World peace and a place on the beach, if you're offering. Of course, with my newfound funds, I think I'm well on my way to achieving the second. How about you? What do you want, Breck?"

"I've got exactly what I want," Breck sneered.

"Really? Because it seems to me, you've gone through a lot of trouble trying to get your hands on these shiny little pieces, but if I'm wrong, we'll just pretend this conversation never happened." Bishop cast his lure.

I waited, nerves strung wire tight, white knuckling the chair. If Breck's greed didn't top his lust, we were screwed.

The snarl coming through the line raised every hair on my body. "Did you see what happened to the last sorry bastard that tried to take what was mine?"

Bishop lost all trace of sardonic humor and his response was a whiplash of anger. "You killed a damn fine man, Breck, hope she was worth it."

"More than you know."

My stomach heaved at the sick satisfaction in Breck's answer.

Even Bishop's jaw tightened and flexed, as his face got darker.

Trying not to let my imagination run wild, I strained my ears, hoping to hear some indication Meli was there in the background, and got nothing.

But Breck wasn't finished. "Now, since you called me, I'm guessing you're looking for a trade." From the arrogance in his voice, it was safe to assume Breck thought he had the upper hand.

"You'd be right," Bishop snapped, playing to Breck's ego. "But I need proof she's alive and well."

The chuckle was dark, twisted. "She's alive, but I can't vouch for the well part. Your buddy didn't do too good at taking care of her."

"Put her on the phone."

Fury lit Bishop's eyes, the same fury curling through me until I shook with it. Under it, cracks snaked their way through my soul. Images of Meli at Breck's hands began to play in sharp, high-def resolution.

"Uh-uh, not yet." Confident he had things where he wanted them, Breck continued to push, "I want a picture of what you have. Once I have my proof, I'll give you yours."

Bishop and I shared a look, then turned to Ricochet. He shook his head indicating we still didn't have a lock on the location.

Releasing the chair, I went over to the backpack, yanked out the gold, and laid the case open on the couch.

Bishop followed, snapped a picture, and sent it. He closed his eyes for a second, blew out a silent breath and put the phone back up to his ear. "It's sent. Where's mine?"

The seconds ticked by, before rustling came over the line.

There was the muted sound of Breck's voice, but it wasn't clear enough to make out words.

Then, broken breathing came over the line. "He...hello?"

My heart seized, and I clenched my fists as my knees buckled. Sheer force of will kept me upright, my gaze focused on the phone in Bishop's hand.

White lines appeared around Bishop's mouth, but his voice was gruff, but steady. "Hey, shrimp."

A broken sob, quickly stifled, then, "Bishop? Is Wolf okay?"

Bishop met my gaze, the regret in his made me want to howl. "I'm sorry, Meli."

A low, shattered moan came across the line, gutting me.

Based on the expressions of Bishop and Ricochet, they weren't doing much better. Bishop squeezed the bridge of his nose between his fingers.

Breck's voice came back on. "You want to trade, you bring me what's mine in three hours. I'll text the directions."

With that the line went dead.

The echoes of Meli's heartbreak wrapped chains of helpless fury around my battered heart. I wanted to rage and strike out, but it would gain me nothing. Instead, I shored up the cracks with grim determination.

She was alive. I had to hold on to that. The rest, the emotional fallout, could be dealt with after Breck was taken down.

Ricochet was busy typing away, and I forced my feet to move. Stopping next to him, I growled, "Anything?"

"Not an exact, but we're within a ten mile radius."

I stared at the laptop, seething. "Too much to cover."

He didn't bother looking away from the computer. "I know, Wolf. I'm sending what I have to Rabbit."

Another damn waiting game. The walls closed in, and the furious noise in my head rose. "I'll be outside, let me know when he gets back to you."

I didn't wait for his nod, but turned and left. Once outside, I had no idea where I was going, but I started walking.

The villas were set up on the edge of a national reserve, which meant I had plenty of space to walk. I headed away from the villas, following a faint hiking trail, forcing my mind only on the next step and the next, unable to cope with the images flooding my head.

Images of Breck and the damage he could do to Meli. It wasn't just the physical threat he posed, it was the emotional and mental.

I kept walking, unable to escape my guilt or fears. It didn't matter that I knew she was strong, even the strong had breaking points, and I worried that Meli had far surpassed hers at this point.

My mind spun, gaining speed and barreling toward the crumbling edge.

Imagination is a horrible thing, especially if it had a great deal of darkness to work from, and mine had it in spades. Besides standing witness to the atrocities humans could render on each other, I had firsthand knowledge of just how twisted a mind could get, and Breck was up there with the best of them.

And that was what fueled my growing nausea and began to splinter my control. Impotent fury and soul searing pain tore through me.

"Wolf."

I spun around to find Bishop standing behind me, gaze wary. My chest heaved, my fists curled and uncurled.

"This doesn't help her."

"No shit," I spat. "Do you think I don't know that? What the fuck am I supposed to do, Bishop? She thinks I'm dead, that I'm not here. The fucker hurt her, and we're sitting here with our thumbs up our asses."

He stepped into my space, his face inches from mine. "We're doing everything we can to find her, you know that."

"It's not enough!" I slammed his chest with my hands, rocking him back a step.

"It has to be," he snarled back, knocking my arms away.

But it wasn't, because Breck was hurting the woman I loved, and I, the one who protected others, couldn't keep her safe. What did that make me?

A failure. The whisper broke through the noise.

My control snapped.

Teeth bared, I charged Bishop. It didn't matter he was my friend, closer than a brother, every fucked up emotion locked on him as a target.

Punches were thrown and taken.

I lost myself in the fight, taking a grim sort of pleasure in the pain and finding a release valve on the storm raging inside me. Bishop's hits barely registered, until finally a sharp jab to my ribs, sent me stumbling back.

My foot caught in an uprooted bush, and I twisted to land on my side, hard. For a moment I lay there, my face inches away from the desert floor, trying to get my lungs to work, while fire scored my thigh and hip.

A shadow fell over me. "You done?"

Flipping over, I found Bishop standing there, watching me. There was a shallow cut over one eye that was beginning to swell, and a trickle of blood eased from the corner of his mouth.

Seeing those brought the aches in my face to life. My cheek was tender, and there was blood in my mouth. Moving my tongue, I found the cuts on the inside of a swollen lip. I prodded my cheek, hissing as it sent needles prickling over my skin. "Yeah."

I lifted a hand, wincing when my ribs and stomach protested as he grabbed it and pulled me to my feet. I stood in front of Bishop, taking stock. Bruised, a bit battered, but overall workable.

Bishop didn't move, but asked, "Feel better?"

Instead of answering right away, I took a moment to check.

The violent edge I'd been riding was replaced by a grim focus. As if the fight purged the worst of it, I found I could think a bit more clearly.

My heart still hurt, but my mind was back in the driver's seat. A damn good thing, because getting to Meli was going to be tricky. Doable, but tricky. "Yeah."

"Good. Now that we got that out of the way, we need to get to work."

We headed back to the villas.

Ricochet looked up when we walked in, and let out a low whistle. "Lovers' quarrel?"

"Jealous?" Bishop headed straight for the kitchen sink and turned on the water, splashing it over his face.

I headed for the freezer and pulled out ice. Digging through the drawers, I found a couple of hand towels, dumped the ice inside, and handed one of the impromptu ice packs to Bishop.

He muttered his thanks, and went to the couch. He sank down, towel to his face, and legs sprawled.

I mimicked him in the chair.

"Thanks to the partial location of the burner, Rabbit found us something." Ricochet didn't mess around.

I lifted the towel so I could see him. "What?"

"A possible location."

I jerked upright, hissing at the flare of pain the move provoked. Still holding the ice against my face, I went to stand behind his chair. On screen was a still satellite image of a neighborhood.

Ricochet kept talking, "Our boy hacked one of our satellites, so we have this."

"Where the hell is that?"

"North end of Vegas, roughly thirty minutes out."

My heart thudded hard in my chest. "How sure is he?"

Ricochet leaned back in his chair, scrubbing a hand over his face, for the first time exhaustion appearing on his normally stoic face. "After ripping through Breck's history for possible local connections, Rabbit's sitting about ninety percent."

He reached out and tapped a finger on the roof of a house sitting at the end of a cul-de-sac. "This used to belong to one of Breck's former teammates. It was lost in a foreclosure, and is now up for auction. Strangely, for an abandoned house, it's still pulling power from the grid. Not much, but enough."

Damn, Rabbit was fucking magic with electronics. "It's enough, all right." Anticipation coiled. Time to bring the fight to Breck, and get Meli out of the line of fire. "Let's get to work."

Chapter Twenty-Seven

Nicholas dropped the cell phone. It landed next to me where I was curled into a ball, grief and rage ripping me apart, while pain thrummed dully in the background. When he slammed the heel of his boot down, obliterating the phone into shattered metal and plastic, I didn't flinch.

"Cocky ass bastard," he hissed, before storming into the kitchen.

While cupboards were wrenched open and slammed closed, I lay there, eyes burning, but there were no more tears.

The echo of Bishop's apology drowned out Nicholas's mutterings, carving a pit of ice in my chest until it threatened to crack open and spill my agony across the scuffed and blood spattered linoleum.

Wolf was dead because of me and my stupid choices. If I hadn't reached out and dragged him into my nightmare, he'd still be here. And it wasn't just Wolf who paid for my weaknesses, so had Eric.

Because I let fear rule my life and my decisions.

My stomach cramped viciously, and my body spasmed, making it hard to breathe.

Back dots danced in front of me, but grimly I held on. They slowed and disappeared until I was able to suck in some air, ignoring the protest of my ribs and back. What the hell was I afraid of? Being hurt by Nicholas? Little late to worry about it now, wasn't it?

My split lips curled in self-disgust.

There wasn't an inch of me that didn't throb or ache. A detached part of my mind was fairly certain I was sporting a set of bruised, if not broken ribs, and my knee where he kicked me, barely worked. Not to mention, one eye was swollen shut, my hands beat in time with my pulse, my back ached, and the pounding in my head was my new norm.

The worst had happened, and I was still here, unfortunately. Alone.

Inch by inch, the ice spread, and in its wake woke a terrible, twisted violent thing. It crawled through my veins, spreading, reaching, taking all of what used to be Meli and leaving behind a single-minded focus.

It was time to make Nicholas Breck pay. Since there was nothing left to lose, the cost didn't matter.

My thoughts were interrupted when a cruel hand gripped my tangled hair, my ponytail a long lost memory, and dragged my heavy body across the floor.

Gritting my teeth, I reached up and despite my broken, ragged nails, gouged the hand in my hair as my heels scrambled across the slick floor for purchase.

Flesh tore under my clawing fingers, and a curse quickly followed.

It didn't take me long to pick up the indicators. I got my arms in front of my face before he smashed me face first, into the floor, his knuckles digging into the base of my skull. "You want to pull that shit again, Meli?"

A sharp shove added another layer of bruises along my forearms.

He yanked my head back, wrenching my neck and leaned in until he was right in my face. "Knock it off."

I didn't even pause, jerking my head forward, uncaring of the burn of my hair as it tore free of his grip, and slammed my forehead into his nose.

He bellowed and reared back.

I threw myself sideways, and took his backhand behind my ear and shoulder. Unable to get to my feet, I tried to crawl, the sharp pieces of his crushed phone slicing open my palms, adding another smear of blood along the floor. My thick and clumsy fingers sent the pieces scattering, but there was one long, thin piece I managed to snag. Just in time.

His foot slammed into my stomach, bringing me momentarily up on all fours, before dropping me to the floor where I fought my spasming diaphragm, my body curling into a ball.

His boots appeared in front of me, and he squatted down, his chest pumping hard, his face carved in stone, his eyes bright with madness. He rested his arms on his knees as he watched me, before a chilling smile curved his lips. "You done yet, babe?"

Pulling my lips back from my teeth, I managed to hurl a mouth full of spit and blood at him.

He lost the grin and wiped a hand down the front of his T-shirt smearing the small drops of bloody spit. He reached out and gripped my chin tightly. His touch set off shock waves of pain, but it was just another layer to the ones he laid before.

Without looking away from him, I gritted my teeth, whipped up my arm and stabbed the slender piece of plastic as deep as I could into his arm.

The hand on my jaw tightened until I thought bone would shatter. His other hand caught mine, trapping my hold on the sharp plastic, and squeezed.

I tried to fight, but his grip was relentless as he forced my hand against the plastic's ragged edges. Blood began to drip from our hands and over his arm.

He watched me with a strange light in his eyes. One I couldn't, didn't want to understand. "I'll let go when you do."

Our silent battle raged on, until finally my hand spasmed.

He tore it away, leaving the blood stained plastic in his arm.

I cradled my savaged hand against my stomach, and watched as he pulled out the plastic and tossed it aside.

He shook his arm and his head. "You just don't learn do you?"

Answering him meant I thought there was something worth saying. I simply watched him watch me.

His head canted to the side and puzzlement furrowed his brow. "I don't get it, Meli. It's like you want me to hurt you." He put his hands on his thighs and pushed until he stood above me. "I didn't want us to start out like this, but you're forcing my hand with this foolish behavior."

He walked away.

I closed my eyes for a moment, gathering my strength because I couldn't stay curled up on the floor. As much as it sickened me, I might actually have to play along, just until I got a chance.

Nausea that had nothing to do with my battered body rose, making my gorge rise. Opening my mouth, I panted through the urge until it dissipated.

The sound of the faucet running brought my eyes open. Slowly, carefully I began to inch my way upright. By the time I managed to drag myself to the wall a few feet away to brace against, sweat had mixed with the blood, the salt stinging my various cuts.

Breathing required concentration.

I dropped my head, letting my hair veil my face. It was a false sense of privacy, but I'd take it.

When a wet cloth was gently placed over the back of my

neck, I started so hard I slammed the back of my head into the wall. My eyes flew open to find Nicholas crouched next to me, his wet hand still raised.

"Relax, Meli."

The soothing note in his voice sent an army of goosebumps racing over my skin. After his unchecked fury, it was creepy as hell.

"We need to get you cleaned up. You can't go out in public looking like this."

As he began to use the washcloth on my face, I held still, tension singing through every muscle, never taking my attention off him.

This abrupt about face should have been terrifying, but the violent animal I'd become simply watched and waited. There had to be a moment, just one, that I could take to destroy him.

Unaware of my thoughts, he kept talking. "We'll head out soon, because I want to make sure everything's in place before our company arrives."

He took the cloth and dragged it along my sore lips, pressing harder than needed. I didn't move. He studied my face, looking for something he didn't find, because he frowned when he continued, still wiping at my face, "Wouldn't do to meet your new friend unprepared."

The rough cloth scraped against the tender skin along my cheekbone and under my eye, and I refused to react.

He shook his head. "Not sure where you found these guys, babe, but they aren't too smart."

He stood, went back to the faucet and rinsed the cloth. Wringing it out, he came back, crouched down, picked up my arm, and began wiping it clean. "If he believes I'd give you or the gold up that easily, he's an idiot."

My stomach pitched, not because of his touch, but because realization hit that he had no intentions of letting Bishop leave the exchange alive.

Oh no, no way in hell was another good man going to pay for my mistakes.

Nicholas went quiet, his concentration centered on cleaning my arms. When he stood up to return to the kitchen, I studied my surroundings, my mind shifting gears. We couldn't leave this house. Somehow, someway, I needed to figure out how to ensure Nicholas ended here.

First I needed a weapon, then a plan of attack. The TV tray wouldn't do me a damn bit of good. Not only was it too far away, but I didn't have enough strength to make it a worthwhile weapon. The table was empty. The scattered pieces of phone on floor were out.

The faucet turned off, bringing my attention to the breakfast bar. The dark handle of the knife he used to cut my restraints lay on the counter.

Nicholas rounded the counter, and I switched my gaze to him. He walked back over, did his strange cleaning thing with my other arm, then rose again to head back to the kitchen. He reached up to scratch his head and his shirt lifted just a bit, just enough to flash the gun at the base of his spine.

Dropping my gaze to the floor to hide my sudden flare of excitement, I considered my two options.

A knife or a gun?

Getting either would be difficult, and required some planning, but I could do it. It was a matter of getting close, real close.

A faint voice in the back of my head warned of danger, but I shut it down. It didn't matter what the cost, I was more than happy to pay it considering there wasn't much waiting for me on the other side.

Besides, it might be the solution to me finally escaping this maw of guilt and pain hollowing out my soul.

Chapter Twenty-Eight

WOLF

We weren't waiting on Breck or his damn meeting, because my churning gut combined with Bishop's prediction, meant we needed to make the first move. Ricochet drove since neither he nor Bishop would agree to hand over the keys.

"Last thing we need is to be pulled over by the cops," Bishop groused, nabbing the keys from me when we headed out of the villas.

Late afternoon was cruising into evening, bringing the gray of twilight with it. One of the side benefits of having shorter days in winter, even here in the desert.

Although each of us carried our personal weapons of choice, each able to support a suppressor, we were short on equipment. Ricochet had one of his babies tucked in the trunk, so we were up one lethally gorgeous M1014, Benelli's specially designed semi-automatic combat shotgun, but our ability it use it was seriously impaired. A shotgun, no matter what neighborhood, would bring cops. Granted suppressors didn't fully mute sound, but they helped minimize how much attention we might attract.

Ricochet wove the car through traffic, faster than the speed limit, but not so fast as to garner unwanted attention.

Confined to the back seat, I was stuck in place, silently cursing the other cars on the road. Meli was running out of time, I could feel it. The sand-filled hourglass in my head dropped grain after grain, each landing with a boulder-like impact.

Bishop lifted his head from the tablet in his lap where he was monitoring any incoming information Rabbit could filter to us on what we would be facing. "I've been asked by Rabbit to remind you to keep this as low-key as possible, since we haven't been able to check in with the colonel."

"Where the hell is she?" Wrong damn time for her to go MIA, yet it hadn't stopped me from moving forward with our plan. Considering what was at stake, it was better to ask for forgiveness than permission.

"At HQ, but she's incommunicado. Jinx had Rabbit track down Cyn and Shaw to report in."

Any other time my curiosity would be off the charts at what was happening behind closed doors in San Diego, but not today. Whatever was going down, I'd deal with it after. For now, since the colonel hadn't called the three of us back, we were good to go.

Ricochet turned into a neighborhood, and I leaned forward so I could watch our green dot on the map in Bishop's hands close in on the red one. Knowing it was a long shot I adjusted my mental shields, thinning them enough to scan the surroundings. We were closing in, and if I were damn lucky, maybe I'd pick up something, probably from the bastard, Breck, since Meli was difficult to connect with. Didn't mean I wasn't going to try.

Of course, first I had to survive the barrage of noise that hit with the force of a battering ram from the random minds currently at home. It was a holiday, and holy shit was the emotional upheaval off the fucking charts.

Wading through the flood of resentment, love, impatience, joy, frustration, and contentment made me grit my teeth.

Why can't she just appreciate what I've done?

Damn, I wish I could pull off an outfit like that.

So glad everyone's here this year. Thank you.

Wonder when I can get away with kicking everyone out? I'm done.

This is so worth it.

On and on it went, the mental clamor growing into a towering wave. It didn't help that my emotional state was chaotic as hell, torn between rage and fear.

Right, so first, I needed to get my shit together. It was the only way to get above the seething masses so I could skim the surface for tell-a-tale signs of Breck or Meli.

It was rough going, and when I finally clawed my way above the din, sweat coated my spine in a clammy grip. My head throbbed as I held my mental position and began to "look" for signs of violence, possession, fear, anything that felt like what hit me outside of Rhyolite.

The car took a turn, and a hand held my shoulder, steadying me physically; psychically, well, that was a different story.

Strange how many different types of fear existed during a season when counting your blessings was everything. Fear of losing someone. Fear of upsetting someone. Fear of failing. Then there was the odd mix of apprehension and self-doubt that seem to afflict families left and right.

The secrets lingering under the layer of smiles and sparkling eyes was massive.

There was an illicit affair, someone was covering their bills with company funds, someone else was desperate to keep the fact their turkey dinner was all thanks to a local grocer and not a testament to their culinary skills.

On and on it went.

Finally a flicker of something much more insidious and vaguely familiar appeared, a self-assured anger bolstered by unshakable confidence and twisted through with avarice, jealousy, and malice.

"Got him." My voice was low, but the car began to slow indicating Ricochet heard me. Keeping Breck's mental signature at the center, I began to gingerly work my way around him, searching for signs of Meli.

Not for the first time I cursed the fact her natural blocks were so damn strong. I just needed a crack, someway in, to let her know we were coming, to hold on.

The second time through I picked up something different, but it was so low key, I wondered if it was my imagination. Considering who she was with, there was no way her mental energy would be that calm—that focused.

Despite my intense concentration, the tension inside the car sang along my nerves. The guys were waiting on me, but there was something… "Hang on."

And then I found it.

Slipping though the hairline fracture fucking hurt. A rough curse came from a distance, and something soft pressed against my nose. I ignored it all because if my attention shifted even the tiniest bit, I'd lose my tentative hold.

Just when the pain hit the blackout level, it disappeared.

It was so sudden, I stilled, afraid to move, but the inky blackness remained, thick and impenetrable.

Cautiously, worried every move I made would shatter this strange emptiness, I attempted a soft psychic scan, trying to capture any thoughts in the vicinity.

At first, all I could hear was the heavy thud of my heartbeat. There was a strange shushing noise as if the darkness was alive and breathing.

As I focused on the soft sound, it began to evolve, gaining definition, until I realized it was two words, being repeated over and over, on an endless loop.

My fault.

My heart shuddered under the suffocating weight of guilt and shame filling that beloved voice.

I managed to find a path into Meli's mind, and the strange void surrounding me morphed into something recognizable— despair, grief, blame, and worst of all—hopelessness.

With that realization slamming home, I worried I was too late to reach her. Even though I managed to connect to her mind, connecting with her was harder than hell, because on some, deep, instinctual level, she truly believed she wasn't getting out of this alive.

Fear spurred anger, and without considering the damage it would inflict, I snarled, "Dammit, Meli, don't you fucking give up!"

For a moment utter silence reigned and the heavy darkness shifted, pulling back.

Then, in a voice so small it brought tears to my eyes, she said, "Wolf?"

Choking back the rage settling in my gut, I forced a teasing note, "Who were you expecting, angel?"

Around me the black began to separate, slowly forming a gauzy wall in front of me. On the other side, something moved, coming out of the shadows.

At first it was another piece of the darkness, but as it moved forward a soft, hesitant glow followed. The wall shifted from wavering sheets of obsidian glass to a smoky filled pane.

Stepping close in mirror of the form on the other side, I sucked in a breath as a half-formed image of Meli appeared, staring back.

It was her, but not, as if I were viewing her through a foggy, distorted lens. Her hands came up to press against the barrier, and I mimicked her movement.

"I'm either losing it, or almost dead, either way works for me." There was bitter humor in her voice.

"How do you figure, sweetpea?" God, I wanted to hold her, but I couldn't get through the wall she held between us. And it was her holding it, because nothing I did budged it.

Her mouth turned down and her shoulders dropped. "I'm talking to the dead."

"I'm not dead, Meli." Desperation added a harsh bite to my reply, but I needed her to believe me. "I wouldn't be here if I was dead."

Her hands fell from the wall and dropped back to her sides. "Wolf can't get in my head. He told me so himself. So it doesn't matter how much you…" She gave a sharp shake of her head and corrected herself, "I deny it, there's no escaping the fact you're not here."

She turned away.

Fear sent my heart into my throat as I lost her. With a roar, I punched at the wall. "I'm fucking alive, Meli! Goddammit, listen to me! You can't give up. We're coming. Just hold the fuck on!"

She stopped, but didn't turn.

"Just hold on, baby, please, for me." There was no hiding the plea in my voice.

Finally, she turned her steps slow and unsure as she came back. When she laid her palms against the barrier, I did the same, wishing I could feel her.

Her soft sob was worse than any torture I could imagine. "I'm so sorry I dragged you into this. Sorry I didn't get a chance to tell you I loved you, Wolf."

She leaned in until her head rested against the wall. I leaned in, only then catching her whispered, "I'm so sorry."

She was killing me. "Just a little longer, angel, please, then I promise it's all over. For me, okay?"

A heartbeat passed before she finally gave a nod. "For you, Wolf. For now."

Relief about dropped me to my knees. "Thank you."

She lifted her head and for a moment the barrier thinned and I could see her—green eyes dark and lost, face drawn and thin, skin nearly translucent, and my gut clenched. She was teetering on the edge, hope almost extinguished.

"I love you, Melisande. Don't let the bastard win, hear me?"

A flash of life returned, and her lips curved into a beautiful smile. "Roger that, soldier boy."

I returned her smile with a fierce grin. "Damn straight."

She reached out and I held my breath as the opaque fog shifted, as if letting her through, then she was jerked backward, a short scream escaping as her hands flew to the back of her head as if struggling against the unseen hand dragging her away.

"Meli!" I lunged forward, but the barrier held, no matter how I hard I beat it. "Meli!"

The only response was a violent jerk as I was shoved back into my body.

"Wolf, dammit, man, get your ass back here."

Bishop's voice acted like a slap to my face, bringing me blinking back into reality. He stared at me from inches away, one hand wrapped around the back of my neck, the other holding a bandana against my nose. A frown carved deep grooves in his face. "You here?"

"Yeah," I mumbled around the wadded up cloth. Reaching up, I took over for him, holding the material against my nose. "Nose bleed?"

He released my neck, sat back, and nodded. "Yeah, kicked in about four minutes ago."

I sat back, tilting my head back. As the blood ran down the back of my throat, I grimaced. I hated nosebleeds. Unfortunately, they were the by-product of over-extending your psychic abilities. Getting through to Meli was akin to digging through marble with bare hands.

"I take it you made it through to her?" Bishop asked.

"Yeah, but she's not in good shape."

"Physically or emotionally?"

The bitter taste of blood was fading, so I felt safe in lifting my head again. "Honestly? Both. She thinks I'm dead, and she's blaming herself."

But there was something more to it, something I was missing, because her guilt and shame went soul deep, and that worried me.

"She'll make it."

I held Ricochet's quiet comment close, needing the reassurance, because my footing was shaky as hell right now. I checked the bandana for fresh blood, found none, and tossed it aside. "We ready to move in?"

"Let's do it." Bishop opened his door, and we all piled out.

Chapter Twenty-Nine

WOLF

Ricochet parked down the block from our target house, because we had no intention of giving Breck any warning of our approach.

While Ricochet melted into the shadows, scouting ahead, Bishop and I strolled down the sidewalk, just a couple of guys out for a walk after stuffing our faces.

Night settled in, and that, with our dark clothing, helped reduce anyone's ability to identify us as potential threats. Porch lights shone in an abstract pattern, because not all of the houses were lit. Here's hoping some of these families were out of town, especially the house just to the left of our target, which remained reassuringly dark.

A cool breeze carried the spice of burnt mesquite, and faint sounds of laughter and music. Everyone was safely tucked inside with their stuffed fowl of choice, wrapped up in the holiday drama of families and friends, which worked for me. Meant less of a chance of being spotted by a Nosy Nelly peeking through a curtain.

We made our way toward the end of the cul-de-sac where the one-story house sat back a bit on the property. Strangely, there weren't many dividing walls in this neighborhood. A few on the larger lots, but most of the homes tended to share backyards.

I suppressed a shudder at the lack of privacy, but tonight, that would work to our advantage. The house we wanted sat on such a lot. Granted, a wall ran along the one side separating the housing development from the road, but on the other side of the road? Nothing but desert.

The long drive was empty.

Since there was an attached garage, that meant dick. The windows were dark, the blinds closed, and there was an air of abandonment hovering around the structure, which made it the perfect hideaway for a sociopathic stalker.

In the front yard, the realty sign was weathered, but there was no missing the FORECLOSURE attached to it.

What a way to advertise to thieves.

Considering we needed to keep this low-key, we skipped the front door and aimed for the cinder block fence running along the far side of the house, keeping the house between us and the rest of the neighborhood.

This close, I didn't dare drop my psychic barriers because it wouldn't put just me at risk, but Bishop, Ricochet, and Meli. It was time to do what I did best—work.

Training rose front and center, shoving the mess of emotional upheaval into a corner. Instead of having me link us together telepathically, we would rely on hand signals.

Worried about my earlier nosebleed, Bishop didn't want to push me into a psychic coma, and Ricochet was always more comfortable when I stayed the hell out of his head. Not that I could blame him. Personally, I was more than happy to stay out their heads, mine was providing more than enough entertainment on its own.

We stepped into the narrow opening wreathed in concealing shadows and found Ricochet waiting for us. There wasn't much space, maybe five or six feet, between the house and the wall, which topped out at around seven feet. The good news, there wasn't much light back here despite the street-lights lining the cul-de- sac and the road on the other side of the wall.

Some lights flickered, triggered by the motion of passing cars, some just failed to respond. A little part of me wished for Rabbit and his electric touch, but the three of us had worked in worse urban environments just fine.

Ricochet did a quick summary, his hands walking us through. "Inside movement. No sounds. Light far window. Eyes on possible entry point."

Sure enough, as I shifted a bit to the side to scan the side of the house and noted a bit of light bleeding around the edges of the window covering, not blinds but the thicker shutters. Based on the window's position and the presence of a drip valve indicated a laundry room or kitchen. And even better, a small concrete pad set in front of a darker shade of dark indi-cated a utility door.

Bishop tucked his firearm into its holster, pulled out a lock pick set, moved to the door, and got to work.

Ricochet slid to the other side, back pressed against the stucco surface, weapon at the ready, eyes on the window, monitoring the interior movement for any signs of threat.

On the door's other side, I held my USP at the ready, atten-tion trained on possible incoming threats.

It took Bishop less than a minute to undo the lock. The ease of his accomplishment didn't lower my tension, it raised it.

I reached over, and held my hand over the knob as he silently moved back and to the side, pocketed the kit, and reclaimed his weapon, aiming it on the door. At his deliberate nod, I grasped the knob, turned it, and gave the door a gentle push.

The door swung open on silent hinges, stopping when

about three feet of space emerged between the door and the frame. Bishop and I checked with Ricochet, got his all clear, and then Bishop began shouldering inside, me on his six. He went right, I went left.

We cleared the garage quickly. There was nothing there except the SUV.

Bishop pulled out his knife, and took care of the SUV's tires. A brutal, but effective way of keeping Breck in place.

I waved Ricochet in, and we came back to Bishop crouched at the door leading into the house.

Now shit was about to get tight.

We had to get inside without alerting Breck.

The house's layout was a mystery and we were going in blind, which made it borderline suicidal to move forward. It wasn't stopping any of us.

Bishop began to work on the lock, and I tapped his shoulder. He looked up. I signaled him to hold. He raised an eyebrow, but I ignored it.

There was one way I could ensure we took Breck by surprise, but it required Meli's help. As much as it grated to ask this of her, I knew she could provide the distraction we needed to get inside undetected.

Going against every instinct I possessed to keep her safe, I retraced the psychic path to her. This time, instead of trying to get past her natural protections, I focused on her unique mental signature.

"Distract him." It was nothing less than an order. I hadn't served as a Chief Warrant Officer for shits and giggles, and all that dominance and discipline whipped through my command. Now, I was banking on her instincts kicking in and responding.

I squeezed Bishop's shoulder, praying Meli heard.

When something crashed to the floor and shattered, I got confirmation my girl was doing what she could. What didn't help was the savage roar that followed, or the sound of something, a body most likely, hitting a wall with a resounding thunk.

Even as Bishop's shoulders tightened under my grip, mimicking mine, my gun was steady, my mind crystal fucking clear.

The sounds of a violent struggle increased, gaining strength and just when I thought my training would break under the strain, Bishop shoved the door open, moving in low and fast.

I followed on his heels as we came through a narrow laundry room that opened into the house.

The sounds of the fight ahead got clearer, and as we swept through the doorway of the laundry room, my stomach dropped, my throat ached with the need to roar, but training prevailed.

The world around me slowed into snapshots.

Meli's battered face covered in a blood-spattered abstract.

Breck's hands wrapped around her throat as he pinned her against the wall.

Her toes barely brushing the floor, but she wasn't struggling.

Breck turning his head toward us, a cold, detached fury leaving a monstrous mask behind.

Meli didn't turn, didn't react, instead, she did something, something I couldn't see because Breck's body blocked my view.

Breck jerked hard, his attention swinging back to Meli, his eyes wide even as his hands tightened on her throat, knuckles showing white.

She didn't look away, but her torn lips curled back, baring her teeth in a silent snarl. Instead of struggling against his hold she looked as if she was leaning in.

Breck slammed her against the wall. Hard.

I lifted my gun, aimed, and fired.

A second shot followed on the heels of mine.

Breck's body jerked as the bullets hit home. His hands spasmed, letting Meli go.

She fell to the floor, crumpling against the wall.

For a moment Breck towered above her, staring at her, then like a puppet whose strings were cut, his legs folded, and he dropped. On his knees, weaving, he looked down and his hands went to his stomach. When he pulled them away they were stained with blood and held a knife.

In front of him, Meli watched, her face blank. Only when Breck held out a hand to her, did she blink, once.

Another shot sounded next to me. Breck toppled to the side.

Time rushed back in, the surreal slowness disappearing under the chaotic wave.

I crossed the kitchen, dropped to my knees the last few feet from Meli, and slid in. I reached out, then stopped, unsure where to touch her without causing pain. There was blood everywhere, and bruises shaded her skin in a sickening pallet.

With her gaze focused on Breck, who was lying in a growing pool of blood, unmoving, she didn't see me. I wasn't even sure how much of what was happening around her was getting through.

Setting my gun on the floor, I scooted around on my knees until I blocked her view of Breck. Then, carefully, in an effort not to spook her, I reached out and drew a finger, feather light, along one of the few unmarred spots on her cheek. "Meli? Angel, can you look at me?"

She huddled there against the wall, her gaze unfocused, her attention centered on something none of us could see.

I could hear Bishop and Ricochet moving around me, but everything I was remained focused on the woman in front of me. I inched closer.

When she flinched, I stopped. Inside, locked where she

couldn't see it, I raged. If I could kill Breck all over again, I fucking would.

I had to clear my throat before I could speak without growling. "Meli?"

Nothing.

As much as I detested doing it, I needed to snap her out of whatever hell she trapped herself in. Using the same tone I used for years on young, wet-behind-the-ears, recruits, I snapped, "Melisande Dwyer, look at me."

A frown marred her forehead, but her gaze jumped to mine, the blankness retreating, and the bands around my chest loosened. She blinked a couple of times, and I waited, giving her a chance to make her way back.

A shudder ran through her, and her tongue came out, touched her swollen lower lip, which caused her to wince, which started a chain reaction, because a soft groan escaped as she raised a trembling hand to cover her puffy eye.

I caught her hand before it could touch anything, and my fingers encountered the warm slide of blood. Lots of it.

Hissing out a breath, I pulled her hand down, as gently as I could, turning it over so I could see what the damage was. It was a mess. "Fuck me, angel."

"It doesn't hurt as much now."

Her voice was a rough rasp, either from Breck's punishing grip that left a raw, red pattern that would darken into ugly bruises, or from screaming.

Thinking of her screaming not only hurt, but made me ill. Holding her hand, palm up, I breathed through it, then called over my shoulder. "I need a cloth or wet towels."

When she tried to curl her fingers closed, I carefully held them open, even as pressure grew behind my eyes. "Not yet, baby, let me see what we're dealing with here."

A wet dishcloth appeared over my shoulder. Without

looking up, I took it and began carefully wiping away the blood.

Bishop settled on his heels next to me, holding another dishrag. "You'll need this to bind it when it's clean."

I nodded and kept on with my delicate work. As I wiped away the blood, a ragged, angry slice was revealed.

Bishop let out a low whistle. "That's going to leave a mark, shrimp."

Another shudder ran through her body as I wrapped up the sluggishly bleeding wound.

"Wolf?"

The tentative hope in her voice about broke me, but I managed to keep it together as I tucked the end of the cloth tight, holding it in place. "Right here, angel."

She jerked her hand out of my grip.

Stunned, I looked up and barely managed to catch her as she threw herself into me. Her arms wrapped around my neck, her head tucked under my chin, her face buried against my chest.

Still worried about the damage I couldn't see, I tried to keep my hold gentle, when what I really wanted to do was pick her up, carry her out of this place, and never let her go.

Her shoulders shook, her breath hitched, and her body kept doing little spasms.

All I could do was tuck her in close and whisper reassurances as I pressed kisses to the top of her hair.

When her first shaky sob snuck out, Bishop met my gaze over the top of her head, remorse and grim resolution plain to see. I got it, God did I get it.

He rose, squeezed my shoulder and went to help Ricochet clean up the mess behind us.

With my back to the room and Meli burrowed in my arms, I closed my eyes, sending a soul-felt thank you to whoever was listening and watching over the precious gift in my arms.

"You're here."

The pressure behind my eyes escaped at her choked whisper. There was so much held in those two words. "I told you I'd come for you."

Her arms tightened, and she pulled back just enough to lift her head up. Tears spiked her lashes, and trickled through the bruises and cuts on her face. "I thought—"

I dipped my head, and touched my lips to hers as carefully as possible, to stop what she was going to say. When I lifted my head, I hid nothing from her, not the fear that set up shop the minute I woke after the accident, not the rage that pounded through me even now, not the belief in her I held to throughout the entire ordeal, not the love and need under it all. "I'm not going anywhere, Meli. Not now, not anytime soon."

Her hold on my neck finally loosened, and she dropped her injured hand to her lap, but her other went to my jaw. She brushed a butterfly touch along it, then slowly traced every feature, including the cut from the accident, and the bruises rising from Bishop's love taps. She ended at my lips, her thumb brushed over my lower one, then dropped to her lap.

She stared at me for a moment, her green eyes darkening with an emotion I couldn't read, before she gave a sad little sigh and leaned back in, her head against my chest.

Something in that sound worried me. "What was that for?"

She didn't answer for the longest time, then, "Nothing, I just want to go home."

If she thought I was buying that, she had another think coming, but right now wasn't the time to pursue it. "Hate to break it to you, sugar plum, but your first stop is a hospital."

"We just have to wait for the police to arrive." Bishop stepped around us and crouched down, a plastic bag filled with ice in his hand. He offered it to Meli. "You need to put this on your eye or your forehead, whichever can stand it."

I took the bag from him and held it against her eye, ignoring her sharp inhale. "You get ahold of the colonel?"

Bishop nodded. "Ricochet just made the call, her orders are to call in the police." In my arms, Meli stiffened and his coffee dark gaze slid to her, his face softening for a moment. "Relax, Meli, you're okay."

"But—"

"I know, but I promise, you're okay."

Okay, I was missing something here. When Bishop turned to me, I arched an eyebrow in demand.

He shook his head once, then explained. "Meli managed to stab Breck in the chest with a knife."

Pride rose, fierce and strong, because that fast, the image of her jerking against Breck's hold when I hit the kitchen made sense.

"However, since he's also sporting three bullet wounds, it's a clear case of self-defense." His gaze held mine, a warning to tread carefully easy to see.

I nodded, letting him know I read him loud and clear.

"EMTs are on their way as well."

"I'm going with her to the hospital." Because no way in hell was I leaving her alone any time soon.

A bit of the tension in his face drifted away. "Ricochet and I will handle things here, you take care of the shrimp."

"That's the plan."

His grin was brief. "Yeah, kind of figured as much."

He shifted to stand, but stopped when Meli reached out and touched his hand. "Thank you, Bishop."

His face softened, and he brought her hand up and pressed his lips to the back of it. "No need to thank any of us. You're a hell of a warrior woman, Meli."

He tucked her hand back in her lap, and stood up. "I'm going to go out and help Ricochet head off our nosy neighbors. You sit tight until help gets here."

I nodded, completely happy to sit right where I was. Meli tucked her face against my chest, burrowing in. For a moment, I breathed her in, cherishing the feel of her in my arms, chasing back the hollow nightmares edging around my mind.

Minutes passed, Meli's weight settling deeper against me as her adrenaline began to recede and her body's demand for escape nudged her closer to blessed unconsciousness.

Faint sounds of approaching sirens broke the quiet. As they drew closer, she spoke, "I'm sorry for all of this, Wolf."

Closing my eyes against the inescapable sound of guilt and sorrow in her whisper, I laid my cheek against the top of her head. "Nothing to be sorry about, angel. Told you that before." I paused, knowing this wasn't the place or time to get into it, but something pushed me. "Why are you apologizing for something that's not your fault?"

Her hand, tangled in my T-shirt, tightened, then relaxed, and her answer was slurred as awareness drew back. "Because it is."

I shifted my hold and bent my head, needing to see her face, only to find her eyes closed. I put my mouth next to her ear, needing her to hear me no matter what, "No, it's not, angel."

A single tear wound its way down her face.

Chapter Thirty

Wolf's house was breathtaking. Not in a model home way, but in the fact that every inch of it showed his pride in creating a home. Something I hadn't expected from him. It was beautiful and heart breaking. Beautiful because it reflected every stupid, foolish dream I held since I was young and looking for Mr. Right. Heart breaking because it wasn't meant to be shared with me.

No matter how I many times I went over things in my head, I couldn't escape the reality that my decisions, my actions led to the hell Wolf went through. Not to mention what my brother endured.

Rage, ugly and thick, curled in my stomach and my aching muscles clenched in protest. I pressed my forehead against the cool pane of glass set in the window seat tucked off the kitchen, rolling my head to the side to avoid putting pressure on the lingering bruise surrounding the slowly receding knot.

In the week since Nicholas's attack, I'd been poked, prodded, and stitched, then bundled into a car and driven to San Diego. At which point, Wolf took me to his house and refused to let me leave. It didn't matter how much I argued with him, he wouldn't budge.

At first, leaving wasn't an option. I spent the first couple of days in bed, sleeping. The doctor assured Wolf it was necessary for healing and I didn't want to admit it was easier to hide in sleep than face him and the questions I knew he wanted to ask.

But it was day five and there was no more hiding.

Earlier, Wolf was called into a team meeting, and should be returning home soon. I wasn't ready. I wasn't sure I'd ever be ready. I knew what I had to do, but it wasn't what my heart wanted.

I spent the last two days going over everything, from the moment Eric introduced Nicholas to the bitter end, when the knife slid in, scraping over bone. I wasn't sleeping more than a few hours at a time.

Memories twisted into nightmares that left me paralyzed and gasping for air. A couple of times the fear that this— Wolf alive, Nicholas dead—was all a dream, forced me out of bed. I snuck into the room across the hall that Wolf took, slipped inside and just touched his hand to make sure he was really there. Surprisingly, he never woke.

A truck pulled up to the curb, grabbing my attention.

I sat there and watched as Wolf climbed out, closed the door, leaned an arm on the window's edge and spoke to the driver. When Wolf turned and caught me watching, he smiled.

I pressed my bandaged hand against the glass, my heart aching, tears burning. There was so much in that look, and I wanted it so badly, even knowing it wasn't safe.

The driver leaned over and waved. Tag Gunderson, Risia's boyfriend, although they were much more than simply boyfriend/girlfriend. They were soul mates, and it was obvious to everyone they came in contact with.

I managed a return wave.

Wolf turned back, said something, and then stepped back. Tag pulled away and Wolf headed up the drive.

As he came closer, I took in the serious lines etched on his face, the small white bandage covering the stitches in his forehead, and the slight limp that the doctor assured him would be gone within a month. It was all that remained from the accident.

Well, and the fact he was now stuck looking for a new truck.

I closed my eyes and listened to the door open, shut, and then his footsteps coming steadily closer. I didn't open them even when I felt him sit next to me, or when he cupped my face in his hand and brushed away a stupid, useless tear that managed to escape.

"Time to talk to me, angel."

I blinked my eyes open, staring into his beloved face, and wondered how I'd survive sending him away. I tried to reassure my splintering heart that at least he was alive, and keeping him that way was what mattered most.

I swallowed against the lump in my throat, but didn't move away from his touch. "I can't stay."

"Why not?" His voice was as quiet as mine, his sea-glass gaze solid and bright.

A thousand inane excuses rushed forward—I needed to get back to my job, he needed to get back to his, I didn't belong here—but my mouth moved ahead of my brain and the truth spilled out, "If I stay, I'll lose you."

He studied my face, a frown marring his forehead. "Want to explain how you figure that?"

I shook my head, because no, I really, really didn't. If I laid it all out there, he'd never look at me like this again.

He sighed and dropped his hand. He looked away, staring over the kitchen for a minute.

I watched, wondering what he was thinking, but too heart-sore to ask.

Finally, he turned back to me. "I saw you, Meli. I saw it all. The guilt, the sorrow, how close you were to giving up."

My mouth fell open as shock rocked through me, quickly followed by soul shriveling shame as he laid one of my darkest sins out. A truth I hadn't wanted to acknowledge, now revealed under a harsh light.

I ducked my head and hunched my shoulders, drawing back, stopping only when Wolf muttered a curse, and pulled me into his arms.

Gently, but firmly, he settled me in his lap, holding me captive. "You have to talk to me. I can't help untangle the mess inside your head, unless you let me help."

"You can't help." I didn't want him to see me that clearly, to see how weak I really was.

He growled in response. "You trusted me once. What changed?"

"Nothing." It came out a whisper.

"Then tell me what's going on." He paused, his hand stroking gently down my spine. "You held on for me when I asked, Meli. I'll forever be on my knees giving thanks for that. Whatever Breck said, whatever he did, it is not on you. It's on him."

Tears, that had been absent for days, came faster and hotter, falling onto his shirt, but there was no stopping them. I felt him press a kiss into my hair before he rested his chin on my head.

"Baby, please take a chance and talk to me."

"I dare you, mouse. Take a chance and see what happens." My brother's advice whispered in my ear.

Unable to fight any longer, I opened my mouth and let it all spill out. "He killed Eric because of me, because my brother was trying to protect me. But I didn't say anything to Eric. I swear! Then he went after you because of me. He planned on killing Bishop because of me." The last came out on a sob.

"I can't figure out what I did, Wolf. I watched you get shot and I couldn't do a damn thing to stop it. He told me it was my fault, and he was right."

Wolf rocked me, his hold tight, keeping me safe. "Oh God, angel, he was a twisted bastard. It wasn't you, it wasn't ever you. There's nothing you did or said that could've ever changed what happened. Breck didn't kill Eric because of you, baby. I promise."

I wanted to believe him, I did, but..."You don't know that."

He sighed. "Actually, I do. With the colonel's help, we were able to confirm that Breck set up your brother's team to be ambushed because Eric figured out he was behind the arms deal and had stolen the gold from the local tribe leaders. Eric was getting everything ready to put Breck away for good.

Unfortunately, because your brother had no idea who all was part of it, he didn't know who to trust, so he sent his only insurance policy to you, which put you in Breck's sights. That's why he was stalking you, that's why he hired others to come after you, he wanted the evidence Eric left behind." He tugged me back until he could see my face, his gaze intent and unguarded, and there was no mistaking he was telling me the truth. "Are you hearing me, Meli?"

I swallowed, nerves jumping as hope, so tentative it was scary, began to flicker to life. "If I hadn't called—"

"You'd be dead." There was so much certainty in his voice, I could only blink, but he wasn't done. "And I'd be left alone."

Holding his gaze, I took in the love and conviction staring back, and offered the last demon for him to see. "Everyone I've ever loved gets taken from me."

"The only way you'll lose me, Melisande, is if you throw me away. Is that what you're going to do? Are you willing to let Breck have the final victory after you've kicked his ass time and time again?" His sea-glass gaze was turbulent. "Are you going to walk away from me?"

From us? He didn't have to say the last aloud; I could hear it in the quiet after his question. I didn't want to lose him, not really. Besides, I promised to stand beside him, and promises were meant to be kept, no matter how daunting. I knew it wouldn't be easy, but then nothing worth having ever was, and Wolf was more than worth the fight.

My hands shook as I cupped his face and took the first step away from my clawing fears and toward something precious. Time to let the rest of the chips fall where they may. "Not a chance in hell. You're stuck with me now."

His grin was fierce and filled with pride. "That's the girl I love beyond reason."

I gave a watery laugh. "I love you too, soldier boy."

Chapter Thirty-One

BISHOP

"It's her."

"You're sure?" I studied the faces gathered around the conference table in the San Diego office. The whole team was here, including Colonel Charlene Delacourt. Her face was tight, but it was the only visible sign of her reaction to the news.

The team's psychic tracker, Kayden Shaw shared a look with his other half and post-cog, Cyn Arden. She was the one who answered, "Yeah."

Good enough for me. "What's the plan?"

"We go in and get her." That was Jinx, who leaned against the wall on the far side of the room, arms crossed across her chest.

In front of her, Rabbit leaned back in his chair, tipping his head back to see her. "We could be walkin' straight into a trap."

She grimaced. "Maybe, maybe not." She turned to the colonel. "How trusted is the initial source?"

"Trusted." The colonel's answer was immediate and definitive.

"They've had her for six months." Ricochet, the quietest of our group spoke up.

Doc ran a hand through his shaggy hair, worry evident in his face. "Six months is long damn time."

"And we have no idea just what kind of shit she's been through," that last came from the team's telepath, Wolf, who wasn't happy being away from his recently rescued girlfriend, Meli.

There was a pool going around on how long the girlfriend status would stick before moving to fiancée. I refrained from placing my bet, because that wouldn't be fair to the others.

"Once we get her back, we can find out." Unsurprising, Tag's answer came across more as a warning than reassurance.

While the team continued to discuss the pros and cons of retrieving former Lance Corporal Megan Rouser, scenarios ran through my mind. Each following a different pattern, and still the outcome remained unchanged.

We needed her back.

Time to cut into the conversation. "Doesn't matter if she went willingly or not, we can't afford to leave her with Falcon."

Cyn tilted her head, studying me, probably trying to get a read on me. Good luck. "How do you figure?"

Since I wasn't ready to share all, I gave enough to make things happen. "If she's still ours, we need to get her out of Falcon's hands. Considering the state their people tend to leave their victims in, we're her last chance at survival."

Jinx narrowed her eyes. "And if she's not ours?"

I caught the colonel's gaze and held it. "We'll have a weak link to exploit with Falcon."

------------◆◆◆------------

Race into FRACTURED BY DECEIT and find out what

happens when Bishop learns Megan may be the biggest threat facing the PSY-IV Teams.
Now available at your favorite bookseller!

PSY - IV Teams Books

Welcome to a world where facing danger requires the unique skill set of the men and women of Jami Gray's PSY-IV Teams. As sparks, and bullets fly, love, action, and adventure will target these unique couples as they race through each breath-stealing operation.

Binge the series today at your favorite bookseller!

HUNTED BY THE PAST

Cyn & Kayden

To escape a killer from their past, can a reluctant psychic trust the man who walked away?

TOUCHED BY FATE

Risia & Tag

A seer's secrets become her only bargaining chip in a high-stakes game of lies and loyalty determining her fate.

MARKED BY OBSESSION

Meli & Wolf

A woman in hiding. A telepath who sees deeper than her scars. Can they forge a bond stronger than the obsession stalking them before time runs out?

FRACTURED BY DECEIT

Megan & Bishop

After a brutal attack by a telepath, Megan turns to Bishop for help, but how does he keep her safe when she's threat?

LINKED BY DECEPTION

Jinx & Rabbit

Forced to play intimate criminal partners, will Rabbit & Jinx risk turning illusion to truth as they race to untangle a web of conspiracies and lies?

About the Author

"This story is an emotional roller coaster, from betrayal, anger, fear, love…" —InD'tale Magazine

Jami Gray is the coffee addicted, music junkie, Queen Nerd of her personal Geek Squad, Alpha Mom of the Fur Minxes, who writes to soothe the voices crammed in her head. Her series combine high-stakes urban fantasy and edgy paranormal romantic suspense into books you don't want to put down. Buckle up and get ready for a wild ride through the fascinating worlds of the Arcane, the Kyn, the PSY-IV Teams, and the Collapse.

Come visit Jami's website at **https://www.jamigray.com** and stay up to date on what kind of trouble she's getting into and when you can expect to join in.

www.ingramcontent.com/pod-product-compliance
Lightning Source LLC
Chambersburg PA
CBHW071118180726
48291CB00007B/2075